THE SACRED STONE

THE SACRED STONE

A Historical Mystery

By

The Medieval Murderers

Susanna Gregory
Simon Beaufort
Bernard Knight
Karen Maitland
Ian Morson
Philip Gooden

Medieval
Murderers

SIMON &
SCHUSTER

London · New York · Sydney · Toronto

A CBS COMPANY

First published in Great Britain by Simon & Schuster UK Ltd, 2010
A CBS COMPANY

This paperback edition first published, 2011

1 3 5 7 9 10 8 6 4 2

Simon & Schuster UK Ltd
1st Floor
222 Gray's Inn Road
London WC1X 8HB

www.simonandschuster.co.uk

Simon & Schuster Australia
Sydney

A CIP catalogue record for this book
is available from the British Library

ISBN: 978-1-84983-453-7

Typeset by Hewer Text UK Ltd, Edinburgh
Printed in the UK by CPI Cox & Wyman, Reading, Berkshire RG1 8EX

THE MEDIEVAL MURDERERS

A small group of historical mystery writers, all members of the Crime Writers' Association, who promote their work by giving informal talks and discussions at libraries, bookshops and literary festivals.

Bernard Knight is a former Home Office pathologist and professor of forensic medicine who has been publishing novels, non-fiction, radio and television drama and documentaries for more than forty years. He writes the highly regarded Crowner John series of historical mysteries, based on the first coroner for Devon in the twelfth century.

Ian Morson is the author of an acclaimed series of historical mysteries featuring the thirteenth-century Oxford-based detective, William Falconer, and a brand-new series featuring Venetian crime solver, Nick Zuliani.

Philip Gooden is the author of the Nick Revill series, a sequence of historical mysteries set in Elizabeth and Jacobean London, during the time of Shakespeare's Globe Theatre. The latest titles are *Sleep of Death* and *Death of Kings*. He also writes 19th century mysteries, most recently *The Durham Deception*, as well as non-fiction books on language. Philip was chairman of the Crime Writers' Association in 2007–8.

Susanna Gregory is the author of the Matthew Bartholomew series of mystery novels, set in fourteenth-century Cambridge. In addition, she writes a series set in Restoration London, featuring the spy Thomas Chaloner. The most recent book in this series is *A Murder on London Bridge*.

Simon Beaufort is a pseudonym for a pair of academics formerly at the University of Cambridge, both now full-time writers. One is an award-winning historian, the other a successful crime-writer. The most recent of their novels featuring the former crusader knight Geoffrey Mappestone is *Deadly Inheritance*.

Karen Maitland's novel *Company of Liars*, a dark mystery thriller set at the time of the Black Death, was short-listed for a Shirley Jackson Award 2010. Her latest medieval thriller is *The Gallows Curse*, a tale of treachery and sin during the brutal reign of King John.

medieval
murderers

The Medieval Murderers would like to dedicate this book to Kate Lyall Grant, our commissioning editor and publisher at Simon & Schuster, who has now shepherded six books to publication, with unfailing courtesy, encouragement and expertise.

The Programme

Prologue – In which Susanna Gregory tells of the discovery of the stone by a band of hunters.

Act One – In which Simon Beaufort describes how the stone causes a rift between Church and State.

Act Two – In which Bernard Knight relates how the stone is invoked to heal a manor lord's sick wife.

Act Three – In which Karen Maitland records how the stone is acquired by a Jewish merchant.

Act Four – In which Ian Morson tells how the stone finds its way to King Henry's bedchamber.

Act Five – In which Philip Gooden reveals how the stone plays a part in the kidnap of Nick Revill.

Epilogue – In which Ian Morson describes the surprise resurfacing of the stone in the present day.

PROLOGUE

Brattahlið, Greenland, 1067

The sound of howling wolves woke Jorund. It was the darkest part of the night, and bitterly cold, so he did not want to leave the house to investigate, but he knew he must. The village had experienced more than its share of bad luck during the past two years, and its inhabitants could not afford to lose any more sheep.

'It is only the wind,' murmured his wife Sigrid drowsily, feeling him stir. 'Go back to sleep.'

The wolves howled again, a mournful symphony in the otherwise silent night. 'Then the wind is hungry for our animals,' he said, speaking quietly so as not to wake the children. 'And I must protect them, or Brand will use the opportunity to make another of his speeches. I do not want to leave Brattahlið, and sail away to find some other place in which to settle.'

Sigrid sat up, pulling the bed-furs around her as she did. Despite its thick turf roof and walls, the little house was always freezing at night.

'So you always say, but why not? Since your father drowned two years ago, we have known nothing but misfortune – healthy animals have sickened and died, our crops have failed, little Ivar's crooked leg fails to mend. If Qasapi had not brought us gifts of seal meat, we would have starved this winter. Perhaps we *should* abandon this place and go home.'

'But this *is* our home,' insisted Jorund. 'We were born here, and our fathers were born here. There is no other place we can call our own.'

'Brand says we could go to Engla lande. He heard from the traders last year that there are fields simply for the taking – we just arrive, choose a good spot and build a farm. The weather is mild, the soil is fertile and the sun shines all year long.'

'Brand is a dreamer,' said Jorund harshly. 'We cannot arrive in some distant country and start claiming great swaths of territory for ourselves – the people already there would object, and we would never know peace again.'

'Are you afraid to fight?' jeered Sigrid, irritated by the reoccurrence of what had become a frequent disagreement. 'You, a descendant of Erik the Red, who settled in this godforsaken spot almost ninety years ago? His blood does not run in your veins, or you would be willing to draw your sword to make a better life for the people you vowed to protect.'

Jorund fought down the anger that surged inside him. He sat on the bed and took her hand. 'I did vow to protect them, and I shall. But not all battles are fought with steel, and I will not drag our people away from their homes just because Brand is restless for adventure. Summer will be here soon – perhaps our luck will change then.'

'Or perhaps it will get worse. I think Brand is right: we should go.'

'No,' said Jorund firmly, pulling his hand away and standing abruptly. 'I am the leader of this village, and I say we are staying. You will see in time that I am right.'

He headed for the door, bringing an end to the discussion. Two years before, no one had listened to Brand and his wild dreams, but Sigrid was right: since Thorkell had fallen through the ice and drowned, things *had* started to go wrong in Brattahliò. Cleverly, Brand was using the problems to confirm his whispering campaign that the settlement was doomed, and many of the village's hundred or so members were beginning to believe him. Unfortunately, those most keen to go were the young, strong men, without whom the village could not manage. Jorund had no choice but to force them to stay.

He sighed unhappily as he fumbled for his boots in the darkness. His father had warned him that this might happen: theirs was a restless race, with a drive to conquer new lands and sail across new seas. They were not farmers, content to eke out a paltry living among scrawny cattle and soil-starved vegetables. Thorkell had told his son that it would not be easy to keep Brattahliò at peace with itself, and he had been right. Jorund could feel control slipping away from him with every day that passed.

He tugged open the door and stepped outside, cursing when a blast of icy wind almost knocked him from his feet. He looked around, trying to gauge which of the various pens might have attracted the wolves' attention.

Brattahliò was not a large settlement. It stood at the head of a fjord, and comprised a tiny chapel – his great, great grandmother had converted to Christianity, and the place was still called Thjodhild's Church, even though she was many years in her grave – and a few houses clustered around it. Sheep, goats and chickens were kept in a range of sheds and outbuildings.

Jorund pulled his cloak more closely around him and began to walk towards the nearest pen. Then the wolves howled again, and he was both annoyed and relieved when he realized they were not close at all – as often happened in the great silence of the Arctic, the wind had carried the sound many miles.

3

'Something is bothering them,' came a voice at his elbow. He smiled. It was Leif, his eldest son, already tall for his nine years and showing the kind of qualities that would make him a good leader one day. 'They do not usually bay at nothing.'

'It is not nothing,' Jorund said, pointing to the sky. It was a clear night, with millions of stars blasted across a vast, velvety blackness. But there was something else, too – the strange, shimmering light that appeared sometimes in the spring months. It hovered like a great green scimitar, shivering and undulating. 'Perhaps God has not forsaken us after all.'

But Leif jabbed his finger towards the east. 'There! Do you see it? Gold in the sky!'

The wind was making Jorund's eyes water, and at first he could not see what Leif had spotted. But then he saw it – a shower of stars that burned brightly, then winked into nothing.

'Treasure!' breathed Leif, gripping his father's arm in excitement. 'God is sending us gold, because He is sorry for all the troubles He has sent us. We will be able to buy anything we want from the traders when they come in the summer, and then it will not matter whether the crops fail and our old animals die. We will stay here and be happy.'

'Perhaps we had better go and look for it tomorrow, then,' said Jorund with an indulgent smile. 'And check the fox traps at the same time.'

Leif grinned in pure pleasure, but then his happy expression faded. 'I cannot. I promised Ivar I would carve him a wooden boat. His leg has been paining him more recently because of the cold.'

Jorund sighed. Ivar had been born seven years before, making his entry into the world at the exact moment that the sun had returned after its winter absence, which the villagers had deemed to be a good omen. But poor Ivar was a frail, sickly child with a twisted leg. Brand often claimed that Ivar's poor health was another sign that they should abandon Brattahliδ and head for more ameliorative climes, but Brand was shameless in using any tragedy, no matter how sensitive, to make his point.

'We shall take Ivar with us,' said Jorund, patting Leif's shoulder. 'We will put him in a sling on my back and collect this gold together. And if we cannot find any, then perhaps we shall come home with a few fox pelts instead.'

White bears were particularly dangerous in the spring, because they were hungry, especially if they had cubs to feed. Two men had been killed by a female the previous year, and Jorund had no intention of sharing their fate. He carried a sturdy sword that had belonged to his father, and asked his friend Qasapi, from the nearby Skraeling settlement, to accompany him – Skraeling was the Old Norse word that the villagers used to describe the local people they encountered. Qasapi, who claimed his people had lived in Greenland since the beginning of time, was a superb hunter, and Jorund was certain no bear would ever catch *him* unawares. Moreover, Jorund needed to repay him for the seals he had given the village during the winter – they would share any furs they collected that day.

Jorund took Brand and his brother Aron on the expedition, too – not because he wanted their company, but because he did not dare leave Brand behind to spread more discontent.

'Did you see the lights last night?' Qasapi asked as they began to climb towards the hills. Leif was skipping ahead, full of energy and excitement; Ivar was a silent weight on Jorund's back; and Brand and Aron were a resentful presence bringing up the rear.

Jorund nodded. 'They have been brighter this year. Perhaps it is a sign that our luck may be about to change. God knows, we need it.'

'No, not the green lights – the falling stars. Did you see the falling stars?'

'It is gold from heaven,' called Leif with great conviction, bending down to poke at a frozen stream with his knife. 'It will make us rich.'

'Rich?' asked Qasapi, laughing. 'How? Will it bring herds of seals and walrus for us to eat?'

'It might,' said Leif archly. 'And then we shall stay here for ever.'

'It will be your death if you do,' said Brand bleakly. He was a powerful man with a thatch of yellow hair and fierce black eyes. 'Brattahlið will be our tomb if we do not leave this year.'

'Stop,' said Jorund wearily. 'It is a glorious day – the first clear one we have seen in weeks. Can you not enjoy it, and forget these dreams of yours? Just for a few hours?'

'I talk to the traders when they come to buy our furs,' said Brand angrily. 'They all say the same thing: that everyone in this region is struggling to survive. Foxes and wolves are getting harder to catch, our own animals are dying, the weather is turning too harsh to grow our crops. It is time to leave this icy wilderness to the Skraeling, who know no better, and sail for Engla lande.'

'Watch what you say,' snapped Jorund, glancing uneasily at Qasapi. They could not afford to offend such a generous neighbour. 'And if Engla lande is such a wonderful place, then why have the traders not settled there? The seas around Greenland are dangerous, so why risk themselves to barter for furs when they could be farming in paradise?'

'Not everyone is suited to agriculture,' retorted Brand. 'Just as not everyone is able to fight.'

Jorund ignored him, knowing perfectly well what he was trying to do. Brand itched to solve the dispute between them with his sword, and he had invited Jorund to win his point by combat on several occasions. Jorund had declined. Brand muttered that this was cowardice, and perhaps it was – he would be a formidable opponent. But it was not just his own life Jorund was afraid of losing, but that of every man, woman and child in Brattahlið, because he knew, with all his heart, that everyone would die if Brand won the contest and led them out across the open seas.

'The gold fell around here,' announced Leif, his chir-ruping voice breaking into the tense silence that followed Brand's remarks. 'Shall we look for it first or check the traps?'

'The traps,' replied Jorund, smiling at him. 'But we can watch for gold as we go.'

The first three traps – the best ones – were empty, and Jorund saw Brand nodding meaningfully at his brother as they bent to inspect them. Worse, one was smashed, and blood indicated that a fox had ventured inside, but something else – a wolf or a bear – had been quick to take advantage. Wearily, Jorund gathered the pieces so they could be carried home and mended. He was acutely aware that the traders would expect at least fifty pelts when they arrived in the summer, to make the journey worth their while, and so far he had only eight.

'The land hates us,' muttered Brand. 'It is telling us to go.'

'Look!' cried Leif suddenly, jumping to his feet and waving something in the air before Jorund could respond to Brand. 'Look what I have found!'

'Is it gold?' asked Qasapi, amused by the boy's eagerness to acquire what seemed to him to be a useless metal. 'To bribe the seals and reindeer to give themselves to us?'

'It is a special stone,' declared Leif, running towards him. 'It is in the shape of a boat!'

He held it out to Qasapi, and the others clustered around to see. The object was about the size of his hand, roughly cruciform, with two longer arms that were straight along one edge and curved along the other. One of the shorter arms was rectangular, while the other was rounded.

'It *is* a boat,' declared Brand. 'Here is the keel, and this square part is the sail. It is a sign that we should load the whole village in one and—'

'No,' interrupted Qasapi. 'It is a bird. The square part is not a sail, but a tail, and the rounded part forms its head. The two longer arms are wings.'

Jorund frowned: it did look like a bird, but he could see why Brand had thought it was a boat. He took it from his son's hand and was surprised by its weight – it felt as though it was made of lead. He took his knife from its scabbard, to scratch it, and was startled when the blade was drawn to the stone's surface, where it stuck. He pulled it away, then let it stick again. When the two surfaces met, they made a light ringing sound.

'It is iron,' he said. 'But like no iron that I have ever seen. It is blacker and smoother.'

'I have heard of rocks falling from the sky in the north,' said Qasapi. 'Although *they* are as big as your church. They are also made of metal, and my people chip pieces from them to use as knives and harpoon heads. We call them sky-stones.'

Leif looked acutely disappointed. 'I thought it was going to be gold.'

'They glow like gold when they fall,' explained Qasapi. 'But they go black or grey when they hit the ground.'

Leif forced a smile. 'Would you like it? It will not make many harpoon heads, but . . .'

'You must keep it yourself,' replied Qasapi. 'A sky-stone is a gift, and you should treasure it.'

'Pah!' Leif made as if to lob it away, but Ivar spoke for the first time that day.

'No!' he whispered from the sling on Jorund's back. 'Give it to me. I will look after it.'

Leif shoved it at him, then turned and bounded away, clearly hoping to discover something more interesting.

'I want to get down,' said Ivar, watching him. 'I want to run, too.'

'I know,' said Jorund kindly. 'And you shall in the summer, when the weather grows warm and your leg becomes stronger.'

'I mean today,' said Ivar, uncharacteristically firm. 'I want to run *today*.'

'Oh, let him down,' said Brand irritably. 'He will soon come snivelling back to you, crying that it hurts. And we will be here for a while, anyway. We need to check another seven empty traps yet, and then discuss why the foxes fail to jump into them.'

Ivar took no notice of Brand's sour temper as his father unbuckled the sling that held him. In truth, Jorund was grateful for the respite, because although the boy was little more than skin and bone, he was still seven years old and no age to be carried. Qasapi helped him, then watched as the boy took several tentative steps, the sky-stone clutched firmly in his hand.

'It is not running, but it is a start,' the Skraeling remarked to Jorund.

Jorund nodded but said nothing. He always found Ivar's pitiful attempts to walk difficult to watch. Why had he not been blessed with two strong sons? The village could not support anyone who was unable to work, but who still consumed valuable resources, and it was only a matter of time before someone like Brand said so. He sensed the man had been on the verge of making an announcement that winter, and might have done had Qasapi not arrived with gifts of meat.

Pushing bitter thoughts from his mind, Jorund turned his attention to his traps, and stared in stunned belief when the next one he inspected contained a beautiful white fox. Its pelt was perfect, and would fetch a good price from the traders – perhaps enough to buy a new axe. And the trap after that contained not one but two animals. He could scarcely believe his eyes! He leaped to his feet, to shout the news to the others, but the words died in his throat.

A bear was suddenly among them, arriving so fast that even Qasapi did not see it coming. Jorund had always been shocked by the terrifying speed of the creatures, and he barely had time to reach for his sword before it attacked Brand and Aron, claws and teeth slashing, and its savage growls terrible to hear.

Aron screamed as the bear's fangs fastened around his head – bears killed seals by crushing their skulls, and this one clearly intended to make short work of the human it had caught. Brand swung his sword at the creature, but panic made him careless and his glancing blow on its shoulder merely served to enrage it. The bear whipped around, and a casual swipe of a talon-laden paw knocked him clean off his feet. As he raced to their rescue, Jorund could see a good deal of blood and knew the wounds were serious, if not fatal.

He reached the bear and raised his sword. It was enormous, and when it growled he could smell its fetid breath. It lunged at him, and the blow he aimed with his sword went wide. He could hear Ivar screaming his terror and Leif howling at him to kill it. But that was easier said than done – one slash of a paw could disembowel a man, not to mention break his bones. He had to stay out of its reach and make sure that, when he did strike, his blow would kill – if it only injured, he would be a dead man for certain.

Then Qasapi arrived. He held a spear, and lobbed it with all his might. Jorund braced himself to take advantage of the bear's distraction, hoping that the wound would slow it down sufficiently to allow him to finish it. If not, the animal would be even more dangerous. The spear hit the bear's head, and Jorund felt his hopes shatter – bear skulls were thick and hard, and even the sharpest of spears would only glance off them.

Thus he was startled when the bear uttered a curious kind of whimper and fell on its side. Cautiously, he edged towards it, sword held ready, and saw the spear had gone through the bear's eye and entered the brain behind. Death had been instant. He turned to the hunter in awe.

Qasapi looked just as astonished. 'I was aiming for its chest,' he explained with a bemused shrug. 'With two men down, it was too dangerous to try anything else.'

But it was no time to congratulate him. Jorund turned quickly to Brand and Aron, steeling himself for sights he knew were going to be grisly. Aron's eyes were closed and his face was waxen; Brand was groaning.

'We must carry them home as quickly as possible,' he said to Qasapi. 'Forget the pelts. We will collect them tomorrow.'

'They will not be here tomorrow,' warned Qasapi. 'The land is hungry this time of year.'

Jorund knew it, but it could not be helped. All the elation he had felt about his luck changing evaporated as he concentrated on how he and Qasapi were to carry two large men all the way to Brattahlið. Was Leif strong enough to tote Ivar? Could they manage their weapons, too? It would be suicide to cross the land without them, but there was a limit to what they could take.

'Hold my sky-stone,' whispered Ivar to the moaning Brand. 'It made me feel strong. Perhaps it will help you, too.'

Brand shoved it and the boy away with an aggressive sweep of his hand. 'I am dying,' he gasped. 'You have your wish, Jorund. You brought me out here in the hope that some accident would befall me. Well, it has. You will not have my advice any more.'

'You are not dying,' said Jorund firmly. But he could tell from the bluish sheen to Brand's face that something was badly amiss. Would he survive the journey home? Would the scent of his blood attract other predators, meaning they would all die trying to help him?

'My belly is slashed open,' whispered Brand. 'I feel my innards spilling hot and wet inside my clothes. Finish it, Jorund. Kill me, because I cannot bear this pain. Then you can carry my brother home. I heard his skull crack when the bear bit it, so he will not survive me for long, but do your best for him.'

'My skull is not cracked,' said Aron. Jorund twisted around in surprise. Aron was standing behind him, and although there was blood on his head it was no more than a smear. 'There was an agony in my head, but Ivar made me hold the sky-stone, and it disappeared.'

'It is true,' said Ivar, standing proudly beside him. He knelt and, ignoring Brand's protests, pushed the stone into his hand. 'You hold it, too. Then you will find your innards are all where they are meant to be.'

'I saw the bear's jaws close,' said Jorund uncertainly. He peered at Aron's head. 'Yet there is barely a mark on you. A few scratches, perhaps, but I have had worse from Ivar's cat.'

'The bear was young,' said Qasapi with another shrug. 'Its jaws were not large enough to go around Aron's head, so instead of crushing his skull the teeth must have glanced off. He is very lucky – few escape such determined attacks.'

Jorund turned back to Brand and began to undo his clothing so he could inspect the damage caused by the claws. Then he stopped, embarrassed. The area around Brand's belly was certainly hot and wet, but it had nothing to do with blood.

'Fear,' said Qasapi, inspecting the mess dispassionately. 'It can do that to a man.'

'I was not afraid!' shouted Brand, mortified. He scrambled to his feet. 'I was slashed! I felt the claws tear through my clothes.'

'Your clothes are torn,' acknowledged Qasapi, while Jorund shook his head in disbelief that both men should have had such narrow escapes. 'But there are no wounds, not even a scratch.'

'It was the sky-stone,' said Ivar, taking it from Brand and clutching it hard. 'It made them well again, just as it made me strong.'

'Perhaps it did,' said Qasapi, while the others regarded the boy uncertainly. 'But we have work to do here. We have a bear and three foxes to skin, and meat to prepare.'

'Bear meat?' asked Brand in distaste.

Qasapi smiled beatifically. 'Why not? The land has made us a gift, and it would be rude not to accept it. We shall take as much as we can carry. But we must hurry: I feel a storm coming.'

The storm raced in from the north as they struggled back to Brattahli∂. Three foxes and a bear were more than Jorund had ever hoped to find, and his heart sang with joy. Leif carried the weapons, while the men staggered under heavy burdens of fur and meat, and – perhaps best of all – Ivar walked by Jorund's side and never once complained that he was tired or that his leg hurt.

The clouds began to gather, thick, black and driven by a fierce wind. Jorund wondered more than once whether they should abandon their spoils and run for home. But the storm held off, and it was only as they pushed through the door to their house that the first flurries of snow began to fall. Perhaps it was yet another sign that the run of bad luck was over, and that the village's fortunes were about to change.

Sigrid cried when she saw Ivar on his feet, and declared his cure a miracle. Together, mother and son went to lay the sky-stone on the altar in the church. Leif, a natural storyteller, was eager to tell everyone about their adventures, and the whole village gathered to eat roasted bear and to listen. They laughed when he described Brand's declarations of imminent death, and Jorund winced – had Leif been older, he might have had the wisdom to omit that particular detail. Brand glowered and slouched out; Jorund sighed, knowing there would be trouble later.

It came sooner than he expected. The following morning Brand approached him, several cronies at his heels. All were burly, powerful young men who were bored and restless living as farmers in Brattahlið. Jorund was not surprised that Brand's dreams appealed to them: most boasted Erik the Red as an ancestor, a man who had been banished from his own country for being a murderous troublemaker. It was unreasonable to expect all his descendants to be satisfied with the sedate life of agriculture.

'We are going,' Brand announced without preamble. 'You cannot stop us, so do not try. We are taking everything we own, plus the boat, and we are heading south. When the traders arrive at the place they call the Western Settlement, we shall go with them to Engla lande.'

'No,' said Jorund firmly. 'We need you – we cannot plant the crops without you. Would you abandon us here to starve?'

'Anyone who does not want to share your fate can come with us,' said Brand. 'They all have a choice, and so do you.'

Suddenly, Jorund was tired of doing battle with Brand. They probably *could* manage without the men who had elected to leave. It would not be easy, but if their luck really had changed, then perhaps it would not be as difficult as he feared. But Jorund did not think he could face another winter of constant recriminations, such as the one he had just endured.

'Very well,' he said, seeing the surprise in Brand's eyes at his abrupt capitulation. 'But do not set out yet. Wait until the weather warms, and there is less ice in the sea. It will be safer for—'

'And give you months in which to dissuade us?' demanded Brand. 'I do not think so! We are going today – we have the boat ready. And we are taking the sky-stone. You have no need of it here, and we can sell it to buy new livestock to get us started in Engla lande.'

Jorund frowned. 'Sell it?'

Brand leaned close towards him. 'You saw what it did yesterday – it cured your crippled son, and then it healed Aron and me of grievous wounds. There are abbeys and priories that would pay a fortune for such a prize.'

'It cured no one,' said Jorund. 'Ivar claimed it did, but he is a child and does not know what he is talking about. His leg healed because winter is over, and he – like all of us – feels better for it. And you and Aron were never wounded in the first place. The bear's teeth glanced off Aron's head, while your clothes protected you from its claws.'

'Then you will not mind us having it,' said Brand. 'If it is just a worthless scrap of stone.'

'I do not, but it is not mine to give. It belongs to Leif, so you must ask him—'

'I will take it now,' said Brand, pushing past him and marching inside the chapel. 'Tell him it is payment for you keeping us here all this time. We would have gone years ago, if you had not forced us to stay.'

He emerged a few moments later with the sky-stone in his hand. Jorund fingered his sword, but he could not hope to fight Brand and six others single-handed. Unfortunately, Ivar and Leif arrived at that moment. Ivar saw what Brand held, and raced forward.

'No!' he shouted, distressed. 'Put it back! It is sacred and belongs on the altar.'

'I gave it to Ivar,' said Leif, gazing defiantly at Brand. 'That means it is his, and you have no right to touch it. Put it back, like he says.'

'Control your brats,' said Brand coldly to Jorund, aware that people were gathering to watch and listen. Several were smirking at the way Leif was laying down the law to his elders. 'They cannot talk to me this way.'

He started to walk towards his friends, but Ivar grabbed his hand to prise the fingers open. Brand swatted him away like a fly. Before Jorund could stop him, Leif leaped at Brand and punched him in the chest. More outraged than hurt, Brand hit Leif so hard that he flew through the air and struck the side of the church. He lay still, and suddenly there was absolute silence.

Stomach lurching, Jorund ran towards Leif and rested a shaking hand against his neck, although he could tell by the way the child had fallen that his neck was broken.

'Leif!' he whispered, cradling the limp form in stunned disbelief. Next to him, Ivar began to cry.

'He should not have touched me,' declared Brand, eyes darting around nervously. 'This is your fault. You should not have let him—'

With a roar of fury, Jorund staggered to his feet, sword in his hand, and launched himself at Brand. Brand was tall and strong, and Jorund had never known whether he would be able to best him, but such thoughts were far from his mind as he attacked his son's killer. Brand stumbled away, shocked by the ferocity of the attack, and Aron darted forward to help him. Someone shouted that two against one was unfair, and another weapon was drawn. Then Brand's friends joined the affray, and the air was full of furious voices and clashing steel. The ground underfoot grew slippery with blood.

Jorund ignored it all, seeing only the hated face in front of him – the man who was determined to spoil the harmony of his village, and who had murdered his beloved son. He did not see Sigrid slide a dagger into Aron's back, or hear Ivar screaming for everyone to stop. Brand was looking frightened, but the man's cowardice acted as a spur, causing Jorund to respond with a series of vicious swipes, one of which caught him just above the ear. It was a killing blow, and Brand toppled to the ground.

Once Brand and Aron were down, the skirmish quickly ended. The bloodlust drained from Jorund, leaving in its place a sense of sick shame. Thirteen men lay dead, some of them Brand's would-be deserters, and some men who had rallied to Jorund's side. Panting hard, he gazed around him and wondered how he had allowed such a situation to come to pass. What sort of leader was he, to draw weapons against his people?

'It does not work,' wept Ivar, and Jorund saw he was trying to press the sky-stone into his brother's hand. 'It will not make him sit up.'

'Why would it?' Jorund demanded harshly. 'It is only a piece of iron. But Brand will have his wish. We will leave Brattahlið today – he said the ship is ready.'

'Today?' asked one of the villagers, startled. 'But we cannot! You said yourself that the weather is not yet warm enough for long journeys.'

'We will go to the Western Settlement,' Jorund replied. 'It is a big place; they will find a corner for us. Release the animals and gather warm clothes. There is nothing for us here.'

'But what about the dead?' asked Sigrid, shocked. 'Wild animals will come and—'

'Leave them,' ordered Jorund, resolutely turning his back on the slaughter. 'Let the land have them. It is what it wanted, after all.'

Twenty years later

'I am not sure this is a good idea,' muttered Jorund, standing next to Ivar as the prow of the boat nosed up the memory-laden waterway towards Brattahlið. 'It was hard living here – Brand was right to encourage us to leave.'

'Our people never liked the Western Settlement,' replied Ivar. Since his lame leg had been cured, he had grown into a tall, strong man; Jorund thought it a pity that he had announced a calling to become a monk, when he would have made a fine warrior. 'They are all pleased to be coming home.'

'Then let us hope they are not disappointed,' said Jorund.

'They will not be,' declared Ivar with great conviction. 'They have been homesick ever since we left. And there is not a soul among them who thinks Brand was right, even if they do remember him. Besides, the green lights were bright in the sky again this year. It is right to come here now.'

Jorund said nothing, but his stomach lurched when the boat's keel scraped on the beach and it was time to disembark. All around, his people were scrambling overboard, calling to each other in unbridled delight as they recognized familiar landmarks. Wordlessly, Jorund and Ivar walked towards the village, leaving the others to unload the supplies. When they drew close to the church, Jorund stopped.

'I cannot go any further,' he whispered. 'We left the dead unburied . . .'

'But Qasapi did not,' said Ivar. 'He sent word to say that he and his people had covered them decently with stones. We shall bury them in the cemetery later, and that will mark an end to the business. This is a good place, and our people will prosper here.'

'I wish you were staying,' said Jorund unhappily. 'We will all miss you. Are you sure you want to go to Iceland and become a monk? I have heard they keep you inside all day, reading and praying.'

Ivar smiled. 'It is all arranged, Father, and I must follow my promise to God.'

'And all because of that sky-stone,' said Jorund bitterly. 'I wish Leif had never found it.'

'It is a great gift, if used properly,' countered Ivar. 'You were sceptical at first, but even you acknowledged its power when it saved Mother after she almost died giving birth to Olaf. And it has brought us luck.'

'Some very good luck, and some very bad,' agreed Jorund. 'But I am glad you are taking it away. It led to fights when the people of the Western Settlement learned about it, and it is unpredictable – it does not always do what one wants.'

'Such as failing to save Leif,' said Ivar sadly. 'And Aron's little son, when he fell in the fire. I suppose it wants to be seen as a boon, not a given. But regardless, the monks will know how to use it wisely, and I do not think we should keep it any longer.'

Jorund smiled, pleased his son had grown so wise. Would Leif have shown the same qualities? And would his third son, Olaf, who was being groomed as village leader now Ivar was making good his promise to take the cowl? He supposed only time would tell.

The following day, while the rest of the villagers mended fences and enclosures, Jorund and Ivar removed the stones Qasapi had laid over the bodies of the thirteen men and one boy who had died so long ago, and began the process of taking them to the cemetery.

Despite the Skraelings' care, animals had been at the bodies, and rain and snow had done their share of scattering, too. It was impossible to tell which bones belonged to whom, so they buried them in a common grave to the south of the church, placing the skulls in a long line against one side.

'We may have put Brand next to Leif,' said Jorund anxiously, staring down at what they had done. 'A killer next to his victim.'

'It does not matter,' said Ivar comfortingly. 'And they were all friends once. Let us put the earth over them and make an end of this dismal business.'

A week later Ivar packed the sky-stone in a bag with some warm clothes and prepared to head south with the traders. He bade a tearful farewell to the parents and brother he would never see again, and watched Brattahliд and its little church until they disappeared from sight. Then he turned his eyes to the seas he would have to cross before he reached his final destination.

In the following days, with his thoughts far away, Ivar did not notice the man from the Western Settlement who watched him intently. Called Saemund, he was not much older than Ivar, and had not dissimilar Norse features. Like everyone from the Western Settlement, he knew all about the sky-stone. He had also heard Ivar telling his father that he intended to give it to a monastery, and he thought it a pity that monks in Iceland should benefit from something that belonged in Greenland. Before they had even sailed, Saemund had decided to kill Ivar and tip his body into the sea; accidents were not uncommon on ships, and it would be assumed that Ivar had been washed overboard.

And the sky-stone? Saemund would grab it before he threw Ivar's corpse into the sea, and then he would keep it safe. When he returned to the Western Settlement the following year, he would take it with him. Of course, he might use it to accrue himself a little wealth in the meantime – such a prize could make a man very rich.

Late one day, with no one else near the stern, Saemund began to edge towards Ivar, but as he pulled out his knife the ship gave a peculiar lurch. He glanced upwards and saw dark clouds scudding towards them. Surely, they had not been there earlier? It had been clear and calm all day, and the captain had been muttering about an unusually placid crossing. Keeping a wary eye on the sky, Saemund eased forward again.

The squall hit the little ship with tremendous force, dousing those on deck with a vicious shower of rain and spray. Saemund blinked water from his eyes. Were the gods providing a diversion for him, so he could take the stone from Ivar without being seen – knowing he would bring the treasure back to Greenland? Or were they warning him to leave well alone?

Saemund took a firmer hold on his knife. There was only one way to find out.

Historical note

In the 1960s archaeological investigations in western Greenland uncovered the foundations of a tiny church. It has been dated to about AD 1000 and is thought to have been built by Thjodhild, wife of Erik the Red; Erik founded the settlement of Brattahlið in the 980s. An unusual mass grave was discovered just to the south of it, containing thirteen adult males and a nine-year-old child. All had been buried at the same time, and, although the skeletons appear to have been deposited fairly randomly, the heads were carefully arranged in a line down the eastern side of the pit. Many show signs of violence, such as hacking injuries to the head and arms.

Several explanations have been offered for why so many men should have died at the same time. Vikings were a seafaring people, and so it has been suggested they were victims of a shipwreck on Greenland's treacherous coast. Alternatively, they may have been the losers in a skirmish, either with a rival clan or with indigenous people. But no one knows, and the fate of these people remains a mystery.

A number of iron meteorites are recorded as having been discovered in Greenland. They were highly prized by the Greenlanders, who fashioned knives, harpoon heads and engraving tools from them. Three large ones landed east of Cape York about a thousand years ago, and, although their whereabouts was a closely guarded secret, rumours of an 'iron mountain' reached the British explorer John Ross in 1818. The American explorer Robert E. Peary found the meteorites in 1894, and the next year took two of them back to the United States. In 1896 Peary led an expedition to remove the largest of the meteorites, which was known as 'Ahnighito' and weighed between ninety and a hundred tons. Peary had it excavated but could not transport it all the way to his ship, so he returned in 1897, when he was able to take it with him back to New York. It is now displayed in the American Museum of Natural History.

ACT ONE

Estrighoiel (now Chepstow), summer 1101

The weathered recluse was frightened. Ever since he had used the sky-stone to save Cadowan's wife, people had been trying to find him, demanding cures. And demanding answers, too. They wanted to know how he had been able to wrest a woman from the jaws of death. Was it by God's grace or the devil's? All that most of them knew was that Nest claimed he had put a curiously shaped stone in her hand and urged it to heal her – and it had. Was it true? Where was this stone? Surely, if it had truly helped her, it should be in a shrine, not in the care of a grizzled, cantankerous hermit in a cave in the woods?

Ivar knew, without the shadow of a doubt, that someone was going to try to take it from him. Nest and Cadowan were good people, which was why he had helped Nest when he had come across her, twisted and broken, after her fall down the cliff. She had promised to keep silent about what had happened, but there had been witnesses – those who had chased her and driven her over the precipice in the first place – and they had accused her of being in league with Satan. To save her, her husband had told the truth, and then Nest had followed suit. Ivar did not blame them; he would probably have done the same.

But it meant that now, after years of solitude, Ivar's sanctuary was under siege. People flocked to him with their questions, pleas and demands, and he knew he could not stay in his refuge much longer. Nest and Cadowan had tried to buy the stone from him, and when he had refused to part with it they had urged him to take it to the monastery in Estrighoiel, where Prior Odo had offered to keep it safe and use it wisely.

Ivar grimaced. Of course he had! The sky-stone would bring the little foundation great wealth, and monks, like the indolent Aidan and the fiery Marcus, would be only too grateful to spend it on themselves. Ivar had learned years ago that the inhabitants of such places were not gentle saints who dedicated their lives to God, as he had been led to believe, but were men with the usual human failings of greed and ambition.

Then there was the constable at the castle, arrived within the last few months – the constable was the man in charge of the fortress and its troops, who held his command directly from the King. Walter de Clare would love to lay his hands on the sky-stone, so he could dole out its favours to those he needed to impress. He was already regarded with fear and suspicion in his new domain, partly because of his ugly character, but mostly because of the mysterious and convenient 'accident' that had killed his predecessor – like Nest, Sir Drogo de Hauteville had gone over a cliff.

Walter would not come for the stone himself, of course: he was too cowardly. He would send his henchmen, battle-honed Norman knights, who would stop at nothing to carry out his orders. Two stood out to Ivar as particularly dangerous: Pigot, who was huge, strong and had a reputation for cruelty, and the angel-faced Revelle, who was too intelligent to serve a man like Walter, and so represented something of an enigma.

Ivar thought back over his life, sorry he had wasted so much of it. He could have achieved great things – it was not as if he had been short of dreams as he grew up on the Greenland farm. But after the shipwreck that had washed him up on the wild Hibernian shore so far from where he had intended to go, he had been confused and frightened. The sky-stone had saved his life, he was sure of that, and he knew it had been for a reason. But what? Everything that had once been so clear to him had become vague and uncertain.

Within days of the four survivors finding themselves thrown on to the shore, an entire army had appeared at the coast to take sail. But its leader lay near death, wounded by a battleaxe. The sky-stone had made him whole again, and suddenly the four were viewed as great healers and men of God. In appreciation, the now-healthy Rhys ap Tewdwr took them with him across a narrow sea, to where he reconquered his lost homeland and reclaimed his title as Prince of Deheubarth.

For five years they remained in Rhys's court at Dinefwr Castle – and Ivar often pondered the safety of the sky-stone – before the Prince was killed by the Normans. Two of the shipwrecked survivors also died in the conflict, and Ivar and the other disappeared into the deep forests and crags near Estrighoiel. There, a quiet, reflective life in a hermit's cave had not always kept the tension from building between the two. So, having always fancied himself something of an explorer, Ivar finally departed, leaving the sky-stone behind only because he sensed it did not want to leave the wooded hills.

He had travelled far and wide, but the sky-stone was always in the back of his mind. It had taken years, but he had returned eventually, and had wept for joy when the stone lay in his hand again. It had not changed – it was still glossy, with the curious shape that might be a bird or a ship. Or even a cross, perhaps. And although he was now the only survivor, the cave was still there, hidden among the ferns and the trees. He found it was a good place in which to live, especially to a man used to polar winters.

When times were very hard, he would venture into Estrighoiel and sell remedies for various minor hurts. But he was always careful to keep the stone hidden when he applied them, so no one would know the real reason why his cures worked. It was better that way, because he sensed there was a limit to the sky-stone's powers – use it too much, and it might not perform in the event that he needed it for himself.

And then, one day, he had happened across Nest and the men who were stalking her with lust in their eyes. Ivar could not be certain, because they kept themselves concealed, but he thought they were knights from the castle. Nest was beautiful, with long black hair and perfect features, and Ivar knew people had been bemused when she chose the plain Cadowan for her husband. But Ivar understood: Cadowan was wealthy, and well able to afford the clothes that showed off Nest's lithe figure and the jewellery that sparkled at her slender throat and on her fingers.

Ivar had watched the men prepare to pounce on Nest, but she had heard the crack of a twig and, sensing danger, had bolted. He had shouted a warning, telling her that the summer rain had turned the track treacherous, but terror had turned her deaf. She had lost her footing near the cliff and fallen, and, appalled, her dissolute pursuers had melted into the trees.

She was dying by the time he reached her. She was so lovely that he found himself wanting her as well, and, determined that such beauty should not perish, he

reached for the sky-stone without thought of the conse-
quences. Unfortunately, the men were still watching,
and they had reported to Walter de Clare, who immediately launched an investigation. Unsurprisingly, no
soldiers were ever brought to book for the intended
rape, although Ivar and Nest were taken to the castle
and questioned.

His memories were suddenly interrupted as a figure
materialized in the entrance to his cave. He was angry and
distressed in equal measure. Why would they not leave him
alone?

'Go away!' he cried. 'I do not want to see anyone.'

'You must come with me,' came Revelle's breathless,
gasping voice. It was a stiff climb to the cave. 'There has
been an accident, and you are needed. Hurry!'

'No!' declared Ivar querulously. 'I do not want to.'

'The victim is a child,' pleaded Revelle, his smooth,
angelic face desperate. 'Walter's six-year-old daughter.
She fell in the river, and now she does not breathe. You
must help her.'

'I cannot,' cried Ivar, alarmed. 'You credit me with altogether too much power.'

'You bring folk back from the dead,' argued Revelle.
'Nest said so. Please cure Eleanor – Walter is beside
himself, and you are the only one who can help.' He hesitated, then forged on. 'He dotes on her, and her death
will turn him bitter. The whole town will suffer if Eleanor
dies . . .'

Against his better judgement, Ivar followed Revelle to
the town, where a crowd had gathered. There was absolute
silence, except for Walter's broken weeping. The townsfolk might not like the constable, with his vicious ways and
unruly henchmen, but everyone adored the little girl with
the gap-toothed smile and dancing eyes.

Revelle pushed the hermit forward. 'You know what you must do, Ivar Jorundsson.'

Estrighoiel, summer 1103

Sir Geoffrey Mappestone had not wanted to travel to Estrighoiel, but his wife had insisted. Geoffrey was not normally a man who could be bullied, but Hilde was a formidable lady, and they had not been married long – he was loath to turn their relationship turbulent with a confrontation. And it was not far to Estrighoiel from Goodrich, especially in summer, when the Wye Valley track was hard, dry and good for riding. He estimated it was no more than thirty miles, and it was not as if he was needed at home anyway – a lifetime of soldiering overseas meant he had scant idea how to run an estate.

A bird flapped suddenly in the undergrowth, and he reined his horse to an abrupt standstill, listening intently as his hand dropped to the broadsword he wore at his waist. It was unlikely that anyone would risk attacking a fully armed Norman knight, but Geoffrey had not survived twenty years of combat by being cavalier about inexplicable noises.

'It is nothing,' said his friend, Sir Roger of Durham, who rode at his side. He had also stopped, one hand on his sword and the other ready to grab the cudgel that was looped behind his saddle. 'Just another nervous pigeon.'

Roger was an enormous man, with a head of long black curls, a bushy beard and expensive clothes that had suffered from being worn too long: they were grimy, smelly and repairs had been made with clumsy stitches. By contrast, Geoffrey, with no mean stature himself, was neater and kept his light brown hair short, in soldierly fashion.

He and Roger had little in common, including whatever the other held dear – Roger was fond of wars and money, while Geoffrey, unusually for a knight, was literate and liked books and art. Nevertheless, they had forged a friendship when they had joined the Crusade to the Holy Land years before. Geoffrey had gone because Tancred, his liege lord, had ordered him to, and because he had had a yearning to learn Hebrew and Arabic, although he had never been convinced of the wisdom of causing trouble in foreign countries. Roger had gone to loot himself a fortune and fight anyone who tried to stop him.

The two had been reunited a few weeks before, when Roger had arrived to enjoy the hunting in his friend's woods. He was a demanding, wearisome guest, with his rough, ebullient manners and unpredictable aggression, and it crossed Geoffrey's mind that Hilde might not have been quite so insistent that her husband travel to Estrighoiel if Roger had not been visiting.

'Why did Hilde want us to come here?' Roger asked as they started moving again. 'I know you have already said, but I was more interested in the lasses in that village of yours, who came to wave us off. I did not listen to you.'

Geoffrey suspected it had been relief that had encouraged the girls from their homes to bid Roger farewell – and that they were hoping his departure was permanent. None were safe from his clumsy advances, and he was regarded as something of a menace.

'Her uncle is a monk at Estrighoiel Priory,' began Geoffrey obligingly. 'And someone tried to kill him with a dagger. He wrote asking her for money, to hire a bodyguard.'

'I can see why she was not very keen on that,' said Roger, who hated parting with cash. 'And your manor is hardly wealthy, anyway. She will not want to squander good gold on keeping some old man alive.'

'Actually, she thought it would be better if we investigated why someone meant him harm in the first place,' said Geoffrey somewhat tartly. Hilde might leave a lot to be desired in a wife, but miserliness was not one of her failings. 'She will find the funds, if necessary.'

Roger sniffed. 'And there was me thinking she is sensible! So that is all we must do in Estrighoiel? Find out why someone tried to murder a monk? With your sharp wits and my sharp sword, we shall have answers in no time, and you will soon be back in the marriage bed.'

He winked salaciously, and Geoffrey winced. He had not wanted to marry Hilde – she was his senior by at least five years and was more manly than most men – but it had been politically expedient to form an alliance with the locally powerful Baderon family. Moreover, Goodrich needed an heir, and the whole manor was watching intently for signs that he had done his duty. He only hoped it would not take long, because going through the necessary procedures was awkward for both of them.

'There it is!' said Roger as they rounded a corner. 'Estrighoiel. We have arrived.'

The Castelle de Estrighoiel was an imposing sight. It comprised a great oblong keep set in a triangular bailey. It was built of pale stone, and its entrance, like all good Norman fortresses, was on the first floor, accessed by a removable wooden staircase. Small round-headed windows made it dark inside, but it was secure and easy to defend. It was further protected by a curtain wall topped by a gallery for archers, and its position, perched at the edge of cliffs that plunged in a sheer drop towards the River Wye, made it all but impregnable.

Beyond the castle was the Benedictine priory. It had a large, striking church built of cream-coloured limestone, and a range of buildings in which the monks ate, slept and worked, all surrounded by a wooden palisade. The town lay between them, centred on its marketplace and the large piers at which several ships were moored. Even from a distance, Geoffrey could see it was busy: carts rolled towards the market laden with goods, and the boats were a hive of activity, as old cargoes were offloaded and new ones taken on.

'It is hot today,' remarked Roger as they left the comparative cool of the shade cast by the woods and ventured into the bright sunlight to approach the town. He wiped his face with a piece of silk that had probably once been pretty but was now stained and rather nasty. 'This fine weather has lasted for weeks now, but it will change soon. I smell a storm coming.'

'I hope you are wrong,' said Geoffrey, squinting up at the cloudless blue sky. 'Rain now will spoil the harvest.'

Roger regarded him askance. 'I cannot believe you said that! You are a trained warrior, who wears the honoured surcoat of the *Jerosolimitanus* – a knight who has saved his soul and had all his sins forgiven by wresting the Holy City from Saracens. And now you sound like a farmer!'

'You will be the first to complain if the crops are destroyed and there is no flour for bread.'

Roger was saved from having to think of a rejoinder, because they had entered the town. People stopped to stare at them as they passed, and Geoffrey wondered whether they should have travelled more anonymously – they wore the half armour and surcoats that marked them as knights. He had not given the matter much thought when they had left the previous morning – he had just donned what he normally wore when travelling outside his estates.

'The landlord of the inn where we stayed last night told me that the Castelle de Estrighoiel is held by the King,' said Roger conversationally as they rode along the main street.

Geoffrey groaned. 'Is it? I thought it was built by one of his barons.'

'It was – William fitz Osbern. But he died in battle thirty years ago, and his son was rash enough to indulge in rebellion. The first King William confiscated all his possessions, and the second King William liked them enough to keep hold of them. Then *his* heir, King Henry, who is a greedy rogue—'

'Not so loud,' murmured Geoffrey, aware that people were listening. It was not a good idea to bawl treasonous remarks in a place where they were strangers, and, not for the first time, he wished Roger were imbued with a little more tact – and sense.

Roger lowered his voice obligingly. 'Well, King Henry, being a man fond of property, keeps Estrighoiel still. Having seen it, I understand why. It is a good fortress – strong and large.'

'Your garrulous landlord did not tell you whether the King is here, did he?' asked Geoffrey uneasily. 'Because if he is, we are turning around right now.'

Roger laughed. 'I have no love for the sly villain myself, but I am not frightened of him.'

'Neither am I,' said Geoffrey stiffly. 'But every time we meet, he uses unscrupulous means to make me do him favours. And as he is never honest about the commissions, they invariably prove to be dangerous or unsavoury. I do not want to meet him, lest he orders me to do something else against my better judgement – or my conscience.'

'It is better not to have a conscience where he is concerned, Geoff lad. But you need not worry. I believe he is in Westminster, plotting spiteful vengeance on those who cross him.'

Geoffrey was relieved: he did not want to be embroiled in any more of the King's dark business. He was about to say so when he became aware of a rumpus taking place in the market ahead of them. It involved two warriors, a pair of monks and a couple from the town. Their disagreement had gathered quite a crowd, although Geoffrey noticed that the onlookers' curiosity seemed more perturbed than nosy.

'There is an atmosphere in this place,' remarked Roger. 'As if everyone is frightened.'

Geoffrey agreed, and imagined it must be powerful, if Roger had noticed it. The big knight was not noted for his sensitivity. The people were cowed and uneasy, and even the children playing in the street seemed restrained.

'He *did* cure her,' one man was declaring. He was a short, red-faced individual with the kind of accent that said his first language was Welsh. His rich clothes indicated he was a merchant. The woman of whom he was speaking was beautiful, with black hair falling in a shimmering sheet to her waist. 'Nest was set to die, and he made her well again.'

'My husband speaks the truth,' said Nest. 'I would not be here today were it not for Ivar.'

'Ivar is sinister,' declared one of the soldiers. Like Geoffrey and Roger, he was a knight, and he wore his weapons and mail with the easy confidence of a man comfortable with them. He was large, black-haired, and his face was marred by a dark scowl.

'Pigot is right: Ivar *is* sinister,' agreed the other knight. He had golden hair, and his face looked far too gentle to belong to a warrior. 'And Sir Walter says we should not have him within the confines of our town. It was better when he lived in his cave.'

'Our prior does not agree, Revelle,' said one of the monks. He was a bulky, affable-looking man with twinkling eyes and a wooden cross displayed prominently against the dark wool of his habit. 'Ivar has been in our fold for two years now and has been no trouble at all.'

Revelle grimaced. 'You often say the town has changed for the worse in the last two years, Brother Aidan. Well, two years ago was when Ivar came down from the hills and took up residence in your priory.'

'And we want him gone,' added Pigot in a growl.

'It corresponds to the time *you* arrived, too,' Aidan shot back. 'You, Pigot *and* Walter de Clare, all conveniently to hand so soon after poor Drogo's death.'

Geoffrey had heard of the de Clare family. They had been present when King William II had been killed in the New Forest, and there were rumours that they had arranged it, so Henry could accede to the throne. Geoffrey had no idea whether the tales were true, but he was certainly aware that the powerful de Clares were not a clan to cross.

'Drogo was murdered,' said the merchant. 'He knew this area well and was not likely to ride over a cliff, as has been claimed.'

'And why was he by the cliff? Because he was visiting Ivar!' retorted Revelle. The promptness of his reply made Geoffrey suspect that it was a debate that had been aired many times before. 'But he never returned. And you wonder why Walter is wary of Ivar?'

'Ivar had nothing to do with Drogo's death,' said Aidan firmly. 'And he is one of *us* now – a Benedictine and a holy man. He is above reproach.'

'Are you saying Benedictines are above reproach, Brother Aidan?' asked Revelle archly. 'After all the unsavoury dealings we uncovered in your priory?'

'They were not unsavoury dealings,' said the other monk hotly, stepping forward. He was roughly Geoffrey's age – mid-thirties – and looked as if he should have been a warrior, not a monk. Unlike Aidan, his cross was gold, rather than wood. 'They were all lies – fabricated by villains in a transparent attempt to discredit us.'

'These tales came from a reputable source, Brother Marcus,' said Revelle. 'And there was evidence to prove that the sacristan *has* misappropriated the funds in his care, that Prior Odo *does* drink too much and that the cellarer *did* entertain women in his quarters.'

'So your spy *claims*,' spat Marcus in distaste. 'Some villain who runs to Walter with tales in return for money.'

'A lot of money,' agreed Pigot with a gloating smile. 'He does not come cheap. But then, his intelligence is worth the expense. And you still have no idea who he might be!'

'I do not know whether the stories from the priory are true, but the ones pertaining to Ivar are lies,' declared Nest. 'He would never do the things he was accused of. He is a saint.'

'He is a grubby vagrant,' countered Revelle, 'with a reason to be frightened by the charges of witchcraft we tried to bring against him. He *did* kill poor little Eleanor, because there were witnesses – myself among them.'

'He did not kill her,' said Aidan tiredly, putting out a warning hand as Marcus started to surge forward angrily. 'He tried to *save* her when she was dragged from the river, but she was beyond his skills. No one, other than you at the castle, blames him for that.'

'He does not cast spells and conjure up Satan, either,' declared Marcus, clearly furious. 'I confess I find Ivar difficult, but we shall stand by him against all lies spread by seculars.'

Revelle shrugged. 'He will show his true colours one day, and then you will be sorry you did not listen to our warnings. The devil will come and drag him down to hell – and will take every single one of you with him. You are a fool to keep protecting him.'

'You are the fool,' muttered Marcus under his breath.

'God's blood!' muttered Roger at Geoffrey's side. 'Quarrelsome villagers, argumentative knights and hot-tongued monks whose comrades cast spells to summon the devil! What sort of place is Estrighoiel?'

Geoffrey led the way towards the priory, supposing he had better make himself known to Hilde's uncle as soon as possible. He dismounted by a wooden gate and knocked. A metal grille set in the door flew open, and he could see a pair of unfriendly eyes on the other side. The fellow's robes indicated he was a lay brother.

'What do you want?' he demanded. 'You cannot come in, whatever it is. We are busy.'

Geoffrey was taken aback. Monasteries were usually hospitable to travellers, especially ones whose surcoats said they had been to the Holy Land. But then, the confrontation in the market suggested something odd was happening in the town, so he supposed he should not be surprised.

'We have come to visit Brother Leger. He is uncle to my wife.'

'He is? Oh, Christ!'

The grille was slammed closed, leaving Geoffrey staring at it in astonishment. Roger's expression hardened.

'That was plain rude. Shall we break down the door and teach them a lesson? Hilde said there are only twelve monks here, and I doubt they have more than six lay brothers. Few will be armed, and we could take the place easily.

And if they harbour Satan-worshippers, then the town and the castle will not object.'

'No,' said Geoffrey, seeing his friend was perfectly serious. 'We are not in the business of sacking monasteries.'

'We did it in Antioch,' Roger pointed out. 'On the Crusade.'

'That was different. We are here to help Hilde's uncle, not besiege his home.'

Roger grimaced, then wiped his face again with his filthy piece of silk. 'We should not have worn armour today – it is far too hot. I am being roasted alive.'

'Wait for me in a tavern,' suggested Geoffrey, suspecting gaining access to Leger might take some time and loath to have Roger complaining while he persuaded the brothers that he was not there to accuse them of drunkenness, dishonesty or failing to save children from drowning. 'I will join you there later.'

'Very well,' agreed Roger. 'But fetch me if there is any fighting. I will not be pleased to hear you have enjoyed yourself without me.'

Geoffrey was relieved when Roger disappeared into a large, neat tavern with a sign outside indicating it was the White Lion. He was about to knock on the priory gate again when the grille snapped open and a different pair of eyes inspected him. This time, they belonged to a monk with white hair, the kind of nose that said he liked a drink, and a large wooden cross around his neck, like the one Aidan wore.

'Who are you?' he demanded haughtily. 'What do you want?'

'I am here to visit Leger,' replied Geoffrey patiently. 'He sent word to his niece, Hilde, that he might be in trouble.'

'That is one way of putting it,' muttered the monk. 'He is dead.'

*   *   *

It was not easy persuading the Benedictine to open the door so that the conversation did not have to take place in a busy thoroughfare. Geoffrey did not like the fact that people were stopping to listen, and if it had not been for his promise to Hilde he might have turned around and gone home.

'It might be better if we had this discussion inside,' he said to the monk. 'A crowd is gathering, and I understand you are already the subject of rumours—'

'All lies, put about by the evil Walter,' declared the monk. But he, too, was eyeing the spectators. Some were muttering that Leger's demise was because the monks harboured a Satanist, while others claimed Walter had arranged the death. A few discussions were growing rancorous. Then the door opened, and a beckoning finger indicated that Geoffrey was to step through it.

'I am Prior Odo,' said the red-nosed monk. 'I am sorry to give you the bad news. Poor Leger died last night, I am afraid.'

'How?' asked the knight. 'My wife told me he is not yet fifty, so it cannot—'

'It is an internal matter,' said Odo stiffly. 'I am not at liberty to discuss it with you.'

'Hilde will want to know what happened,' warned Geoffrey. 'So you can either tell me, or you can tell her – because she will descend on you herself if she is not satisfied with my answers. If you have ever met her, you will know I am right.'

Odo gulped. 'I *have* met her, and there is nothing I would like more than to furnish you with the information that will keep her away. But I cannot, because I have no idea what happened.'

'Then tell me what you do know.'

'A few days ago, Leger said someone was trying to kill him, and grew very agitated – he wrote to your wife, begging for help. He claimed there was poison in his food, and the cat *did* refuse to eat it when offered, but it is a fussy creature and may not have been hungry.'

'He told Hilde someone threw a knife at him.'

'He told me that, too. But we live a very secluded life here. We have no enemies.'

'Are you saying he died of natural causes, then? Or that he killed himself?'

Odo crossed himself. 'He was stabbed in the back, which is decidedly unnatural.'

'It is not easy to do if you are trying to commit suicide, either,' remarked Geoffrey. 'And that leaves murder, which means he had at least one enemy and that he was perfectly justified in being afraid for his life.'

'I suppose it does,' acknowledged Odo reluctantly. 'Perhaps I should have heeded his concerns.'

Geoffrey regarded him askance. 'After two attempts on his life? Yes, you should!'

Odo looked sheepish. 'Would you like to see his body? You are obviously a soldier, so you will be familiar with wounds. Perhaps it might tell you something.'

Inspecting corpses was not a way Geoffrey would have chosen to spend a summer afternoon, but he followed Odo across a cobbled yard to the church. It was a beautiful building, with one of the finest carved doors he had ever seen. He stopped to admire it, but the prior was disinclined to spend time on pleasantries and indicated impatiently that he was to enter.

The building was blessedly cool after the heat outside. It was also dark, and Geoffrey tripped over several uneven flagstones as he followed Odo to one of the transepts. Leger, dressed in a clean habit and with his hands folded over his chest, lay in a plain wooden coffin. It was a kindly face, browned by the sun, and Geoffrey had the immediate impression that he probably would have liked him. The insight surprised him, because he did not care for many members of Hilde's large and bellicose family.

'This is where he was stabbed,' said Odo, hauling the body into a sitting position and sliding the robe down its back so Geoffrey could see.

It was not a large wound, although a faint bruising around it suggested it had been delivered with considerable force. Geoffrey peered at it in the gloom and imagined it went very deep. He had no doubt at all that it would have killed Leger all but instantly.

'Where did he die?' he asked, watching the prior lay the corpse back down again. 'You said it was last night. Was he asleep?'

'He refused to come to the dormitory with the rest of us – said he would be safer here.'

'He was dispatched in a church?' Geoffrey was shocked. He was not particularly devout, but the notion of committing murder on consecrated ground was anathema, even to him.

Odo nodded. 'As he knelt to pray in this very lady chapel. The rest of us retired to bed after compline, and we found him dead at matins. Ergo, he was struck down during the night.'

'He sounded terrified in his letter, so I am sure you would not have left him here alone while you went to sleep,' said Geoffrey. 'Who was with him?'

Odo looked sheepish. 'No one.' He became defensive when he saw the knight's disapproval. 'He said he would be safe in here. We tried to persuade him to come with us to the dormitory, but he refused. In the end we gave up – we are busy men and need our sleep.'

'Then who was in the priory, other than you and your monks?'

'No one – the lay brothers go home at dusk. We lock the gate behind them and do not open it to anyone until the following morning. No one can come in or go out.'

Geoffrey frowned. 'So one of your monks killed him.'

'No! They are all as shocked by this as I am.'

'Leger's wound was not self-inflicted,' said Geoffrey, 'and clearly it was no accident. That leaves two possibilities: he was killed by a monk, or he was killed by an intruder. You say no one can come in or out . . .'

Odo swallowed hard. 'What are we going to do? Leger was loved in the town, because of his kind heart. People will demand answers – but we have none to give!'

'Do you have any idea *why* he suddenly became so fearful?'

Odo tried to calm himself with several deep breaths. 'None at all, although I suppose I should not be surprised that the current feud with the castle has ended in bloodshed.'

'What feud?'

'Estrighoiel was a peaceful, happy town until a little more than two years ago, and we all liked Drogo de Hauteville, who was the constable. Then he "fell" over a cliff, and Satan's spawn arrived very quickly to take his place. Immediately, things began to change. He has spies everywhere, even in the priory, and there is an atmosphere . . .'

'Satan's spawn?'

'Walter de Clare – and his henchmen Revelle and Pigot. I would not be at all surprised to learn that they murdered Leger.'

'Why would they pick on him? Did he speak out against them?'

'He did not approve of them, certainly. And then there is Cadowan and his wife Nest. They wanted to buy Ivar's sky-stone and were bitterly disappointed when he refused to sell.'

Geoffrey was confused. 'What is a sky-stone?'

'A piece of star that fell to earth in some godforsaken land to the north. Ivar brought it here, and it is said to be able to heal people.'

Geoffrey thought about what he had overheard at the market: Nest saved, but not Walter's child. Was this why Walter and his men seemed to hate the priory? If so, it was unfair to pick on Leger. Why not Ivar, who owned the thing?

'Where is it?' he asked, wondering if it was in the church and if Leger had been struck down as someone attempted to make off with it.

Odo grimaced. 'Ivar declines to say, despite my cajoling over the last two years – such a thing belongs in a shrine, not in whichever wretched hiding place he has chosen. But he maintains that God gave it to him, so he should decide its fate. It is difficult to argue with such conviction.'

'So no one else knows where he has put it?'

'No one. Ivar never leaves the priory these days, lest someone lays hold of him and tries to force him to tell. I do not blame him for being wary – Walter would tear him to pieces for failing to save Eleanor, while Cadowan and Nest are eager to own the stone.'

'So these are your suspects for killing Leger? Walter and his men, and the town couple?'

Odo nodded. Geoffrey turned abruptly and walked back to the gate. It was sturdy and secured by two heavy bars that slotted into the wall on either side. Clearly, an intruder was not going to enter that way. Then he began to walk around the perimeter, and his heart sank. There were several places where an agile man could scramble across, and he

43

saw that anyone could have invaded the monks' domain and committed murder while Leger's brethren slept.

'What do you plan to do about this, Father Prior?' he asked.

Odo shook his head slowly. 'I do not know. We have barely had time to gather our thoughts.'

'May I speak to the other monks?' asked Geoffrey.

'Why?' demanded Odo suspiciously. 'None of us heard or saw anything amiss.'

'Sometimes there *are* witnesses – they just do not know what they have seen.'

Odo stared at him. 'Are you saying you intend to look into the matter on our behalf?'

'On Hilde's behalf,' corrected Geoffrey.

'Then thank you,' said Odo. He gripped Geoffrey's hand. 'I shall take you to see my flock now, and you may ask them anything you please.'

Odo conducted Geoffrey to a refectory, where ten monks were sitting down to a meal. Lay brothers served them, and he saw that the Benedictines had carved a comfortable existence for themselves. Their habits were made of finest wool, although a concession to poverty was made in the simple wooden crosses that hung around their necks. The only exception was Brother Marcus, one of the pair Geoffrey had seen in the market, who sported a fine gold one.

Most of the monks were in their thirties or forties and seemed sleek and well fed. Geoffrey had been expecting older men, and it occurred to him that any of those now present would possess the strength to ram a knife between Leger's shoulder blades, despite Odo's contention that the killer was someone from outside.

One sat slightly apart from the others, and looked as if his life had been much harder than theirs. He had a shock of prematurely grey hair, and his skin was brown and wrinkled, as if he had spent many years out of doors. Although he was now stooped, his size and shape indicated that he had once been a formidable man. The knight saw tears glittering on his cheeks.

'That is Ivar,' murmured Odo. 'He was a hermit in the woods for years before taking the cowl. Ivar and poor Leger were particular friends.'

'Ivar?' asked Geoffrey, regarding the man at the centre of such controversy with interest.

Odo narrowed his eyes. 'Have you heard the horrible lies Walter has spread about him?'

'I heard his magic stone failed to save Walter's daughter.'

Odo waved a dismissive hand. 'Ivar has explained that – the stone can cure but not raise from the dead. And poor Eleanor was dead long before Revelle dragged Ivar from his cave to tend her. But I was not referring to *those* lies. I was asking whether you had heard the others – about the bad things that have happened since Ivar decided to take the cowl.'

'Not really.'

'Poor crops, flooded rivers and now this suspiciously nice weather. But Walter and his creatures arrived at the same time that Ivar took his vows, so I believe *they* are responsible for our downturn in fortunes. They say Ivar has been seen worshipping the devil, but he is a monk now, so clearly they are lying.'

'Do you think Walter killed Leger to give credence to their tales?' asked Geoffrey. 'The murder of Ivar's friend would certainly damage his reputation further—'

'It damages *them*,' declared Odo fiercely. 'I would not have believed they would stoop to such wickedness, but perhaps you are right. They will almost certainly say Ivar did it. And their spy will fabricate "evidence" to prove it.'

'You have no idea about the identity of this spy?'

Odo suddenly looked old. 'No. I have charged Brother Marcus to find out, because he is a dedicated and thorough man. His questions have seen him arrested and held prisoner at the castle on several occasions, but he has no answers yet.'

'It seems a sorry state of affairs,' mused Geoffrey. 'Castle and Church bandying accusations back and forth like fishwives.'

Odo glowered. 'They started it!'

'Where does the town stand in this dispute?'

Odo's glower intensified. 'The sensible ones see we are the wronged party, but the lunatics support Walter and his villains.'

'In other words, the feud is pulling the place apart.'

Odo continued to glare but made no other reply.

'I had better ask my questions,' said Geoffrey, wanting the case solved as quickly as possible. With such a bitter quarrel, it would not be wise to risk becoming embroiled in it.

'We shall say a psalm first,' said Odo piously. 'And then a prayer. And then you may ask us anything you like.'

Geoffrey studied the monks as they stood and allowed their prior to lead them in their devotions. They sang lustily – with the exception of Ivar, who did not seem to know the words – and clearly enjoyed impressing their guest with their chanting. It confirmed Geoffrey's initial impression: that the priory put great store in outward appearances. But what lay within?

'Brother Leger thought someone was trying to kill him,' said the large, amiable monk who had been addressed as Brother Aidan in the market. His companion, the hot-tempered Marcus, sat next to him. 'We were

disinclined to believe him, because we did not imagine for a moment that Walter and his henchmen would
murder any of us.'

'He hates us all,' said Marcus, fingering his gold cross.
'But I still refuse to accept that he stooped so low as to
stab a monk in a church. I think Cadowan and Nest did
it. They were probably looking for the sky-stone. Leger
caught them, so they killed him.'

'Did Leger see who threw the dagger at him earlier?'
asked Geoffrey. 'Or who tampered with his food?'

'Not that he told me,' said Aidan. 'And I questioned him
about both incidents.'

'Then what explanation did he give? He must have had
some notion as to why someone meant him harm.'

'He thought it might be something to do with our feud
with the castle,' replied Aidan. 'Meanwhile, we heard and
saw nothing of his killer. We all retired to bed, and everything was quiet and peaceful until we rose to pray before
dawn. Finding him with a dagger in his back was a terrible
shock.'

There was a chorus of agreement, but Geoffrey could not
tell how much of it was sincere. Would one stab a comrade,
just because it would be assumed that Walter had done it,
and thus topple the constable from his seat?

'Did you keep the dagger?' asked Geoffrey, wondering whether it might be identified and its owner traced.
It would not be the first time an inexperienced murderer
had made a careless mistake.

'I threw it in the river,' said Marcus. He shot Geoffrey a
defiant look, as if daring him to criticize. 'It was a hateful
thing and had no place in our holy precinct.'

'It did not occur to any of us that it might be needed,'
added Aidan.

'Is it retrievable?' asked Geoffrey.

'No,' said Marcus immediately. 'The Wye is fast and muddy, and it will be long gone by now. That is why I deposited it there – I did not want anyone else to touch the filthy thing. It is tainted and evil, like the hand that wielded it.'

'What did it look like?'

Marcus shrugged and would not meet the knight's eyes. 'Just some cheap, nasty thing that can be bought in the market.'

'I think Walter, Revelle or Pigot is responsible for Leger's murder,' said Aidan quietly. 'Because he was Ivar's friend, and we all know they would do anything to hurt Ivar.'

'But we have no evidence to make such a claim,' said Marcus bitterly. 'Like my belief that Nest and Cadowan are the guilty party. Both theories are just suspicions – ones that may well prove true, but not ones we can prove.'

'I am surprised you do not leap at the chance to accuse Walter,' said Aidan, turning to the younger monk and raising his eyebrows. 'After all the grim nights you have spent incarcerated in his dungeons.'

'I hate him,' acknowledged Marcus. 'But there is no *evidence* that he or his henchmen killed Leger.'

Odo sighed as he turned to Geoffrey. 'This case will not be easy to solve.'

Geoffrey had a bad feeling he might be right.

While the Benedictines began to talk among themselves, Geoffrey went to sit next to Ivar, who had not taken part in the discussion. He was reading a book, but when Geoffrey looked at it he saw it was held upside down. His first thought was that the monk's eyes were failing, but Ivar regarded Geoffrey sharply enough, and the knight supposed he was just one of many monastics who was illiterate, but who did not like to admit it.

'Walter de Clare likes to tell tales about me,' the monk said softly. 'He thinks I commune with the devil. But if I did, why would I have come to live in a priory? It would be difficult to speak to my familiar in a community of Benedictines.'

'Perhaps he means to malign all the priory's residents,' suggested Geoffrey. 'And chose you as a scapegoat, because . . .' He faltered.

'Because of Eleanor,' said Ivar bitterly, and Geoffrey saw tears sparkling in his eyes. 'If I could have saved that little angel, I would have. But it was beyond me. Walter thinks I failed deliberately, but he is wrong. He says the town's problems started that day – and he is right. I decided to join the priory, and castle and Church have been at logger-heads ever since.'

He had a curious accent – one that Geoffrey had heard before, when he had joined men from many nations to march towards Jerusalem. 'You sound as though you hail from the kingdom of the Danes.'

Ivar smiled. 'I have been told that before, although I have never been there. Many years ago, I lived in a village in a country far to the north. I was called Ivar Jorundsson then.'

'Greenland? My father had some gaming pieces made from Greenlandic ivory.'

Ivar inclined his head, still smiling. 'It is rare to meet someone who has heard of my homeland. Most cannot believe such a place exists – a land of ice and snow and mountains.'

'So how do you come to be here?'

'When I was a young man, it was arranged that I would take the cowl in Iceland, but there was a terrible storm during which many sailors were lost, including the naviga-tors. We drifted aimlessly for weeks, never in sight of land.

Then pirates took us prisoner, but another storm wrecked *their* ship, and I was washed up on the shore of Hibernia.'

'I see.' Geoffrey wondered if Walter might have a point when he claimed Ivar had brought bad luck. One storm was bad enough, but two *and* pirates was remarkably unfortunate.

'There were few survivors,' Ivar continued. 'But we were brought to the west of this land by the noble Prince Rhys of Deheubarth. When he was killed in battle and his territories taken by the Normans, I continued east with another survivor of the shipwreck, and when we found this perfect country of woods and rivers we took it as a sign from God that we should settle here.'

'How long ago was that?'

Ivar shrugged. 'Ten years or so; I cannot recall exactly. Later I followed the crusading call of Peter the Hermit, and accompanied his glorious force to Constantinople and beyond. There I witnessed the great battle where so many of his followers fell.'

'Near Civetot?' asked Geoffrey. He had heard stories of that particular massacre, which many felt had been avenged several years later when the forces of which he himself had been a part had besieged, taken and pillaged the Holy City of Jerusalem.

Ivar nodded. 'It was pure slaughter, and shocked me into returning here. I found the cave I had sheltered in previously, and decided to remain. After seeing all of those terrible things, I liked living away from the world of men, and wish I was there now.'

'Then why did you leave it?'

'Because of Eleanor.' Ivar looked away. 'Some people turned against me then, and Prior Odo suggested I would be safer here. He was right: Walter might have killed me, otherwise.'

'You took holy orders?'

'Yes – as I should have done years ago. It was always my intention, but I was happy in the cave. The forest provided fruit, berries and nuts, and the river is full of fish. And when times were bleak, I healed people in exchange for food.'

'Healed them of what?'

Ivar shrugged. 'Small things – warts, aching joints. I helped just enough folk to keep me from starving. I pretended to heal them with my remedies, but it was really the sky-stone.'

'Odo mentioned that you had hidden it,' said Geoffrey. 'Is that wise?'

'Are you suggesting that I should tell someone else in case I drop dead? Or because Walter's hatred means that I have not much time left?' Ivar shrugged again. 'Then it will be God's will.'

There was no point in arguing once God was mentioned, and Geoffrey did not try. 'How did you come by it?' he asked instead.

'My brother found it when we were children. I was taking it to the Church in Iceland when I was shipwrecked, but God obviously did not want it to go there. Anyway, the sky-stone cured me of a crooked leg, then healed two men of terrible wounds from a white bear.'

'Then it does have remarkable power,' said Geoffrey. 'So why do you keep it hidden? Why not use it to help people?'

'Because it does not always work, as was shown with Eleanor. And because it might wear out if it is overused. Besides, God did not tell me to tout it about, and I am loath to offend Him – I do not want to suffer more storms, shipwrecks and pirates.'

'But it saved the lives of three people,' argued Geoffrey. 'Surely, that must mean it—'

'Two were killed the following day, because they tried to take it for their own ends.'

Geoffrey was bemused. 'You killed them?'

Ivar was appalled. 'No, of course not! I was seven years old – too small to hold a sword, let alone use one. It was my father's doing. He was a gentle man mostly, but he knew how to fight.'

'I see,' said Geoffrey, not seeing at all. But Ivar's rambling discourse was doing nothing to forward his enquiries. He stood to leave, but the man reached out and pulled him back down.

'I told Leger where I hid the sky-stone. He was the only one, because I dare not trust anyone else. I told him last week.'

Geoffrey frowned. 'Last week was when he started to say someone was trying to kill him.'

'I know.'

'Are you saying Leger was murdered because you told him of the sky-stone's whereabouts?'

Ivar looked out of the window. 'Hermits do not have friends, and it was difficult to adapt to life in a priory. Leger helped me, with patience and understanding. He was the closest I have had to a true friend in my life. I trusted him completely. So I asked him what should be done with this gift from God. And I told him where it was hidden.'

'What did he say?'

'That he needed time to think and confer with others. He left the priory that day but would not say where he had been. And that night he began to say that someone had designs on his life.'

'You think he conferred with someone who then tried to kill him? Who?'

'I do not know, but I wish with all my heart that I had kept my mouth shut. There are many who would kill for the secret. Walter, Revelle and Pigot are soldiers, used to blood. Nest and Cadowan are good folk, but the sky-stone has a way of bringing out the worst in people. And my brethren here are worldly, and love money and power. I do not trust any of them.'

'It will be easy to know whether Leger revealed the secret – go to where you hid the sky-stone and see whether it is still there. If it is, then he did not tell anyone. If it is not, then he did.'

Ivar winced. 'I moved it within moments of his going out. I am afraid I did not like the fact that he could not give me an immediate answer, and I grew uneasy.'

'In other words, someone might have killed him because he revealed the location of the sky-stone, but it was not where he said it would be,' concluded Geoffrey.

Ivar nodded slowly. 'It is certainly possible. I tried to talk to him about it, but he became distant and worried. I have told you this because I want his killer found – you must question Walter, Odo and Cadowan, and demand to know where they were last night.'

'Perhaps you should write down where you have hidden this stone,' suggested Geoffrey. 'Because if anything happens to you, then it really will be lost for ever.'

'Not for ever,' said Ivar. 'These objects have a way of putting themselves in the place where they mean to be. It may lie hidden for decades – centuries, even – but it will emerge in the end.'

Geoffrey was silent for a moment, thinking about what had been said, but when he turned back to Ivar his eyes were closed and he appeared to be asleep. Odo approached before the knight could wake him.

'Leave him,' the prior said softly. 'He is distressed by what happened to Leger, and it is good that he sleeps. I do not suppose he confided where he hid the sky-stone, did he? If so, you must tell me. You will appreciate that it belongs here, in the hands of the Church.'

Geoffrey shook his head, watching the flash of disappointment in the prior's eyes. 'He said he told Leger, but no one else.'

Odo looked angry. 'Did he? Then why did Leger not tell *me*? I was his prior – I am used to making weighty decisions, and he was not. It was his duty to tell me, as one of my monks.'

It was not a question Geoffrey could answer, so he did not try. 'Ivar does not seem like a man who would fit well into your community,' he observed. 'I am surprised you took him.'

Odo glared at him. 'And what do you mean by that, pray?'

'He is illiterate, for a start.'

Odo continued to glare. 'How do you know?'

'First, he was holding his book upside down, and, second, when you sang your psalm he stumbled over the words. He has memorized some, but not all, and cannot read to jog his memory.'

And there was also the fact that most of the elegant, self-assured men in the priory would not seek out the company of grubby hermits, so Geoffrey could only suppose that Odo and his monks must want very badly to lay hands on the sky-stone, and thought earning Ivar's gratitude for good food and comfortable lodgings was the best way to go about it.

Odo regarded him with an unfriendly expression. 'He fits in well enough.'

Geoffrey changed the subject. 'Just after Ivar shared his secret with Leger, Leger went out. When he returned, he began to be concerned about his safety. Where might he have gone?'

Odo narrowed his eyes. 'Are you suggesting he told someone outside the priory about the sky-stone's whereabouts, and that person began to threaten him?'

'It is impossible to say without more evidence. Who might he have visited?'

'Anyone!' declared Odo, angry and distressed. 'Perhaps he told Walter, because once the constable has the stone, he might leave the priory alone. Leger hated discord and might have gone to Walter in the hope that giving away the stone would heal the rift between us.'

'Surely, then Walter would have killed him at the castle?'

Odo gave a short, bitter laugh. 'He would not – it would have laid him open to accusations, and Satan's spawn is nothing if not clever. It would be entirely within keeping with his sly character to kill Leger later, in his own church. Of course, he would not do the deed himself – that is what Pigot and Revelle are for.'

'Did Leger have any friends outside the priory who—'

'Cadowan and Nest!' exclaimed Odo. 'They are desperate to have the stone, too, and he was fond of them. Perhaps he told them the secret, and they killed him to make sure he did not tell anyone else.'

'I doubt they would have waited a week,' Geoffrey pointed out. 'There would be no point in dispatching him then.'

Odo pressed his lips together in a long, firm line. 'So you say, but there is no accounting for what folk might do when they are determined.'

There was little point in arguing with him. 'We discussed the possibility earlier that Walter has a spy in the priory—'

'Walter has spies everywhere,' declared Odo angrily. 'But he does seem to have recruited one who sells him sensitive information about us. I am *not* a drunkard – I like a little wine on occasion, but who does not? And our sacrist is *not* dishonest, nor our cellarer debauched. But these lies are spread around the town, so we become a laughing stock.'

'Perhaps this spy learned what Ivar had told Leger,' suggested Geoffrey. 'He is clearly adept at listening to conversations not intended for his ears, so perhaps—'

'Leger and Ivar would have taken more care,' interrupted Odo. 'The spy is not one of my monks, and the lay brothers are beyond reproach, so I imagine it is some sly dog from the castle or the town. God knows, Walter has enough of them in his pay.'

'May I inspect Leger's possessions?' asked Geoffrey, doubting there would be much to find but supposing he had better be thorough.

'Not today,' said Odo. 'It is almost time for vespers, and I would like to be present when you do it. Come tomorrow, after dawn prayers.'

'It would be better to start now,' objected Geoffrey, not liking the delay. If the culprit *was* in the priory, then it would give him hours to eliminate crucial evidence.

'I have spoken,' declared Odo loftily. 'Return tomorrow. I shall be expecting you.'

'You cannot investigate this,' said Roger irritably, sitting in the White Lion with a jug of cool ale. 'It is none of your business.'

'I cannot return to Hilde without answers,' replied Geoffrey. 'Leger was her favourite uncle. She will want to know that his killer has been brought to justice.'

'Then let the constable do it,' argued Roger. 'You have no jurisdiction here, and the whole thing sounds far-fetched, anyway. I have never heard of sky-stones.'

'Nor have I, but that does not mean they do not exist.'

Roger sighed. 'This is a bad idea. Let Hilde come to ask questions, if she is going to be curious. I do not like it here and want to leave. It feels like a place where trouble is brewing.'

'Then you should feel at home,' said Geoffrey. 'You thrive on trouble.'

'I like fighting,' acknowledged Roger. 'But I only like doing it with enemies I can see. Here, I feel they are all around me and I cannot tell who they are. I do not like it, Geoff. We should leave this place. Tonight. I would rather sleep under the stars than stay here after nightfall.'

Geoffrey raised his hands in surrender. 'Then go. Return to Goodrich and tell Hilde what has happened, and that I am trying to investigate. But do not let her come.'

'Why not? She is the one wanting answers.'

'Because you are right: there is something strange going on, and I would rather she stayed well away. She *is* my wife, Roger.'

'Yes, but I have never met a lass better able to take care of herself.' The admiration was clear in Roger's voice, and Geoffrey wondered whether *he* should have married her. 'I have rarely seen such skill with a battleaxe.'

'You are not easily unsettled, and if you do not feel safe here then neither will she be.'

'And neither will you,' Roger pointed out.

Geoffrey went on as if he had not spoken. 'Besides, I do not trust what Odo and his monks told me, and I do not understand Ivar. There is a peculiar story to be unravelled, and I would like to do it. For Hilde and for Leger.'

'It is—' began Roger, but stopped speaking abruptly when the door opened and Revelle and Pigot shoved their way inside. The tavern immediately divided between those who made for the rear door and those who exchanged nods and smiles with the two men. Three others followed Revelle and Pigot – two more knights, and someone who was obviously their leader. The leader was smaller than the others, with reddish hair and eyes oddly close together. Geoffrey suspected, from the richness of his clothes and the shine on his sword, that his spurs had been earned because he was nobly born, not because he had proved himself in battle.

The newcomer peered around, letting his eyes become accustomed to the gloom after the bright sunlight outside, then strode towards the table at which Geoffrey and Roger sat.

'I understand you visited the priory,' he said icily. 'Why?'

'What business is that of yours, little man?' demanded Roger, unwisely hostile in his turn.

'I am Sir Walter de Clare, constable of the castle,' the man replied. 'I am ordering you to leave Estrighoiel immediately. My family holds the favour of the King, so you will do well to do as you are told.'

'I have never heard of you,' said Roger rudely. 'I know Gilbert and Roger de Clare, who are always hanging around the royal courts. But who are you? Some distant cousin?'

'I am their younger brother,' said Walter, angered by the insult. 'And a knight in my own right. Now, are you going to leave peacefully or do my men have to use force?'

Geoffrey supposed Walter did bear a resemblance to the de Clares he had met when serving the King. He had not taken to them, although he suspected his dislike stemmed from the rumours regarding the peculiar death of King William II in the New Forest – and the fact that the archer who had loosed the fatal 'accidental' shot just happened to be married to one of their sisters. He found them sly and secretive, and he could tell that Walter was cast in the same mould.

'Force?' asked Roger, his voice dripping scorn as he looked Walter and his four knights up and down with calculated disdain. 'You think they can best two *Jerosolimitani*?'

The loutish Pigot reacted immediately by drawing his sword, but Revelle stepped between his friend and their quarry.

'Wait,' he muttered. 'Give them a chance to go peaceably.'

'My men can best you with ease,' said Walter to Roger, ignoring his henchman's efforts to calm the situation. Geoffrey was amused to note that he did not include himself in the challenge.

'Can they indeed?' asked Roger dangerously. 'Perhaps we should have a wager on that.'

'Why?' snarled Pigot. 'You will not be alive to pay it.'

'Why do you object to us visiting the priory?' asked Geoffrey, cutting across the furious rejoinder Roger started to make. 'Did we upset someone?'

'I am not prepared to wait and find out,' said Walter. 'I know you were asking about Leger's murder and the whereabouts of the sky-stone. These are not matters that concern you.'

Geoffrey raised his eyebrows. 'Your intelligence network is impressive, but—'

Walter looked pleased with himself. 'I know everything that happens in my town.'

'Then who killed Leger?' pounced Geoffrey.

'Pigot! Elias! Escort them out!' ordered Walter. 'Revelle and Seine bring up the rear. I do not have time for this nonsense.'

'We are not going anywhere,' said Roger. He seemed to have forgotten that he had been eager to leave not many moments before. 'We are free men; we have the right to go where we please.'

'Not in Estrighoiel,' replied Walter. There was a cant in his eyes that was every bit as dangerous as Roger's, and Geoffrey saw it would be unwise to antagonize him any further.

'We are leaving,' he said, standing. 'We do not want trouble.'

Anger suffused Roger's face. 'I am not being ousted by this upstart. And his henchmen can try to make me leave if they dare. It would be a pleasure to skewer them.'

'We will not be gone long,' murmured Geoffrey in his ear. 'Just follow me now. I will explain later.'

'There is something bewilderingly perverse about you,' grumbled Roger, deliberately knocking into Pigot as he followed Geoffrey outside. Pigot staggered, and it was only Revelle's warning glare that prevented him from drawing his sword. 'I never know what you are going to do next.'

But he was used to deferring to Geoffrey in tactics, so he let the matter lie. Walter's men had already been in the stables, and the horses were saddled and ready. To make the point that he was not to be bullied, Roger began to make a fuss about the way his bags had been secured.

'The strap is broken,' he declared. It had been fine earlier and Geoffrey wondered whether he had cut it himself. Roger looked directly at Pigot. 'You had better mend it for me.'

'Mend it yourself,' snarled Pigot. 'I am no man's servant.'

'No?' responded Roger. 'I thought you were the constable's lackey.'

Pigot's sword was out of its sheath in seconds.

There would have been bloodshed had not Revelle stepped in front of Pigot, then clicked his fingers to several men in the crowd that had gathered to watch, ordering them to mend the strap.

'Do not annoy Pigot,' whispered a man who stood near Geoffrey. It was the red-faced merchant called Cadowan, his pretty wife Nest at his side. 'And tell your friend he is pushing Walter too far. Our constable is a dangerous man.'

'In what way?' asked Geoffrey. A messenger had arrived, claiming the attention of Walter, Revelle and the other two knights, while Pigot continued to banter words – but at least not blows – with Roger.

'We are fairly sure he killed his predecessor – Drogo de Hauteville,' replied Nest. Her voice was low and pleasant, and Geoffrey found himself wishing Hilde had some of her looks. 'Drogo plummeted over a cliff in the woods, even though he knew the area well and was unlikely to have lost his way.'

'He was killed instantly,' added Cadowan, taking up the tale. 'And within hours, Walter arrived. He said he just happened to be passing when he heard the news, and he stepped into Drogo's shoes because no one else was to hand.'

'The King must be satisfied with him or he would have been replaced.'

'Walter put down a small rebellion,' said Cadowan, his voice dripping disgust. 'Although we suspect it was engineered by Revelle to give his master an opportunity to shine.'

Geoffrey frowned. The whole affair *did* stink of treachery.

'We suspect Walter killed Leger, too,' whispered Cadowan. 'Although I imagine he will have blamed the monks in the priory. Or even us. Am I right?'

Geoffrey shrugged, unwilling to gossip. 'I have been listening to accusations all afternoon. It is difficult to keep them straight.'

Cadowan shot an angry glare towards Walter. 'Nothing has been right since that devious dog arrived. He blames it on Ivar, but it was hardly Ivar's fault that he could not save Eleanor – the sky-stone does not work for everyone. Thank God it did on Nest.'

'I could feel myself dying,' said Nest quietly, 'but then Ivar put the stone in my hand, and the life began to course through me again. Walter can say what he likes, but the stone *is* sacred.'

'The monks want it badly,' said Cadowan. 'But they are not very saintly men, and I would not like to think of such a pure thing in their hands. I tried to buy it from Ivar, so I could take it to a monastery with devout monks, rather than this worldly horde. But Ivar will not sell.'

'Does he explain why not?'

Both shook their heads. 'He said he would wait for God to tell him who to give it to,' said Nest. 'But—'

'Enough,' roared Walter, finishing with the messenger and seeing Geoffrey speaking to the merchant and his wife. 'Get on your horses and leave. You have wasted enough of our time.'

Eager to avoid further confrontation, Geoffrey mounted up. But Roger once again had to have the final say.

'Perhaps you could bend down so that I could step on your back to mount,' he said to Pigot.

The other knight's face was a mask of unbridled hatred as he reached for his sword. But Roger struck him on the forehead with the metal hilt of his dagger, and Pigot dropped senseless to the ground.

The constable squawked in alarm as all the knights immediately assumed fighting stances. In a move born out of sheer terror, he lobbed his sword at Geoffrey. It was an unconventional manoeuvre, and not one any sane knight would perform – it would leave him effectively unarmed. But because of its very nature, it took Geoffrey by surprise, and there was a burning pain in his arm – his armour had leather sleeves, and the blade had sliced through one of them. He struggled to raise his shield as first Elias and then Revelle began a series of hacking blows.

'The King will have your head for this,' Roger bellowed, realizing too late that the odds were not very favourable. 'He will not appreciate his agents being murdered.'

'Agents?' asked Walter, making an abrupt gesture that stopped his knights from attacking, although they remained alert. 'What are you talking about?'

'Geoffrey is one of his most trusted officers,' said Roger loudly.

'Geoffrey?' asked Walter uneasily. 'Not Sir Geoffrey Mappestone? Of Goodrich?'

'The very same,' shouted Roger. 'Which you would have known, had you bothered to ask.'

'My cousin, William Giffard – who is the Bishop of Winchester – mentioned Geoffrey Mappestone in a letter he wrote to me,' said Revelle, sheathing his sword. 'And his description matches this man. Giffard said Geoffrey has helped the King with a number of difficult problems.'

'Then why did you not tell us who you were?' said Walter, expansive and oily. 'Your reputation goes before you, and His Majesty has often sung your praises. Elias! Seine! Why are you standing there like great apes? Welcome our new friends. We must amend this silly misunderstanding.'

Geoffrey did not want to step inside Castelle de Estrighoiel – not because it was the lair of a man who had lobbed a sword at him, but because it was owned by the King. He had learned from bitter experience that it was safer to stay well away from anything under Henry's control.

'We will stay in an inn,' he said, trying not to show how painful his injury was.

'Nonsense,' declared Walter. 'They are likely to be full by now, and there is plenty of room at the castle. Besides, it is the least I can do. You *do* understand that I would never have tackled you had you told me your name, do you not?'

Geoffrey nodded, although he was not much comforted. It meant Walter was not averse to ambushing other innocent visitors, which hardly made Estrighoiel a place of safety.

'Then we will stay at the priory,' he said. 'There is no need for—'

'You will not be safe there,' said Walter darkly. 'Please, Sir Geoffrey. You will be much more comfortable with us. And you know I mean you no harm – if I had, you would be dead by now. And you are still very much alive.'

'Why did you stay your hand?' asked Geoffrey. The King would be vexed to lose the services of a retainer, but no more – Geoffrey might be useful to Henry, but Henry did not like him, and the feeling was wholly reciprocated.

'Because the King told me you were a good man to call in times of trouble,' replied Walter. 'And this is a turbulent region. If I am to maintain my hold on Estrighoiel, then I shall need all the allies I can get.'

'Your hold on Estrighoiel is insecure?'

If that were the case, then Geoffrey was disgusted, because defending such a mighty fortress should have been child's play. Then he looked at the constable's shiny mail and untried sword, and understood the situation: Walter was but a shadow of his older brothers. Estrighoiel was his chance to make a mark, but it was unlikely that he would be equal to the task.

Walter shot him a furtive glance. 'Treachery is rife. No one can be trusted, with the exception of these four knights – Revelle, Pigot, Seine and Elias.'

'Why is treachery rife?' asked Geoffrey. 'There will be grievances between Normans and locals – both English and Welsh – but you should be able to manage those with diplomacy.'

'People will not do as they are told,' said Walter sullenly, and Geoffrey saw he was a petty despot – that he ruled by fear.

'It is not an area that responds well to force,' Geoffrey said carefully. 'Bribery works much better.'

'Why should I yield to the demands of peasants?' snapped Walter angrily. 'I am above such paltry dealings. But why did you come to Estrighoiel? What did you want here?'

It was on the tip of Geoffrey's tongue to remark that he should have asked that before trying to throw him out of the town, but he managed to suppress the instinct.

'I came because my wife's uncle wrote to say he was in fear of his life. Unfortunately, I arrived too late to help him.'

'Leger,' mused Walter. 'Odo or one of his brethren will be responsible for Leger's death. It is a pity – Leger was the only reasonable fellow among them and I am sorry he is dead. But the culprit will not remain free for long. He will be a monk, and lay brothers gossip.'

'Your spy in the priory is a lay brother?' asked Geoffrey, supposing that would narrow it down. There were only six of those, as opposed to ten monks and a prior.

Walter smiled enigmatically. 'I am not such a fool as to reveal my sources to anyone who asks. Suffice to say that nothing happens in that priory without my knowledge – and that is important, given that the wicked child-killer and devil-lover Ivar lurks there.'

'A Satanist would hardly take up residence on conse-crated ground,' said Geoffrey reasonably. 'It would cramp his style, to say the least.'

'You assume the priory is holy,' said Walter curtly. 'But it is not. Ivar's demonic evil has rubbed off on them, and they are all wicked now, even if they were not before. It is a pity they are not *all* stabbed in their church. But never mind this. Let me ask you a question: what were you hoping to learn about Leger's death?'

'Just who killed him,' replied Geoffrey simply.

'I have just told you who killed him – a monk. Any of them is strong enough, although my money is either on Odo or Aidan, on the grounds that they are the biggest and meanest. Or perhaps Ivar summoned a demon from hell to do it. And if you want to know *why* Leger was murdered, it will be something to do with that damned sky-stone. Ivar has hidden it and refuses to say where. My spy has done his best to find out, because I would like to get it myself.'

'It seems a number of people would.'

Walter smiled, although the expression was not a pleasant one. 'Yes, but they intend to charge the desperate huge amounts of money for cures. I mean to destroy it, so it cannot be used to deceive anyone else. It killed my daughter, you know.'

'I thought she drowned,' said Geoffrey, then winced. His wits were not functioning properly, because he would never normally have made such a blunt remark to a man who was clearly still grieving.

'She fell in the river,' said Walter softly. 'But Ivar could have saved her, had he wanted. She was only six. The Satan-lover killed her, and I will never believe any different.'

When they reached the castle, Walter was immediately claimed by a clerk who declared there was urgent business for him to attend. It was left to Revelle to conduct Geoffrey and Roger to their quarters. These comprised a tiny chamber off the main staircase, little more than a cupboard built into the thickness of a wall. But it was palatial compared with some of the places in which they had been obliged to sleep, and reassuringly private.

'My cousin Giffard wrote a lot about you,' Revelle said, sitting uninvited on the bench that was the only piece of furniture, other than two straw mattresses and a tiny chest.

'Did he?' Geoffrey wished he would go. His injured arm ached, and he wanted to lie down.

'He said you have helped him on several occasions, and that he considers you a friend. He was fond of Drogo, too – Estrighoiel's previous constable. But he detests Walter. He advised me against going into his service.'

'So why did you? Giffard is a wise and intelligent man.'

'I wish I had listened,' said Revelle. He glanced towards the door, then went to close it. 'I have been asked to do things . . . Walter was never pleasant, but he has been worse since the death of his daughter. It is a pity for everyone that Eleanor died – she had a sunny, gentle disposition, and would have kept him from some of his depredations.'

'What depredations?' asked Geoffrey. 'Ordering the death of unarmed monks in churches?'

Revelle looked pained. 'I am not sure what happened to Leger.'

'Who is the spy – the man who tells Walter the priory's secrets?' asked Geoffrey. 'He would be a good person to interview tomorrow.'

'I do not know,' said Revelle, and Geoffrey had the feeling he was telling the truth. 'Walter says he trusts us four knights, but there are only so many secrets he shares with us. And the identity of the spy is not one of them – Walter says it must be so, to protect the man. It is unsavoury – I have never approved of spies, personally.'

Neither had Geoffrey, but he said nothing, and Revelle began speaking again.

'Other crimes are overlooked, too. Have you heard how Nest fell over a cliff and the sky-stone brought her back to life? Well, she was being chased by soldiers from the castle who were intent on rape. Pigot was among them – it was he who told Walter how Ivar saved her. But their actions were overlooked with a wink and a nod.'

'That will not make Walter popular with the townsfolk.'

'He is popular with those he pays generously to spy. But others *hate* him. Unfortunately, it is not always easy to tell which is which. I plan to leave his service soon. Perhaps Giffard will find me something to do, and Winchester sounds like a nice place to live.'

'He is not in Winchester at the moment – he is in the midst of a lengthy stay in Exeter.'

'Then I shall go there,' determined Revelle. 'Soon, before I am asked to do anything else that plagues my conscience. Like arresting the hapless Marcus every other week.'

'That is you? The priory objects to the frequency with which he is detained, and so does he. I am surprised Walter dares – the Church does not like seculars imprisoning its members.'

'I know, but he is well treated, despite what he claims afterwards. He stays in this room, in fact – where Walter keeps guests, not prisoners.'

'It feels like a prison to me,' growled Roger, speaking for the first time since they had arrived in the castle. He was still angry with himself for not besting Seine at the skirmish earlier. 'I do not like it here. I like Giffard, though, so if you are his cousin, you must be all right.'

Revelle smiled, which made him more angel-like than ever. 'My whole family likes Giffard, and I appreciate the fact that he takes the time to write to me. Unfortunately, Walter's clerks are usually too busy to read his letters to me – and I like to hear them more than once. He has a nice way with words.'

'Geoff can read,' said Roger brightly. 'I try to keep it quiet, because it is hardly something worthy of a knight, but it comes in useful sometimes. He will read them to you.'

Smiling, Revelle pulled a bundle of missives from inside his surcoat, while Geoffrey scowled at his friend. He wanted to sleep, not squint over Giffard's tiny writing by lamplight.

'I happen to have the most recent ones here,' Revelle said, 'because I was going to ask Leger to interpret them for me. Unfortunately, he died before I could approach him.'

Geoffrey forced a smile and unfolded the first one. Giffard *did* have a way with words, and both Revelle and Roger listened spellbound at the prelate's accounts of journeys he had taken and people he had met. There was a reference to Geoffrey, flattering enough to make the knight blush. Then there was a description of Estrighoiel during Drogo's rule. Giffard had been there when Drogo's accident had occurred, and he expressed reservations about Walter's role in the affair.

Drogo set off to see the holy man, Giffard wrote. *But he knew the land well, and it was no act of God that sent him over the precipice. Beware of your liege lord, cousin.*

'Drogo was going to see Ivar,' explained Revelle, looking at Geoffrey. 'But Walter has always claimed Giffard was mistaken – that Drogo did not know the cliffs as well as my cousin said he did. I have never been sure who to believe.'

'Giffard would not lie,' said Roger. 'He is annoyingly honest.'

'A mistaken belief is not a lie,' Revelle pointed out. 'Read the next one.'

'It is not from Giffard,' said Geoffrey. 'The handwriting is different.'

'Oh, that one,' said Revelle dismissively, peering over his shoulder. 'That is some missive he included with one letter, probably by mistake. I have never bothered to have it interpreted, because I am not interested in the ramblings of anyone else – and Walter's clerks charge me a fortune for their services. I am loath to squander good money.'

'It is addressed to Drogo,' said Geoffrey, his interest piqued. 'And dated five years ago.'

'What does it say?' asked Revelle. There was a pained expression on his face: he found the diversion tiresome and wanted to get back to Giffard's epistles. 'And who is it from?'

'It is unsigned, but from someone who feared for his life. It is also in peculiar English, as if it was not its writer's native tongue. Perhaps he was Welsh. It reads: *The killer hunted me in darkness, and it is not long ere my light is gone. The great battle turned an already evil mind and Satan walks the earth.*'

'Lord!' breathed Roger with a shudder. 'That is unpleasant. I wish you had not bothered. There is a seal, too, at the bottom of the letter.'

'It is not a seal,' said Geoffrey. 'It is a shape filled with red ink. It looks like an angel.'

'Not an angel,' said Roger, frowning. 'It is some archaic weapon. Or perhaps Satan!'

'Actually, it is a boat,' said Revelle. 'There are a number of families in Estrighoiel who have made their fortunes from shipping – like Cadowan and Nest. Perhaps one of them has taken this symbol to represent them. Regardless, it means nothing.'

But Geoffrey was not so sure.

Revelle left eventually, to Geoffrey's relief. The pain in his arm had settled down to a dull nag, and he wanted to sleep. Or should he? He did not feel safe in the castle.

'I will take first watch,' said Roger, reading his mind, 'and wake you later.'

Geoffrey lay down and fell into a doze immediately, having the soldier's ability to nap anywhere and in almost any conditions. He felt better when he awoke, although his arm still throbbed unpleasantly. He supposed he should inspect it, but that would entail removing his armour, and he was reluctant to do that as long as he was in the castle. He decided to leave it until later.

To take his mind off it, he thought about what he had learned of Leger's death. Unfortunately, it was pitifully little. He knew there were suspects in the town, the castle and the priory, and that all blamed the others for the man's murder. He also knew Leger had probably been killed because Ivar had trusted him with a dangerous secret. Who had Leger gone out to see immediately after Ivar had confided his tale? Was *that* person the killer? Could it be assumed that it was no one at the priory, because Leger had left soon after the discussion with Ivar?

Geoffrey frowned. He could assume nothing, because the evidence was not there. He let his mind wander to Giffard, and hoped the bishop was enjoying his sojourn in Exeter. Then he thought about Ivar and his cave, and how dismal it must have been in winter, even for a man used to Greenland weather. And he thought about the sky-stone. Could it really heal? Why had it helped Nest and not Eleanor? Was it really because it would help only the living, and those who had already passed into death were out of luck?

Bored with waiting for dawn to come, he began to count the stones in the wall, working out patterns and multiples in his mind. He noticed that one stone stood slightly proud of the others, and the longer he looked at it the more he became sure that something was odd about it. He stood, and the movement disturbed Roger, who, rubbing sleep from his eyes, rose to see what his friend was doing.

It did not take Geoffrey long to see that the brick was loose. He tugged it out. Beyond it was a recess, in which was concealed a small box. It was beautifully made, and boasted three red chevrons, the de Clare family symbol. Geoffrey opened it. Inside was a crude wooden cross and several gold coins. Roger's eyes gleamed.

'Treasure!' he exclaimed. 'Who would have thought it? Give it to me. I shall put it somewhere safe, although you can keep the cross.'

'No,' said Geoffrey. 'It is evidence.'

Roger did not look impressed. 'Evidence for what?'

'Evidence that Marcus is the spy at the monastery.'

Roger gaped at him. 'How in God's name did you reach that conclusion?'

'Because he, alone of the monks at the priory, wears a gold cross around his neck – all the others wear wooden ones like this. I suspect he was given a better one to wear in its place.'

Roger looked doubtful. 'That is weak, Geoff. You are not thinking clearly.'

But Geoffrey had not finished. 'He is arrested often, but is not put in a cell. He is brought here, where guests are housed. Why, if he is a prisoner? The answer is that he is not a prisoner at all, but a guest. He provides information, and Walter provides money. But Marcus cannot take it back to the priory, where communal living would give him away.'

'So he keeps it here,' finished Roger, 'in a special box Walter has given him. I think you had better have a word with him at first light.'

Clouds had blown in from the west during the night, and the sky was a dark, ominous amber-grey. It was a shock after so many days of gentle sunshine. Roger regarded it uneasily.

'The storm will be a bad one,' he predicted. 'They always are when clouds have that nasty yellow sheen. Perhaps you were right to be worried about your crops.'

Geoffrey was eager to talk to Marcus before Walter awoke; he did not want the constable to know he had guessed the identity of the spy. He left the castle and walked briskly towards the priory. His arm still ached, but there was no time for such matters, because all he wanted was to identify Leger's killer and leave Estrighoiel as quickly as possible – preferably before Walter decided Geoffrey was not the sort of ally he wanted anyway.

There was a flicker of lightning, followed by a distant growl of thunder as he knocked on the gate, although it was a long way off. The same lay brother peered through the grille at them, but this time he opened the door and indicated that Geoffrey and Roger were to enter. They were not the only ones to visit: Cadowan and Nest had arrived before them. They nodded at the knights, although there was no warmth in the greeting, only unease.

Dawn prayers had just finished, and the monks were filing out of the church. Some, seeing the state of the weather, headed for the dormitory to collect hoods and cloaks before the deluge, while others drifted towards the scriptorium or the kitchens. Odo had cornered Aidan and was talking to him in a low, urgent voice, while Marcus turned and shot back inside the church when he spotted Geoffrey.

'Where is he going?' asked Roger suspiciously.

Ivar, who was passing and overheard, answered. 'I noticed his mind was elsewhere during the Mass. I imagine he has gone to say a few more prayers, to salve his conscience.'

'It needs salving for more than that,' remarked Roger before Geoffrey could stop him. He spoke very loudly, and monks, Cadowan and Nest turned to listen. 'He is the one who has been telling your priory's secrets to Walter de Clare.'

Ivar gaped at him. 'Marcus is the spy? No! It is far more likely to have been Odo.'

'Odo? Why him?' asked Geoffrey, watching as the prior broke away from Aidan and disappeared around the side of the church. His affable monk went in the opposite direction and was soon lost to sight among the chicken coops.

Ivar lowered his voice. 'Because he pretends to be pleasant, but there is a black heart beneath his habit. My other suspect is Aidan, who alone of the monks likes to wander the town on his own. None of us knows what he does, and he gets testy when we ask. And the spy cannot be Marcus, anyway, because he is the one who is most vocal about the damage the spy does with his tales.'

And that, Geoffrey thought, was exactly what Marcus *would* say when he was confronted with the evidence of his treachery. He was about to say so when Ivar, seeing Cadowan and Nest indicate they wanted to speak to him, turned and broke into a run. They followed, making a comical procession as they rounded the church.

Then the gate opened again and Walter strode inside, holding a cloth-wrapped bundle; his four knights were at his heels. Their arrival was oddly timed, and Geoffrey wondered whether they had heard Roger's pronouncement from outside – it had certainly been loud enough. Pigot's dark face creased into a scowl when he saw Roger, although Revelle smiled a friendly greeting. Walter grinned when he saw Geoffrey, all teeth and no sincerity.

'You are up early,' the constable remarked. 'I expected you to sleep late, given that you must have been tired after yesterday's exertions. I am sorry business claimed me last night, depriving us of the opportunity to chat, but we shall rectify that today. I am eager to make better acquaintance with one of the King's agents.'

Odo appeared suddenly from the direction of the church. He was breathless and looked flustered; Aidan was not far behind him. Odo stopped dead in his tracks when he heard Walter's words.

'You are the King's agent?' he demanded, regarding Geoffrey with alarm. 'You did not mention that yesterday.'

'He is a modest man,' provided Roger when Geoffrey said nothing. 'It is usually left to me to do the bragging. And it was as well I did yesterday, or you might have killed him.' He turned to glower at Walter, who had the grace to look sheepish.

'Walter tried to harm you?' asked Odo. An expression of gleeful malice crossed his face. 'Then it is a matter that must be reported to the King. I shall write this morning and—'

'Please do not,' said Geoffrey tiredly, unwilling to have his name brought to Henry's attention for any reason. 'It was a misunderstanding.'

Odo's eyes narrowed. 'I do not believe you. And you do not look well today. You—'

'He said it was a misunderstanding,' snarled Walter, coming to stand close to the prior and insinuating enough menace into his words to make Odo step back in alarm. 'So that is an end to it. You would do better to pay heed to your own business – for example, establishing which of your monks murdered Leger, who, incidentally, is uncle to Sir Geoffrey's wife.'

'That means Geoffrey is Leger's kin, and you are in serious trouble,' added Pigot provocatively.

'How dare you make such accusations,' shouted Odo. 'You know perfectly well that the villain was one of the brutes who stand at your heels. They have killed before and—'

'I came to return this,' interrupted Walter. He pulled the cloth from the parcel he held, to reveal a large altar-cross. 'It was found in the possession of a local thief, and I imagined you would be pleased to have it back. However, I did not come here to bandy words with you. I am above such indignities. With your permission, I shall take it to the church.'

He turned and strutted away, without waiting to hear whether he had permission or not, leaving Odo grinding his teeth in impotent rage. It was a clever piece of manipulation – coming to present the priory with stolen property, and then manoeuvring himself into the position of injured party during the exchange that followed – although Geoffrey saw through it. But Walter's games with the priory were not his concern.

'We need to talk to Marcus,' he told Odo, watching as Walter and his henchmen opened the church door and disappeared inside.

'He is your spy,' added Roger, presenting the little box and its contents with a flourish. Geoffrey closed his eyes. He had imagined the thing had been left where it had been found and would have stopped Roger, had he seen him removing it.

Aidan snatched it from him. 'Walter owns a lot of these. I know, because when we say Masses for his daughter's soul, the coins come in one. And here is one of our wooden crosses. It looks like Marcus's – his was chipped when he dropped it once, and here you can see a small piece is missing.'

'But Marcus told me he lost it,' said Odo, bemused. 'And that his family had sent him a gold one as a replacement. He asked my permission to wear it, because he said a gift from his family helped alleviate the sorrow he felt at losing the one he was given at his ordination.'

'If this cross was at the castle,' said Aidan, staring at his prior with worried eyes, 'then it means Walter stole it. Marcus would not have parted with it otherwise. Or it fell off when he was in their dungeons.'

'Fell off into a box?' asked Roger archly. 'Which was then hidden in a wall of the room allocated to him when he is at the castle? And in company with gold coins?'

'There are no gold coins in here,' said Aidan, peering into the box doubtfully.

'They must have fallen out,' said Roger smoothly.

'We should confront Walter,' said Aidan, watching as the constable left the church. Walter was walking briskly, giving the impression of being a busy man. 'He is here anyway.'

'No,' said Odo, reaching out a hand to stop him. 'We will talk to Marcus first. Where is he?'

'Asking forgiveness for his sins in the church,' replied Roger piously, ignoring the fact that he had some sins of his own to confess, the most recent being theft.

Odo set off towards the building, the others at his heels. It was far darker than it had been the previous day, because of the gathering thunderclouds. As if to accentuate the point, there was a flash of lightning and another growl of thunder, this time closer.

It illuminated Marcus, who was in the Lady Chapel next to Leger's coffin. He was lying on his face, and there was a dagger protruding from his back.

Odo released a strangled cry and ran towards him, while the blood drained from Aidan's face. Geoffrey dropped to one knee beside the prostrate monk but could see he was past all earthly help. Like Leger, he had been killed neatly and proficiently with a single, efficient blow.

'Walter!' exclaimed Aidan. 'He was just in here. *He* killed Marcus!'

'He might have done,' acknowledged Geoffrey. 'However, you can see from here that the cross is back on the high altar. Perhaps Walter really did just replace it and leave.'

'Then why did he not raise the alarm when he found Marcus?' demanded Aidan.

'Because you would not be able to see a body on the Lady Chapel floor from the high altar,' explained Geoffrey. 'And Walter is not stupid, anyway: he is unlikely to commit such a bold murder when he is the obvious suspect.'

Or, he wondered, was that what Walter was hoping everyone would think? That the clever constable would be more subtle in dispatching his enemies? But Marcus was not an enemy – he was a much-valued spy. Of course, Geoffrey thought wryly, he had probably heard Roger's stentorian announcement, and so knew the monk would no longer be of use to him – worse, that he might be a liability, should Odo decide to write to the King. The knight rubbed his head, not sure what to think.

'Well, we know the killer is not Odo or Aidan,' muttered Roger as the two monks began deliberating how best to confront Walter. 'First, you can see they are shocked. And, second, we saw Marcus enter the church, and they were outside until we came in here.'

'It is easy to feign horror,' Geoffrey murmured back. 'Moreover, both Odo and Aidan disappeared from sight briefly after you announced that Marcus was the spy, and I can see from here that there are another two doors they could have used – one at the back of the building and one at the side.'

'They would not have had time,' objected Roger. 'And they would be drenched in blood.'

But Geoffrey shook his head. 'You know as well as I do that it takes but a moment to plunge a knife into a kneeling man's back – and that leaving the weapon in the wound reduces spillage.'

Roger frowned. 'But this means our suspects for Marcus's murder are the same as the ones for Leger – Walter and his creatures, and Odo and all his monks. We cannot eliminate anyone.'

'No,' agreed Geoffrey. 'And you can add Cadowan and Nest to the list, too. They also disappeared from sight after you bawled our findings to half of Wales.'

Roger looked indignant. 'I merely spoke the truth. But which of these villains do *you* think is the culprit? You have a sharp mind: you must have some theories.'

'Not really,' said Geoffrey. 'However, while all our suspects had the opportunity to dispatch Marcus, they do not all have a motive. I understand why Walter might have done it – and the monks will certainly want to avenge themselves on the spy who has been selling embarrassing secrets to the castle. But Cadowan and Nest?'

'They are obsessed with getting the sky-stone,' said Roger. 'Perhaps they think the spy at the priory is one reason why Ivar is so distrustful. In other words, Marcus's death will mean everyone likes each other again, and Ivar will relax enough to part with the thing.'

It did not sound very likely, but Geoffrey was acutely aware that there was a lot they did not know about Estrighoiel and its inhabitants. Cadowan and Nest might have a motive that had not yet been uncovered. He winced when there was a particularly loud grumble of thunder. It rattled the glass in the window frames, and the lightning that flashed just before it was enough to turn the twilight gloom into bright daylight.

'Which of those dogs did it, do you think?' Aidan was asking Odo, clearly having dismissed Geoffrey's reasons for why Walter might be innocent. He was fingering a dagger. Monks were not supposed to carry weapons, and Geoffrey wondered where it had come from.

'Revelle, probably,' replied Odo bitterly. 'He will obey any order, no matter how repugnant. Or his stupid friend Pigot. Walter would not have delivered the fatal blow himself. But one thing is clear: we shall not sit back and do nothing while a second monk is murdered.'

'A monk who was a spy,' Roger pointed out.

'But a monk nonetheless,' said Aidan coldly. 'Yet some good will come out of this dreadful business: the King will have no choice but to remove Walter from office now.'

Geoffrey stared after him as he stalked away. Having Walter under suspicion of murder would put the priory at a significant advantage, and was yet another reason why the monks should remain on his list of suspects.

While the Benedictines started moving Marcus's body to an outbuilding for washing, Geoffrey began to feel that the odds of solving the crime were too great, and he seriously considered riding away and telling Hilde that her uncle had been killed by a lunatic who randomly slaughtered monks at their prayers. Unfortunately, she was unlikely to be satisfied with such an answer, and he also knew that the mystery would gnaw at him if he did not stay to solve it.

As they exited the church, Walter returned, this time with a contingent of soldiers as well as his knights, and offered to set them to investigating the latest crime. Odo's jaw dropped in astonishment at what he declared was mind-boggling audacity, while Cadowan and Nest watched the scene with expressions that were difficult to read. Geoffrey was not sure what to make of any of them.

'You asked yesterday to examine Leger's possessions,' said Aidan, handing Geoffrey a box. 'He did not have many – he followed our order's policy of poverty, obedience and chastity.'

The knight was acutely aware that everyone was watching as he began to sort through the chest's contents. Cadowan and Nest were blank-faced. Odo and his monks were vengeful and angry, although Ivar seemed more distressed than enraged. And the men from the castle were alert and tense; Geoffrey realized uncomfortably that they seemed full of pent-up violence,

He doubted there would be anything useful in Leger's belongings – not so long after his death, and with the entire priory aware that he had asked to inspect them. There was a spare habit, another plain wooden cross and some letters from Hilde. Odo's eyebrows drew together in disapproval when he saw them: monks were not supposed to hoard keepsakes.

'Nothing,' said Roger in disgust.

Absently, Geoffrey unfolded one or two of the letters, half listening to a tension-loaded discussion between Walter, Odo and Cadowan about who might have committed the second murder. None of them said anything new: Odo thought the suspect hailed from the castle, Walter claimed it was a monk or a townsman, while Cadowan pointed out that the priory and the castle held the most obvious suspects. Tearfully, Ivar announced that *he* distrusted everyone, and even included Geoffrey and Roger in his accusing glare. The bald declaration silenced the clamour of the others, and so did the growl of thunder that followed it.

A tiny piece of parchment had been hidden in the third letter Geoffrey opened. The spidery writing looked as if it had been penned by the same hand as the desperate letter to Hilde. The knight had no doubt that it was Leger's. He began to read:

Brother Ivar shared a terrible secret with me today. He told me the location of the sky-stone, which lies at the base of the great oak below the cliffs from which Drogo fell. I urged him to set it on the altar, because it comes from God, but he is afraid. Perhaps it would be best if it stayed hidden, because it brings out evil in good men. I fear for my life now. It is

There was no more, and Geoffrey could only assume that the monk had been interrupted before he could finish. He became aware that people were regarding him expectantly, so he handed the letter to Odo, who read it with narrowed eyes. The prior glared at Ivar.

'You concealed the sky-stone under a tree?' he demanded angrily. 'You stupid fool! Why did you not bring it here, to be safe?'

'No!' cried Ivar, blood draining from his face. 'Leger promised never to reveal my secret – not until we had discussed together what was to be done. He *promised*!'

'That was before he knew it might cost him his life,' said Aidan angrily. 'Why did you burden him with this knowledge? Why not Odo or me? We are men who know how to look after ourselves, but he was not. You killed him with your nasty games!'

Ivar looked ready to cry, while Geoffrey considered the information with interest; Odo and Aidan knew how to look after themselves, and he had seen Aidan with a dagger. Did that mean they were not averse to shedding a little blood for whatever cause they believed in?

'We had better go and lay hold of it,' said Odo to his monks. 'We do not want it falling into the wrong hands.' He looked pointedly at Walter, who bristled.

'What do you mean by that?' the constable demanded. 'And why should you have it? If Ivar had wanted it to go to the Church, he would have given it to you when he took holy orders.'

'I do not want *any* of you to have it!' shouted Ivar. 'I have kept it safe for years, and *I* shall decide where it goes when my death is near.'

'Then you had better make a decision soon,' growled Pigot. 'Or you may run out of time. Like Leger.'

'Is that a threat or an unintentional confession?' demanded Odo. 'It sounded like the latter. In other words, *you* killed Leger, because you guessed Ivar had confided in him, and you wanted the thing for yourself.'

'We do not want it,' said Walter contemptuously, while the black-haired knight blanched at the accusation. 'Why would we, when it failed to save Eleanor?'

'Because it saved me,' said Nest quietly. She looked directly at Pigot. 'When I was being chased by men with harmful intent.'

Pigot flushed guiltily, although Walter was incensed. 'That incident had nothing to do with us, as I have already told you.'

'But Pigot has not,' said Cadowan, who had not missed the knight's reaction. 'Let him hold Leger's cross and deny it. If he lies, he will be struck down. Here – take it.'

'Perhaps we did follow Nest when we saw her alone by the cliffs,' snarled Pigot, putting his hands behind his back when Cadowan tried to thrust the cross into them. 'But you cannot prove our intentions were dishonourable.'

'It does not matter,' said Nest quietly, pulling her husband away. 'It was a long time ago, and all forgotten.'

'Not by me,' hissed Cadowan. 'It will never be forgotten by *me*.'

'Never mind this irrelevance,' said Walter briskly. 'As constable, it is my duty to find this stone and smash it before any more evil is done. I shall prepare a search party.'

'No!' cried Ivar, darting forward. 'You cannot destroy it! It is a gift from God.'

'Get away from me, you devil-lover,' snarled Walter. 'Your stone will soon be dust.' Then he snapped his fingers to indicate his men were to fall in behind him and left the priory without another word.

'We had better make sure we reach it first,' said Odo grimly. He looked around at his monks, who were already donning cloaks against the looming storm. 'We cannot stand by and see a gift from God destroyed. You had better stay here, Ivar – you will slow us down.'

Geoffrey raised his eyebrows. 'You will have to hurry: if Walter reaches it first, it will not be easy to wrest it from him. He and his men are armed.'

'There are many ways to the base of the cliff,' said Aidan. He grinned wildly. 'And I believe I know a faster way than Walter.'

They hurried away, and Geoffrey looked around to find that he and Roger were alone. Cadowan and Nest had also disappeared, while even Ivar, apparently loath to stand by while his treasure was seized, had hobbled after his brethren.

'It looks as if they all mean to have it,' said Roger, amused. 'It is a pity they know these cliffs, because I would not mind owning a healing stone myself – to use on you. You do not look well.'

'I am all right,' said Geoffrey, although his arm now throbbed so badly it was difficult to think of anything else. He winced when the next thunderclap started. 'I suppose all we can do now is wait to see who returns victorious.'

'Not here, though,' said Roger, looking around in distaste. 'We shall visit a tavern.'

The glimmer of a solution was beginning to form at the back of Geoffrey's mind, and he knew he had enough information and clues to identify Leger's killer. Unfortunately, the pain in his arm was distracting, and he did not feel equal to the serious thought such an analysis would entail. He followed Roger out of the priory, more than happy to sit in the White Lion until he felt better.

'You cannot let Walter destroy the sky-stone,' said Revelle, intercepting them as they walked towards the tavern. Geoffrey blinked, wondering where the angel-faced knight had come from – and why he was not with the bevy of soldiers he could see moving at a rapid lick along the path out of the town. 'It cured Nest, and there is great good in it.'

'Probably,' Geoffrey agreed tiredly. 'But Aidan knows a faster way, so perhaps he will reach it first. Moreover, Cadowan and Nest have disappeared, and I imagine they also intend to claim it. Thankfully, there is no room for more contenders, because I do not feel—'

'But Ivar did not head for the base of the cliff,' said Revelle urgently. 'He was plodding towards a route to the top and farther west – towards the cave where he used to live. I know, because I went there when Eleanor needed his help. I think the sky-stone is not where he told Leger it was.'

'Then go,' suggested Geoffrey, recalling that Ivar had said as much himself – that he had moved the sky-stone after confiding in Leger, because Leger had not given him an immediate answer about what should be done with it. 'Claim it for yourself, and give it to whichever contender you think the most worthy.'

'Ivar will not have left it out in full view,' snapped Revelle. 'He will have buried it or shoved it in a crevice, and it will take me an age to search for it alone. By then, Walter will have realized the story was a fabrication, and will search the cave as well.'

'He is your liege lord,' said Geoffrey. 'Reason with him if you feel so strongly that—'

'You do not *reason* with Walter,' interrupted Revelle contemptuously. 'As you should know from yesterday. He will destroy the stone, and we will all be the losers. But if you two come with me now, we can save it together.'

'But which of us gets to keep it?' asked Roger acquisitively. 'Or do we break it in three?'

'We give it to my cousin,' said Revelle, ignoring Roger's pained look and addressing Geoffrey. 'Bishop Giffard will know how to use it justly.'

'He will,' acknowledged Geoffrey. 'But—'

'Good,' interrupted Revelle. 'Then we must hurry. We shall use a goat-track and will arrive before Ivar is even halfway up.'

The last thing Geoffrey felt like was scrambling up cliffs, but Revelle and Roger were already setting a cracking pace, so he followed as quickly as he could. Once at the woods, Revelle began to follow an almost invisible trail that angled sharply upwards. Geoffrey doubted many human feet had trodden it.

'How did you discover this route?' asked Roger, panting as it grew steeper.

'Hunting for wild boar,' replied Revelle between quick breaths. 'It was how I reached Ivar so quickly after Eleanor drowned.'

Geoffrey was breathing heavily, and his vision was becoming blurred, made worse by the fact that the clouds overhead were so black that the morning was more like twilight. He began to wish he had risked removing his armour to inspect his arm the previous night, because now he was developing a fever. He tried to push his discomfort to the back of his mind, but his misery intensified when there was another roll of thunder and rain began to fall.

At first, it was just a few drops, but then the heavens opened with a ferocity the knight had rarely seen. Even the trees did not protect him, and the track underfoot became slick and dangerous. His feet skidded constantly, and, each time he fell, pain shot up his arm. He could not recall when he had last felt so wretched.

'I cannot continue,' he gasped to Roger. 'You go. I will wait here.'

'Watch out!' yelled Revelle from above them, and Geoffrey only just managed to leap to one side as a stream of brown water shot by, full of foliage, mud and small stones. The intense rain was washing away the soil that anchored trees and bushes to the ground.

'You cannot stay here,' said Roger grimly, grabbing his good arm and hauling him on. 'You will be swept away. You have no choice but to climb.'

'Do you think the sky-stone is driving this weather?' called Revelle uneasily. 'Is it summoning the help of the elements to ensure it is claimed by the party it wants?'

'No,' said Geoffrey, refusing to contemplate such a wild notion.

It felt like an age before Revelle shouted that they were near their destination. Geoffrey was exhausted, his arm burned and he could not catch his breath.

'The cave is there,' Revelle said, pointing with one hand and reaching down to pull Geoffrey up with the other. The cave's entrance was well concealed, and Geoffrey would not have known it was there had Revelle not identified it. They fought their way through a curtain of creepers and found themselves in a surprisingly spacious cavern, with a dry, sandy floor. Immediately, the sound of the storm faded.

But they were not alone: Ivar was there. He was breathing hard, as if he, too, had endured a fierce scramble. He had lit a fire and was sprinkling something on it that made it burn a curious blue colour. He was also chanting.

'What are you doing?' demanded Revelle. 'And how did you get here before us?'

The former hermit's face wore a peculiar expression, halfway between malice and triumph. 'I know these cliffs better than anyone: you could never outrun me. And I am about to summon some help, so I can keep what is mine.'

'He is calling on Satan!' cried Roger in alarm. He was about to stride forward and grab Ivar, but stopped when the crazed-looking man pointed a gnarled finger at him.

'Stand back!' Ivar ordered. 'Or you will be sorry. I *have* called Satan, and he has sent this storm to help me. I control it, and I will use it to destroy you if you come any closer.'

As if to prove his words, a blaze of lightning lit the entire hillside and the loudest crack of thunder Geoffrey had ever heard crashed outside. Several trees burst into flames. Revelle and Roger regarded Ivar with stunned expressions, while answers clicked smartly together in Geoffrey's mind. He leaned against the wall of the cave and supposed his fever had prevented him from seeing them before, because they were obvious.

'Ivar is the killer,' he said, surprised at how feeble his voice sounded. '*He* killed Leger.'

'Keep back,' warned Ivar again. 'Or you will die.'

Geoffrey saw him hold something above his head. It was a little smaller than his hand and unevenly shaped, bearing the same mark as the symbol on the letter that Giffard had forwarded to Revelle. The sky-stone, thought Geoffrey, gazing at the item that had caused so much trouble.

'I conjure Satan!' shouted Ivar wildly. 'Come, my dark lord!'

'Get out, quickly!' hissed Roger, grabbing Revelle's arm and hauling him backwards. 'It is not safe in here. Do not just stand there, Geoff! Move!'

But Geoffrey had no strength to move. It was all he could do to lean against the wall of the cave, when his legs threatened to buckle and deposit him on the ground.

'I thought Walter was being perverse when he accused Ivar of witchcraft,' said Revelle from outside the cave. 'But he was right all along! He—'

But suddenly there was a tremendous crash and a huge tongue of flame shot into the cave. It knocked Geoffrey from his feet, and he could feel heat licking his armour. Then it faded as quickly as it had come, leaving behind it a rank stench of burning. He looked at the front of the cave, but there was no sign of Roger or Revelle, and the vegetation where they had stood was blackened and smoking. Geoffrey had no doubt that they were dead.

Still staring at the ruined foliage at the mouth of the cave, Geoffrey tried to clamber to his feet. He found he could not do it.

'Are you still here?' asked Ivar. He sounded surprised. 'Well, no matter. You are in no condition to hinder me – you will not take the sky-stone, and nor will anyone.'

'You killed Leger,' said Geoffrey dully, not letting himself think about Roger. 'But not because you told him the location of the sky-stone, since that was a fabrication – it was here all along. You told him a deeper, more terrible secret. And he was appalled and at a loss about what to do, and *that* was why he asked for time to consider the matter. You do not trust anyone, and you thought he was going to betray you.'

'He *did* betray me,' said Ivar bitterly. He barely glanced at Geoffrey, busy with something over his fire. 'He wrote down what I said about the sky-stone, for anyone to read. And when he left the priory after we had talked, it occurred to me that *he* might be the spy – that he was running off to tell Walter de Clare all the things I had confided to him.'

'He was not the spy,' said Geoffrey, trying again to stand and failing. Another roar of thunder shook the cliffs. 'He was innocent of everything except befriending a monster.'

'I should have kept him at a distance,' spat Ivar, 'as I have everyone else since I arrived in this godforsaken land. But I had one moment of weakness and confessed that . . . But that is none of your affair. I realized immediately that I had made a mistake, so I hastened to confuse him by making up a tale about the sky-stone. Then he rushed off, saying he needed time to "reflect". You cannot blame me for killing him when his behaviour was so suspicious. *Why* did he want time to reflect?'

'Because he thought the matter you had entrusted to him was important,' explained Geoffrey tiredly. 'He wanted to pray – not in the priory, but alone. But you, who only pretends to hear God, cannot understand that. You tried to stab and poison him when he returned.'

'I wish I had succeeded,' muttered Ivar venomously.

'He did not share your secret with anyone,' Geoffrey went on. 'And that means no one was trying to kill him for it. So he knew *you* were the one trying to take his life. He stayed in the church, thinking that holy ground would stay your hand. He was wrong.'

'He was a pious fool,' said Ivar dismissively. He raised his hands again, and almost immediately there was a flicker of lightning outside that seared into Geoffrey's eyes and forced him to look away. The following thunder was deafening. 'No one will miss him.'

'My wife will,' said Geoffrey. He tried to see what Ivar was doing, but the man's hands were a blur of practised movements: whatever it was, he had done it before. He changed the subject when he saw that Ivar was not listening, hoping to win time and summon enough strength to prevent whatever diabolical mischief he was creating. 'You killed Marcus, too.'

'Your friend said *he* was the spy,' said Ivar with a careless shrug, as if the death of a man was nothing. 'Marcus had no right to take priory business to the evil Walter de Clare.'

'*Walter* is evil?' muttered Geoffrey, taken aback. 'You are the one summoning the devil.'

'My evil is pure,' declared Ivar. 'His is born of malice.'

Such warped logic was beyond Geoffrey's understanding. 'You killed Roger,' he said as anger gave him the strength to stagger to his feet. 'There was no need to harm him.'

Ivar barely glanced at him. 'Was there not? He was a greedy man, who would have stolen my stone without a moment's hesitation. Him *and* Revelle. But I will show you all what happens to men who cross me.'

'What are you doing?' asked Geoffrey uneasily as Ivar tossed more powder on the fire, which burned blue. Outside, the storm continued to rage; the rain was a white veil across the entrance.

Ivar stopped his conjuring to grin. 'I am avenging myself on all those who mean to steal from me. Do not come any closer, or you will not live to witness it – and I promise it will be impressive. I feel Satan strong within me today.'

Geoffrey again tried to distract him. 'You probably searched Leger's belongings, hunting for evidence that he betrayed you.' He took a step forward, supporting himself on the wall. 'But you cannot read, so you have no idea what he wrote in—'

Ivar rounded on him. 'Enough about Leger. I am tired of Leger!'

'Then let us talk about Ivar Jorundsson instead,' said Geoffrey, fighting off the dizziness that was beginning to claw at the edges of his vision. The ache in his arm had spread to his whole body, and he knew he would not be able to stay upright for long. 'You killed him, too.'

Ivar gaped at him. 'So Leger *did* betray my secret!'

'No. It was revealed in a letter that was sent to Drogo de Hauteville five years ago. Bishop Giffard must have taken it after Drogo's death, then sent it to Revelle. Its sender talked about a killer hunting him in darkness, and a mind lost to evil. The writer was Ivar Jorundsson, and he was referring to you.'

'How do you know?' demanded Ivar. He was not fiddling with his potions now, and all his attention was focused on Geoffrey.

'Because it was penned by a non-native speaker of English, and because it had a drawing of the sky-stone. Clearly, the real Ivar sent it, warning Drogo about you – the man who would kill him, steal his stone and use it for selfish purposes. Moreover, Ivar Jorundsson left Greenland to become a monk, which means he was devout and almost certainly literate. You are neither.'

'Is that the sum of the "evidence" you have?' sneered Ivar.

'No,' said Geoffrey, leaning more heavily against the wall when he felt himself reel. 'It was obvious from your own story that you were the "other survivor" of the fall of Deheubarth. You probably craved the sky-stone for years, even before the shipwreck, but it was not until you witnessed the slaughter near Civetot seven years ago that your mind turned totally to getting it. And as the last piece of evidence, there is *that*.'

He pointed to an alcove behind Ivar, whose eyes grew wide with horror when he saw the skeleton that was huddled there. It had been buried, but the explosion that had killed Roger and Revelle had loosened the earth around it, exposing it for all to see.

'And you probably murdered Drogo,' Geoffrey went on when Ivar turned back to his fire and began to chant with renewed fervour. Outside, the storm reached new heights of fury, so it felt as if the whole cliff-face was shuddering under its impact. The knight took another step forward.

'Drogo had met Jorundsson,' said Ivar. 'He had to die if I was to assume Jorundsson's identity, and I am glad he fell over the cliff.'

Geoffrey lunged at him. The madman punched him, using the hand that held the stone. Geoffrey felt a blinding pain in his temple, and then a curious floating sensation. Lights exploded behind his eyes, and he was not sure if it was his imagination or more lightning. Ivar was poised to hit him again, but Geoffrey grabbed his wrist, wrenched the stone away and, after stumbling a few steps, threw it as hard as he could out of the cave's entrance.

'No!' howled Ivar, haring after it.

Geoffrey supposed he should not let him escape. He staggered to the entrance, and winced when there was a terrible scream, followed by the kind of crashing that suggested someone cartwheeling down the tree-studded slope.

'Geoff!' exclaimed Roger, appearing suddenly in front of him. 'I am sorry to abandon you with that villain. I was coming back for you, but that thunderbolt hit and knocked me out of my wits.'

'Where is Revelle?' asked Geoffrey. He found he was able to stand unaided.

Roger's expression darkened, and he looked away. 'The thunderbolt must have blown him to pieces. And then Ivar went over the cliff – he just tore out of the cave and plunged straight over, trying to catch the sky-stone.'

Geoffrey stood straighter. 'Did he succeed?'

Roger shook his head. 'And I am afraid there is no point hunting for the stone, because it will never be found in all that undergrowth. What a pity! I am sure we could have sold it for a handsome price.'

'It was not something to be haggled over,' said Geoffrey. He flexed his arm, aware that it no longer throbbed and his wits were clear. He supposed his tussle with Ivar must have dislodged some pocket of poison and allowed his humours to rebalance themselves.

'The rain has stopped,' said Roger, squinting into the sky, where a brilliant rainbow was beginning to shimmer. 'So I recommend we leave, because if anyone else comes up here I am not sure how we shall explain what has happened.'

Nor was Geoffrey.

'I hate to say it, but Walter was right,' said Roger as they neared Goodrich the following afternoon, glad to have left Estrighoiel and its warring inhabitants behind. 'Ivar *was* evil, and he *did* try to summon demons from hell.'

'He did try,' agreed Geoffrey. 'But he did not succeed. All he did was light a fire, throw some handfuls of coloured sand at it and mutter a lot of gibberish.'

Roger gaped at him. 'But he called up that terrible storm – which seems to have destroyed crops as far as the eye can see.'

'The storm was brewing long before he went to his cave,' countered Geoffrey. 'It was coincidence that it broke when we happened to confront him.'

'If you say so,' said Roger, unconvinced. 'But you cannot deny that he was a selfish, wicked villain. He murdered Ivar Jorundsson to get the sky-stone in the first place, having coveted it for years. He must have killed Drogo, and he stabbed Leger after he had second thoughts about confiding in him. Then he dispatched Marcus because he was the priory spy. Why did he do that, Geoff? He felt no loyalty to his Benedictine brethren.'

'Probably because he was afraid that a man who snooped might have the skill to learn the whereabouts of the sky-stone and the identity of Leger's murderer.'

Roger nodded. 'And Cadowan, Nest, Odo and his monks, Walter, Revelle and Pigot were innocent. However, I confess that I am disappointed that we could not find something with which to accuse Walter and his henchmen. I did not take to them.'

'The feeling was mutual. But I am sorry we found no trace of Revelle to bury. He was a good man, and I do not like to think of him lying scattered down the cliff.'

'Unlike Ivar – or whatever his real name was,' said Roger. 'Walter found *his* body.'

They rode silently for several moments.

'Why do you think the sky-stone helped Nest but not Eleanor – a sweet child whom everyone liked?' asked Roger.

'I am not sure it did save Nest. She was probably stunned by her fall, then regained her senses when Ivar reached her and began to call her name.'

'It cured you,' Roger pointed out. 'The arm Walter sliced through, and the fever.'

Geoffrey shook his head. 'The injury must have been in my mind – I never removed my armour to look at it, so there is no evidence that it was ever there. And the so-called fever was the result of a poor night's sleep.'

'It was more than that, Geoff lad! Let me see your arm again.'

Geoffrey pulled up his sleeve to reveal a limb that was smooth and unblemished. 'See? There was never any wound.'

'You had a scar there,' said Roger, pointing. 'From the battle to take Jerusalem. And another below it from our adventures at Goodrich last year. But both have gone.'

'They were fading anyway,' said Geoffrey. 'The sky-stone had nothing to do with it.'

'You can think what you like,' said Roger, kicking his horse into a canter. 'But I know the truth.'

A few miles away, Revelle was also urging his horse forward, eager to put as much distance between him and Estrighoiel as possible. He smiled as he slipped his hand inside his tunic and felt the reassuring bulk of the sky-stone within. He had thought he was a dead man when the thunderbolt had blown him over the cliff, and he had been lying on the ground, sure his back was broken and his innards crushed. And then a miracle had occurred. The sky-stone had sailed through the air and landed next to him. He had managed to grab it, and within moments he had felt the strength surge back into his limbs.

Had it saved him, or had he just had the breath knocked out of him by the fall? He had dropped a long way – farther than Ivar, and *he* had been smashed to a pulp. No, Revelle thought, there *was* power in the sky-stone.

He felt a little guilty at making off with it, but it was for the best. There would never be peace between the castle and the priory if the sky-stone was in Estrighoiel, and he was doing them a favour by spiriting it away. It was not theft, but an act of selflessness – of taking upon himself a burden that was too great for them to bear.

He was glad to be away from Walter and was looking forward to seeing his cousin again. Even if Bishop Giffard could not find him a post, Exeter was said to be a fine city, and the Revelles were a powerful force in the area. It would be a good place in which to settle, and let the sky-stone keep him fit and healthy as he enjoyed the rest of what he hoped would be a long and happy life. And there were others who might benefit from the touch of the stone – an old aunt, crippled with pains in her back, and another cousin who was afflicted with fits.

Or would its effects be weakened if he shared it? Revelle clutched it tighter and decided he had better keep it to himself. After all, he needed all the good graces he could muster, given his sins. He smiled when he thought of Nest. He had almost had her that day in the woods, and it was a pity she had fallen before he could reach her. And then there was Drogo – he had rather enjoyed pushing him over the cliff so Walter could step into his shoes as constable. These were grave crimes, but the stone would save him. Would it not?

Historical note

Storms were always a part of medieval life, and they ruined crops on a regular basis. But the one on 10 August 1103 must have been particularly spectacular, because it was recorded by several contemporary chroniclers. It damaged the harvest so badly that starvation was widespread the following winter.

Odo was an early leader of the Benedictine Priory in Estrighoiel (Chepstow). It was founded by William fitz Osbern, who also built the first Norman castle there. William's son rebelled against William the Conqueror in 1075, and Chepstow was taken from him in retaliation. It was held directly by the Crown until about 1115, when it was passed to the powerful (and loyal) de Clare family. There were several de Clare brothers, including Gilbert, Roger and Walter. The older two were present at the hunting accident in the New Forest that saw William II (Rufus) killed, leading to Henry I taking the throne. Their sister was married to Walter Tirel, who loosed the fatal arrow.

ACT TWO

North Devon, September 1236

The woman and the girl trudged wearily along the rough track in the gentle warmth of an autumn afternoon.

'I'm feared that he will come back unexpectedly and follow us, mother,' whined Gillota, the fourteen-year-old who was leading their only cow on a rope halter. 'He'll surely beat us and perhaps try to have his way with me again!'

Matilda Claper, strong in nature as well as in arm, tried to reassure her daughter. 'Don't worry, girl, Walter Lupus has gone to the Goose Fair in Tavistock. He'll not be back home for three or four days – longer if he gets heavily into the drink.'

Only partly consoled by the thought of their manor lord being far away, Gillota trudged on. A large pack was strapped to her back, containing some food and all the clothes they possessed. In her free hand she dangled a wicker cage containing their tabby cat, a threadbare mouser with one ear shredded in many fights. In the cloth scrip on her girdle, she had five pennies and a cheap tin crucifix, the sum total of her possessions.

Her mother walked a few paces behind the skinny brown cow, a rope around her shoulders dragging a crude sledge of hazel withies lashed together with twine, piled with their bedding and a few cooking pots. Matilda was a handsome woman, dark-haired and slim – in fact, too thin for her height – but there was a sadness in her face that told of recent hard times.

She looked with affection at her only child, all she had in the world now that her husband Robert was dead. He had been a good thatcher and a good man, but God had taken him away three years ago, when he fell from the roof of the church and broke his back. Matilda had been taken in by her father, who was the manor reeve, elected by the serfs to represent them and to organize the work on the strip fields and on the lord's demesne. Matilda and her daughter worked his croft alongside him, except when he gave his villein service to the manor three days each week.

She sighed as she thought again for the thousandth time of all that had gone wrong in the last two years. First, their manor lord, Matthew Lupus, had died of a gnawing cancer of the throat, leaving his evil son Walter to inherit and make their life a misery. Then her own father, Roger Merland, had died six months ago of lockjaw, contracted when he jabbed his foot with a pitchfork. Soon afterwards, Walter began trying to seduce the attractive widow. When she repulsed him, he turned his attention to her virginal daughter and Matilda was hard-pressed to keep him at bay. Now she had endured enough, and they were stealing away illegally from Kentisbury, a village a few miles from the north coast of Devon, heading far inland for Shebbear, which lay south of Torrington. Their opportunity came when Walter Lupus, together with his steward and bailiff, went off for a few days to the great fair at Tavistock. Matilda and her daughter left covertly before dawn, and, though many of the villagers knew of their departure, they were willing to look the other way and plead ignorance when Walter returned home. He was an unpopular successor to his father, being dour, selfish and arrogant, and Matilda's sympathetic neighbours were well aware of the harassment that they were suffering.

Matilda, leading a pregnant goat on a cord, whistled to their hound Chaser to round up their two pigs, which were snuffling in the undergrowth at the side of the track. They could not be far from their destination now, as it was about twenty-five miles between Kentisbury and Shebbear and this was the second day of their flight. They had spent the night under a wide elm, well away from the track, to be out of sight of the footpads and thieves who infested the fringes of Exmoor. With the cow and goat tethered to a tree and the pigs hobbled with cords, they passed the night in uneasy and fitful slumber, after eating the bread and cheese they had brought with them.

Ahead of them the track lay through a stretch of deep forest, the last before they reached Shebbear. This was the sort of place where outlaws lurked, ready to steal, ravish and kill, so they entered the gloomy tunnel of oaks and beeches with trepidation. There were few people travelling this lonely road, but Matilda hoped that this might discourage robbers, who would get thin pickings from such sparse traffic.

'Why has God treated us so badly?' said Gillota suddenly. 'We have done no evil that I know of! I go to confession with Father Peter, but I have little to tell him – not that he seems interested, anyway.'

Matilda smiled to herself. Her daughter was naive, certainly, but she was intelligent and always seeking for truths that neither her mother nor anyone else in the village could give her.

'There is little opportunity for folks like us to sin, child,' she called at Gillota's back. 'Sin is for men, who drink and lust and cheat – and for the lords, who fight and kill!'

She knew that the girl was perplexed by the misfortunes that had overtaken the family. Her childhood had been secure, albeit impoverished, until her father died. Even living with her grandfather was tolerable, but after his death Matilda and Gillota had to scrape a living from the half-acre toft that he left them, existing on their few animals and growing vegetables for their staple diet. Though at thirty-two she was comparatively young, Matilda also had a reputation as 'wise woman', so she was all the village had by way of health care and a midwife, which brought her in a few pennies for her poultices and herbal potions.

In spite of their fears, the few miles of forest were crossed without incident, and they emerged only a couple of miles from Shebbear, where the road dipped down into a small valley and strip fields began to appear on each side. This was a King's manor, having no lord but a bailiff who administered several such parcels of royal land in this part of Devon.

'Do you know where your aunt lives, mother?' asked Gillota as the first tofts and cottages began to appear at the side of the road.

Matilda shook her head. 'I've never been here before – in fact, this is the first time I've ever left Kentisbury,' she confessed.

It was her husband Robert Claper who had been a Shebbear man, being sent to Matilda's village years before when the two bailiffs exchanged a thatcher for a blacksmith – and as an unfree villein he had no more say in the matter than if he had been an ox or a sheepdog. However, his good fortune was to meet and marry Matilda and to father Gillota before death claimed him.

'How will we find her, then?' persisted her daughter, fearful of this unfamiliar place that was opening up before them. A stone church faced an alehouse, the inevitable pair of buildings seen in almost every English village.

Suddenly their attention was attracted by something on the grass verge in front of the church. It was just a very large boulder, probably weighing a ton, lying under an old tree. Though nothing remarkable, the mother and daughter stared at it and then at each other, and something unspoken passed between them. Increasingly as she grew older, Gillota showed that she was becoming as 'fey' as her mother, both having the rudiments of 'second sight', knowing things that were outside the normal five senses. It was this that allowed Matilda to function as a 'wise woman', though she was careful never to let it be known, in case of accusations of witchcraft. Now that Gillota was showing the same hereditary gift, her mother worried that she might not yet be mature enough to hide these sporadic but powerful insights.

'That's a work of the devil!' said the young girl impulsively, looking at the greyish rock.

Her mother nodded but pushed her daughter onwards. 'None of our business, my girl! We have more urgent matters to deal with.'

'So how will we find Aunt Emma?' persisted Gillota

'Your father always said she had a toft just beyond the church,' answered her mother. 'We will ask the first person we see.'

This proved to be an old woman, bent almost double over a gnarled stick, who came out of the churchyard gate as they passed. The crone stared at the procession of animals and muttered a greeting through toothless gums, which Matilda answered with a question.

'Mother, can you please tell us where Emma, who was once called Claper, lives?'

'Claper? It's many a year since I heard that name. Emma married a man called Revelle, but he ran off to the wars and was never heard of again.' She cackled at some private secret.

'So where can we find her dwelling?' asked Gillota politely.

The old woman raised her stick and pointed up the track. 'The last cottage on the right side. But she's not well, you know.'

Matilda stared. Only three weeks ago she had had a reply from Emma by word of mouth via a friendly carter, saying that she would welcome them into her household, and there was no mention of illness then.

'Not well? What ails her, then?'

'She had a seizure last week,' answered the crone with morbid satisfaction. 'Lost the use of an arm and her speech, though I hear tell she's past the worst. Her neighbours are looking after her as best they can.'

Numbed by yet another catastrophe, Matilda murmured some thanks and set off rapidly up the last few hundred paces to the toft that the woman had indicated.

'What do we do now, Mother,' snivelled Gillota tearfully. 'How can we stay with a sick woman? Will we have to go back to Kentisbury?'

'Stay out here with the beasts!' she commanded as they reached a rickety gate in a fence around the croft. 'I'll go inside and see what's happening.'

Shrugging off her sledge ropes, she went up the few paces to the door. The cottage was a square box of oak frames, filled in with wattle and daub, a mixture of lime, clay, dung and horsehair, plastered over woven hazel panels. The thatch was old but in good condition, and two shuttered window spaces were set each side of the open front door.

Matilda tapped on the half-open door and peered in. In the centre of the single room she saw a large matron standing over the fire-pit, stirring the contents of an iron pot resting on a trivet over the glowing embers. Beyond her, an older woman was slumped on a stool, supporting herself against a table. One arm rested uselessly in her lap, and the corner of her mouth drooped as if part of her face had melted.

The neighbour looked around questioningly as Matilda entered. 'Who are you, woman?' she snapped. 'You're a stranger!'

'I'm Matilda, widow of Emma's nephew. I've come with my daughter to live here.'

Shebbear, August 1237

Gillota threw down the pile of dry grass in front of their cow, which had filled out well since the previous autumn. Served by the village bull, she had recently produced a calf and now munched away contentedly at the feed that the girl had cut with her sickle from the verges outside the village.

Matilda came out of the cottage with turnip peelings for the goats, and for a moment mother and daughter stood looking with satisfaction at their livestock. Their pigs were penned behind hurdles at the bottom of the half-acre plot, though in a month they would be let loose in the woods beyond the pasture, to root for beechnuts, on payment of a halfpenny-a-week pannage fee to the bailiff. A dozen fowls and four geese paraded around the back of the house, and in a distant corner half a dozen ducks splashed in the muddy water of a large hole dug in the ground.

They had worked hard since that day last summer when they came to find Aunt Emma struck with the palsy. Helped by the neighbours, they had nursed her back to reasonable health, and, though her arm was still weak and her speech a little slurred, her legs were sound and after a month or

two she was able to do a share of the work in both cottage
and on the croft outside.

Emma was a strong character, of formidable appearance. Tall and bony, she looked younger than her sixty-five
years. The grey hair that strayed from under her head-rail
still had streaks of russet in it, and she had kept many
of her teeth, albeit discoloured and crooked. A devout
woman, she was not given to much humour but was always
even-tempered and tolerant of the two younger women
who now shared her home.

'You may stay here for as long as you need,' she
announced within days of their arrival. 'And when I die,
the toft will be yours, for I've no child to hand it to.'

Her gratitude for the attention that Matilda and her
daughter gave her during her illness was muted, but nonetheless sincere, and as the months went by the all-female
household became strongly bonded. Thankfully, it was a
mild winter, with little snow and ice, though by the spring
their stocks of food were running dangerously low. By
March they were living on turnips and carrots stored in
clamps in the yard, winter cabbage, onions and a few eggs
that the fowls managed to produce off-season. The cow
had a drain of milk left from last year's pregnancy, but did
not come into full flow until the calf was born.

It was a lean time, but they survived. Matilda again acted
as a midwife and herbalist to the village and was paid for
her services in kind: a loaf of bread, a pat of butter, a pan
of wheat or a rabbit poached from the village warren. As
they were acknowledged as free from serfdom in Shebbear,
they had no allotted strips in the surrounding fields as
did the villeins, who paid for the land allotted to them by
the manor by the three days each week they worked for
the bailiff on the King's demesne, plus many other 'boon
days'. With Gillota's help, Matilda dug and planted half

the ground behind the cottage, keeping the rest for the animals, though each day Gillota led the cow down to the common pasture to graze.

One winter evening, when the aunt had recovered fairly well, the three women had crouched around the fire-pit, Emma and Matilda on the two stools and the daughter on the bracken-covered floor.

'I still don't understand how you say you are a free woman,' muttered Emma thickly. 'Your husband Robert was a villein when he left this village to go to Kentisbury.'

Her speech was improving, but the other two had to listen hard to understand her. Matilda frowned as she worked out the complicated family relationships.

'Yes, all the Clapers were serfs, but that wasn't the way we became free,' she explained. 'Robert, God bless his soul, married me, a Merland, who were unfree ever since William the Bastard conquered at Hastings.'

The aunt interrupted rather testily. 'So was I, like all the Clapers, until Alan Revelle married me. He was a soldier and was freed for his service, so that made me free as well.'

'Did he die, Aunt Emma?' asked Gillota innocently, getting a lopsided scowl in return.

'No, he went off to fight in the barons' armies against King John. That was twenty years ago, and I've not heard a word of him since. Thank God I had this freeholding to live on, or I'd have starved.'

Matilda had waited patiently to finish her story. 'Your nephew Robert came to Kentisbury, married me and worked both as a thatcher and in the fields, like all the villeins. My father was the manor reeve for many years, and he worked so well and was so popular that our lord, Matthew Lupus, freed him about three years ago.'

'That wouldn't have made Robert free – and you were his wife,' objected Emma.

The younger woman nodded her agreement. 'No, not then. We remained in serfdom and worked for the lord as usual. But when Robert died, I became unencumbered by a bonded husband and so, as the daughter of a free man, became free myself.'

Emma thought about this for a moment. 'Can your lord testify to his freeing Robert?'

Tears sprang to Matilda's eyes. 'This is the problem! Matthew Lupus died last year, and his son Walter refuses to accept the situation. He denies that his father freed mine, and, especially since my father also died, he claims that I and my daughter remain in his servitude. He made us carry on in bondage as before, working for the manor and paying our boons the same as the other villeins.'

Emma poked the small logs in the ring of whitewashed stones with a rod held in her good hand. 'Was there no document to prove the act of manumission?' she asked.

Matilda shook her head sadly. 'No one in the village apart from the priest can read or write. The king's steward from Barnstaple comes with a clerk every quarter to record all the village payments and debts.'

'But surely the village knew that your father had been freed?' objected Emma.

'When it came to the test, Walter Lupus denied it,' said Matilda sadly. 'How can you go against what your manor lord says?'

Gillota looked from her mother to her great-aunt as the dialogue swung from side to side. She was still anxious about being dragged back to Kentisbury, even though months had passed.

Emma was still raising objections to Matilda's story. 'But the manor steward and the bailiff would have known about the manumission of your father by this Matthew Lupus,' she declared. 'Could you not have appealed to them?'

Matilda shook her head. 'The bailiff at that time left for a better post in Suffolk, and when his father died Walter got rid of the old steward and appointed another, younger man, Simon Mercator, who was always eager to do his bidding.'

'The manor court, then!' said the old lady. 'Could you not have appealed to them?'

'I did, even though the new reeve who replaced my father was reluctant to put my case forward. But when it came to the hearing, the new steward held the court, with Walter sitting alongside him. They dismissed my plea with contempt, saying it was a frivolous lie.'

Over the following months they had this conversation several times, but nothing could be resolved, and as they had now escaped it seemed pointless to keep reviving the issue.

The winter turned into spring, then summer, and the two refugees settled into the steady routine of life in Shebbear. With one exception, everyone accepted them, and they became part of the village community. The exception was Adam the carter, a freeman who made a living from his ox-cart, in which he carried goods and material all over North Devon.

Much of his trade was in transporting grain and wool from the King's manors to Barnstaple and Bideford for shipment, but he would take anything anywhere for a few pennies. For some reason he took against Matilda from the start, scowling at them in the road and muttering under his breath. In the alehouse he would complain about these foreign interlopers coming to his village.

'Escaped serfs, that's all they are!' he would whine. 'Absconded from their master and pretending to be free!'

As the rest of Shebbear became quite fond of the pretty woman and her daughter, they took little notice of him, but he persisted in his dislike of the women. This feeling was mutual, as Adam was a scrawny, ugly fellow with a face like a weasel and a nature to match.

When there was additional work to be done in the fields, Matilda and her daughter pitched in with the rest, even though as free women they had no obligation to do so. Matilda also continued to gain her neighbours' favour by dealing with sickness and childbirth, her knowledge of herbs being welcome, since the previous 'wise woman' had died of old age a year before.

She noticed that Gillota's gift of unusual perception was increasing, and sometimes they would exchange a swift glance when something came into their minds simultaneously. On one occasion, after a heavy rainstorm, they both knew that something was badly amiss at the little footbridge over the stream. Both ran towards it and found that one of the village children had fallen into the swollen brook and was in danger of drowning. Having rescued him, they explained away their presence by saying that they happened to be passing, not to arouse any suspicions, but Matilda guessed that several villagers had a shrewd idea that they were 'fey'.

Another example of their shared powers was in the matter of the little stone that lay on a shelf in Emma's kitchen. At the back of the square room that occupied the whole cottage, there was a crude lean-to, entered through a gap in the rear wall. Here food was prepared on a table, and the task of dealing with the day's milking was carried out, skimming some for cream in a wide earthenware dish. Emma's few pots and pans sat on a plank shelf fixed to the wall, and as soon as Matilda entered for the first time she knew that something powerful was concealed there.

As she reached up, Gillota came in and their eyes met in complete understanding. 'What is it, Mother?' she asked breathlessly. 'It's strong and good, whatever it is!'

Alongside a pottery jug, Matilda's finger found a hard, cool object, and she lifted it down carefully. Though it looked like a stone, it was too heavy and had a metallic feel. She held it out to Gillota. 'I've never seen the like of this before.'

Her daughter took it almost reverently and laid it across her palm. It was the size of her hand and had four irregular arms.

'It reminds me of a flying bird or a funny-shaped cross,' she said wonderingly. 'But I don't think it's meant to be anything other than itself.'

Her mother took it back and looked at it closely, turning it over in her hands. 'It's telling me that it came from far away, perhaps beyond the sky itself.'

'It's not just a strange stone; it has a life of its own,' said Gillota, crossing herself. 'Let's ask Aunt Emma where it came from.'

Her great-aunt was dismissive of the stone. Both Matilda and her daughter were well aware that Emma had no trace of their gift.

'My husband had it from somewhere,' she muttered. 'He said it had been in the Revelle family for years. No one knows what it is, but I kept it as a curiosity. You can have it, Matilda, if it takes your fancy.'

Matilda readily accepted it and kept it under her mattress to keep it near her, curious to learn what its properties might be. This was the second strange stone they had come across in Shebbear. Soon after they arrived, Matilda enquired casually about the large stone that she and Gillota had seen near the church and which had triggered some primitive fear in both their minds.

'That's the Devil's Stone,' she was informed. 'He threw it there when he was turned out of heaven by St Michael.'

In November they joined the rest of the village in an ancient ritual, standing around the stone well after dark in the light of a blazing bonfire, to watch some of the men turning the massive boulder over with stout poles, while the church bell clanged out a racket to frighten off Satan.

'No one knows why we do it,' admitted their neighbour. 'But it's always been done, to avoid bad luck for the coming year.'

After the turning, there was food and drink provided by the bailiff, a pleasant tradition that was repeated throughout the year, usually on saints' days, when a holiday was declared and an 'ale' held in the churchyard. The weak beer brewed and drunk in large quantities got its name from these 'ales', when eating, drinking, dancing and flirting were conducted in equal measure.

Several men became interested in Matilda, a comely widow, but she was older than all the unmarried men and did not fancy the prospect of wedding an old widower. However, Gillota was a different matter and, at almost fifteen, was well into marriageable age. A number of the village youths showed their interest, though having managed to shrug off their serfdom Matilda was concerned that her daughter might fall for a villein again and lose her freedom.

In August harvest-time arrived, as the weather had been good this year, a welcome change for some recent bad summers. This was the culmination of the farming year, and everyone turned out to help bring in the wheat, barley and oats that together with the beans and root vegetables would hopefully see the village through the next winter.

Matilda and her daughter joined everyone else in the fields, following behind the men who reaped with scythes and sickles. They collected and bound the cut corn into sheaves and stooked them to dry. Older women came with wide wooden rakes to collect the fallen stems, even Emma managing to drag one behind her with her good hand. Children were put to gleaning, squatting to pick up fallen grains into bags tied around their waist, as every speck of food might mean the difference between starvation or survival by next February.

The strips belonging to the King's manor were harvested first, then the rest of the corn was tackled, of which a tenth would go to the Church as tithes, as did a similar proportion of almost everything else that the villagers produced, be it eggs, ducks or lambs.

For three days they worked from first light until dark, the stooks cut on the first day now being dry, thanks to the good weather. As Matilda followed the reapers, Gillota gathering behind her, the ox-carts rumbled past, piled high with yellow sheaves, headed for the tithe barn and the barns at the manor barton, ready for winnowing the grain from the straw.

Both men and women sang as they worked, looking forward to noon, when they could rest for a few minutes and eat the bread and cheese or scraps of meat they had brought and replace their sweat with weak ale. Then they carried on until the sun was sinking, when eventually the reeve called a halt and the workers began streaming back to their homes to eat and then collapse on to their beds until dawn, when the whole exhausting routine would begin again.

But for Matilda and her daughter, daybreak would bring a very different scenario.

Just as the early summer dawn was breaking, Emma awoke and, using her good arm, levered herself up from the palliasse on the bracken-covered floor. She went to the fire-pit and blew on the embers under the white wood-ash, then added a few sticks, so that she could warm the iron pot of oat gruel that sat on a trivet.

She shook Matilda and Gillota awake and soon they were sleepily eating the gruel and some bread smeared with pork dripping that was their breakfast. They slept in their working clothes, calf-length shifts of coarse cloth, clinched at the waist with a rope girdle, so they were ready to be off as soon as they had washed down their food with some small ale.

But as they moved barefoot to the door, it suddenly flew open and Adam the carter burst in.

'There they are, the runaway serfs!' he shouted triumphantly and stood aside as two rough-looking men entered and advanced on the women. Behind them came another, dark-haired man, dressed in a short tunic, breeches and riding boots, of a quality that marked him as being from a higher station in life.

'Walter Lupus!' screamed Gillota and ran to hide behind her mother. Aghast, Matilda shielded her with her body, but one of the men dragged her aside and began snapping rusty iron fetters on the girl's wrists, while the other did the same to Matilda.

Wriggling and shouting, she began protesting at the top of her voice. 'Why can you not leave us in peace? We are free, don't you understand?'

The lord of Kentisbury pushed his way further into the room. 'Be quiet, woman!' he shouted. 'You are absconders, do you understand? You're going back where you belong.'

The manacles were attached to long chains, and the two ruffians, whom Lupus had obviously brought from Kentisbury, began dragging the two women out of the door, with Emma stumbling behind them, shouting for help at the top of her damaged voice.

By the time the disorderly procession had reached the gate, neighbours were beginning to congregate in the road outside.

'What's going on here?' demanded the man from next door. 'Who are you and what are doing to those women?

For answer, one of the roughs pushed him in the chest, making him fall against the fence.

'Mind your tongue, fellow!' bellowed Walter. 'Then mind your own business, for this is none of yours.'

There was a growl of anger from the small crowd, which was growing as more villagers congregated at the house.

'Leave our women alone. What right have you to invade our village?' shouted the smith, who had always been very friendly to Matilda and her daughter.

Lupus raised a riding crop he carried and smacked the man across the face, raising a red weal across his cheek.

'Keep a civil tongue in your head, man, or I'll have it cut out!' he snarled.

The crowd fell back a pace, alarmed at this early show of violence. They could see that this was a man of substance from his demeanour and quality of clothing – and some of them had seen the fine horse that was tied up outside Adam's cottage.

'Send for the bailiff – and the sergeant!' screamed Emma from the yard. 'They'll know how to deal with these outlaws!'

Her damaged voice carried well enough for some of the neighbours to start running back towards the centre of the village, but Lupus ignored her and began striding up the track towards Adam's house.

The two louts followed, dragging the woman and the girl behind them by their chains. Matilda thrashed and struggled, calling out all the time for Lupus to let them go, but Gillota just stumbled along sobbing, tears streaming from her eyes.

Adam followed behind, but he was jostled and abused by his fellow villagers, several of whom managed to get in a punch or kick against this traitor in their midst.

They reached Adam's dwelling, a cottage with large yard and a thatched byre where he kept his oxen. He hurried ahead and pulled open the crude door to the shed, revealing a heap of soiled straw and a manger where he fed hay to his two beasts. They were tethered in the yard, so the byre was empty, and the two men Lupus had brought from Kentisbury dragged the women inside and pushed them roughly down on to the straw. One of them secured the loose chains to one of the roof supports with a rusty nail-spike, which he hammered in with a large stone.

'That'll keep you from wandering until we're ready to leave!' he jeered.

By the time Walter Lupus had inspected the chains, new arrivals had appeared in the yard. The bailiff, Ranulf de Forde, and the Sergeant of the Hundred, Osbert de Bosco, had been summoned by the villagers. The first administered the King's properties in the area, and de Bosco was responsible to the sheriff for law and order in the part of the county centred on Shebbear.

'What's going on here?' demanded the bailiff. 'Why are these women being shackled like this?'

Walter was not disposed to being questioned in such a peremptory fashion by a bailiff. 'It's none of your concern. I would have thought you would be aware that I am the lord of Kentisbury. I am merely recapturing two serfs who ran away last year. It has taken me this long to discover where they were, thanks to your carter Adam. I had thought that they had run to a borough like Barnstaple.'

This was a reasonable assumption, as most absconding villeins made for a town, where, if they could evade recapture for a year and a day, they were entitled to their freedom.

The sergeant was not happy with the situation. 'I feel it is not right for you to just ride into our village with your men and seize two of our women without a by your leave or any gesture of courtesy to us.'

Walter turned on him angrily. 'Damn you and your courtesy, fellow! These are not "your women", as you call them – they are my serfs and I need every person to help with the harvest. This is nothing to do with you or this miserable vill of Shebbear!'

His arrogance annoyed them, but they recognized that he probably had the ear of the sheriff or one of the Devon barons, so they were afraid to antagonize him.

'What are you going to do with them?' asked de Bosco in a more conciliatory tone.

'They are going back to my manor in chains,' snapped Lupus. 'Your carter Adam, who told me of their whereabouts, is taking them back today. I am angry that you gave them shelter here, when it must have been obvious that they were fugitive serfs.'

'They claim they were freed, sir,' objected the bailiff.

Walter Lupus gave a laugh that was more like a derisive bark. 'They would, wouldn't they! Liars, both of them. The woman's father was my father's reeve, from a long line of villeins.'

He turned his back on the two officials and snapped a command at Adam, who was lurking in the byre, trying to keep away from his irate neighbours.

'Give these women a bucket and something to eat before you leave. I shall expect you in Kentisbury tomorrow night.'

An ox-cart moved at the pace of a man's walk and would take two days to cover the miles between the villages.

Walter left one of the guards he had brought in Adam's yard, then he and the other man walked back to the church and rode away on their horses, leaving a disgruntled but powerless community behind.

Emma marched into the ox-byre, defying the lout who tried to prevent her. 'Get out of my way, you heartless swine,' she screeched. 'I need to see my niece and her daughter.'

A few of the village men pushed into the yard and stood threateningly around the man. Though they dare not defy the lord of Kentisbury by rescuing the women, they had no scruples about harassing his servant.

Emma went into the shed and spent a few minutes trying to console Matilda and especially Gillota, who was devastated by this reversal of their fortunes.

'You'll have to go back, but we will do all we can to get you home again,' Emma promised. 'I will ask the bailiff, sergeant and our priest what can be done.'

She went back to their cottage and put the few spare garments that the women possessed into a cloth bag, together with some food for the journey and a purse with a few pennies, all she had to give. At Matilda's pleading, she also added the strange stone that her niece kept under the end of her mattress.

'Something tells me that I might be needing it,' she told Emma grimly as they were pushed on to the cart to start the long journey to Kentisbury.

Just as it had been in Shebbear, it was now harvest-time in Kentisbury, though it had started a week later there.

Once again, Matilda and Gillota were in the strip fields, toiling alongside their old neighbours, gathering sheaves, stooking and raking. The first shock of their kidnapping had worn off, to be replaced by sorrow and despondency, especially at the loss of their old home.

When their long and uncomfortable cart ride was over, they were turned off at Walter Lupus's manor house, a grey-stone block set inside a wide compound surrounded by a wooden stockade. The surly guard dragged them by their chains around to the back of the house, where the huts of the servants lay between stables and barns. As he released their fetters by knocking out the rusty pins that held them, Matilda protested that they were in the wrong place.

'Our home is further up the road!' she complained.

'Your home is here now!' came a voice from behind her. Turning, she saw Simon Mercator, the steward to Walter Lupus, the man who had previously denied her attempt to establish her freedom at the manor court. He was a narrow-faced man with sandy hair and cold eyes, which roamed over her body as if he could see through the thin woollen smock that she wore.

'We have our own croft, where I was born!' retorted Matilda defiantly.

'Not any longer,' sneered Simon. 'My nephew lives there now, so you'll live here as the servants you are. When the harvest is over, you will help with the domestic work around the manor.'

He ignored her loud protests and pushed her into the hut that acted as one of the servants' dormitories. The earth floor was strewn with rushes, and much of the space was occupied by a wide mattress, a hessian bag stuffed with hay and ferns. Apart from a milking stool and a couple of planks fixed to a wall to act as a shelf for their meagre belongings, the hut was bare.

'This is where you will sleep with two of the other women,' snapped the steward. 'You will eat with the servants in that hut over there.' He pointed nonchalantly at one of the other thatched buildings that clustered at the back of the compound, then walked away, oblivious to Matilda's loud complaints.

The lout who had accompanied them back from Shebbear pushed her back into the hut. 'If you know what's good for you, you'll shut your mouth and keep it shut!' he growled. 'Enjoy your last evening while you can, as from now on it'll be work every daylight hour.'

Matilda was no stranger to that, as before her father was granted his freedom she was accustomed to the life of a villein – but then she at least had her own home, first with her husband, then with her father. Now they were back labouring in the fields, alongside the folk they had known all their lives until they escaped eleven short months ago. Their neighbours were sympathetic to their plight, but as the new arrivals were no worse off than themselves, apart from the loss of their croft, there was nothing they would or could do to help them. However, there was universal dislike and even fear of both the new manor lord and of his steward.

'Mean, grasping bastards, both of them!' muttered the man who used to live in the next cottage to them. 'Walter is a totally different man from his father Matthew, God rest his soul! He is dour and bad-tempered, thinking of nothing but the weight of his purse. He has brought that bloody man Simon Mercator here, as well as those surly ruffians to enforce his will. I reckon they are outlaws from the moor that he's allowed back in, as long as they do his every bidding.'

Each evening, when the work ceased as dusk was falling, they plodded back to the village with the others and made their weary way to the manor house, where an unappetizing meal was provided in the eating hut. Then, like the rest of the villagers, they slumped on the bed with two of the younger serving girls and slept the sleep of the exhausted until daybreak.

Matilda tried endlessly to think of ways to escape from this nightmare, but there seemed nothing she could do. It would be impossible to run away again – and where could they go, anyway? They no longer had their few animals to live on, and it was impossible to think of getting back to Aunt Emma a second time. Barnstaple was too small a borough to hide in for a year and day, even if they could reach it undetected – and Exeter might as well be at the other end of the world for all the hope they had of getting there.

Gillota seemed devastated by the change in their circumstances, and, although their former neighbours were kind to her and tried to cheer her up, she was quiet and withdrawn, her former bright nature crushed. She seemed permanently fearful of either Walter Lupus or his creepy steward accosting her, in spite of her mother's constant assurances that she would protect her. As it happened, they saw little of either of these men, the daily work routine being directed by the manor reeve, her father's successor, who seemed a reasonable fellow, though weak in spirit.

Thanks to continued fine weather, the end of the harvest came little more than a week after they arrived back in Kentisbury. When the last sheaf was stored in the barn, ready for winnowing, it was traditionally the time for the celebration of 'harvest home', the expected right of both villeins and freemen to be fêted by their lord in thanksgiving for the land's bounty.

'If it's like last year, don't expect much from this mean bastard!' muttered the village smith, in gloomy anticipation of the 'ale' to be held in the churchyard that evening.

The whole village turned out, many bringing what spare food they could manage, to add to the victuals and drink grudgingly provided by Walter Lupus. Trestles were set out to carry the bread, cheese, pasties, shellfish, boiled salmon and some sweetmeats. A pig was being spit-roasted nearby over an open fire, and in spite of the smith's pessimism there seemed plenty of ale as well as some cider.

The mood was subdued until Walter and his steward left after a token appearance, when their departure and the effects of the drink began to loosen up the atmosphere. Music was provided by a set of bagpipes, a drum and a fiddle, to which the younger folk began dancing. Even Gillota brightened a little when several of the village boys began flirting with her and soon dragged her into the ring of dancers.

Matilda went to the table to take some food, the labours of the day making her hungry even through her tiredness. She was breaking a piece off a barley loaf to eat with a piece of hard, yellow cheese when someone at her elbow spoke gently.

'The mussels are good – I suppose they're from Combe Martin.'

She looked around and saw a face that was vaguely familiar, though for a moment she couldn't place it. It was a man a little older than herself, tall and broad with a pleasant, open face below his wiry brown hair. He wore a long tunic of good broadcloth, with a wide leather belt carrying a long sheathed dagger at the back.

'You've forgotten me, haven't you? We used to play in the barns when we were little!'

Enlightenment lit up her face. 'Philip? Philip de Mora! I've not seen you in twenty years!'

He grinned at her mischievously. 'I've been away at the wars, a foot soldier and then an archer. But those days are over, I'm afraid!'

He held up his left hand, two of the fingers of which were missing and the others twisted, with an ugly scar across the wrist.

'A French sword ended my military career, so I came home a few months ago. But I gained my freedom over it.'

His face became serious. 'I have heard of your misfortune in that respect, mistress. It is a scandal. Something must be done about the situation in this manor.'

Philip lowered his voice as he muttered the last few words. Then he brightened again and held out his good hand to her. 'But tonight is for revelling, so let's join the dance. Your daughter should not have all the fun!'

He pulled her towards the increasing number of people stamping and twirling to the tune of the pipes and rebec and the thump of the drum. For a time she almost forgot her troubles, as they danced, then ate again and danced some more. She kept a wary eye on Gillota, but she also seemed to be enjoying herself with a group of younger boys and girls.

As it grew dusk, the older people began to make their way home, but many stayed in the churchyard, some drunk, others flirting and yet other couples vanishing into the growing darkness beyond the yew trees behind the church.

The large harvest moon was almost at the full as Matilda and Philip de Mora sat together on the grass in the pale light.

'Where do you live now? Are you married?' she asked him. She recalled now that he had gone off as little more than a boy to become a squire's servant during the troubles early in King Henry's reign.

'I never married. I was always away at the wars,' he replied. 'My mother and father died years ago, but when I was wounded last year the knight for whom I served granted me my freedom. I decided to come home, at least for a time. I pay the manor a rent for our old house at the end of the village and will stay until I decide what to do with the rest of my life.'

They talked for a little while longer, until Matilda noticed that some of the lads with Gillota were getting too frisky from the amount of ale they had drunk. She decided it was time to go home, if one could call it that. Gathering her daughter up and ignoring her protests, she bade good-night to her new friend.

'I'll see you safely to the manor house,' he offered gallantly and escorted them back to the big gates set in the stockade around the Lupus stronghold.

As she watched him wave and turn away, Matilda felt a small glow of contentment at having made a new ally and possibly a champion.

Matilda preferred the hard labour of harvesting to the menial tasks that she and her daughter were given around the manor house. For the first week the steward set them to work in the large kitchen shed, where far from being allowed to cook they were forced to scour iron pots with wet sand, carry wood for the fires and scrape and clean vegetables. There was a cook and a baker, who lived in their own houses, together with the pair of young girls who shared their barren quarters in the sleeping shed. They all ate at a side table in the kitchen, and as Matilda and Gillota knew them well there was at least a friendly atmosphere, unless Simon Mercator saw fit to come prowling around, when he seemed to enjoy ogling Matilda.

The two ruffians who had captured them in Shebbear acted alternately as gate guards during the day, the heavy wooden gates of the stockade being shut and barred from nightfall to dawn. However, they did not challenge Matilda when one evening, after all the kitchen work was finished, she went out with Gillota to walk around the village. They stopped outside their toft and gazed sadly at the building and the plot of land around it. Two infants were playing in the dirt outside the front door, and a young woman, presumably their mother, stared at them as they stood looking in. She was a stranger to the village and must have been imported from wherever Simon Mercator came from.

They walked on, exchanging greetings with other villagers, some of whom enquired discreetly if there was any hope of their regaining their freedom. Then, with nowhere else to go, they sadly retraced their steps, Matilda rather hoping that she would meet Philip de Mora as they passed what had been his parents' cottage at the top end of the village street. There was no sign of him and, forlornly, they went back to the room they shared with the younger servants and went to bed.

The only other occasions when they could leave the manor house were on Sundays, when virtually the whole village went to Mass. Though it was not strictly obligatory to attend church, very few failed to appear, unless they were very old, sick or infirm. In any case, going to church was a social event, where they could gossip to their friends and for an hour or two shrug off the dull, repetitive pattern of their claustrophobic lives.

St Thomas's was a century old, built of stone on the site of a previous wooden Saxon church. The oblong nave was just large enough to take all the villagers, who stood shoulder to shoulder on the floor of beaten earth, apart from the old and infirm who 'went to the wall' to squat on a narrow ledge.

The chancel was up a single step, carrying a plain altar with a brass cross and two candlesticks. There was a small sacristy through a door on the left of the chancel where the priest kept his robes and the makings of the Host. Matilda and Gillota stood right at the back, as even in church there was a pecking order. Walter Lupus and his pale, sad-looking wife were in the front, with his bailiff and steward on either side. The manor lord himself had no family, and it was widely whispered that his wife was barren, as well as ill.

On the first Sunday that they attended, Matilda whispered to her neighbour while they waited for the parish priest to appear from the sacristy.

'Who is the parson now? I heard that old Father Peter had died since we left the village.'

'He went to God just after Easter,' was the reply. 'We have another old one now, Father Thomas, the same name as our patron saint. He is a prebendary from Exeter Cathedral, a very learned man, they say.'

'So what's he doing in an out-of-the-way place like Kentisbury?' murmured Matilda. Perhaps someone more learned, instead of the usual dullard or drunk posted to the more remote parishes, might be able to give her advice about her problem.

'He's really retired, but the bishop sent him here until they can find someone more permanent.'

As she spoke, the sacristy door opened and a small man, probably aged about seventy, appeared, stoop-shouldered and with a slight limp. The lank hair below his tonsure was grey, though some darker streaks still survived. Matilda peered between the heads of the people in front and saw that his face was narrow, with a pointed nose and a receding chin. In spite of his unprepossessing appearance, her sixth sense told her that there was something kindly about his nature and she resolved to try to speak to him as soon as she had the chance. Perhaps confession would be the most opportune time.

The Mass began and, as always, was conducted entirely in Latin, which not a soul present could understand.

However, as a departure from what most were used to, when it came time for the congregation to be called up to receive the Eucharist of bread and wine, Father Thomas included a few words in English, to explain the significance of what they were doing. One of the last to kneel on the step, Matilda looked up at the priest as he passed from Gillota to her to offer her the scrap of pastry, which by transubstantiation became the body of Christ. Something passed between them as their eyes met, each being well aware that this was more than a friendly exchange of glances between a parson and a parishioner. She looked sideways at her daughter and caught a slight nod, telling her that Gillota was also aware of something significant.

Canon Thomas de Peyne, for that was his full title, then preached a short sermon in English, explaining in clear, easy terms the meaning of this particular Sunday in the Church calendar, and followed it with a gentle homily about respecting one's neighbours. His words were free of the usual blood and thunder about the tortures of hell that were the wages of sin, a favourite theme for so many parish priests, who had little insight or imagination.

When the service was over, the congregation parted to allow their lord and his wife to pass to the door, followed by his senior servants. They strode out without a word to anyone, then the villagers straggled out into the churchyard and began a marathon of gossip, before going home to their dinner. No farm work was done on the Sabbath, apart from caring for livestock, but the manor-house servants had to hurry back to serve the meal to Lupus and his wife, two of the cooks having stayed behind all morning.

Matilda and Gillota were considered too lowly to serve at table, but they had other tasks in the kitchen and especially afterwards, when the clearing up was done. By late afternoon they could take their ease, walk around the village or go to their bed until it was time to prepare supper. Again, Matilda haunted the village street, hoping to come across either Philip de Mora or the priest, but neither of them appeared.

A couple of weeks after the harvest was finished, she tackled the steward again about her situation.

'I wish to bring my complaint to the manor court again,' she said stubbornly when he came into the kitchen to check on everyone's work. 'It is not right that our lord treats us in this way. There must be some way to appeal against his treatment of me and my daughter!'

Simon Mercator glared at her and for a moment she feared that he was going to strike her.

'Be quiet, woman! You have been to the court and it was dismissed,' he snarled contemptuously.

'Dismissed? It was not even discussed! It should be considered by a jury of the villagers; they have the right to offer their opinion.' Her face was red with indignation, but the steward was unmoved.

'There is nothing to discuss!' he shouted. 'You were born a serf and a serf you will remain for the rest of your days!'

'His father declared mine free!' she replied stubbornly. 'Why do you persist in denying it?'

Simon thrust his angry face near hers. 'Because it never happened! Every villager could suddenly decide to claim that they had been freed, so why do you think that your particular lies should be heeded?'

'You were not even here when my father was released from his bondage!' she blazed.

Simon pushed her out of the way, making her stagger back. 'I want no more of this nonsense, do you hear?' he snarled. 'If you open your mouth about it once more, I'll have you back in chains again – and that brat of yours!'

He stalked out of the kitchen, leaving Matilda close to tears and Gillota trying to comfort her, as did the cook and one of the serving wenches. Later that day, she sat on her thin mattress and tried to think of a way out of this nightmare. Escaping again was impossible, and it seemed equally impossible to get justice at the manor court – and she knew of no way of seeking it elsewhere. She took her cloth bag that lay on a shelf on the wall and took out the strangely shaped stone, wrapped in a rag. To her, it still had an aura of power about it, which she could not describe but which she felt in her very soul. Yet it seemed unable or unwilling to translate its potency into action.

She turned it over in her hand and studied the strange marks on its surface, which meant nothing to her. Rubbing the steely-hard surface with the rag burnished it slightly, but had no other effect. Yet when she held it close to her chest, she fancied she could feel the slightest of vibrations deep inside. With a sigh, she wrapped it up again and was about to place it back in the bag when two crystal-clear images came unbidden into her mind. One was the face of Philip de Mora and the other was that of Father Thomas. They shone brightly in her mind's eye for a moment, then merged together and faded.

Conscious that something unusual had taken place, she turned towards the door and saw that Gillota was standing there, watching her.

'Those two men are our only hope, Mother,' said the girl, not needing any words to know what Matilda had just experienced.

Though Walter Lupus had ignored her until now, a week later Matilda came to his attention once more. She was squatting outside the kitchen hut one morning, scouring cooking pots with wet sand and a rag, trying to remove the ever-present rust, when a pair of leather shoes suddenly came into her vision. Looking up, she saw Walter standing over her, staring down with his usual dour, inscrutable expression.

'Come with me, woman,' he commanded with a beckoning gesture. Reluctant and somewhat apprehensive, she rose to her feet and followed him towards the steps that led to the back door of the manor house.

'What do you want with me now?' she asked defiantly. 'Have you reconsidered your bad treatment of me and my daughter?'

He ignored this and led her up into the hall of the house, which occupied most of the ground floor, apart from two small rooms partitioned off to one side. It was now early September and a fire smouldered in the large chimneyed hearth on the opposite side of the hall. Alongside, a doorway led to a narrow staircase set in the thickness of the wall, and she followed him up the stone steps, uneasy at this new departure from her routine. There were several men in the hall, merchants and tradesmen by their appearance, so she could hardly be ravished there, but going up the dark stairs was another matter.

'Where are we going?' she asked, trying to conceal a tremor in her voice.

'To see my wife,' was the surprising reply, but at the top it proved to be true. The upper floor, beneath a sloping roof of stone tiles, was divided into a solar overlooking the front of the house and behind it, through a door, a larger bedchamber.

Walter stopped with his hand on this door and spoke in a low voice. 'My wife Joan is ill and needs constant attention,' he revealed. 'She is cared for mostly by Alice, the housekeeper, who needs more help. You will work here now instead of the kitchens.'

He said this with an air of finality that did not invite questions, but Matilda was not satisfied. 'Why me? I am no nursing nun. I know nothing of running a sickroom.'

'You will fetch and carry at Alice's direction. You need know nothing of physic!' he snapped. 'An apothecary comes each week from Barnstaple for that. Not that he's of much use.'

Walter sounded bitter, and for a moment Matilda had a pang of sympathy for him, until his next words set him against her again.

'In spite of your insolent nature, you have the glimmerings of intelligence and are preferable to those other slatterns in the kitchen. Now, go in and make yourself known to my wife and Alice, who recommended you.'

He pushed his finger through a hole in the door to lift the latch and shoved her inside before vanishing down the stairs.

A wide bed occupied much of the room, raised on a wooden plinth, instead of the usual position on the floor. Beneath covers of heavy wool and sheepskin lay Joan Lupus, staring listlessly up at the dusty rafters high above. Alice the housekeeper, a fat woman whom Matilda had known all her life, sat on a milking stool at the side of the bed, holding a pewter cup of posset, trying at intervals to tempt the lady to drink the honeyed mixture of milk and spiced wine.

'Here's Matilda, a nice young woman to help me look after you, my lady,' coaxed Alice, but the pallid wraith in the bed gave no more than an uninterested nod, then turned her head away. Soon she was asleep, and Matilda took the opportunity to question the housekeeper.

'What's wrong with her? I saw her in church the other Sunday. She looked ill then, but not as bad as this.'

'She is losing blood down below,' said Alice primly. 'She has been for months, but it's getting worse and she's getting weaker all the time. That apothecary is useless, so I thought you might be able to help. You have a reputation, Matilda. We sorely missed you when you went away.'

'I'll do my best for her. Anything is better than working as a skivvy. But I'll not be diverted from my fight to regain my freedom!' she added in a fierce whisper.

For several days she helped Alice, mainly in changing the soiled bed coverings, cleaning up the sick lady and fetching and carrying anything needed in the sickroom. She took turns in feeding her, trying to coax her to eat a variety of tempting morsels, but Joan Lupus seemed oblivious to their presence for much of the time, sleeping a great deal. Her husband came several times a day and tried to exchange a few gruff words with his wife, with little response.

'Is she dying?' he asked bluntly one day, speaking to Alice, but with Matilda standing alongside.

The housekeeper tried to reassure him, but Matilda was more honest.

'She has lost so much blood that unless it stops she cannot survive,' she said firmly.

Walter glowered at her. 'That's not what I wanted to hear,' he said. 'So what can be done? Shall I send for a physician? The nearest one of any substance would be in Bristol.'

Matilda shrugged. 'I doubt any doctor could do much. Her strength needs to be built up, so that she can replace the blood she loses. And then you need a miracle to cure whatever is the root cause!'

The lord of Kentisbury turned on his heel and vanished down the stairs.

'You are risking yourself, speaking like that,' admonished Alice. 'And what can we do to build her up, as you call it?'

'Give her pig's liver and green herbs like Good King Henry and cabbage,' suggested Matilda. 'An infusion of periwinkle may help to slow the bleeding. I'll go out along the lanes with my daughter and see what I can find.'

This was partly an excuse to get out as much as possible, and also to get Gillota away from the drudgery of the kitchen hut, as she persuaded Alice that she needed her to search for the various medicinal herbs and plants that flourished in the hedgerows and woods. But the image of the priest and the former soldier was always in her mind, and she single-mindedly strove towards meeting them again.

Towards the end of that week, part of her hope was realized when she was grubbing in a ditch for wild spinach and a voice made her spin around.

'Are you trying to dig your way out of the village?'

It was Philip de Mora, with a pack on his back and a long staff in one hand. He explained that he had been in Barnstaple, attending the burial of his old godmother, who had left him some money in her will, which explained why Matilda had not seen him around the village.

They sat on the verge for a while and she brought him up to date with her fortunes, such as they were.

'At least I've managed to get away from slaving in the kitchen – now I need to get Gillota away from there, too.'

Philip listened thoughtfully to her tale. 'Walter seems to have lessened his persecution of you. Perhaps he will come around to acknowledging your freedom – or at least letting it be heard properly in the manor court?'

She shook her head. 'I doubt it – that foul man, Simon Mercator, seems to hate me, and he controls the court. He has a strong influence over Walter Lupus.'

De Mora thought for a moment. 'The sheriff has to come twice each year for the view of frankpledge. That might be a chance to raise the matter with him and get it taken to the county court or even to the King's court in Exeter.'

The 'view of frankpledge' was the six-monthly inspection by the county sheriff of the system whereby the population was divided into 'tithings'. Each tithing was made up of all males over twelve years of age, from about ten households. All the members were held collectively responsible for the behaviour of the others and, if one committed an offence, all the rest were punished, usually by a fine.

'A good idea, but I doubt if the steward would let me get within a hundred paces of the sheriff,' said Matilda bitterly.

'We'll see when the time comes – he must be here by about Michaelmas or soon after, less than a month away.'

Matilda then told him of her idea to try to speak to Thomas the priest about her predicament. 'Surely I can insist on making my confession,' she said. 'That would give me the chance to raise the subject. He seems to be a sympathetic man.'

Philip agreed with her, knowing something of the man in question. 'He was once the clerk to the famous coroner Sir John de Wolfe, back in Richard the Lionheart's time. He was well known for his honesty and love of justice, so maybe some of that rubbed off on to his clerk!'

They walked back to the centre of the village together, and Philip promised to think further about her problems and to see her after church next Sunday. She left him feeling much more cheerful than usual and, back in their dormitory, she took out the stone and sat looking at it with Gillota.

'Maybe it's working its will slowly?' suggested her daughter.

She took it from her mother and held it tightly against her head. 'Though I don't feel anything special today. Maybe it has to rest, just like us.'

The rest of the week did not go so well for Matilda. She spent a lot of time trying get Joan Lupus to take the various concoctions she had made, from the herbs she had collected to potage made from meat and liver, in an effort to improve her blood.

Alice explained to Walter on one of his daily visits that Matilda had been looked on as having special skills, inherited from her mother, and he seemed vaguely content that something was being attempted to save his wife. This did not translate into any increase in friendliness towards Matilda, and she dismissed any hope that his gratitude might extend to reversing his attitude towards her bondage to the manor.

It was Simon Mercator who was the main problem, for he obviously resented the softening of Walter's regime that held the two women in strict bondage.

'You've wheedled your way out of the hard work, I see,' he sneered at her as she passed through the hall with a bundle of clean clothing for the invalid. 'It won't last, I assure you. You'll be back scouring pots and chopping firewood before long.'

At every opportunity he scolded her and made threatening remarks about her, but worst of all he began badgering Gillota when her mother was occupied upstairs. The girl came to her one day, weeping because Simon had cornered her behind the kitchen shed and kissed her roughly while he groped his hands over her breasts and bottom. Gillota had broken away and run off, leaving the steward laughing at her distress. Infuriated, Matilda went running to seek out Simon, unsure what she was going to do when she found him, but it came to nothing, as he was nowhere to be found. Then she went looking for Walter Lupus, but again he was away, said by the stablemen to have ridden to Ilfracombe.

Frustrated, she went back to Gillota, who was being comforted by the cook, who sounded as if she was ready to use her biggest knife on the steward if he crossed her path.

'He's well known to have molested several of the girls in the village since he arrived,' she said indignantly. 'In a few months there will already be two babies who could call him father!'

According to her, the village gossip claimed that he had had a wife where he lived in Taunton, before coming to Kentisbury, but that she had run away from him.

Gillota recovered rapidly but vowed to keep well out of his way in future, if that was possible. Once she had settled down and was being kept company by two of the other girls, Matilda resolved that the time had come for resolute action, if she was to save her daughter from more harassment and eventual shame.

As soon as the lady of the manor was made comfortable for the night and Alice had said that Matilda could go, she threw a shawl over her kirtle and went out into the evening twilight. The first chill of autumn was in the air as she hurried down to the centre of the village and pushed open the gate into the churchyard. Passing the porch, she carried on along the path to the small house on the further side of the yew-encircled graveyard.

The parsonage was little bigger than the cottages in the village, but it had two rooms under the steep thatched roof. Summoning up her courage, she knocked on the frayed boards of the front door. Getting no answer, she knocked again several times, with the same lack of response. Feeling deflated after her impulsive gesture, she turned away from the door and slowly made her way back towards the gate. However, just as she was level with the porch again, she heard some coughing from inside the church and hurried into the nave to find their priest brushing away with a birch besom at some loose leaves on the hard floor.

He greeted her cordially, leaning on his brush. 'Hello, my child! The autumn has started early this year. These leaves are down already.'

'I am Matilda Claper, father,' she answered. 'I work at the manor house, more's the pity.'

The small priest looked at her quizzically. 'That's an unusual introduction, at least. Tell me more about it.'

She felt his soft brown eyes on her and knew instinctively that here was a man with compassion in his heart. 'Sir, I came to ask if you would hear my confession – and the first thing I would have to confess is that it was but an excuse to seek your advice.'

Thomas de Peyne smiled, his old face lighting up so that he looked decades younger. 'You don't need an excuse for that, daughter! That's what parsons are for – or should be!'

He dropped his brush and led her to the stone shelf around the wall, sitting down and motioning her to perch beside him.

'Tell me your troubles, Matilda. I have seen you and your daughter at Mass but know nothing of you.'

Feeling secure with this mild-mannered man, she explained her whole predicament from start to finish. At the end she said, 'They will not allow me to be heard at the court-baron and I doubt I can get the sheriff to listen to me when he comes for his view of frankpledge. Now this vile behaviour of the steward towards my daughter makes it all the more urgent that we leave this village.'

Thomas listened gravely to all she said and now sat with his chin in his hand, considering the problem.

'It is true that this is not a happy manor, compared with most I have known,' he conceded. 'There is little I can do about that, being an outsider who is here only on sufferance until a new priest is appointed. I will speak to Walter Lupus, but from past experience he is not a man who accepts any view but his own.'

He sighed and placed a consoling hand on her shoulder. 'You do not need me to tell you that the nub of the matter is proof that Matthew Lupus did in fact grant your father his freedom.'

She nodded, fearful that in spite of her hopes this man would also side with those who dominated the manor. 'But at the time, most of the village heard about it and accepted it,' she pleaded. 'If there was a genuine hearing before a jury, surely they must confirm that?'

'Was there no document of manumission provided, as there should have been?' asked the priest.

'I don't know. My father never showed me one, but what would be the point? No one except the priest could read or write.'

The prebendary pondered this for a moment. 'There should always be a document of manumission, properly witnessed by one or preferably two people. As those in holy orders are usually the only literate ones, the witnesses are usually priests. Then the document should be confirmed by the county court. Do you recall your father ever going down to Exeter for that purpose?'

Matilda shook her head. 'The furthest he ever went in his whole life was Combe Martin, a few miles away.'

'The priest who was here before me must have been involved,' he murmured. 'Father Peter, God rest him. But he left no parchments behind. This house was bare of anything but a few sticks of furniture.'

'Perhaps Walter Lupus took them – maybe he destroyed them?' suggested Matilda, but Thomas shook his head.

'I doubt that, because any document should have gone to Exeter for ratification, as I said.'

He stood up and extended a hand to politely raise up the woman from the bench. 'I have to go to Exeter on the Monday after the next Sabbath, so I will make enquiries, as I still have good friends there. I will be back in time for the following Sunday, in case I have any news of this matter.'

Matilda dropped to her knees and bowed her head before this good man, who made the sign of the cross over her as he blessed her.

'Come to me at any time for advice – or for that confession you mentioned,' he said with a grin.

'I fear my confession would be full of uncharitable thoughts towards those who hold this manor in their grip,' she whispered.

When Matilda had gone, Thomas finished his brushing of the nave, then went back to his gloomy dwelling, where he lit a pair of rushlights and sat at his small table. He poured himself a cup of cloudy cider, for he had never been a lover of ale, and began to think about the sorry tale that the woman had related. He had noticed her at Mass, for there was something about her, and to a lesser degree her daughter, that was different from the usual run of villagers. He was intelligent and well read, having been educated at the cathedral school in Winchester many years before, but had no pretensions to second sight, only a sharp awareness of character, and was convinced that these two women had some occult gift.

Sadly, he felt that Matilda's predicament was insoluble, unless some tangible proof could be produced of her father's release from bondage – or if the villagers organized a mass protest and forced the matter into the manor court. Given the tyrannical way in which Lupus and his odious steward held the levers of power, this seemed unlikely.

As he sat in the twilight, with the smoky flames of the grease-soaked reeds flickering on each side, he thought of the absolute authority that men like Walter Lupus had over the inhabitants of a manor. Though most were not great barons, often being mere knights or even successful merchants with the ear of the King's court, they wielded the power of life and death over their subjects, some even erecting their own gallows at the village crossroads. No one could leave the village, accept an inheritance, get married or enter the Church or a trade without their consent – almost invariably dependent on a fee. These lords held their fief from the King, who owned the whole of England, keeping about a third for himself, as with royal manors like Shebbear, apart from the huge estates owned by the Church. These greater barons often sublet manors to lesser lords, taking either military knight-service or a rent from these other vassals. The latter passed this despotism down to their own subjects, so it was no wonder that Lupus could dictate to that poor woman and ignore her demands for justice.

Yet, thought Thomas, there had to be a balance between manor lord and villagers, for each was dependent on the other. In return for the lord's promise of protection from marauding barons and bands of robbers, as well as his organization of the production of the food that saved them from starvation, the inhabitants supported him and his family by working for him year in, year out. The free men paid a rent, either in money or in kind, and the bondsmen – the serfs or villeins – had to work his fields for at least three days each week, as well as many extra 'boon' days, plus providing him with extra support throughout the year in the form of eggs, fowls, pigs and other produce. For that, the lord gave them a 'toft', a cottage and a croft, as well as several acres of strips in the fields to work on their free days. Below those were the cottars, a poorer class who had a cottage but no land and paid for their home by working at ditching, hedging, thatching, herding and other menial labour.

Thomas knew that being a serf was not necessarily degrading, as they could own personal property and pass it on to their heirs – in fact, some bondsmen were richer than their free man neighbours. But he accepted that none of this solved this poor woman's problem. He would do what he could for her, even if it incurred Lupus's displeasure – at least his incumbency of the parish did not depend on the lord's gift, as so many did. And, he thought as he pinched out the lights before going to his bed, it did not matter if Lupus got rid of him, as he was only here as a favour to the bishop and would be quite happy to go back to his comfortable lodgings in Exeter.

In spite of Matilda's attempts with herbs and her advice to Alice to put more green cabbage and especially spinach in Joan's diet, there seemed no change in her condition and she continued to lose blood. The day after her meeting with Canon Thomas, Matilda sat on the palliasse in their mean sleeping hut and wondered what else she could do for the lady of the manor. Though she detested Walter Lupus for ruining her life, her natural compassion for anyone who was ailing made her concerned for Lady Joan, for she was afraid that death could be the only end result, unless something radical was done.

As a last resort, she felt under the head of the mattress where she and Gillota lay with the other two maids and pulled out the little stone from its hiding place. For the hundredth time, she held it in her palm and studied it. Though it seemed so inert, something told her that it was a force for good. Unlike the great rock in Shebbear, which was alleged to be the work of the devil, the cross-shaped stone seemed benign, though Matilda sensed that in spite of its suggestive shape it had nothing to do with the Christian faith, being infinitely older.

'If this can work any miracles, then they'll not be like any of those that the priests tell us are described in the Scriptures,' she murmured as she slipped the stone into the pouch on her belt.

Going up to the sickroom, she waited until Alice had gone out on some errand, then, while gently putting Joan's pillow more comfortably under her head, slipped the stone under the mattress. 'It's three times thicker than mine,' she thought to herself. 'But if it has any powers at all, a few inches of goose-feather won't stop it!'

Next day was Sunday and Matilda had the chance to speak to Philip when they mingled in the churchyard after Mass. She told him of Canon Thomas's kind words to her and his promise to see if there was any sign of a document of manumission in Exeter. Then she went on to describe Simon Mercator's foul behaviour towards Gillota, and the effect on the former soldier was remarkable. Normally placid and amiable, he instantly reddened with anger.

'The bastard! He can't be allowed to get away with that! I know of his bad reputation with women, but when it concerns someone you know and respect it's not to be tolerated.'

She put a hand on his arm in alarm. 'Philip! Gillota and I are villeins, at least to him, to do with as he likes! We must avoid him as much as we can, that's all that can be done.'

Philip was not to be mollified, his face set in a grim scowl of determination. 'I will warn him, for I am a free man – and one used to fighting and confronting enemies. I will make him understand that, if he approaches Gillota again, he will have me to contend with!'

He glowered in the direction of Walter and his steward, who were just leaving through the churchyard gate.

'I will go to Walter Lupus as well. He is supposed to be the man's master, though sometimes I wonder who is in charge of this manor!'

Now Matilda was really worried, for she recognized the stubborn streak in Philip and knew he meant what he said. For a moment she wondered if this violent reaction to an insult to Gillota meant that it was her daughter, rather than herself, who interested him, but their ages were so far apart that it would be ridiculous.

'Please do not be hasty,' she pleaded again. 'They are powerful men and the likes of us cannot hope to prevail against them. My daughter and I will just make sure we avoid him at every turn.'

The churchyard had emptied now, and they were obliged to leave as well, though they arranged to meet in the early evening near the mill. Many villagers, especially youngsters and courting couples, paraded the village on a Sunday, as all work, even on their own crofts, was forbidden on the Sabbath, other than tending the animals.

Philip de Mora was a man of his word, and after he had eaten his solitary dinner of thin potage, bread and salted fish, he set off for the manor house, which was on a side turning from the main track that ran through Kentisbury towards Combe Martin.

There was a dry ditch around the outside of the stockade, which Philip crossed at the big gates on a wooden ramp that could be quickly removed as a further defensive measure. No one had attacked the village in living memory – the main danger was from marauding pirates coming in from the coast. The Severn Sea was rife with marine bandits, some based on Lundy Island, as well as from Wales, Ireland and even as far afield as the Mediterranean, but as Kentisbury was a few miles inland, the coastal villages suffered most.

One of the thugs imported by Lupus was lurking inside the gate and demanded to know his business. He was known as Garth, a hulking man with shaggy black hair and a rim of beard around his face and chin, widely suspected of being an Exmoor outlaw who had crept back into the village with Simon's connivance.

'I'm seeking the steward,' snapped Philip, fingering the hilt of his long dagger. 'Where is he?'

He was in no mood to be questioned further by some low-life servant and strode straight past as Garth pointed towards the door of the hall. This was up some wooden steps, the hall being built over the undercroft, a semi-basement used for storage.

Inside he found the steward sitting alone at a table, though several servants were nearby, clearing dishes and scraps of food from other trestles. A pewter goblet of wine was in front of him and a small wineskin lay nearby. There was no sign of Walter Lupus, who was upstairs with his wife.

'What do you want?' growled Simon, looking up at the new arrival. 'You can't just walk in here on a Sunday. Come back tomorrow, if your business is urgent.'

If the former archer had not been a free man, the steward would have called for Garth or his fellow thug Daniel to throw him out, but he knew that this Philip de Mora had been a member of the King's army. He needed to be treated with circumspection in case he had some influential friends, as he had been under the standard of Baldwin de Redvers, Earl of Devon.

'My business *is* urgent,' snapped Philip, becoming flushed with anger once again at the steward's dismissive manner. He was a tall, powerful man and hovered threateningly over Simon Mercator. 'I came to warn you that if you act indecently again with that young maid Gillota, you'll have me to contend with! Understand?'

The steward shot to his feet, his stool clattering over behind him. He was shorter and slighter than Philip, but his years in office as a right-hand man to manor lords gave him an arrogance that compensated for his physical disadvantage.

'You insolent swine!' he howled, quickly outdoing Philip for the redness of his features. 'Get out of here at once, before I have you flogged!'

'You have no power over me, Mercator,' snapped Philip. 'I am not one of your serfs to abuse and torment. I only rent a dwelling from your master, and I can walk out of this village tomorrow – and perhaps I will, except that I need to stay to make sure you behave yourself!'

Several of the hall servants were starting to smirk at their hated steward's discomfiture, and Simon, suddenly realizing they were present, turned to scream at them to clear off. Then he began to yell for one of his creatures, Garth or Daniel, to rid him of this interloper.

Philip jabbed him in the chest with a finger of his good hand. 'Think on what I've said, steward!' he rasped. 'Lay a finger on that girl or her mother, and I'll find you and beat you senseless! Is that clear?'

Simon's flushed face now drained into a pallor of rage, as he could hardly credit that any villager was rash enough to speak to him in this manner, especially in front of gossiping servants.

Any caution because of the man having been a soldier was thrown to the winds in his fury. He began to rant and threaten Philip with every punishment from mutilation to branding, but Gillota's champion had turned on his heel and was making for the door. As he reached it, Garth lumbered up the steps and, at the steward's screeched command, tried to grab the archer. Philip gave him a hefty push in the chest, which sent him stumbling back to fall over a bench, and by the time he got to his feet the visitor had vanished.

Quivering with rage and damaged pride, Simon Mercator threw down the rest of his wine in a savage gesture.

'The insolent swine, he'll regret this!' he snarled, mainly to himself, as Garth had no idea what was going on. 'I'll see him swing for this.'

When they met near the watermill that evening, Matilda's concern for Philip increased when he told her of his warning to the manor steward.

'He's an evil, vindictive man,' she said. 'He'll not take such an insult to his rank lightly. He will plot your downfall somehow.'

She even suggested that Philip should leave the village and seek his future elsewhere, though this was the last thing she wanted from a purely selfish point of view. Even on their short acquaintance, she felt drawn to him, the first time since her husband died that she had even entertained the thought of marrying again.

But he shook his head deliberately. 'I'll not stir from here until I know that you and your daughter are safe from this man, even if it takes me years!'

They sat on the grass above the millpond and looked at the big wheel, now silent on a Sunday. It was another example of the hold that a manor lord had over his subjects, as everyone was forced to use the mill to grind the corn that they grew on their crofts, just as they had to use the lord's baking ovens to fire their bread – all for a fee, of course.

'They say in the village that you have special gifts, Matilda,' he said. 'I recall when I was a lad, there was a wise woman in the village who used to treat everyone's ills, but it was not your mother, was it?'

She shook her head. 'No, it was old Sarah, wife of the farrier. I just happen to have picked up some knowledge of herbs and suchlike – no magic about it!' Matilda played the matter down for her own protection, though a number of the villagers, who had known her all her life, suspected that she had unusual gifts. That ability was now niggling at the back of her mind, worrying that this brave man was heading for serious trouble if he persisted in antagonizing the steward.

As it grew dusk, Philip walked her back to the manor house and then went back to his empty cottage, determined to strengthen his position with Matilda by ensuring that no harm came to her or her daughter.

It was two days later before Alice noticed the first change in the appearance of Joan Lupus. When she awoke, the invalid seemed to be brighter in the eye and sat up in her bed to take more interest than usual in the food that was brought. When Matilda and the older nurse came to change the cloths that staunched her bleeding, they found them dry for the first time in weeks. Next day, her colour was noticeably better, the pallor of her inner eyelids having changed to pink – and the following morning the lady of the manor declared herself strong enough to get out of bed and sit for a while in a leather-backed chair in the solar.

Everyone was delighted, as, unlike her husband, his wife was popular – or perhaps pitied – by the villagers and manor servants. Alice was commended by them for her expert care, and Matilda was content to keep well in the background, wondering if her stone had had any effect or whether this recovery would have happened anyway. She decided to leave it in place under the bed for the time being, in case it was still working its charm.

However, a few days later Joan was so much better that Alice said that there was no need for Matilda to help her any longer, as the lifting and general bed-care now seemed unnecessary. Afraid that she might not be able to recover her stone if she no longer had access to the bedroom, she retrieved it and put it back in its old hiding place. This was in the morning, when she reluctantly went back to her previous toil in the kitchen, but in the afternoon the village was hit by the equivalent of a thunderbolt.

The first Matilda knew of it was when she was returning to the kitchen after tipping a wooden bucket containing turnip and carrot peelings into the pigsty. As she crossed the bailey, she saw Parson Thomas hurrying from the gate towards the hall door, his limp accentuated by his haste. For a brief moment hope surged in her breast that he was coming with some news of her father's manumission, but then she remembered that it was next week that he was going to Exeter. However, even the faintest hope of some development made her seize some clean platters from the kitchen and use them as an excuse to go to the back door of the hall and lurk just inside, where shelves held the dishes and utensils for meals. Walter Lupus, his steward and bailiff and the miller were sitting at a table within earshot and she could hear the grey-haired priest's high-pitched voice quite clearly.

'It was there the day before yesterday, for I cleaned it myself!' he announced in an agitated voice. 'Together with the chalice, it's always stored in that aumbry in the chancel.'

Matilda knew that he was referring to an oak chest near the altar, where the priest's vestments and the sacred vessels for the Eucharist were kept.

'And you've looked everywhere else, father?' rumbled Walter Lupus.

'Of course I have!' snapped Thomas, for once made irritable by his concern. 'Three times, in fact. And there are precious few hiding places in that bare little church.'

Keeping as still as possible in the shadows, Matilda soon gathered that what was missing was the paten that held the scraps of pastry that were used to offer the body of Christ during the Mass. Walter Lupus rose to his feet and thumped the table with his fist.

'That plate was silver! My father, God rest him, donated it to the church at the time of my birth, in thanks for a son, after having had three daughters!'

Simon Mercator leaned back on his bench to look up at his master. 'That makes it all the more terrible, sir, for it has sentimental as well as monetary value!'

'It was good Devon silver fashioned by smiths in Exeter and cost more than nine marks, so my father was fond of telling me,' ranted Walter. 'It must be found! Turn the village inside out if needs be!'

The steward and bailiff were on their feet now, Simon trying to reassure the manor lord that it would be retrieved.

'It has to be in the village. No one from outside has been here these past few days,' he brayed. 'I'll find the thief, have no fear of that!'

'What about that poxy carter, that Adam from Shebbear?' roared Walter. 'Though he was useful over those women, he's a shifty character. I'd not trust him with a stale loaf, let alone a silver plate!'

The bailiff shook his head. 'I've not seen him here for weeks. I think he may well have fallen foul of the villagers over that affair and taken his trade elsewhere.'

Simon Mercator persuaded Thomas de Peyne to sit down and poured a cup of wine for him. 'I'll not rest until we have got your plate back, Father!' he said placatingly.

'That's the problem. It's not *my* plate,' replied Thomas. 'I am but a temporary incumbent here and have betrayed my stewardship of this church's sacred property!'

'Not betrayed, Father. It is not your fault, but the fault of the evil, sacrilegious robber who has dared steal from the house of God!' replied the steward. 'But never fear, we'll find him!'

He walked towards the main door and yelled for Garth. By now, other servants had sensed that something was going on and had crowded near Matilda, so she no longer needed to hide. She whispered an account of the theft of the Eucharist plate and there were murmurings of outrage at such an impious crime. Its value of nine marks was almost beyond their comprehension, as a mark was worth more than thirteen shillings.

Garth came clumping up the steps into the hall and, before Simon could speak, Walter Lupus had taken over. 'Start a hue and cry around the village! Call in everyone who is in the fields, and we will set up a search. Let not a single stone go unturned – every croft and toft is to be ransacked! Look in every barn, cow-byre and fowl-house! Understand?'

Garth gaped at him and looked at the steward, who usually gave him his orders. 'But what are we to search for, sir?'

'A silver plate, stolen from the church!' snapped Simon. 'Tell everyone that if it is not found by sundown, there will be trouble such as they've never known before!'

The Communion paten was found well before sundown, mainly because two of the searchers knew exactly where it had been hidden.

All normal community life had come to an abrupt halt, as everyone over the age of six who was not bedridden, senile or sick was turned out to comb the village. Matilda, Gillota and Philip kept together, as an added opportunity to enjoy each other's company. They used sticks to beat the verges and search the ditch between the church and the further end of the village street, prodding between the withering weeds of autumn for the glint of silver plate.

For more than an hour Kentisbury looked like an anthill, swarming with figures poking in and out of every cottage, barn, pigsty, ox-byre and privy. For the fifth time Thomas de Peyne made a futile exploration of his church and grounds, peering into every nook and cranny of his house, knowing that he was wasting his time but afraid to give up.

About an hour before sunset a sudden cry went up from one of the cottages.

'It's here! I've found it!' came a stentorian bellow from one of the searchers.

There was a stampede of all those within earshot, followed by the rest of the villagers who had seen them running. Those first through the gate in the fence around the croft were rewarded by the sight of Garth brandishing a shining disc the width of a large handspan. He held it above his head, as Walter Lupus, Simon Mercator and the manor reeve came pounding from the various points where they had been searching.

'It was pushed into the thatch, here!' yelled the steward's servant. Proudly, he indicated the frayed lower edge of the straw-covered roof, where it ended at head height, overhanging the whitewashed wall of cob.

Garth pushed his fingers between the layers of the six-inch-thick thatch, then slid the plate back into the crack to show how it had been concealed.

Hearing the commotion, Matilda and her daughter began trotting down the track towards the growing crowd, Philip close behind. Then, as they got closer, they slowed in horror.

'That's my cottage!' howled Philip. 'The bastards have trapped me!'

Without even a sign from Lupus or Simon Mercator, Philip de Mora was grabbed by Garth and Daniel the instant he set foot through his own gate.

Though he struggled violently, he was no match for the two large ruffians, who forced him to his knees before the manor lord and his steward, who were standing at the corner of the cottage where the plate had been found.

'You contemptible thief!' snarled Simon. 'Stealing from a church is a blasphemous sacrilege, as well as a common crime. You'll hang for this!'

Struggling, the former archer howled back at him. 'You set this up, damn you! To pay me back for accusing you of running your dirty hands over young virgins!'

For answer, the steward kicked the helpless man in the face, causing blood to stream down from a cut over his eye. 'Keep your mouth shut! Don't add lies to your other sins,' he hissed vindictively.

Walter Lupus regarded Philip impassively but did not interfere. Just then, the village priest limped up, great concern on his face.

'You've found it, then, thanks be to God! Where was it?'

The steward gave Philip another kick, this time in the ribs. 'This rogue stole it, canon. He hid it in the thatch of his cottage, no doubt until he could smuggle it away to sell.'

Thomas de Peyne, though greatly relieved at the restoration of the sacred plate, was nonetheless concerned at the steward's behaviour. 'You must not mistreat the man like that! He is innocent until proved guilty – which I find very hard to believe. In fact, now that the paten is restored, I do not wish to bring charges against anyone.'

Walter now came to life. 'I am afraid that cannot be done, Father. This is a serious crime, both against my authority in my own manor and against the King's peace, as well as being a serious sin against the Church.'

'You were a coroner's clerk yourself for many years,' added Simon craftily. 'You must be well aware of the law. That plate was worth at least nine marks – many, many times more valuable than the twelve pence that defines a felony.'

Thomas frowned. He already suspected that there was some conspiracy afoot here, but what the steward said about the law was correct.

'But you must prove him guilty first. There is no call for arbitrary judgement – nor for the violence I just saw you commit upon this man.'

'There is little doubt of his guilt,' snapped Simon, who did not take kindly to being reprimanded by some ancient priest. 'The stolen article was found hidden in his house – who else would do such a thing? He is a soldier, accustomed to looting. He has no land to work, so he needs money to live. He is guilty. Any trial would be a waste of time.'

Walter Lupus seemed to tire of his steward making all the decisions.

'There *will* be a trial – at a special manor court tomorrow,' he snapped. 'Then he can be hanged!'

There was a general muttering from the crowd clustered around the gate and standing along the fence to the street. It was hard to tell if they were agreeing that this obvious thief should be summarily executed or whether they found it hard to believe that a man they had known since he was born in the village could have committed such a blatant and uncharacteristic act. Many already suspected that the unpopular steward and manor lord were involved in some scheme of their own.

'How did that fellow of yours know to look so quickly in such an unlikely hiding place?' asked Thomas suspiciously. But no one answered him, being too concerned with hustling Philip away, his arms locked behind him by the steward's two acolytes. They marched him away down to the turning where the manor house lay, leaving the crowd of villagers staring after them, many as dubious about this performance as the parish priest had been.

Near the gate, Matilda and Gillota were almost paralysed by what was happening, unable to believe their own senses. One moment they were in Philip's pleasant company, the next he was on his knees, assaulted and bleeding, before being dragged away to imprisonment and the promise of the hangman's rope.

Several of their former neighbours tried to console them, knowing of their friendship with Philip. Many of the villagers were muttering about the high-handed actions of the men who ruled their hamlet with such severity, but it was to Thomas de Peyne that the woman and her daughter turned to for solace.

'Father, they cannot hang him for this! It is such an obvious falsehood, to pay him back for accusing the steward of his foul behaviour,' cried Matilda, her arm around her sobbing daughter.

Thomas knew about Simon Mercator's indecency with Gillota and was shocked. As a young man, he had been falsely accused of the same offence with a girl pupil at the cathedral school in Winchester, which had blighted his life for several years until he was proved innocent. But now, the villagers who surrounded him were keen to confirm the steward's reputation for such lewdness, and he had no reason to doubt them.

'This sounds like a gross injustice!' he agreed. 'I will do what I can to stop this charade, but I have little influence here. I am not even the regular parish priest.'

'Can't you threaten to excommunicate them, Father?' asked Matilda, almost beside herself with anguish.

Thomas gave a sad smile and shook his head. 'It would require someone far higher than me to do that – and no grounds for such action exist in this secular matter.'

'But it was a sacred vessel that was stolen from a church!' she persisted. 'Surely that is sacrilege?'

'Yes, but as it stands Philip himself is the culprit and I fail to see how we can prove who else might be to blame.' He sighed and gathered the skirts of his cassock together. 'I will speak to Walter Lupus and try to make him see the truth – though I fear he seems too loyal to this Simon fellow for me to have much effect.'

With the drama over for the time being, the villagers began drifting away and, disconsolately, Matilda and her daughter trudged sadly back to the manor house. One of the other servants told them that Philip had been thrown into an unused stable and that Garth was standing guard outside. They went around to the side of the stockade where the horses were kept and tried to speak to Philip, but were chased off by the thickset thug who stood outside the door.

'Clear off, will you!' he shouted. 'No one speaks to the prisoner until they hang him!'

Later, Matilda tried again, bringing some food and ale purloined from the kitchen, but this time Daniel was squatting outside and refused even to let her leave the victuals for Philip.

She went back to their sleeping place and sat on the mattress alongside Gillota, the other two girls already sound asleep on the other side of the bed. It was almost dark, but she and her daughter had one of those episodes where each knew the other's thoughts.

'Take it out, Mother. Maybe if it worked on Lady Joan, it can do something now,' whispered Gillota. 'It seems at its best when there is urgency, like the decline of Lady Joan!'

Matilda felt under the hessian palliasse and pulled out the stone. As she held it in her hands, she thought she felt that slight vibration again, though perhaps it was the quivering of her own nervous muscles.

Mother and daughter stared at it in the dim light, both uncertain what to do next.

'Maybe if we send our thoughts and pleadings into it together, it might respond,' suggested Gillota in a whisper.

Matilda rose from the bed and motioned to the girl. 'Let's go outside. We cannot risk waking these maids.'

They went out into the fitful light of the moon, which now and then broke through the drifting clouds, and went quietly around to the back of the hut.

'We must both hold it,' said Matilda, holding the stone out by one of the wings so that her daughter could grasp the other one. With no more words needed, they merged their thoughts and tried to project them into the strange little metallic object that joined them. For five long minutes they visualized justice, rescue, salvation and love together with an image of Philip's features. Again, Matilda wondered if the tiny tremors she felt in her fingers were from her own tense muscles or the stone itself.

'I think it is quaking more rapidly, Mother,' said Gillota, reading her thoughts. 'Let's keep pleading with it.'

They stood in the cool night air for a further ten minutes, until something told Matilda that they had done all they could.

'Leave it for tonight, child,' she said eventually.

'What shall we do with it now?' asked the girl. 'It seemed to work with Joan when it was very close to her.'

'I shall leave it as near Philip as I can – tonight, at the court and, God forbid, near the hanging tree if it comes to that!'

She sent Gillota back to bed, then crept along the backs of the huts until she came to the stable where the prisoner was kept. At the back wall, she quietly pushed the stone into a hollow where one of the rough planks had rotted against the ground and covered it over with crumbled wood fragments and a clod of turf.

'Do your magic until morning and I'll come back for you,' she said in her mind before creeping back to her bed.

The manorial court, or 'court-baron', was held at varying intervals in different manors, but in Kentisbury it was normally a three-weekly event. Most of the business was usually about mundane matters concerning land, disputes over crops and livestock, seeking consent for marriages and inheritance affairs, as well as minor offences like drunkenness, fighting, domestic disputes, short measures, poor ale and the like. Today it was a special court called by Simon Mercator on behalf of his lord Walter Lupus, though as usual the steward conducted the proceedings. Unusually, Walter sat on a bench to one side of him, together with Thomas, the parish priest, with the bailiff and sergeant standing behind them.

Normally, the court was held in an empty barn, but after the recent good harvest these were all full, so it was convened in the yard in front of the manor house itself. A chair and a couple of benches were brought out of the hall and placed below the entrance steps, the jury of twelve men being ranged before them. A large crowd of villagers had left their work in the fields and had pushed through the gate to stand in the stockade behind the jury.

Though legally all the men in the manor over twelve years of age were supposed to attend the court, usually only those who had any business there as jury or witnesses were obliged to turn up. Today was different, and a restive, truculent crowd came to see what was going on.

The jury were reluctant to take part, as though the steward was not supposed to act as a judge, the verdict being left to the jury, in practice this was often ignored, and there was a strong suspicion that this would be the state of affairs today.

As Matilda and Gillota were already in the compound, they had little difficulty in sidling around to the edge of the crowd, as close to Philip as they could get, when he was dragged out by Garth on the end of a chain attached to his fetters – probably the same ones by which they had been hauled back from Shebbear. The former soldier was dishevelled and gaunt from his night in a stable without food or water, and Matilda's heart went out to him. She had retrieved the stone early that morning and now had it safely in the cloth pouch on her girdle, but she could detect no vibrations from it at all, much to her chagrin.

Simon Mercator stood up from his chair and yelled at the crowd to be silent, a task he had to repeat several times before the villagers grudgingly obeyed him. He knew that strong feelings and resentment were rife, from the obvious attitude of both the freemen and the villeins and from the visit of Thomas de Peyne earlier that morning.

The priest had come to see Walter Lupus, not the steward, but Simon pushed himself into the meeting in the hall and Walter had not denied him.

'I am extremely unhappy about your determination to try this man Philip in such an arbitrary way,' said the canon firmly. 'I have had long experience of the legal system in this county and know that such a grave accusation should be placed before the King's judges or his Commissioners of Gaol Delivery.'

He was a such a small man that it was difficult for him to assert himself adequately in front of these powerful men, but he was adamant about Philip's right to be tried in Exeter before an experienced and independent tribunal. As he had expected, neither man was impressed by his demands.

'With respect, parson, this is none of your business, whatever you may have done in the past,' sneered Simon. 'The issue is so simple that it should be dealt with summarily, as my lord Walter is quite entitled to do. We must make an example of such blatant thieving, to prevent anyone getting the idea that such a crime may be repeated with impunity.'

Walter Lupus, silent until now, nodded gravely. 'A manor lord has a responsibility to his tenants to safeguard their lives and property,' he said ponderously. 'I am surprised that you think fit to object, considering that such a valuable and venerated object such as your Communion plate was the thing stolen by this man.'

'You have already judged him, then?' retorted Thomas bitterly. 'I thought that was the function of the jury and that until they offer their verdict a man is considered innocent?'

'You are too naive, father,' brayed Simon. 'Of course the damned fellow is guilty – the facts speak for themselves!

No jury can think otherwise – and if they do, I will put them back on the right road!'

And so it proved within a very short time. The steward had Philip dragged in front of him by Garth and Daniel, who stood one at each side, pulling on his chains, while he harangued the prisoner and the jury.

'We need waste no time over this!' he shouted. 'The sacred platter was found to be missing, this felon cannot account for his whereabouts at the time, and most damning of all, a search soon discovered it hidden in the thatch of his own house. There is no need for any more evidence!' He glared at the discomfited line of men who formed the jury.

'The verdict is yours, but you can have no other answer than to declare him guilty!'

However, Simon Mercator was not to have it all his own way. The blacksmith, daring to contradict the man who had his livelihood in the palm of his hand, stood forward to object.

'Steward, we need time to discuss this! Not to beat about the bush, the whole village knows that this man was in bad odour with you. To be fair to him, you should not be trying him here yourself. The matter should be heard in Barnstaple or even Exeter.'

A few yards away, Matilda heard the brave words and her heart leaped with hope – but when she gripped her pouch, she felt nothing from the stone hidden there.

The steward was almost apoplectic with rage at the blacksmith's defiance. Red in the face, he screamed at the man. 'Have a care, Edwin Pace! Lord Walter will not stand for your insolence and pig-headed obstinacy and neither will I! You will take the course of common sense or it will go hard with you and your family in this manor!'

The threat was undisguised, and after a few nudges from his fellows Edwin gave in, for he knew his own survival and that of his wife and children depended on the tolerance, if not goodwill, of the steward and, through him, Walter Lupus himself.

There were catcalls from the crowd when after much shuffling and muttering the jury capitulated and shame-facedly agreed that the prisoner was guilty of the theft.

Instantly, Simon translated that into the sentence. 'Philip de Mora, you have been found guilty by a jury of your peers. The holy plate which you so sacrilegiously stole from our own house of God was worth many marks, far above the value of twelve pence that constitutes a felony. You will therefore be hanged at noon this day from the oak tree used for the purpose.'

There was an outcry from the crowd, who began to surge forward, but Walter Lupus drew his sword, and the steward, bailiff and sergeant closed around him, brandishing heavy staffs and cudgels.

'Get out of this bailey!' roared the manor lord. 'Clear the yard, damn you all!'

Incensed as they were at this tyrannical behaviour of their masters, the villagers knew that they had no real redress, short of starting a peasants' revolt, which would soon bring down the wrath of the sheriff and the King upon them and lead to far more necks being stretched on the gallows.

Still shouting, cursing and protesting, they backed away through the gates, which Daniel ran to close securely, leaving Garth to hold the prisoner.

Philip seemed bemused by the whole proceedings, standing with his head bowed, accepting the inevitable. The servants were chased away by the bailiff and in tears, Matilda and Gillota went back to their labours in the kitchen.

'The stone has failed us,' said Gillota miserably as they stood chopping vegetables to add to the cauldron of potage. 'Perhaps it never worked anyway and Joan would have improved of her own accord.'

Her mother wiped her eyes, her misery made more obvious by the onions she was peeling. 'I'll not give up yet . . . How long has he got, poor man?'

Though telling the time was sheer guesswork, by the sun it was mid-morning, so noon could not be much more than an hour away.

Some minutes later, with the connivance of the cook, Matilda crept out and looked into the bailey. Now that the crowd had dispersed, the gate was open again. Taking an empty leather bucket and reaping hook as camouflage, she went out unchallenged, as Garth and his fellow thug were keeping a strict guard on the condemned man in the stables.

Matilda walked down the road from the manor house to where the track to Furzepark forked south of the village. Here was the notorious oak tree, large and gnarled, which had stood there since before the Normans arrived. The thickness of the massive trunk was so great that four men would be needed to touch hands around it. Fifteen feet above the ground, the first thick branch stuck out, from which the hangings took place. At one point a dozen feet out from the trunk, grooves rubbed in the bark by ropes were a sinister reminder of the number of men who had died there over the years.

In this early autumn the leaves were already turning colour, but there was still a thick canopy of green and gold shielding the sky. No one was around yet, and quickly Matilda found the hole she remembered from her childhood days, about shoulder high in the rough bark. She recalled that birds used it for nesting and squirrels left nuts there, but now she quickly thrust the little stone into the crack and covered it with a handful of moss pulled from the other side of the tree. With a last glance to make sure she had not been observed, she hurried back to the manor after cutting some wayside herbs to put in her bucket.

Meanwhile, Walter Lupus and his steward had again shrugged off Thomas de Peyne's impassioned plea for mercy for the condemned man and his repeated request that the matter be sent to the justices in Exeter.

Thomas was uncertain what Walter was thinking about this issue. He remained silent and just shook his head at all the priest's supplications, but it was the steward who did all the talking, almost as if he had the manor lord under his thumb, instead of the other way around.

'You're wasting your time, parson – and mine!' snapped Simon. 'Better if you employed it in shriving the man and getting his confession. Time is rapidly running out for him.'

Despondently, Thomas took this advice and went to the stable to spend the last hour with Philip, who seemed dull and apathetic, hardly answering him. He made a mumbled confession, which did not ring true to the priest's ears, though Philip firmly denied stealing the Eucharist plate.

Soon, Garth came in to jerk on his fetters and pull him out to lead him down the road to the hanging tree, followed by Walter Lupus, Simon and the other officers and senior servants of the manor such as the bailiff, sergeant, huntsman, hound-handler and hawker. Thomas de Peyne walked alongside the alleged felon, talking earnestly to him and saying prayers for his soul, which seemed to fall on deaf ears. A few villagers were waiting at the gates, but the majority of the manor deliberately kept away. This was unusual in a hanging, as when a known criminal or outlaw was to be dispatched it became almost a festive occasion.

Now, however, the absence of most of the village was intended as a mute protest against the tyrannical behaviour of the lord and especially his evil steward.

By the time the dismal procession reached the large oak, Daniel had already gone ahead to throw a rope over the large branch and form a noose in one end, which hung down ominously at about head height. Where permanent gallows were erected, such as those in Exeter or Tavistock, the condemned were either made to climb a ladder and were then pushed off with a noose around their neck – or stood on an ox-cart, which was then driven away, leaving them dangling. Here the execution was performed more simply, by hauling them up until their feet left the ground.

Without any delay, Philip was marched across to stand under the branch, which was as thick as a man's waist where the rope ran over it.

Thomas, his eyes moist with compassion, stood alongside the doomed soldier, continually intoning Latin prayers. Well back, Matilda and Gillota, with a handful of villagers, stood weeping as they watched the noose being placed over Philip's head by Garth.

Through her tears Matilda tried to concentrate her willpower on the winged stone, though she was beginning to despair of its powers. She felt Gillota doing the same and, with a surge of mental effort, they both urged the artefact to help them.

'Get out of the way, Father!' called Simon Mercator. 'You've done all you can. Now let justice take its course.'

Daniel and Garth went to the other side of the branch and grasped the free end of the long rope, taking up the slack until the noose was dragging Philip's head erect. Simon moved towards the trio, holding his hand up in the air, ready to give the fatal signal.

'Now, pull!' he shouted, letting his hand fall. As Thomas made the sign of the cross in the air and despairingly chanted a last valediction, the two ruffians hauled on the rope together. Philip made a gargling noise as he was lifted from the ground by his neck.

The next moment there was a creaking groan and then an ear-splitting crack as the sturdy branch tore away from the trunk of the great oak and thundered to the ground in a blizzard of dust and leaves. There were screams from Daniel and Garth as the falling branch swept them aside like dolls. Miraculously, Philip was untouched, rolling well clear with the rope still around his neck. The further end of the branch landed on Walter Lupus, the foliage and smaller branches flattening him to the ground, bruising and scratching much of his body.

But it was Simon Mercator who fared worst, as he was standing midway between the two thugs and the manor lord. The half-ton of wood fell directly upon him, pinning him to the ground and breaking both his legs.

With much shouting and screaming, the onlookers ran towards the chaotic scene, though no one seemed in a hurry to tend to the steward. The bailiff and sergeant of the Hundred hastened to aid Walter Lupus, whose clothing was ripped and whose face and hands were bleeding from superficial wounds. He seemed to have been struck on the head, as though he was conscious he was groaning and unable to stand or speak.

Gillota and Matilda raced to help Philip, who was on his hands and knees, tugging to get the rope from around his neck.

'Are you hurt?' asked Gillota, who was first to reach him.

'No, but it was a miracle! I thought my last moment had come,' he gasped. 'What happened?'

Thomas de Peyne put a helping arm around him as he staggered to his feet. 'A miracle indeed!' agreed the priest, still bemused by what had happened. He had suspected for some time that there was more to Matilda than met the eye, but as a devout Christian he had to eschew anything outside his faith, so he held his tongue for fear it might land her in serious trouble.

By now, more people had appeared, streaming down from the centre of the village, having heard the commotion. They stood and marvelled at the huge fallen branch. Several went behind the mass of foliage that lay on the ground and dragged out Daniel, who had a broken arm, and Garth, who was unconscious from a blow on the head. Then they attended to the steward, as the bailiff and sergeant were still fussing over Walter Lupus. The branch was across Simon's legs, and it took eight men to shift it off him.

'He'll never walk again without sticks,' said the blacksmith, the strongest man there when it came to lifting trees. 'If he survives this, he'll be no use as a steward or anything else. Maybe it's God's retribution!'

The injured men were propped against the bole of the great oak until it was decided how to move them, and together with some of the villagers Philip and Thomas stared up above them at the yellow-white scar where the branch had come away from the trunk.

'It doesn't look rotten, so why did it fall?' asked Philip. He was thankful yet mystified at being snatched from the brink of death.

'No rot there. The wood's as healthy as me!' declared the village wheelwright, an expert in anything to do with timber. 'A little tug on a rope wouldn't snap that! You should have been able to swing a pair of oxen from that branch.'

Matilda, now openly clinging to Philip's arm, gave her daughter a look of triumph, and in return Gillota gave her a nod of secret delight.

'I can hear the stone singing from here,' she whispered.

A month later Emma's cottage in Shebbear had a visitor. A docile pony arrived at the gate and an elderly man in a priest's cassock under his black cloak gingerly slid from the saddle.

'Father Thomas!' cried Gillota in delight as she rose from her weeding to greet him. Inside the toft, he was regaled with food and drink, as he was introduced to Emma, who had recovered almost completely from her earlier stroke. Matilda and Gillota sat at his feet as he told her his news.

'I've finished my penance in Kentisbury at last,' he said. 'The bishop found someone who was willing to live there permanently, so I'm on my way back to Exeter but came out of my way to see you, as I have news.'

'We have news, too, Father Thomas,' said Matilda proudly. 'I am soon to be wedded to Philip and live here. That will make me and Gillota free women again, against any challenge!'

The canon smiled roguishly. 'I am delighted to hear it, Matilda – but as to becoming free by that route, there is no need, for you are already free!'

He explained that, as he had promised some time ago, he had searched the county court records in Exeter for any evidence of a document of manumission for Matilda's father. He found nothing, but by chance had spoken to a parish priest in Exeter who remembered witnessing such a document from Kentisbury when he was in Barnstaple several years before, though he could not recall the name of the freed man. The next time Thomas was in

Barnstaple, he called on the chaplain of St Peter's Church who, searched the archives and produced the parchment which confirmed that Matthew Lupus had indeed given Roger Merland his freedom!

Matilda threw her arms around Thomas's neck and gave him a very un-ecclesiastical hug of delight.

'That means we needn't have run away again, if only we'd known!' she exclaimed.

After the chaos and confusion of the miracle at the hanging tree, Philip had hustled Matilda and Gillota away before Walter Lupus or any of the surviving officials could recover their wits. Abandoning his house, he had set off with them for Shebbear that day, and after three days' walking they had arrived at Emma's croft, who welcomed them with open arms. Reunited not only with their aunt, but with their cow, pigs, cat and dog, they settled back into the life they had enjoyed for almost a year until Walter had kidnapped them.

Philip worked their croft with them and was negotiating to rent several acres more from the bailiff, having some money put by after his military service. For decorum's sake, he was lodging with a family at the other end of the village until the wedding. Gillota was delighted to have him as a stepfather and teased her mother that he had only proposed to her because she was carrying the stone in her pouch at the time!

Before Thomas left to return to the city, Matilda asked him a question that had been worrying her ever since their second escape from Kentisbury.

'Is Philip still in danger from the law? He was still under sentence of death when that branch fell.'

The little priest shook his head. 'I think you can rest easy on that score. That evil steward is crippled for life. He lives in his nephew's house – your house, really – and I doubt he'll ever walk again. Walter Lupus seems subdued since then and has got himself a new steward, an older man who seems to have plenty of sense and tolerance. The villagers know well enough what the real truth was, and I have spoken to the sheriff about it, so if, God forbid, the matter should ever be raised again, it will go before the justices in Exeter, who will undoubtedly condemn what happened in Kentisbury.'

He would dearly like to have asked Matilda about the small stone he had seen her covertly take out of the hole in that oak tree and slip into her pouch when she thought no one was looking – but he decided to let sleeping dogs lie, though he noticed that it now sat in a place of honour on a shelf over the door lintel.

A little later, as he rode sedately out of Shebbear on his way home, he passed the great rock lying outside the church. He knew of the legend and of the pagan ceremony of turning it each year and hastily averted his Christian eyes.

'There are too many strange stones in this part of Devon – sacred and profane!' he muttered, crossing himself as he passed and reciting St Patrick's Shield under his breath until he was out of the village.

Historical note

This story, including the names of the main characters and the places involved, is based on an actual case recorded in the rolls of the Crown Pleas of the Devon Eyre of 1238, the forerunner of the later Assizes and now Crown Courts. Though the later part of the story is fictitious, the records show that Matilda Claper's complaint brought Walter Lupus before the King's justices at Exeter

Castle in June 1238 and that after initial denials he admitted that he had brought her back to Kentisbury in chains and that she was free. He was found guilty and fined twenty shillings.

The Devil's Stone does lie outside the church in Shebbear and is turned by the villagers to the accompaniment of the church bells at eight o'clock in the evening on each 5 November, though this has nothing to do with Guy Fawkes!

ACT THREE

*Norwich, May 1241, the Jewish
month of Sivan, 5001* CE

The old merchant twisted around in the saddle of his
horse and glanced back uneasily down the narrow street.
He couldn't see the Black Friar behind him, but with such
a throng of riders and travellers all eager to crowd into
Norwich before dark, it was hard to be sure that the tall,
hunched stranger was not lurking somewhere in the shadows. Jacob raked his fingers through his long white beard
and tried to ignore the tightening band of pain gripping
his chest. He told himself that he was imagining things.
There were a hundred reasons why a man might journey
from Exeter to Norwich. The Black Friar wasn't following
him: why should he? What business would a friar have with
a Jew? It was mere coincidence that they had travelled the
same roads.

And yet the old man still felt a prickle of fear, for each
night on the journey he had turned aside to seek lodgings with Jewish families in the towns along the way, but
somehow, the next morning, the cowled figure on the grey
gelding always appeared on the road behind him, creeping after Jacob like his own shadow. And however slowly or
rapidly Jacob had ridden, the mounted friar always kept
pace with him, never overtaking him. Was that nothing
more than chance? Whatever it was, the merchant knew

he would not feel safe until he was inside his own house with the door stoutly barred.

On any other day Jacob would have been carefully watching each person in the crowd for signs of mischief; you didn't reach seventy years and five without learning to keep a sharp lookout for cutpurses and thieves. But on this particular evening the old man was too preoccupied with searching for the friar to notice that someone else was taking a keen interest in his progress through the busy streets. Three youths, slouching in the shadow of the tower by Nedham Gate, had signalled to each other as soon as they spotted Jacob entering the city, and as the merchant rode past them they peeled themselves off the wall and began to weave through the crowd behind him.

In his younger days Jacob had always felt a sense of relief as soon as he was within the walls of Norwich under the protection of the royal castle guards. Jews were after all chattels of the King, and though there had been riots against them from time to time, forcing them to flee to the castle for protection, for the most part Gentiles dared not risk attacking the Jewish merchants, for to do so would be robbing the King himself and the penalties for that were enough to make even the battle-hardened shudder.

But what Jew was safe anywhere these days, even in his own city? Since the Pope had commanded all Jews to wear the badge of shame, the two white strips on their clothing over their hearts, which represented the tablets of stone, they couldn't even hope to pass unnoticed on the road as once they did.

Last year monks had stormed into Jacob's house and burned his books and scrolls in front of him, declaring them the work of the devil. They had even destroyed the scrolls of the Old Testament, because they were written in Hebrew, not Latin. The monks had tried to toss the old merchant on their bonfire, too, but the soldiers from the castle had at least prevented that, for now anyway. After they'd gone, Jacob had offered up prayers of gratitude that the men had not discovered his most precious books and scrolls stored in the genizah, a concealed cupboard in the upper chamber of his house, though he was at a loss to understand why the Eternal One should have spared his books when so many of his fellow Jews had lost everything.

Then, just a few weeks ago, Jacob had received word from Leo, a Jewish pedlar in Exeter, concerning a strange and wondrous stone that had come into his possession. As he read the message, the old merchant's hands began to tremble with excitement. He found himself on his feet dancing and swaying around his chamber like a young bridegroom at a wedding. Jacob had waited his whole life for such a sign, praying for it, longing for it, without ever knowing what form it would take.

In these last few years, with old age gnawing at his bones, Jacob had begun to fear he would never see the sign in his lifetime. But as soon as he read Leo's words he knew for certain that this stone was what he had been searching for, and he, Jacob, had been chosen to deliver it to his people. Now he understood why the Eternal One had hidden his books from the eyes of the monks. The books had been spared so that he could use them to buy that stone. And he would use them. He would give all he owned if he had to, just to bring that stone home.

It had not been an easy journey to Exeter. No honest man was safe from cutpurses and outlaws on the lonely tracks and roads that spun a tangled web through heath and forest, hamlet and marsh. Once Jacob would have joined a band of fellow travellers for such a journey, but now few Christians were willing to be seen in the company of a Jew, and he was as much in danger of having his throat cut by other merchants as from any outlaw on the road. So the old man had been forced to make the long journey alone, seeking out the hospitality of fellow Jews in towns such as Thetford to at least give him a place of safety to sleep and food that had not been spat in or worse by a surly innkeeper.

Jacob had found the pedlar waiting for him in his filthy lodging in the very worst quarter of Exeter. They were old acquaintances, but still Leo had driven a hard bargain for the stone, not that Jacob blamed him for that. Leo had once been a merchant himself with a dozen men working for him, and Jacob had done much business with him over the years, but the massive taxes against the Jews, the community fines and the ever-increasing restrictions on their trade had combined to ruin the man, so that when finally pirates seized a ship carrying his cargo to Flanders, Leo had been left with nothing but debts. Now he was forced to tramp from village to village hawking cheap buckles, thread and anything else he could sell for the price of a night's lodgings. The man was bitter – and little wonder.

The pedlar had carefully unwrapped the stone and laid it on the rough wooden stool between them. At first Jacob could see nothing unusual about the stone except perhaps its shape, but when Leo tilted it at an angle to the candle flame, Jacob gasped in wonderment. He stared at it, not daring to touch it, suddenly aware of his unwashed hands.

'Where did you find it?' Jacob whispered, unable to tear his gaze away.

'Shebbear. You'll not have heard of it – a piss-poor village, full of lice-pickers,' Leo said sourly. 'I was selling door to door, or trying to, but those muck-grubbers wouldn't part with a clipped farthing. Finally, this woman at the end of the village took pity on me and invited me in for a bite to eat. I thought the angels were smiling on me; for once you get inside a house you can usually persuade a woman to buy something just to get rid of you.

'Anyway, that's when I spotted the stone up on a shelf above the door lintel. Noticed it straight off, strange shape, bit like a bird if you squint at it the right way, but even so, not what you'd expect to find on a shelf. Those crofts are so small there's scarcely room for their pots and pans. Who'd waste space on a stone? So I looked closer, and that's when I saw the marks. I could tell the woman had no idea what they were; doubt she'd even noticed them. Those villagers can't even read their own names. So I told her an alchemist in Exeter might pay a few pennies to melt it down for iron. It feels like iron, and those crofters will believe anything you tell them about a city.'

'So she sold it to you?' Jacob asked.

Leo shifted uncomfortably on his seat. 'She wouldn't. Said something about it bringing her and her husband together. You know what fools women can be. So I hung around until she and her daughter were busy, then I tackled the husband when I could get him alone. Men aren't sentimental, not when they can smell money. But he was as stubborn as she was and said if his Matilda didn't want to part with it, he wouldn't sell it, not for a king's ransom.' Leo shrugged. 'So what could I do? The next day was Easter Sunday. I knew there'd not be a soul about with all the villagers in the church, so I took my chance then, while the croft was empty. Put another stone in its place, so they'd not notice the gap straight away, especially if they came home merry after the feasting.'

'You stole it?' Jacob was shocked. In all his years as a merchant he had prided himself on never knowingly buying or selling anything that was stolen.

'There was no danger,' Leo assured him, misinterpreting Jacob's frown. 'She could hardly raise the hue and cry over a worthless stone, and it is worthless to them, but to us . . .' He gestured towards the stone. 'You think this should be allowed to stay in the hands of Christians? If one of their priests should chance to see and recognize the marks, they wouldn't hesitate to defile it. They'd spit and piss on it before they smashed it to pieces. Look what they've done to our holy books. You think I should have left it there so that they could commit such a blasphemy?'

'No . . . no,' Jacob finally conceded. 'You did right to rescue it. It is a sin to steal, but the rabbis tell us that the commandments may be broken to save a life, and I am certain that this stone will save not just one life but the lives of all our people. Such a *kemea* . . . such a sacred sign has not been granted to our people since we were driven out of the land of Israel.'

For once Jacob hadn't haggled over the price, and as soon as he felt the weight of the stone in his scrip pressing against his body a great peace seemed to wash over him. He left Exeter that same day, travelling as fast as he dared in order to reach Norwich before the feast of Shavuoth, the celebration of giving the tablets of stone to Moses on Mount Sinai.

He had arrived just in time, for the eve of Shavuoth was just two days off and what better day could there be to unveil this stone in the synagogue, a sign that the Eternal One would deliver them from the misery the Christians had imposed on them, just as He had delivered their forefathers from the Egyptians. Jacob's gnarled old fingers reached up to cup the stone concealed beneath his cloak. If he could spend his last few months on earth meditating on those marks on that stone, his soul would truly find eternal bliss.

Smiling to himself, the old merchant dug his heels into his horse's side, trying to urge it on apace, but the narrow alley was crammed with the stalls of bellowing bakers desperate to sell the last of their pies and bread to the housewives who elbowed each other aside to snatch a bargain. In all the commotion there was scarcely room for a beggar's brat to squeeze between the stalls, never mind a horse. But he wasn't far from his home now. Most of the Jews lived in Mancroft, around the synagogue and close to the castle, where they could flee if they were attacked. But Jacob's father had been wealthy enough to build a stone house near the river in Conesford Street, where the air was fresher and goods could more easily be transported to and from the boats.

At the crossroads, Jacob glanced behind him as he had done many times over the past few days looking for the Black Friar. Satisfied that there was still no sign of him, the old man was turning his horse's head in the direction of home when he felt the reins being torn from his fingers. Before he could even cry out, he was dragged from his horse and bundled into a courtyard. Moments later he found himself pinned against the wall with the point of a knife pricking the wrinkled skin of his throat. Three unkempt youths crowded around him.

The one holding the knife thrust his face close to Jacob. 'Gold, Jew, that's what we're after. Give it to us and we might let you live.' The lad was short and stocky, his legs so bowed he could have straddled three whores at the same time, but he could move as rapidly as a weasel.

Jacob swallowed hard, reciting a silent prayer. 'I've . . . only a few coins – you can have them all – but . . . I've no gold.'

'He's lying, Gamel,' one of the boys told Bow Legs.

'I know that, you cod-wit!' Gamel grabbed a handful of Jacob's beard and wriggled the knife against his throat. 'We know you've got gold. All you filthy Jews have got gold. We saw you leave days ago with a full pack, been waiting for you to return. You've no pack now, so what did you sell it for? How much?'

'I didn't sell it for money.'

'What, then?' Gamel demanded.

'A . . . s . . . stone.' Even as he stammered out the words, Jacob knew no one would believe that, but it was the truth. What else could he tell them?

The young men laughed mirthlessly. Gamel's knife flashed upwards, its blade slicing across the old man's mouth. Blood gushed from Jacob's lips, staining his white beard crimson.

Gamel took a step back. 'Search him,' he ordered his companions. 'He'll have the gold ingots strapped to his chest.'

Jacob caught sight of faces peering down at them from the upper casement of a house overlooking the courtyard. He shrieked out to them that he was being robbed, but almost at once heard the sound of a door being bolted shut. It was plain the witnesses to his plight were going to stay safely locked inside and ignore the trouble until it was over.

Frustrated at finding neither discs of gold nor of silver strapped to the old merchant's chest, Gamel punched Jacob viciously in the stomach. The old man doubled up and sank to the ground. Something muffled but heavy hit the cobbles of the courtyard. Gamel pounced and in a trice had cut the leather thongs of Jacob's scrip. He held up the weighty leather bag in triumph.

'Told you he had gold. Lying bastard.' He kicked the old man in the ribs, and his two companions grinned as they heard the bones crack.

Jacob rocked on the ground in puddles of piss and muck, his arms hugging the agony of his chest, his mouth gaping like a fish as he struggled to breathe. The three youths all tried to make a grab for the scrip, fumbling with the fastenings. Finally, Gamel wriggled his hand inside and pulled out the heavy lump. For a moment the three youths gaped at the black stone in his hand.

Gamel's two companions glanced at each other, fear gathering in their eyes. 'If we go back with nothing,' one muttered, 'she'll feed our balls to the hounds—'

'—while we're still wearing them,' the other finished.

With a howl of fury Gamel hurled the stone at Jacob. It struck him on the shoulder, and though the old man cried out in pain he reached out and grasped the stone. With what little strength he had left, he lifted it to his bleeding mouth and kissed it. '*Shma . . . Yisrael*,' he breathed, but that was all he had time to whisper. For the three youths with a single shout of rage ran at Jacob, kicking and stomping on the old man as if he was an insect they wanted to obliterate.

It is hard to know exactly when the old merchant lost consciousness, but mercifully he was dead long before the youths had finished battering his head to a bloody pulp.

As the youths ran off, Gamel glanced up at the frightened faces peering down from the casement above. He paused to press his finger first to his lips and then slowly and pointedly drew it across his throat, before he followed his companions out of the yard.

As soon as he was sure the youths had gone, a tall stooped figure dressed in a Black Friar's habit edged cautiously around the entrance to the courtyard and began to pick his way towards the crumpled figure lying in the corner. He had almost reached the body when he heard the sound of the bolts being drawn back on the door of the house. He hesitated, gazing longingly at the black stone still grasped in the dead man's hand, but before he could reach it the door opened and a maid rushed out screaming and shouting. The friar turned and fled from the yard, empty-handed.

Judith tore through the streets, running after Nathan and her brother Isaac. Her brother yelled at her to go back, but she ignored him. As a small child, she'd been able to beat any boy of her age in a race, but now, at seventeen, she was hampered by her long skirts, and the two young men were already inside the courtyard by the time she caught up with them.

A huddle of women stood just inside the archway to the yard, clutching each other and chattering shrilly like starlings. Judith edged past them and walked over to where Isaac and Nathan stood. As she looked down, it was all she could do to keep from retching. She reached inside her kirtle and grasped the silver amulet in the form of a hand which her mother had given her for protection. She held it so tightly the metal cut into her palm, but she didn't feel it.

The district bailiff was bending over what looked like a heap of blood-soaked rags, but when he caught sight of the white badge on Nathan's chest he straightened up and stepped aside. 'He's one of yours. You know who he is?'

Nathan pressed his hand to his mouth as if he was about to vomit. 'Zayde? *Grand-père?*' he whispered.

He sank to his knees in the muck and began shaking the old merchant as if he was sleeping and had to be woken. Tears streamed down the young man's face. He gently eased the black stone from the old man's fingers and, grasping the gnarled hand, pressed it to his lips, kissing it over and over. Judith felt the tears stinging her own eyes. She grasped her brother's arm. Startled to find her at his side, Isaac pulled her into his arms, hugging her so fiercely that Judith knew it was as much to comfort himself as her.

'Well, who is it, then?' the bailiff demanded gruffly. 'His name'll be needed for the records.'

'The merchant . . . Jacob ben Meir . . ,' Isaac said. 'Have you caught the bastard who did this to him?'

The bailiff grimaced. 'Hue and cry's been raised. There's men out looking, but I don't reckon we'll find anyone, No idea who we're looking for.'

'Someone must have seen something,' Isaac insisted. 'What about the people who live here?'

The bailiff shrugged. 'Didn't see anything. All busy about their duties. Was a maid found the body, and by then whoever did this was long gone. I dare say he brought it on himself. Might even have been the Jew who started it. Look there.' He nodded to the black stone in Nathan's hand. 'The old Jew was holding that when he was found. Could break a man's skull, could that. Maybe he tried to hit someone from behind to rob them and they were just defending—'

Nathan gave a bellow of fury and outrage. He was on his feet in a flash, the stone raised in his hand. But the bailiff was a burly man, well used to dodging the blows of drunks and desperate men. And as Nathan struck out, the bailiff grabbed his arm, twisted it and sent him sprawling face down in the yard across the body of his grandfather.

'Get him out of here,' the bailiff growled at Isaac. 'I'm only letting him get away with that 'cause I can see the lad's upset, but if he threatens me again . . .'

Isaac hastily dragged Nathan upright and bundled him towards the archway. All the fight had drained out of Nathan; though he was still grasping the stone tightly, he offered no resistance. All eyes followed the sobbing young man as he stumbled over the cobbles, his grandfather's blood dripping from his hands.

Wednesday 22 May, the fourth day of Sivan

'At least you had the sense to stay away from my inn until morning.' Magote scowled. 'So the old Jew's dead, is he? I hope for the sake of your necks there were no witnesses.'

The innkeeper's widow glanced sharply at Gamel and his two friends, but they merely shuffled their feet and grunted. The courtyard of the Grey Goose Inn was empty, but Magote had been long enough in her game not to take any chances. She gestured the lads into the long low lean-to that served as her brewing room and followed them, taking care to leave the door open just a crack so that she could observe anyone entering the yard.

'I asked you if there were any witnesses?' she repeated in a dangerously quiet tone.

Gamel jerked his chin defiantly. 'I made sure they told the bailiff they saw nothing. They know what'll happen to them if they talk.'

'Good lad. You're learning.' Magote nodded approvingly.

There was an art to handling these boys: reward and punishment, praise and terror in equal measure. The trick was to keep the lads off balance; never let them guess what was coming. Over the years, she'd worked up quite a gang of them; nearly a dozen lads under her control now. She'd lost a few from time to time – some who'd got themselves knifed, others hanged for thieving – but not one of them had ever fingered her, not even to save their own miserable skins. She was feared far more than the gallows, for even the slowest hanging was as quick as a cut-throat's knife compared with what she could do to those who betrayed her. If the condemned lad kept his mouth shut, she'd see his family had a fat purse to comfort them for their loss and he'd have someone to pull on his thrashing legs to bring a merciful end to the slow strangulation of the rope. But if the lad was foolish enough to talk . . . Widow she might be, but those who had the misfortune to cross her knew her better as the *widow-maker*.

Magote had made good use of the inn after her whore-mongering goat of a husband abruptly and mysteriously departed this life. Innkeepers always know what travellers have in their purses, and what the pedlars and camelots will buy with no questions asked. But Magote had her rules: guests in the Grey Goose were left unmolested for just as long as they remained in her inn enjoying her hospitality. As she told her lads, only a fool plucks a bird while it's still laying eggs, but once it's finished laying, then it's fair game.

Magote narrowed her eyes. The lads were too quiet, shifty. There was something they weren't telling her. She folded her huge muscular arms across her ample breasts. 'Well, where is it? Hand it over.'

Gamel looked in mute appeal to his friends, but they were staring fixedly at the rushes on the floor as if they'd never seen anything so fascinating before.

Gamel swallowed hard. 'The old man, he'd nothing on him . . . nothing. Searched him and his horse too.'

'What!' Magote spat the word out with such venom that all three lads cringed. 'Did you lose him, let him stop off somewhere in the city? Did he speak to anyone?'

'Never out of our sight, he wasn't, from the time he came in through the gate,' Gamel protested.

'Don't lie to me, you miserable little pig's turd. The old man left with a full pack. Rumour was he was to sell his finest books. This was to be his last trip. He'd have brought back enough gold to see him through for the rest of his days. So where is it?' She seized a hank of Gamel's greasy black hair, twisting it and pulling his head back until she forced him down on his knees. 'If you're trying to cheat me, boy ...'

'I swear there was nothing ...' he squealed. 'Nothing except a lump of stone, that were all, a lump of black stone.'

'Heavy?' Magote demanded.

Gamel nodded as best he could with her fist still gripping his hair. Magote slowly raised her calloused hand. Gamel saw what was coming, but had no way of avoiding it. She struck him so hard across his cheek that it made his head ring.

'Mutton head! Haven't I taught you anything? These Jews cover gold in black wax or tar, even dip it in lead to disguise it from cod-wits like you. That trick's so old, Adam was pulling it.'

Gamel's eyes were watering with pain. 'But it didn't feel like—'

'You couldn't feel your own arse unless someone kicked it for you.' Magote spat in disgust. 'Now you get out there and find out who's got that stone. You fetch it here, and I promise you'll be living like a lord on your cut of the gold. But if you fail I'll be taking my cut from you, and I don't mean in coins.'

Judith peered out of the casement on the upper floor of the synagogue, checking that the garden below was empty. Few men came to study this early in the evening, especially on a weekday, which is why her brother and his friends met here. Satisfied that she would not get caught, Judith laid down her broom and tiptoed across the wooden floor towards the tiny study chamber at the far end.

Her brother and his friends had entered the study chamber from the outside staircase at the back of the building. They didn't dare risk coming in through the main synagogue entrance in case the rabbi or one of the elders should see them. A year ago Rabbi Elias had closed the Talmudic school and forbidden the study of the Kabbalah after their teacher had been forced to flee abroad with his wife. It was dangerous to provoke the Christians, Rabbi Elias said; they were already suspicious enough of the Jews, and regarded the mystical symbols and charts of the Kabbalists as sorcery.

Besides, Rabbi Elias did not approve of these new ideas from Spain and Germany with their strange meditations, which had been known to drive young men into states of dangerous melancholy or mad ecstasy, which was almost as bad.

'Read the Torah, pray and work hard to earn a living. That is enough to occupy any young man,' he declared.

But Judith's brother Isaac and his three friends, including the rabbi's own son, Aaron, had continued to study in secret in defiance of the rabbi's instructions. Aaron swore that he for one was not going to be intimidated by the Christians even if his father was too cowardly to stand up to them.

Judith edged her way along the wall of the chamber until she found the familiar spot where there was a small hole in the wooden partition. She hunkered down and pressed her ear to the gap. She did not need to squint through it to know who was talking. She'd been eavesdropping on this room for months, listening to their fierce debates, and by now she had learned almost as much as they had.

Her brother Isaac was speaking. 'But Jacob must have told you why he wanted the stone. He was no fool, not when it came to business, anyway.'

'What more can I tell you?' Judith heard the exasperation in Nathan's voice. 'His old friend in Exeter sent him a message, and the next thing I knew Zayde was setting off. My mother told him it was dangerous to make such a journey at his age and with such valuable books, but he said when Moses saw the burning bush he went to it without hesitation, and where would our people be if he had not?'

'Now you're telling us he thought he was Moses?' Aaron said mockingly. 'That proves the old man was crazy.'

'You talk to me about crazy,' Nathan snapped. 'Last week you were certain that a new prophet had been born that hour, because the fish you had for dinner had a glass bead in its belly.'

Judith heard the scrape of a chair as if someone had pushed it violently backward.

'Enough!' Benedict's voice rang out hard and commanding. Benedict was only eighteen, two years younger than her brother Isaac, but he had a certainty about him that made others listen. 'We've tried every test of the alchemist's art on the stone. It transforms nothing, and it will not itself transform into anything but what we see.'

Benedict was already a skilled apothecary, having learned the trade from his father, but since his father had been hanged, Benedict had been forced to learn what he could from books. He could read Latin, German and French as well as Hebrew and, according to her brother, Benedict's room beside the apothecary's shop was stuffed with books on every subject from alchemy to brewing cordials for coughs. Not that Judith had ever seen them, of course;

an unmarried girl did not visit a man in his chamber, not even her future husband.

She and Benedict had been betrothed for two years now, and Judith had not thought it possible to be more infatuated with a man than she was on that day they gave each other their pledge. But as the months passed that youthful adoration had matured into a deep and solid respect, and a love that sometimes burned so fiercely in her she thought she would be consumed by it, if they did not soon become man and wife.

'So,' Aaron said, 'if Benedict is right, and the stone is not valuable, then what . . .' Suddenly his voice took on a new excitement. 'This scroll, what is its value?'

Judith put her eye to the hole in the partition and peered into the room. The rabbi's son was brandishing a small leather scroll under the nose of Nathan.

Nathan tugged at the small wisp of hairs on his chin which was struggling to proclaim itself a beard. 'Three, four shillings,' he hazarded.

'No, I mean what makes it worth three shillings? Is it the leather?'

Nathan snorted. 'What? An old piece of leather like that? A penny or two at most. It's what's written on . . .'

He broke off as Aaron snatched up the stone from where it lay between them on the table. Trembling with excitement, Aaron pulled a candle towards a solid-glass globe to intensify the light of the flame and tilted the stone upwards. The others crowded in to peer over his shoulder. For a long time all four men stared at it.

'Is that . . .' Isaac began. 'No, it's nothing.'

'Wait . . .' Aaron turned the stone around. 'There! There! Do you see it? Where the blood lies. It's the Hebrew letter – *Shin*. And that mark there. It's the letter *Mem*.' The stone was wrenched from hand to hand as each of the four young men pored over its surface.

'And there ... there's another. Is it ... could it be a *Hay*?' Nathan cried out, almost dropping the stone in his excitement. '*Shin, Mem, Hay*, or is it *Mem, Shin, Hay*? Moses! The letters spell *Moses* in Hebrew.'

'You are useless, Nathan,' Aaron yelled, ripping the stone out of his hand. 'That is a final letter *Mem*. It can only be written at the end of a word. *Hay, Shin, Mem*. Don't any of you see it? The letters spell *HaShem*. It means *The Name*. That is what is written on the stone – *The Name*. That is what the Eternal One was called at the climax of creation when He made Adam; only when creation was complete could *HaShem, The Name*, be known. And it is the title that the Eternal One used of Himself when He gave us the Torah on Mount Sinai. *I am HaShem that brought you out of the land of Egypt, the house of slaves*. Don't you see this is a sign that He is going to deliver us from those who oppress us. A sign written on stone, just as the law was written on stone. And tomorrow night Shavuoth begins, when those tablets of stone were given to Moses. It all fits.' Aaron grasped the white strips on the front of his cloak. 'This badge will no longer be our badge of shame; it will be our symbol of triumph.'

In the distance the church bells of Norwich began tolling for the evening service of compline. Aaron was prancing around the room holding the stone above his head like a banner.

Isaac caught his arm. 'It's late. Your father will be here soon, Aaron. We'd better go before he arrives for evening prayers.'

Aaron grimaced. 'Prayers! "Have patience and pray for the Messiah to come, my son",' he mimicked. 'All these centuries watching our people get slaughtered, and we are still waiting. My father will still be praying when the Gentiles are setting light to the bonfire under his feet. The

Jews of Norwich will never stand up for themselves as long as my father is rabbi. We have to find a way to destroy our enemies before we all end up like poor Jacob. And this! This—' he brandished the stone again '—will show us how to do it.'

'Not if your father finds us here with it,' Isaac warned. 'Does your mother know about the stone, Nathan?'

Nathan nodded miserably. 'But she won't tell anyone. She thinks the old man was tricked into giving away his wealth for nothing. She couldn't bear the shame of her friends and neighbours thinking her father had lost his wits.'

As he spoke, Nathan took the stone from Aaron's hand and began to wrap it in wool.

'What are you doing with it?' Aaron demanded indignantly.

'I'm taking it home,' Nathan told him, 'where I should be right now. I shouldn't have let you talk me into coming here. I should be sitting with my poor mother in mourning.'

'But you can't take the stone,' Aaron protested. 'I need to spend the night studying it and meditating on the letters. I told you letters are only the sign, but there is a message hidden in them, something that will show us what to do.'

'You don't need the stone to meditate on the letters. You know what they are.' Nathan thrust the stone firmly into his scrip.

'But suppose your mother finds it and throws it out,' Aaron said.

Nathan pressed both hands tightly against the leather scrip. 'It belongs to me. I am Jacob's grandson. I'll keep it under my pillow at night and with me all day. If my zayde thought it was worth giving everything he had for it, then

I won't part with it for a king's ransom. This stone is all I have left of him.'

Aaron's face was flushed with fury. 'But it's wasted on you! Jacob would want it to go to the person who can use it. You haven't the wit to discover the riddle in it. I'm far more advanced in the mystic path than any of you. I'm the only one who can read it.' He tried again to wrest the scrip from Nathan's grasp, but Nathan fought back. Isaac and Benedict stepped in to separate them.

'It belongs to Nathan,' Benedict said firmly. 'It's stained with the blood of his family. Besides, it's safer in his house than in yours. Your father may be set in his ways, Aaron, but he is not stupid, and if he found it in your possession he wouldn't rest until he found the letters on it. Now make haste. Let's separate and get out of here before the elders arrive.'

Judith didn't wait to hear what Aaron replied. She fled across the room and resumed her sweeping. Footsteps clattered down the back steps, and moments later the door connecting the study chamber to the synagogue opened and Benedict emerged alone. He stopped as he caught sight of her.

'Cleaning at this hour, Judith? It's very late,' he said with a frown.

'I was late arriving,' Judith lied. 'I had to walk to the far end of Fish Quay to find good herring for supper and then there was such a crowd.'

Benedict stepped closer, taking the broom from her and bringing both her hands to his lips, kissing each hand in turn.

'You work too hard,' he told her. 'But as soon as we are married, all that will end, I promise. Just a few more months and I will have the money.'

Judith sighed and tried to force a smile. Marriage had been set to follow within a year of their betrothal, but a year ago, just weeks before the wedding, Benedict's father had been hanged along with two other men. They were three of the sixteen men and women accused of the forced circumcision of a convert's little son ten years before. The whole Jewish community had raised the money demanded to pay for a mixed jury of Jews and Christians. But the King had taken the money, then declared that Jews were barred from sitting on the jury, because they would not convict one of their own.

Judith's own parents as well as the Kabbalah teacher had been among those accused, but they had wisely fled to Germany before the trial and could never return for they had been declared fugitives, but at least they were alive. Benedict's father had foolishly put his faith in the King's justice, and now he was dead and all his property forfeit to the Crown. Benedict was forced to work for a Christian master in the shop his father had once owned and rent a tiny chamber between the shop and the storeroom to sleep in.

Judith had repeatedly assured Benedict that she would gladly wed him without a penny between them, for she loved him more than her own life, but Benedict was too proud to accept that. When he could afford to marry her, he said, he would, but as Judith lay awake at night with every fibre of her body aching to be lying in his arms, she began to fear she would be wearing a shroud before a bridal gown.

They heard the sound of laboured footsteps on the wooden stairs below. Benedict grabbed Judith's cloak and thrust it around her shoulders as Rabbi Elias shuffled into the room. The rabbi stared in puzzlement at the sight of the young couple alone in the synagogue. Judith could see the question forming on his lips.

Before the rabbi could ask it, Benedict said quickly, 'Judith's brother couldn't come for her tonight. He was concerned that she shouldn't walk home alone, so he asked me to escort her.'

The rabbi's frown relaxed. 'Troubled times, troubled times.'

Benedict hastily ushered Judith towards the stairs.

'You are a close friend of the boy Nathan?'

Benedict turned. The rabbi was gazing not at him but at the closed doors of the ark where the scrolls of the Torah were kept.

Rabbi Elias continued without looking at Benedict. 'I know that Jacob ben Meir went to Exeter to bring back some special object for this community, something he believed would protect us, give us hope. That much he confided in me before he left. Jacob said he was willing to give everything he owned for that chance for us all to live in peace. I believe that had he known what that object would really cost him, he still would not have hesitated to bring it here. Yet the universe is created in pairs. For every light there is a corresponding darkness, and what brings peace can be used to bring destruction, if it falls into the wrong hands.'

The rabbi turned and fixed Benedict and Judith with his piercing blue eyes. 'I am only in my forty-second year, and if it pleases the Eternal One I might live for some years yet, but my son is not willing to wait until I am old to replace me as rabbi. He believes that like our fore-fathers, the Maccabees, who rose up against the occupying Greeks, we can rise up against our masters and overthrow them. But this is not Israel and we cannot fight the whole of Christendom! If we try, they will utterly destroy us. Our only hope is to put our faith in the Eternal One, as we have always done. Benedict, you are a man known for keeping your own counsel, so I will not ask you if you know what object Jacob brought back or where it is, but ask you this – do all in your power to ensure it does not fall into the hands of my son, Aaron, and those like him, or it will mean the end of all of us.'

Thursday 23 May, the fifth day of Sivan, the eve of the Festival of Shavuoth

The flames in the oil lamps guttered each time the synagogue door opened to admit more men and boys hurrying in from the chilling rain. The benches around the little tables were filling up fast, and Nathan found himself squashed between Benedict and a stout red-faced butcher who, though he had washed, still stank of blood and dung.

'Have you brought the stone with you?' Benedict whispered.

Nathan nodded reluctantly. He hadn't had any choice but to bring it. Aaron and Isaac had both arrived on his doorstep as dusk was gathering and insisted on watching him put the stone in his scrip before escorting him like a prisoner to the synagogue.

'I don't see what good it will do you,' Nathan told them. 'We can't discuss the meaning of the letters this evening. Every man in the community will be in the synagogue tonight.'

But Aaron had exchanged a knowing wink with Isaac, and Nathan realized at once that they were planning something. Whatever it was, he wanted no part of it. So it was much to Nathan's relief when Aaron and Isaac left him at the synagogue door and went to join the other groups of men.

It was the tradition for the men to gather on the eve of Shavuoth to study all night, until dawn proclaimed the time for morning prayers and the main services of the festival would begin. Debates over the holy texts were always lively, as each man deliberately offered a counter-argument to that of his companions so that all possible interpretations of the verses could be explored.

But as the evening wore on, Nathan became aware of two voices loudly raised above the general buzz of discussion in the room. With a sick feeling gathering in his belly, he realized the two voices belonged to Aaron and Isaac. Gradually, the other conversations died away as the whole room stopped to listen. The arguments Isaac and Aaron were posing were so bizarre that several of the older men in the congregation leaped to their feet in outrage, shaking their fists and banging the tables. Finally, Rabbi Elias threw up his hands and ordered an end to the unseemly debate. Glaring furiously at his son, the rabbi dismissed everyone to their homes to let tempers cool. But even so, it wasn't until Nathan saw the look of undisguised triumph on Aaron's face that he realized this was exactly the outcome he and Isaac had been planning.

Nathan squeezed past the grumbling elders and bolted out of the door. He had every intention of going to see his beloved Eleanor and trying to forget for a few brief hours that he was a Jew, that's if her father wasn't around to prevent it. But Nathan had not gone far along the street before his arms were seized on either side and he found himself being steered around the back of the synagogue to crouch in the darkness under the outside steps to the chamber. All four men waited, shivering in the rain, until they heard the sounds of the synagogue door being locked and footsteps shuffling away across the flagged path. Then they climbed the steps to the study chamber. Nathan knew it was useless to protest. The other three were determined to resolve the riddle of the stone, and even he was forced to admit that there could be no more fitting night on which to do so.

Aaron barred the door between the synagogue and the study chamber in case his father should return, then, taking the stone from Nathan, placed it carefully on the table between two lighted candles. He fumbled at his waist and unfastened a piece of long red cord with which he formed a circle on the table around the stone and candles. When he was finally satisfied that the circle was as perfect as he could make it, the four of them took their places on the stools, one at each corner of the table. The room was in darkness save for the flickering twin flames. No one spoke. They all knew what to do. They concentrated simply on the rhythm of their own breathing until it slowed almost as if they were sleeping.

Then Aaron, keeping his voice low and even, spoke from the shadows. 'Look at the letters on the stone *Hay, Shin, Mem*. Stare at each letter in turn until they start to move. Watch them weave in and out of each other, growing bigger and smaller, changing their colours. Let yourself dissolve into the letters – become the letters.'

Nathan knew the meditation well. Their former teacher had often made them practise it, but always before they had visualized words in their heads. They had never stared at letters written on anything. Nathan had never been any good at it, not even when they were students. You were supposed to breathe each word until it lost its meaning and new words and new meanings danced in your head, but the only thoughts that ever came into Nathan's head were certainly not spiritual. Mostly he spent the time dreaming up ways of being alone with the voluptuous, flaxen-haired Eleanor without her father finding out.

But tonight, as Nathan stared at the stone glistening in the trembling yellow candle flame, it was only too easy to see the letters moving. The letters first began twisting and undulating, then they seemed to be crawling off the stone and scuttling across the table towards him. He could hear the word stalking around him in the darkness, *Ha-Sh-em*, *Ha-Sh-em*. His three companions were breathing rhythmically in and out on the syllables of the word. Though he couldn't tear his gaze away from the letters, Nathan was vaguely aware that the others were standing now, folding and unfolding their bodies to the rhythm of their breath, *Ha-Sh-em*. The word slithered through the shadows.

The letters were changing colour. *Shin* was glowing red as if it had caught fire. *Mem* had turned ice-blue and was running like water over the table, yet where the blue water touched the ruby flame it seemed only to make the flame burn more fiercely.

Aaron's breathing had deepened as if he was trying to suck all the air from the room. He was chanting a different word now – *Raziel, Raziel*. The other two joined in, calling on the name of the angel who reveals the secrets of heaven and the knowledge of the future. *Raziel, Raziel, Raziel*. Nathan became aware of something growing in the corner of the room, blacker than a hangman's shadow, deeper than the pit of Gehenna, a total absence of light so thick and heavy it was as if the very darkness from which the world had been created was reforming in that room. It was swelling up, uncoiling and reaching out . . .

Nathan yelled in panic and dashed his hand across the table, sweeping stone, cord and candles crashing to the floor. For a moment he could see nothing while his eyes adjusted to the thin shaft of moonlight filtering in through the hole in the shutters. But Nathan didn't need any light

to tell him that whatever it was that had entered that room
had vanished and the four of them were alone.

'You clumsy imbecile, Nathan,' Aaron raged at him.
'We'd almost succeeded in summoning the spirit that
would have given us knowledge of the future. Do you realize what a miracle that was? Not even the greatest mystic
teachers have succeeded. Just think what power . . .' Words
failed Aaron, and he slammed his fist into the table in
frustration.

'But didn't you see it?' Nathan asked them. 'That thing
didn't come from the light . . . Didn't any of you see what
it was?'

It was too dark to make out the expressions on their
faces, but he could sense their anger and bewilderment.
But if they hadn't seen it, how could he begin to explain?

Nathan sank down on the stool, his hands trembling.
'Just go. Get out of here and leave me alone.'

He heard the door close behind them and their footsteps on the wooden staircase, but he didn't move. He sat
staring into the corner, trying to understand what he had
seen. There had been nothing there, and yet that nothing
had been so dense, so massive, so full of rage and hate, it
felt as if that nothing had been the only solid thing in the
room, and the table, the walls, even he himself had been
mere wisps of smoke in its presence.

Somewhere out in the city a dog was howling, and then
he heard a single set of footsteps slowly climbing the
wooden staircase outside. It must be Isaac, Benedict or
Aaron come back to see if he was all right and walk him
home. Nathan rose and started across the room to meet
them. A finger came through the hole in the door, lifting
the latch, and the door swung open.

Friday 24 May, the sixth day of Sivan, the Festival of Shavuoth

Judith leaped to her feet almost before she had opened her eyes, startled by the shouts and cries in the street outside. For a moment she thought she had overslept and the market was already open for the day, but then she realized the room was still dark. Isaac was standing by the tiny casement and peering out through the open shutter, shivering in the cold damp air. A thin grey light crawling up over the rooftops showed that dawn was not far off. Judith joined her brother at the casement, draping his cloak around his shoulders against the cold, though it still felt damp from the night's rain.

'What's the noise?' Judith asked.

Men were spilling out of the houses on either side of the street, still rubbing the sleep from their eyes. Women and children leaned out of the casements trying to see what was going on.

'They're calling the hue and cry,' Isaac sighed. 'I'd better go and help.' He stooped, struggling to pull on his wet shoes. They were caked in mud.

Judith frowned. 'Why didn't you put those near the hearth when you came in? Anyway, when did you come in? It must have been very late. I didn't hear you.'

But Isaac was already halfway out of the door. Judith turned back to the window and saw her brother emerge on to the street to join the other men who were rapidly dispersing in threes and fours in different directions hunting whoever was being sought by the law. She waited until Isaac had reached the end of the street, then she could contain her curiosity no longer and, slipping into her kirtle, cloak and shoes, ran outside. By now the women, hugging themselves against the sharp morning air, were gathering on the street.

'Been a murder in Little Orford Street,' they told her. 'Jew it was and no mistaking it – found him naked as the day he was born.'

Judith felt her throat tighten. There wasn't a Jew in Norwich she didn't know, at least by sight. Now that they were all forced to wear the white strips, they could recognize everyone, even those who didn't come to the synagogue. She found herself praying that it would not be one of her own friends, then reproved herself sharply; after all, it would be some poor woman's father or brother or son. Another one of their community murdered. Where would it all end?

She allowed herself to be swept along by the crowd into Little Orford Street, where a mass of people had gathered around a small gap between two of the houses. At first Judith couldn't see anything, but then a man caught her arm and dragged her forward through the throng.

'Here's another of the Jews, bailiff. Go on, you look, girl, see if you know him.'

A figure was lying stretched out on the ground on his back, his arms raised above his head. He'd been covered by someone's cloak, but one of the men kneeling beside the corpse pulled it back far enough to allow Judith to see the face. She closed her eyes briefly, steeling herself to look. The dark brown eyes of the corpse were wide open as if in shock, and the lips were drawn back from the yellowed teeth in something approaching a snarl, but despite the contorted expression Judith was certain it was not a face she knew.

She felt her stomach relax in relief. 'I've never seen that man before. Besides, he's not Jewish. He has no beard, and look at his hair.'

Though the victim had dark stubble on his face, he had certainly been clean-shaven not much more than a week ago, and there was something else. A circular fuzz of new hair in the centre of his head indicated that in the not-too-distant past the man had been tonsured.

'Probably trying to pass himself off as a God-fearing man,' one man in the crowd muttered. 'Trying to cod innocent folk into giving him alms or get into an abbey, so he could steal from them. Typical of their tricks.' The others nodded.

Judith pressed her nails into the palms of her hands, trying to keep her anger in check. 'But what makes you think he is Jewish?' she persisted.

The men grinned at each other. With a magician's flourish, the bailiff whipped the cloak from the naked body. A livid stab wound in the chest showed that there was no mistaking this was murder, but the bailiff was not pointing to the man's wound. His spiteful smile deepened as he watched the hot blush spread over Judith's face.

'Good Christians don't go around chopping the heads off their sons' manhoods,' he sneered.

The bailiff was right, and there was no mistaking that the dead man was circumcised.

Sunday 26 May, the eighth day of Sivan

A shaft of lemon-sharp light darted into the synagogue as Judith threw back the shutters. Yesterday the synagogue had been crammed with people for the Shavuoth services, but the door and shutters had been kept firmly barred in the hope that their muffled prayers would not reach the ears of the passers-by outside, and the synagogue was still fugged with the stench of sweat, oil and tallow.

Judith breathed in the cold morning air gratefully. As soon as the sun warmed the streets they'd be stinking of rotten vegetables, fish, dung and offal from Saturday's markets, but for now a stiff breeze from the river carried with it the subtle scents of thyme, mint and bergamot growing in the synagogue garden below the window. Church bells from the scores of churches and chapels were pealing out over the city, calling the faithful to Mass.

Judith pulled the star-shaped oil lamp towards her and set about scraping the sticky residue of oil and wick fragments from the five spouts before refilling the reservoir. She remembered that the lamps in the study chamber would also have been burning and, with the flask of oil already in her hand, thought that she might as well refill those before she started her sweeping. But to her annoyance she found the door between the chamber and the synagogue barred on the other side.

Irritated by having to make the extra walk, Judith trudged out of the synagogue and climbed the back stairs that led to the separate chamber entrance. She unlatched the door and pushed it open. As in the synagogue, the shutters in the little chamber were tightly fastened, but the light from the open door was just enough for Judith to make out the figure of Nathan crouching in the corner of the room. His legs were drawn up to his chest, and his forehead rested on his knees. He didn't look up, obviously so deeply asleep that even the sound of the door opening didn't arouse him.

Judith closed the door as quietly as she could and was about to tiptoe back down the stairs when she stopped. There was something about the room that was not right. She was used to the study chamber being in disarray – the tables usually heaped with untidy piles of parchment, scrolls, discarded quills and even forgotten garments – but this was different. And there was a foul smell in the room, too, more than just the stench of tallow, sweat and stale air.

She cautiously opened the door again. Flies were buzzing against the shutters. Parchments and scrolls were strewn across the floor like autumn leaves. One of the trestles was overturned. Had Nathan thrown it over in a passion of grief?

'Nathan?' she called softly. Still he did not stir. She almost gagged, the stench was so overpowering. She had taken a step inside the room to open the shutters, when the breeze caught the door behind her and slammed it shut. She heard something thump down on to the wooden floor. She wrenched the door open again and saw that Nathan had slumped over on to his side. It was only then that Judith glimpsed the thick cord cutting deep into the flesh of his neck. What she could see of his face was purple and grotesquely swollen. His eyes were bulging wide. Nathan was dead.

Judith ran down the steps, half slipping in her haste. Someone was standing in the shadow of one of the apple trees in the synagogue garden. She was about to shout to them when it occurred to her that the watching figure might be Nathan's killer. She started to run back up the stairs, but she knew she couldn't bring herself to go back into that room, whatever danger lay outside. She turned again, trying to get a better glimpse of the person under the tree, but the place where they had been standing was empty.

Judith edged across the garden, then she picked up her skirts and ran the few streets to her home, praying that her brother would still be there. It was the Christian Sabbath, so Jews were not permitted to work in the workshops, but Isaac usually continued to sew in secret at home, for they needed the money. But when she burst in, she found the room empty. She tried to think. Where would he be? He must be with Aaron or Benedict. She hurried to the rabbi's house, her heart still thumping so loudly in her chest she thought it would burst. But though she hammered for several minutes on his door, neither Rabbi Elias nor Aaron answered.

'Judith,' a voice called behind her. She turned to see her brother Isaac hurrying along the street towards her. Almost crying with relief, she ran to him.

'Isaac ...' she panted. 'You must ... come at once. It's Nathan ... I've just found him in the synagogue ... He's ... he's dead!'

'No, no, that's not possible!' Isaac turned and ran towards the synagogue. Judith followed more slowly. Her legs felt as weak as a newborn calf, and it was all she could do to walk, never mind run. Isaac had already raced up the stairs and was flinging open the door of the study chamber before Judith had crossed the garden.

Almost at once he emerged again at the top of the stairs. 'I thought you said Nathan was in here.'

Judith pulled herself up the stairs. As she stepped cautiously inside the chamber, Isaac followed. Everything was exactly as she had left it, except for the body. Nathan's corpse had vanished.

'But ... he was right there in the corner,' Judith protested, turning in bewilderment to her brother.

Isaac gently squeezed her shoulders. 'Perhaps you only thought Nathan was dead. He may simply have fainted and then recovered and has taken himself home.'

Judith closed her eyes tightly. 'You didn't see his face, Isaac, his eyes. There was a cord tied around his neck, cutting into his throat.'

'A cord? Aaron was using a red cord two nights ago. He left it here, after Nathan ...' Isaac's gaze darted around

203

the room. 'Are you sure you saw a cord? It's not here now.'

'Of course I am,' Judith yelled at him. 'And the stench. Can't you smell it?'

Her brother sniffed. 'That rotten stink from the butchers' market – everyone can smell that. Look, little sister, dead men don't get up and walk. A corpse can't just vanish.'

'Isaac, listen to me. I thought I saw someone watching this chamber. What if it was Nathan's murderer and he came back while I was gone and moved the body?'

'But why risk discovery by moving a corpse in broad daylight when they could simply leave it here?' Isaac suddenly clapped his hand to his mouth and began frantically to search the room, tossing parchments aside, flinging out the contents of the small chests. 'Is there something else missing, Judith? Something you saw in the room before that isn't there now?'

'Like what?'

But he didn't answer her and she didn't need an answer. She knew he was looking for the stone. And if the stone was missing . . .

'Isaac, you said that Aaron had a red cord in this chamber. Is it possible that Aaron could have . . . *murdered* Nathan?'

Her brother gaped at her. 'Aaron is the rabbi's son. We've all grown up together. They may have quarrelled but . . .' Isaac hesitated. He shook his head as if trying to rid himself of the idea and said firmly, 'No. This is nonsense. You must have imagined it. You were always seeing monsters in the corners of the room in the dark when you were a child. You probably ate too much cheese last night.'

He bent over to kiss her forehead, but Judith furiously pulled away. It was the closest she had ever come to slapping him since they were children.

'And what about whatever you were searching for: is that here?' she demanded.

Isaac gnawed at the skin of his needle-calloused finger. 'Nathan must have taken it home with him. I'll go to his house straight away. That'll put your mind at rest.' He tried to smile. 'Nathan's probably sitting there right now swigging his ale, and all your fears will be for nothing.' But he didn't sound convinced by his own words.

Nathan was not in his house or his shop, and by the time the city gates were closed for the night and fires damped down in hearths he had still not returned. Anxious enquiries among all the Jews in the city revealed only that no one remembered seeing him since the eve of Shavuoth. There was no doubt that, dead or alive, Nathan had vanished and he was not the only one missing; Aaron likewise had disappeared.

Monday 27 May, the ninth day of Sivan

Isaac and Benedict came in from the yard, their hands still dripping with water from the ritual washing before meals. Judith ladled the thick bean and mutton potage into rough wooden bowls, fishing out an extra piece of mutton from the iron pot to put into Benedict's bowl. There were more green herbs in the potage than meat or dried beans, for the stores in her kitchen were dwindling fast. Shavuoth may have been the wheat harvest festival for their ancestors in Israel, but here in the northern lands it was a time of hunger, for it would be many weeks before grain and fruit were ready to harvest.

Judith took her own bowl and sat at the end of the table. She could see that Benedict was bursting to say something, but silence had to be kept between the washing of hands and the blessing over the meal, so he was forced to bite his tongue until Isaac had finished mumbling the prayer. Then he burst out, 'But what if Aaron's been murdered, too?'

Isaac glanced uneasily at his sister. 'We've no proof that *Nathan* is dead. Judith was probably mistaken in what she saw. It's very dark in the study chamber.'

'I know exactly what I saw,' Judith blurted out furiously. 'I'm not a child.'

Benedict held up his hands. 'We believe you, don't we, Isaac?' he said, kicking his friend hard under the table. 'The point is,' he continued hastily, 'both Nathan and Aaron have vanished. What if they were both killed in that room and the murderer had time only to move one of the bodies before Judith arrived?'

Isaac pushed his bowl aside. 'Look, just suppose that my sister is right and Nathan has been killed. Then the murderer would have to be the same bastard who killed Jacob, but he'd not have been able to take the two of them. Aaron never left the house without a knife. No, most likely when Aaron got home, his father blistered his ears over that business on Erev Shavuoth and Aaron stormed off. He's just lying low somewhere until the old man calms down.'

Benedict shook his head. 'I spoke to Rabbi Elias and he said he hadn't seen Aaron since he told him to go home that night. Anyone can tell he's worried sick about his son.'

Judith nodded and turned to her brother. 'If you're so sure that Aaron isn't dead, then he must have run off for some other reason, and why would he do that unless he'd killed Nathan?'

Isaac sprang to his feet. 'No, if Nathan is dead then this is the work of the Christians.'

'And what would Christians want with a stone?' Benedict asked quietly. 'The stone is missing – or have you forgotten?'

'The stone is here,' a shaky voice whispered from the doorway.

All three of them turned around. Aaron was standing in the low doorway, one hand clinging to the door frame as if he feared he would fall if he didn't hold on to something. His face was pale, a dark bruise stained his cheek and one of the seams of his cloak had been ripped open, but in his right hand he held the sacred stone. Judith knew she should go to help him, but she couldn't move.

'I killed him,' Aaron said, almost in wonder. 'I didn't mean to, but I couldn't let him take it . . . you understand that. He was a traitor, a blasphemer. I couldn't let him take this stone from us, too. You would have done the same, wouldn't you, Isaac? Benedict?' he begged desperately.

He staggered forward and would have fallen had Benedict not caught him in his arms and lowered him gently on to the bench.

Judith hurried across the room to the flagon of wine they kept for the Shabbat meal on Friday evening and swiftly returned with a large measure. Benedict gently prised the stone from Aaron's fingers and laid it on the table before clasping the man's stiff fingers around the beaker of wine. Aaron stared at it as if he couldn't understand what he was holding, then he lifted it and drank so fast Benedict had to pull it away from him to stop him choking.

Isaac opened his mouth as if he was going to speak, but no words came out.

Judith could contain herself no longer. 'What did Nathan do to betray us? He couldn't, not Nathan. He was such a gentle, honest man.'

Aaron turned to her, his gaze unfocused. 'What do you mean, Nathan? Nathan's a bloody fool at times, but he's no traitor.'

'But you said you killed him.'

Aaron buried his head in his hands. 'I told you, I didn't mean it. They'll hang me. Worse than that. Who knows what they'd do to a Jew who killed a man in holy orders. You have to help me get out of Norwich before they find me.'

Judith knelt down on the rush-strewn floor and stroked his arm gently. She could feel his whole body shaking. 'What happened, Aaron? Just tell us from the beginning.'

He took another gulp of wine and sat staring at the table. 'I . . . I went back to the study chamber on Erev Shavuoth after we parted. I wanted to try the meditation again on my own. Just as I got there, I saw someone hurrying down the stairs. I could see it wasn't one of you. The figure was too tall, walking all hunched over, and he was wearing a long robe, though I couldn't make out its colour in the dark. So I hid, but just as he drew level with me Nathan came staggering out of the chamber holding the side of his head. He was standing at the top of the stairs yelling, "Thief, thief." The man took to his heels. I chased after him and managed to grab him on the corner of Little Orford Street. As soon as I turned him round, I realized he was a friar, a Black Friar, and he was trying to stuff the stone into his scrip. I told him to give it back and I'd let him go, but he just laughed. He said he'd rather destroy it than let a Jew have it. The whole story burst out of him like pus from a boil.

'Apparently, the Black Friar had heard rumours about the stone in Exeter. A pedlar was spreading the word among the Jews, wanted to sell it to the highest bidder so that he could buy passage on a boat. The friar arrived just an hour too late. The pedlar told him that Jacob had already bought it and was on his way home. The friar knew that Jacob wouldn't sell it to him, but he thought that once Jacob was home he could talk his way into his house and steal it.'

'Jacob would never have allowed a friar across his threshold, not unless he had soldiers with him,' Isaac said.

'That's what I told him, but he said Jacob would let him in if he thought he was a Jew. I laughed. That's when the little weasel told me.

'He said, "Do you think I've always looked like this? I was born one of you, a Jew. My fool of a father scraped a living from the leavings of the Gentiles all his life and still they spat on him in the street. You think I wanted to spend the rest of my life being kicked out of the way and treated like pigswill? I knew there was only one way out: if you can't beat them, become one of them. So I converted to the true faith and joined the order as soon as I was twelve. They were pleased to have me at first, a convert plucked from the burning, but that didn't last long. They were never going to let me forget I was born a Jew. But if I bring them the stone they'll have to accept me. We'll destroy it and then we'll destroy the rest of you vermin. When there isn't a Jew left in England, then they will forget I'm one of the accused tribe." '

Aaron clenched his fists. 'I pulled my knife. I didn't mean to use it, just to threaten him, but he wouldn't listen. He wouldn't give up. He just kept taunting me. There was a struggle. The ground was slippery from the rain. I don't know if I pushed the knife into him or if he fell on it, but the next thing I knew he was dead.

'I didn't know what to do. I was about to run off when it occurred to me that if I stripped him, it might take longer for them to work out who he was and buy me a little more time. Besides,' he added savagely, 'I wasn't going to let them find a Jew in a friar's robes.'

Tuesday 28 May, the tenth day of Sivan

Judith stood in the doorway of their house, throwing the crumbs from the morning bread to the squabbling chickens in the yard. The pale primrose light gave promise of a fine day to come, which was as well for she needed to tend the synagogue garden. Weeds were sprouting everywhere after all the rain.

As if he could read her thoughts, Isaac paused in the act of pulling on his worn leather shoes. 'Promise me you'll stay out of the study chamber today. I don't want you going back in there until I've had a chance to straighten it. We don't want you imagining any more bodies or demons, do we?'

Judith rounded on him furiously. 'I didn't imagine it and Nathan is still missing, isn't he? And his poor mother's going out of her mind with worry.'

Isaac raised his eyes to heaven. 'Give me patience. You heard Aaron last night. He said Nathan was standing on the stairs yelling, "Thief." So the Black Friar can't have killed him when he stole the stone. And before you start accusing him again, Aaron couldn't have done it either; he was too busy chasing after the friar. Look, little sister, I didn't want to tell you this, but Nathan has been seeing a girl, Eleanor. He's besotted with her, but she's a Christian, so they have to meet in secret. Nathan's mother would kill herself if she found out about it.'

'You think they've run off together?'

Isaac shrugged. 'It's more than possible, especially if the girl's father got wind of it. He'd hardly give the couple his blessing, now, would he? But I can't tell Nathan's mother that. So be a good girl and stay out of that room. I don't want you upset again. We've enough to worry about with a real body, without worrying about imaginary ones. If the authorities realize that corpse was a friar, not a Jew, they'll turn this town upside down looking for his killer.'

Judith swallowed hard. She hadn't dared tell Isaac that she had drawn the bailiff's attention to the man's tonsure. She prayed that the bailiff would dismiss what she said, as he did all Jews.

Beads of sweat prickled on Judith's forehead. Although the afternoon sun was warm for May, she was hoeing with unnecessary vigour between the bushes of rosemary and hyssop in the synagogue garden to try to keep her thoughts off that study chamber. But it wasn't working, and she kept glancing up at the casement. Isaac was right; the most likely explanation for Nathan's disappearance was that he and this Christian girl had fled the city together.

As a little child, Judith been too terrified to cross the yard at night, convinced that she could see a demon with glowing eyes lurking in the corner, though her father had shown her it was just the light from her own lantern glinting off a piece of metal. Even now she sometimes thought she saw her mother sitting hunched in the chair before the fire. Perhaps she had imagined Nathan's body, too. If she could just see what it was in that room – a shadow, a piece of cloth, something that had made her think she'd seen Nathan – she could forget the whole thing.

Judith's heart gave a lurch of relief as she pushed open the door of the chamber. She'd half expected to see Nathan crouching there again, but the corner was empty and bare. Almost at once, relief was replaced by disappointment. Someone had already tidied the room, her brother or Benedict, no doubt, for it was a man's hand that had tidied it, she could see that at once. Tables and benches were now upright, but not neatly aligned, and armfuls of books and parchments had been scooped up and stacked in drunken piles without any attempt to sort them or put them back in their places on the shelf. It was as if someone had straightened things just enough to create a space to work. Several sheets of parchment lay spread out on one of the tables, close to a candle stub with a quill pen and pot of black ink.

Judith lifted one of the sheets. It was a random list of words written in Hebrew – *gold, fire, citadel.* Other Hebrew letters were written beside each word, but these letters didn't make words. Judith glanced at the rest of the table, searching for the book or scroll that the person had been studying. It was the custom to take a passage from the Torah and study each word and phrase in depth, looking for the different meanings. Usually that passage would be in front of the scholar as he studied, but there were no scrolls or books on the table.

Judith glanced up sharply as she heard footsteps pounding up the wooden steps outside, but before she could cry out the door burst open and Aaron rushed into the room. If anything, he looked paler than he had done the day before, and he was certainly trembling as much.

He doubled over, gasping for breath. 'Isaac . . . Benedict . . . where are they? I . . . thought they might be here. They said at the tailor's that Isaac had gone to the warehouse at the river to fetch cloth, but I thought he might have come here.' He glanced repeatedly at the door as if he was fearful that someone might be following him.

'What is it? Has something else happened?' Judith asked, beginning to feel as scared as he looked.

Aaron took a deep breath. 'I need to show you something. Come, please come.'

'Where to?'

Aaron shook his head as if he couldn't trust himself to speak, and after an anxious glance through the half-opened door he urgently motioned her to follow him. Judith was outside before she realized she still had the pieces of parchment in her hand and quickly stuffed them in her scrip before running after Aaron.

He strode rapidly, his hood pulled far down over his face as if he feared to be recognized. Judith had to keep breaking into a trot so as not to lose sight of him. When they reached Conesford Street, Aaron finally stopped. The breeze from the river was stronger here, and Judith was glad of it for she could feel the sweat running down her back.

They were standing in front of Jacob's house, a fine stone building with a heavy oak door guarding the entrance. Aaron withdrew a large iron key from under his cloak and slid it into the lock. As the door swung open, he pushed Judith through the door, locking it behind them. It was dim inside the small entrance chamber. All the shutters were closed, and the only light came from two small slits in the thick stone walls either side of the door. Judith shivered. It had been just a week since Jacob's death, but with no fires lit in the house the air felt damp and chill.

She rubbed her arms uneasily. 'What are we doing here, Aaron?'

'Upstairs . . . please,' he begged her.

He led the way up the stone steps to the upper hall. A huge fireplace occupied one wall, but the logs in it were blackened and dead. A long table stretched down the centre of the room, set about with chairs. Chests and side tables were ranged along the walls. The lower half of the walls was wainscoted with timber panels, painted green and dotted with gold stars, while the stones on the upper half were lime-washed white. At the far end of the room was a wooden partition.

Judith hovered uneasily by the door. 'We shouldn't be in here. How did you get the key?'

'I went to Nathan's house to find out if there was any news of him. I saw the key on a shelf and guessed what it was. It was too big for any lock in that cottage. Nathan's mother must have taken it home with her for safe-keeping when she dismissed Jacob's servants after his death. I suppose the house would come to Nathan, in due course, unless Jacob bequeathed it to another relative.'

'So Nathan's mother knows you are here.' Judith felt more comfortable knowing that.

Aaron looked wretched. 'I took . . . borrowed the key when she was out of the room. No, wait, please, Judith,' he pleaded. 'Rumours are beginning to spread that the corpse was a monk. I even heard someone say he was a wealthy abbot. If the justices believe that, they won't rest until his killer is caught. I have to get out of England. But I need money to buy a passage.

'I can't go to my father. He always puts his principles before anything, even his own son. He'd hand me over to the bailiff himself. I was sure Jacob would have something valuable in the house. I persuaded myself that Jacob didn't need it any more and Nathan had run off with Eleanor. Who knows if he would ever come back to claim his inheritance? I wasn't going to take much, just a few coins or something I could sell. But I couldn't find anything small enough to carry. Nathan's mother probably took anything of value to her own house in case of thieves breaking in.'

'And it seems she was right to do so,' Judith said pointedly, but Aaron ignored her.

'Then I remembered once, when I was a child, I was playing here with Nathan and your brother and Benedict. Old Jacob was out and Nathan showed us the place where his grandfather hid his most treasured books. I thought there might still be something in the old hiding place.'

'And was there?' Judith asked.

Aaron nodded. Without saying anything more, he led the way behind the partition. Here a large bed, draped with hangings against the cold, occupied most of the centre of the room. Aaron went to the far wall and paused in front of the wooden wainscoting. Taking a deep breath, he ran his hands over the panelling until he found what he was searching for, then lifted the section away. There, set into the stone wall, was a long, low recess lined with wood, an ideal place in which to conceal books or anything else of value.

And it was filled with something covered in sacking, but from her position at the end of the bed Judith couldn't make out what it was. She was aware only of a terrible stench filling the room. Her guts had turned to iced water, but she forced herself to move closer and then stifled a scream as she caught sight of what was lolling out of the top of the sack. The face was blackened now where the blood had congealed, the skin was beginning to peel, but for all that there was no mistaking that the body in the hidden recess was that of Jacob's grandson, Nathan.

Judith didn't know how long she stood there staring at that nightmare vision, but then cold fear pushed her into action. She'd been right all along. Aaron had killed Nathan and now he was going to do the same to her. That's why he had lured her to an empty house. She ran back through the hall towards the stairs and clattered down them, slipping on the final steps in her haste and having to grasp the rail with both hands to stop herself crashing backwards on to the stone. She flew at the door, twisting the great iron handle, but the door wouldn't budge. She could hear Aaron pounding down the steps behind her and she turned, trying to make for the door to the lower chamber, but at that moment Aaron reached the bottom of the stairs and stood barring her way.

He held out his hands. Terrified, she backed away. A look of bewilderment crossed his face.

'I'm sorry, Judith. I should have warned you instead of showing you, but I didn't know how to say it. I thought you wouldn't believe me unless you saw for yourself. Judith, you're the only one I can trust now. I must leave today, before the city gates close. I'd take you with me if I thought you wouldn't be in even greater danger if they come after me, but I couldn't leave you here with them without warning you.'

'You think I'd go with you, a *murderer*?' Judith screamed at him.

'I told you I didn't mean to kill the friar.'

'Nathan! I'm talking about poor Nathan lying up there. What did you do, go back and strangle him after you'd finished butchering the friar?'

Aaron sank down on to the bottom step. 'Is that what you think, that I killed Nathan? Judith, I swear that Nathan was alive when I left him, and I did not go back. I thought . . . I really thought he'd run off with that girl, until this afternoon when I removed that panel and found him there. I swear to you on my life, I did not kill him.'

'Who else could have done it? Who else could have put him there?' Judith raged at him.

Aaron covered his face with his hands and moaned. 'I wish for your sake I had killed him, Judith, because the alternative . . .' He raised his anguished eyes and looked at her. 'Only five people knew of the existence of that recess. Jacob, Nathan and the three little boys Nathan was playing with that day. There was no one else Nathan would ever have shared the secret with except me, Isaac and Benedict. I know I didn't kill Nathan, so that leaves only two others who could have done so and hidden his body here – your brother or your future husband.'

Judith sat shivering in her room. It was growing dark, but she hadn't bothered to stoke up the fire or prepare supper. She couldn't seem to think how to carry out even the simplest of tasks which she had been performing since she was a child.

Aaron had left Norwich. She had given him the small silver amulet in the shape of a hand that she wore around her neck. She didn't suppose it would fetch much, but it was all she had, and Aaron had been grateful. Her mother had given her the amulet the day she and Judith's father had fled before the trial. Judith remembered the fierce hugs. How she'd clung to her parents, desperate for them to stay, but urging them to go, scared that if they didn't leave at once it would be too late. She'd felt that same fear again that afternoon when she hugged Aaron and pleaded with him to go quickly. His last words to her had been, 'Take care of yourself.' Her mother's last words had been addressed not to her but to Isaac. 'Look after your little sister, Isaac. You must be father and brother to her now.'

Was it true that her own brother had killed their best friend? She could not, she would not believe that, but if it wasn't Isaac, then the man she loved even more than her brother, the man she had pledged her life to, must be the murderer. And that was equally unthinkable.

She tried to reason it out. Why had Isaac been so desperate to convince her she had imagined the corpse? Was he the shadow she'd seen under the apple tree? He could have waited until she left and then moved the body while she was searching for him. Not to Jacob's house – there wouldn't have been time – but he could have dragged the corpse from the chamber into the synagogue and moved it to Jacob's house later that night. But why would he want to kill poor harmless Nathan?

She tried to visualize the room as she'd seen it that day, but all she could remember clearly was how it had looked this morning. The jumbled parchments and books piled up hastily as if someone had been impatient to get on with another task – those lists of words!

She reached into her scrip and pulled out the sheaf of parchments. Lighting a candle from the embers of the fire, Judith examined them again. *Temple, burned offering, consume.* Some of the words had been crossed out and different words written over the top. But the random letters alongside the words made no sense at all. Then, with a sudden flash, it came to her. Hebrew letters were also numbers. The letter *Dalet* was the number 4 and the letter *Resh* was the number 200. Every word on the list had a number beside it, and that number was the combined value of the letters in that word. The letters written on that stone – *Hay, Shin* and *Mem* – each had a numeric value too. *Hay* was 5, *Shin* was 300, *Mem, 40;* that made a total of 345. Was that important?

Judith glanced up. It was dark outside now, and Isaac still hadn't returned. Something was wrong. She stuffed the parchments back into her scrip and, snatching up her cloak, hurriedly left the house. The streets were almost deserted, save for scavenging dogs. A couple of drunks reeled out from one of the taverns, holding each other up.

One of them called out to her, but Judith kept her arms tightly crossed over her chest to hide her white badge and hurried on. The synagogue and the study chamber were in darkness, and there was no sign of Isaac there. She prayed she'd find him at Benedict's lodging and turned to retrace her steps.

The wooden shutters on the apothecary's shop, like all the others in the street, had been dropped down, sealing off the shop entrance, but Judith slipped along the alley to the side of the shop and knocked tentatively on the narrow door. Silence. *Please be at home, Benedict, please.* After the third time of knocking, the door opened a crack and Benedict peered out.

'Is my brother here?' Judith asked.

Benedict stared at her distractedly as if he wasn't really taking in what she was saying.

'I have to talk to you. It's about Isaac. I'm worried he may be about to do something stupid, dangerous even. Benedict!'

He finally jerked out of his reverie and, with a worried frown, gestured for her to enter. Judith followed him through the storeroom, threading her way between barrels and great earthenware pots. Shelves were crowded with phials of green, brown and gold liquids, some opaque, some as transparent as the coloured glass in the windows of churches. Sacks of dried herbs lay in dusty corners and bunches of them hung from the beams, thickening the air with a potage of spicy scents. Roughly hewn tables were scattered with yellowing animal bones and black wizened roots like tiny shrivelled babies.

Benedict held aside a leather curtain that separated his own small chamber from the workroom. His bedding was rolled up in one corner, and a small table with two stools occupied another, but the rest of the room was taken up with piles of scrolls, sheaves of parchment and teetering stacks of books. Judith wondered where Benedict found space on the beaten-earth floor to lay out his thin palliasse when it came time to sleep.

He gestured to one of the stools but remained standing himself, hovering awkwardly in the doorway and wiping his grimy hands repeatedly on his sacking apron. Judith realized she had interrupted him grinding up some herbs for the shop.

'What's this about Isaac?' Benedict prompted. 'It must be serious for you to come here alone.' There was a reproving note in his tone. Though they were betrothed, tongues would flap if she was seen entering his room at night, and such things mattered to Benedict, Judith thought with sudden irritation. She tried to ignore his frown. She had to tell him about Nathan, but she was unsure how to begin. If he disapproved of her coming to his room alone, he would certainly not like the idea of her going off with another man to an empty house.

'Aaron has left Norwich, but before he left he told me he found the body of Nathan.'

Benedict stared at her in horror, then his legs seemed to give way and he crumpled against the door frame, pressing his fists to his eyes. Judith wanted to throw her arms around him and hold him, but she knew she had to keep talking or she'd never bring herself to tell him what she feared.

'Nathan's body was hidden in Jacob's house in a secret recess that only you, he and Isaac knew of. Aaron swore that he didn't put him there, so he reasoned it had to be either you or Isaac. And I've been thinking: when I told Isaac about the body, he ran straight to the study chamber, not the synagogue where I told him it was. Then he did everything he could to persuade me that I had imagined a body.'

Benedict thrust his hands palms out as if to push away the very suggestion. 'You can't believe your own brother is guilty of murder.'

'I don't want to believe it, but who else could have known about the hiding place? Isaac went to Nathan's house that very afternoon. He must have seen the key there and taken it, just as Aaron did, then slipped it back when he returned later to ask if Nathan had returned.'

'But why would he want to harm Nathan?' Benedict asked.

'I think he wanted the stone. Maybe he didn't know that the Black Friar had already taken it. There's something else.' Judith pulled the lists of words out of her pocket. 'Look, he has been practising gematria. I think he is trying to find words that add up to the same numeric value as the word on that stone.'

Benedict lunged forward and snatched the lists from her and examined them closely. 'How . . . how do you know about gematria or about the word on the stone?'

Judith shook her head impatiently. 'I overheard you all talking, but that's not important. What matters is what Isaac is going to do with these words.' She pointed to the lists.

Benedict took a deep breath and spoke without looking at her. 'On Erev Shavuoth we were trying to meditate. We had almost succeeded in raising a powerful spirit, one who has the knowledge of the future, at least that's what Aaron and your brother believed. But Nathan panicked and sent everything crashing to the floor before the spirit could materialize properly.'

'Did you see it?' Judith asked

Benedict shook his head. 'I felt something, a force. It was as if I was hollow and a great wind had roared through me, and for a moment I felt such . . . but I saw nothing.

There was nothing coming to our aid,' he added bitterly. 'Isaac wants to try again. But he is not as skilled in the art as Aaron. And it's dangerous to attempt these things alone. Your brother doesn't have the strength or knowledge to control what he might raise, and such a powerful spirit can take possession of you or even destroy you if you cannot master it.'

Judith leaped up. 'We have to stop him. But I can't find him. He didn't come home, and he's not in the study chamber.'

'I think he will try to raise the spirit somewhere in the heart of the Christians' world, so that it can destroy them. He will have used the words as a sign of where he should go.' Benedict rifled through the lists, then he pounced on one and held it up. 'This is the one. *Cup* – that is 170, *gold*, 14, *temple*, 65, *idol*, 148, *daybreak*, 508. They all add up to 905, the same number as the letters on the stone.'

Judith frowned. 'But the value of the letters in *HaShem* is only 345. I worked that out myself. Never mind how I know,' she added impatiently, seeing the astonishment on Benedict's face.

Still staring at her in disbelief as if she was a cock that had laid an egg, Benedict said slowly, 'Isaac was using the mystic numbers. If *Mem* is a final letter it has a greater value – 600, instead of 40.'

'But even if these words add up to 905, what do they mean?' Judith asked. '*Temple, cup, idol* and *gold* – that could be a church; they have statues, gold and chalices in the churches, but there are fifty or sixty churches in Norwich. We can't search them all.'

Benedict studied the words again. '*Daybreak.*' He shook his head. '*Cup* – that must be it,' he said finally. 'All churches have chalices, but the cup is the specific emblem of one of their saints, John the Evangelist. There is only one church in the city with that name, and it's in Conesford Street, not far from Jacob's house.'

'Then we must go there at once.'

'This is no task for a woman,' Benedict told her firmly. 'You shouldn't even know about the stone, much less the numbers. Alone, I can reason with Isaac quietly. If you're there, his pride might make him do something foolish. You go home and wait for us. I'll find him and bring him to you.'

As if to show that he would not be swayed on this, Benedict walked ahead of her out of the room, holding the lantern. Without really thinking what she was doing, Judith scooped up the pieces of parchment and followed him outside.

'You will find him?' she begged. 'Whatever evil he's done, he's still my brother and I love him. He can't have meant to kill Nathan. He must be ill or maybe whatever was conjured in the room that night . . .'

Benedict squeezed her shoulder. 'Go home. I have to hurry!'

Judith crossed to the casement for the hundredth time that night, but there was still no sign of Isaac and Benedict. The curfew bell had long since sounded, signalling that all house fires must be damped down for the night and made safe, but still her brother had not returned.

Suppose Benedict had been too late or had gone to the wrong place? Could *cup* mean something else? But she couldn't think what else it could mean. Frantically, Judith pored over the lists again. If only Aaron was here – he was more skilled in the art of the mysteries than any of them. She wondered where he was sleeping tonight. She prayed he was safe and the silver hand amulet would protect him; if only Isaac had such protection.

She began adding the words again, looking at each list in turn. None of the other lists added up to 905. Then finally she saw it: there was a second list that added up to that number. She'd almost missed it because of the repeated crossings-out. Two words on this other list were the same as the first, *gold* and *daybreak*, but the others were different. *To cross, or pass over*: the number 272 had been written beside this; and next *burned offering*: against that had been written 111.

To pass over, to cross: what did you pass over? A river, a bridge. You crossed over a river using a bridge. But which bridge? Coslany, Blackfriars, Fye, Whitefriars, Bishop's Bridge? They were scattered right across Norwich. She stared at the other words, *gold, burned offering, daybreak*. These weren't the names of any of the bridges. A bridge of gold? None of the bridges was made of anything but wood and stone, though some said the Bishop's Bridge was paved with gold, given the money he gathered in tolls from those entering the city. That had to be the answer! Bishop's Bridge was the only one of the bridges that formed an entrance to Norwich. And the tolls from this entrance went not to the city but straight to the bishop's coffers. That's what Isaac would want to destroy, not some little church. Benedict had gone to the wrong place.

Judith snatched up her cloak and a lantern and rushed out into the streets. Most of the houses were in darkness, though here and there a pinprick of light shone between the cracks of the shutters. The alehouses had long since emptied, and the brothels were silent. Norwich was sleeping. A mist was creeping up from the river and ditches, rubbing and curling around the houses. There was a squeal behind her and Judith whirled around, but her lantern caught only the great green eyes of a cat with a mouse dangling from its mouth. The cat glared at her before bounding lightly over a wall and disappearing.

Fog hung over the river like a white prayer shawl. Judith could hear the water rushing below her, but she couldn't see more than an arm's length in front of her. She crept as quietly as she could across the bridge, clinging on to the side to guide her way in the mist. Below her was nothing but swirling whiteness, as if the stones were floating on clouds. The bridge had never seemed as long as it did now. She hadn't thought the river so wide.

Judith stopped with a gasp. She had almost walked straight into the wooden hurdles on the far side. Two of the bishop's soldiers lay with their backs to her on the other side of the hurdles, their task to see that no one entered or left by that bridge until after prime in the morning when the tollbooth was open for business. She could hear the men snoring, confident in the knowledge that no one could drag those hurdles aside without waking them.

Judith backed away as quietly as she could. She had been so sure that Isaac would be here. How could she have been so arrogant as to think she had worked out what Benedict could not? He had already shown her to be wrong once that evening over the number. There was nothing for it but to return home and wait, as he had instructed her.

Then, as she had almost reached the city end of the bridge, she heard a scraping as if something heavy was being dragged over stones. She stopped and listened hard. For a moment or two she could hear nothing more over the sound of the rushing river, then she heard the noise again. It was coming from beneath her feet. It was probably just a piece of driftwood being ground against the pillars of the bridge by the force of the river. All the same, suppose Isaac was under the bridge, not on it.

Where the bridge joined the road on the city side, Judith left her lantern hanging on a tree and scrambled down the bank, sliding on her bottom until her foot encountered solid ground. Pressed against the wall, she edged forward gingerly. The mist billowed in waves, curling away, then closing in again. She thought that she could see a thin strip of flickering yellow light and someone or something moving. But each time her eyes fastened on the shape, the mist would obliterate it again. She edged forward, afraid that she would walk straight into the river, but just at that moment the white fog parted.

Hard against the bridge, a small wooden jetty projected out from the bank into deeper water to enable the boats to unload their cargoes when the river was low. Someone was standing on that jetty muttering to himself in a slow rhythmic chant, as if he was breathing every syllable. *Ha-Sh-em. Ha-Sh-em.*

'Isaac, no, don't. Please don't try to conjure it,' Judith whispered, trying to make him hear without her voice carrying to the two guards at the far end of the bridge.

Startled, the man whipped around, but it was not Isaac's face she saw staring at her in alarm, but Benedict's. His hands were trembling.

'Go home, Judith. You shouldn't be here. This is too dangerous. I don't want you to get caught.'

'But what are you doing here? I thought you were looking for Isaac at the church.'

Benedict sighed. 'I couldn't tell you, because I wanted to keep you safe. Isaac doesn't have the stone. I do. It was me who wrote those lists of words. Aaron was right: we have to stand up for ourselves. We have to show them that we can fight back. The Eternal One is supposed to defend the innocent, but where was He the day they hanged my father in front of a jeering crowd? I learned something that day. Heaven will not send down fire to slay our enemies or part the water to save us unless we first do something for ourselves. We must fight for our own survival. If we fight, He will give us victory, but if we simply sit there praying and wailing, He will not hear us.'

'So you mean to conjure up a spirit to destroy your father's murderers?' Judith asked.

He shook his head impatiently. 'I am no more skilled than Isaac, as I told you. Even if I did possess Aaron's ability to call up a spirit, what good would it be if I couldn't control it? The stone was a sign, a sign that we had to rise up and take matters into our own hands. *HaShem, The Name*, the title the Eternal One used of Himself when He delivered us from slavery in Egypt. Our people had to force the pharaoh to let them go. They had to start walking before the Red Sea parted. Now we must do the same. The stone has told me what to do; there can be no mistake – *the crossing of gold, the burned offering.* It is so clear, Judith.' Benedict's eyes glittered in the lanternlight.

As he moved, Judith noticed three small barrels behind him on the jetty, stacked against the arch of the bridge. Benedict pulled the wooden bung out of one of the barrels. A thin stream of black powder began to trickle out across the wooden jetty under the bridge. It looked like the same powder that Judith had seen him dusting from his hands that afternoon.

'What is that?' Judith asked fearfully. 'Is it a dried herb?'

'It's a mixture of substances; a little charcoal and sulphur, but mainly saltpetre, scraped from the walls of cellars. My father taught me to make it to treat running sores and cankers of the skin. Alchemists say it's an elixir of life and will remove corruption from metals. But a few weeks ago I discovered in a book a list of recipes for making different kinds of fire. It was written that if the correct proportions are mixed, when a flame is touched to it, it will burn more fiercely than a blacksmith's fire. And more than that: for the fire ignites so suddenly and with such force that it can bring walls crashing down. They say it is like a mighty thunderclap and flash of lightning together.'

For a moment Judith couldn't grasp what he was saying; such a thing sounded impossible. Then she looked again at the three barrels stacked against the pillar of the bridge.

'You mean to start such a terrible fire now, don't you, and cause this bridge to tumble into the river?'

'Yes, yes! Imagine it. Oh, they will rebuild it in time, but it will take a very long time, and think of the money the Church will lose. Think of the terror they will be in, knowing that we have such power. They will not dare lift their hands against us again, for this weapon will strike such fear into them, just as did the plagues of Egypt. And I want to hurt them, Judith, hurt them in the only way they will understand. Make them pay for what they did to my father and the others. All these years they have been bleeding us dry. Now they will know what it feels like to have what they value torn from them.'

'And do you mean to smite the firstborn, too?' Judith said furiously. 'What of the innocent men, women and children crossing the bridge when you unleash this plague on them? Do you intend to drown them in the river like the pharaoh's soldiers?'

Benedict looked shocked. 'No. You know I would never kill anyone. The sign was clear – *daybreak, dawn*. The fire will be lit as the first rays of the sun light up the sky, long before the bridge is open. No one will die, I swear to you.'

'But *we* will die, Benedict. Do you think they will allow you or me or any of us to live if they discover we possess such power and pose such a threat? There will be such an outcry in this land that the Christians will not rest until every Jew in England is burning. And what then, Benedict? What if they let you live to watch me burn on a bonfire and our neighbours and our friends, the old women and little children, too? If they let you live to witness that, how will you take revenge then for those innocent lives?

'Your father went to the gallows still believing in justice; would he have wanted you to take revenge? Old Jacob gave all he had for a stone that he thought would bring peace and hope to all of us. He would be appalled at the thought of you using this stone to bring more destruction and misery.' She abruptly halted in her tirade as an even more terrible thought flashed into her head. 'The stone . . . If Isaac doesn't have it and you do, then you must be the one who killed Nathan for it.'

Benedict threw his arms over his head. 'Judith, how could you think that of me?'

'You are standing there threatening to bring a bridge crashing into the river, and you ask me how I could think that you were a murderer. What else should I think?'

'But I didn't kill him! I discovered Nathan's body in the chamber, but I heard someone in the synagogue, so I slipped away and hid. Then I saw you enter the chamber and come running out. Like you, I assumed Aaron had killed Nathan for the stone. You know how hot-tempered he is, and he was convinced he was meant to interpret the letters. I knew that if the authorities learned of a body in the synagogue they'd start arresting Jews for the murder. They didn't bother for Jacob, because they guessed his killer was a Christian, but if they thought they could pin a murder on a Jew they wouldn't hesitate to hang half the synagogue and claim we'd all had a hand in it, so that the Crown could claim all our property, just like they did when they hanged my father. I hid the body, Judith, to protect Aaron and the rest of us, but I am no murderer.'

'And that's why you'll never have the guts to go through with this,' a voice behind them sneered.

Judith spun around. A tall, muscular woman was leaning against the wall of the bridge, her arms folded over her pendulous breasts as if she was trying to keep them from straying.

'He's right, lady. He didn't kill your friend; I did. My boys had been keeping a watch on this Nathan, but I told them to fetch me when they were sure he was alone. They'd already lost the stone once when they gave that old Jew a hammering, so I wasn't going to trust them again. If you want something done properly, you need a woman to do it.

'But young Nathan insisted he didn't have the stone, even when I half throttled him with a piece of cord, so I finished the job and searched the room. As it turns out, the stinking piece of worm-meat was telling the truth; it wasn't there. But I figured that if I left the body in the room, the stone would come to me. Your lover there knows what would have happened right enough. They'd have rounded up every Jew in Norwich and thrown them in the castle keep until they could decide how many to hang. The stone had to be in one of your houses, so all I had to do was wait, then send my lads round to search while you lot were rattling your chains and begging for mercy. But you had to go and move the little runt's body, didn't you? Still, no matter.'

Magote suddenly unclasped her arms and, too late, Judith saw the flash of metal. With the agility of a cat, Magote sprang forward and in one practised movement had grabbed Judith's arm and spun her around to face Benedict, twisting the arm behind her back. Judith felt the point of a dagger pressing up between her ribs.

'Now, lad, you give me that stone and I might just be persuaded to let your little sweeting live.'

'I'll . . . I'll give it to you. Wait. Don't hurt her, I beg of you,' Benedict pleaded.

With shaking hands he struggled to pull the heavy stone from his scrip. After what seemed to Judith like a lifetime, he finally placed it on the wooden jetty next to his lantern so that it was in plain sight.

Holding Judith tightly in front of her, Magote pressed back against the wall. 'Now, my pretty lad, you walk past me nice and slow and climb up the bank. When I have the stone safe I'll let her come to you. But you try and make a grab for her and this dagger will be in her body up to the hilt afore you can bless yourself.'

Benedict edged past Judith, his face a mask of fear. Judith heard him trying to scramble up the wet grass, slipping and sliding in a frantic attempt to carry out the woman's instructions to the letter.

'You're coming with me, my sweeting,' Magote hissed in Judith's ear, 'just in case your lover there changes his mind and tries something.'

She slid the dagger around to Judith's back and, using it as a goad, forced Judith to walk forward on to the slippery boards of the jetty. Without warning, Magote grabbed Judith's shoulder and pulled her violently sideways. Judith's feet slid from under her and she crashed into the river. She didn't have time to take a breath before the icy water closed over her head, as her heavy skirts pulled her down and down into the blackness.

Free of Judith, Magote reached out for the stone, but she moved too quickly and slipped on the slimy boards. The edge of her gown caught the lantern and sent it crashing over. The candle rolled out on to a thin line of black powder, which instantly flared up like a rearing snake. Magote stared at it. She'd never seen the like of it before. The flame raced along the trail of powder and seemed to leap into the hole in the barrel. For a moment nothing happened, then there was a bang. Magote, screaming in agony, tottered backwards clutching at her face. Her gown, soaked in grease from the fat of the many meals she had cooked at the inn, blazed up like a tallow candle. For a few moments she teetered blindly on the edge of the jetty, flames leaping up around her head, before she toppled over into the river with a great splash and hiss.

It was the woman's screams more than the dull bang that woke the guards, for the black powder was too damp and loosely packed to create a loud explosion and the bridge didn't even tremble. By the time the guards got to their feet there was nothing to be heard but the sound of rushing water. They searched the length of the bridge but, finding nothing amiss, concluded that their duty was done and, yawning, returned to their posts and their dreams.

Benedict had slid back down the bank as soon as he heard the bang and the cries. But both women had vanished. Only a small blaze on the wooden jetty under the bridge marked what had happened. He knelt by the water's edge, frantically calling Judith's name, but there was no sound save for the gurgling of the oily black water.

With tears blinding his eyes, he desperately ranged up and down the bank, trying to peer through the mist for any sign of life. Then he heard something. At first he thought the sound was merely an echo of his own sobs, but as he held his breath he heard his own name. The sound seemed to be coming from under the arch in the middle of the river. But there was no means of getting to the place by land.

'Judith! Judith, wait, I'm coming.'

Benedict stripped off his cloak and climbed down off the jetty, shuddering as the icy water crept up his body, and struck out to where he thought he had heard her calling. The noise of his own splashing and the water crashing against the stones drowned out any cries. The mist swirled above the water. He twisted and turned this way and that, trying to find her. Then he spotted something pale against the dark water. An arm, a single arm stretched out above the river, clinging to an iron mooring ring embedded in the stones of the bridge. Even as he struggled against the current to reach her, he could see her fingers slipping from the ring.

'Please hold her up,' he prayed desperately.

He must have said the words aloud, for Judith stirred at the sound, reaching out to him with her other hand. He swam towards her, but, as he had almost reached her, Judith's fingers slid from the iron ring and she sank without a struggle beneath the rushing black water.

Desperately, Benedict pushed himself downwards, groping around until his fingers closed on some cloth. With a great heave he lifted Judith to the surface. He had enough strength only to reach out again for the iron ring and, with one arm locked tightly through it, he pulled her head on to his shoulder. Her eyes were closed and her skin was frog-cold.

Benedict pressed his face against hers, holding her tightly against his body, his eyes stinging with water and tears. He cursed himself and prayed in equal measure, begging, almost screaming for a miracle. Then he heard a cough and a gasp, her head moved slightly beneath his chin and, looking down, he saw her eyelids fluttering. Judith, his beloved Judith, was alive.

Wednesday 29 May, the eleventh day of Sivan

Just after dawn, fishermen pulled Benedict and Judith from the water. The men assumed that the couple had stumbled into the river in the fog, and Benedict did not disabuse them. The fire on the jetty had long since burned itself out, and those who noticed the scorch marks assumed that boys had wantonly lit the fire from mischief or to cook a supper of fish. They grumbled that young lads these days were out of control; they had no respect for property or their elders. And with Magote dead, there was no one to contradict them.

As Benedict helped Judith up the street to her home, Isaac came running out of the house towards them. He swept his sister up in his arms and carried her inside, almost sobbing with relief that she was unharmed. He seemed to have aged ten years overnight.

Isaac told them that the previous evening he had gone to the inn owned by Eleanor's father. It had occurred to him that if he could discover that Eleanor was also missing, it would confirm his suspicions that Nathan had indeed run off with her and then he would be able to put Judith's fears to rest.

Isaac had hung around the inn until late that night trying to pick up any gossip about the girl, for if Eleanor had vanished it would be dangerous for him to be heard asking questions about her. But he'd discovered nothing. Then, just as the inn was closing, Isaac glimpsed Eleanor in the yard throwing out the slops and he knew that wherever Nathan was, he was not with her.

With a heavy heart, Isaac had returned home, only to find his own house empty and no sign of Judith. Fearing that she, too, had been attacked like Jacob and was lying hurt somewhere or worse, he had spent the rest of the night frantically searching the streets for her, though it had never occurred to him to look under a bridge.

Judith and Benedict could delay the tragic news no longer. When they finally told him that Nathan's body had been found, Isaac tore his shirt and cried like a little child in his sister's arms.

That same afternoon Benedict returned to the bridge, as soon as he had assured himself that Judith was resting safely, being cosseted by her brother and an endless stream of neighbours bringing nourishing possets and potages to her bedside.

Just before he left her, Judith seized his hand and whispered, 'Remember the vow you made in the water last night. You must keep it now, you know.'

'I thought you couldn't hear me,' Benedict said in astonishment, blushing furiously as he recalled just what he had been murmuring through that long hour until dawn.

'A woman can always hear what she wants to.' Judith managed a tired little smile. 'I love you, Benedict. Though goodness knows why, for you are the most irritating, stubborn, obstinate, foolhardy muttonhead I've ever known, save for my own brother. And no other woman would put up with you, so I suppose I must, for you need someone to keep you from your own folly.'

Benedict humbly acknowledged the truth of that with a wry smile and quickly slipped away before she could think any more of his faults to add to her list.

The miraculous stone still lay on the jetty among the charred remains of the barrels. Even if anyone had noticed the dark stone in the shadow of the bridge, no one would have troubled to take such a commonplace thing. What value would it have had to anyone?

Benedict took the stone straight to the home of Rabbi Elias and placed it on the table in front of him.

'This is what Jacob went to Exeter to fetch.'

Rabbi Elias lifted it up, his face registering surprise as he felt the weight of it. He turned it over in his hand.

'So Jacob sells everything he values for something that looks like a child's carving of a bird or maybe he thought it was a boat. But . . .' A smile of wonderment spread over the rabbi's face. 'There is a great sense of peace in this stone, a sweetness, like the moment when the world stops and we pause to light the Shabbat candles.'

'Perhaps in the right hands, rabbi, but mine are not the right hands,' Benedict said, shuddering, as once more he was overcome by shame at the thought of how close he had come to killing the one person in the world that he truly loved with all his soul.

'There are letters on the stone, rabbi, if you examine it closely.'

Rabbi Elias nodded. 'I dare say, but I think sometimes it is better not to examine things too closely. Let us be content with saying it is nothing more than a bird or a boat; after all, it was an ark and a dove that brought us hope once, and it was enough then. May it be so again.'

'Amen,' Benedict breathed. He grinned bashfully, remembering what Judith had said about holding him to his vow. 'One thing more, rabbi. I would like to marry Judith just as soon as it can be arranged.'

The rabbi's mouth's split in a broad grin. 'It's about time. You've waited far too long,' he said, slapping

Benedict firmly on the back. 'And after a wedding night, we hope, comes the blessing of a new generation. What better memorial to your poor father than that he should have grandchildren and great grandchildren to carry on his name.'

Benedict smiled. For the first time since his father had died he felt at peace. The bitterness and hatred which had festered in him for so many months seemed to have drained away in that river and been carried far out to sea. Benedict reached out to touch the stone one last time. Maybe old Jacob had been right and there *was* something in that stone which could save a man, even if that man didn't know he needed saving.

Downriver a group of small urchins, wandering home after a day of fishing and mischief-making, saw something stranded in the mud among the reeds. The creature was lying face down, naked above the waist. Its back was blistered so that it almost looked as if it had scales. The hair was burned away, leaving livid red patches on the skin of the head. The boys cautiously prodded it with long sticks, but it didn't move. Each dared the other to turn the creature over, and finally one plucked up the courage to do so. There was no mistaking that this monster was a female, for though her breasts were as burned as her back, they were massive enough for there to be no mistake. But a female what? The swollen, charred face, covered with cuts and tiny fragments of wood, did not resemble anything human.

The bravest of the boys went closer and poked the creature again, giggling and showing off to his friends. But the laughter changed to a shriek of terror as a hand shot out and seized his ankle with a grip as strong as an iron manacle. He fell over, yelling and struggling as the monster dragged him towards her across the mud. His companions seized their playmate's arms and pulled with all their strength, until the creature's fingers slipped from the boy's muddy leg.

The urchins took to their heels and ran to their parents, yelling that they had just seen a hideous mermaid who'd tried to drag them into the water and drown them, for hadn't their mothers told them often enough that it was just what these evil river monsters do. But none of the adults came to look, for only last week the same boys had sworn they'd seen a serpent as big as a tree trunk slithering through the marshes.

And later, when the boys crept back, like brave knights, to slaughter the monstrous mermaid with their sticks and borrowed axes, they found that, like the giant serpent, the creature had vanished; which, though they'd never admit it, was a great relief to them all, for none of them would really have been brave enough to strike the first blow.

Historical note

The incidents in this story concerning the sacred stone are, of course, fictional, but the hanging of Benedict's father and the exile of Judith's parents are based on a recorded incident. In 1234 thirteen Norwich Jews were accused of having unlawfully circumcised a five-year-old Christian child, Odard, in 1231. The first trial before the religious authorities in Norwich found all guilty except one, and twelve were sent to stand trial before the King and Archbishop. The Jews paid a gold mark to the King to have the boy publicly examined to prove he had not been circumcised, which suggests that they had not been involved. However, the child was found to be circumcised.

In around 1237 the accused paid two hundred pounds for a trial and a further fifty marks for bail. But they were not brought to trial until 1240, when they paid another twenty pounds to be brought before a mixed jury of Jews and Christians. Having taken the money, the King then instructed the justices that Jews could not sit on the jury, since a mixed jury would fail to agree. At least three of the Jews were hanged and one died in prison awaiting trial. Another eleven were listed as fugitives from justice, having fled before the trial. Clearly, more Jews were convicted than had originally been charged in 1234.

It has been suggested that Odard was the son of a Jewish convert to Christianity, and one possible explanation for this bizarre incident might be that his parents may have been crypto-Jews who had converted under duress or to improve their circumstances but were still practising their Jewish faith in secret. It was common for 'hidden Jews' to circumcise their children. However, if a Gentile had noticed that the child was circumcised and threatened to report the matter to the Church, the father might well have claimed that the boy had been abducted and circumcised without his consent in order to save his own life and that of his family.

Gunpowder had been used for many years in China, both in fireworks for entertainment and as a deadly weapon in battle. Although gunpowder was not employed in European warfare until the fourteenth century, it was in use by the twelfth century in the West as a medicine and as a purifier in alchemy. In the first half of the thirteenth century a number of books came into circulation in Europe giving recipes for creating different kinds of fire and small explosions using 'black powder'. In the early days black powder was not a reliable explosive. Saltpetre, which has to be dissolved in water then crystallized out, was often contaminated with impurities. Other factors such as the powder being packed too tightly or loosely or getting damp often resulted in the powder producing only a small bang like a firework, which would cause great injury to anyone standing immediately next to it but was not sufficient to damage buildings or anyone standing a few feet away.

ACT FOUR

Westminster, 1272

His Majesty King Henry of Winchester, the third monarch of England to bear that name, was dying. At his bedside in the Palace of Westminster sat a grizzled man shabbily dressed in a worn black robe that had seen better days. His unruly tangle of tight grey locks spilled out from under his round cap, a university master's pileum. The room was silent, save for the ragged breathing of the King. The atmosphere was oppressive, weighed down with the heavy odours of one near to death. The King's own wavering voice broke the silence.

'But who killed him?'

'Work it out for yourself.'

The master's bedside manner was not of the best, and he spoke before recalling whom he was addressing. To soften his tones, he leaned forward to tidy the embroidered cushions that had slipped out from behind Henry's back. He studiously ignored the sharp intake of breath that his abrupt response had drawn from the only other occupant of the room. Sir Thomas Dalyson, the King's chamberlain and most obsequious courtier, would not have dared to speak to the King of England so. He had expressed his disapproval but remained standing, half hidden in the long shadows cast by the Burgundian drapes that hung across the window arch. The bright and sparkling sun was not to be allowed to spoil the funereal atmosphere of the death room.

The master leaned forward and whispered something in the aged King's ear. It brought forth a rasping wheeze of laughter that angered Dalyson. What was this upstart tutor saying about him? This William Falconer – so-called detector of murderers, regent master at Oxford, and now the King's favoured pet? Dalyson suddenly became aware that Falconer had turned his penetrating blue eyes on the chamberlain.

'The King requests we speak alone.'

There was a moment when the two men's gaze locked like two rutting stags then, pale with rage, Sir Thomas left the room. The master turned back to the feeble man on the bed, who was fighting for each breath in his reluctance to give up his temporal realm.

'Now remember my guiding rule of deductive logic – the syllogism. Two lesser truths, when brought together, can reveal the greater truth being sought.'

Henry was still vexed as he struggled in vain to find a starting point. Falconer began to speak, but the King imperiously waved a skeletal hand to stay him.

'If only I had the sky-stone. I felt clear-headed when I touched it.'

Falconer sighed, wishing he could please the King in his desire. After all, being King gave him the right to be waited on as he pleased. It was 1272, and he had been King of England for well nigh fifty-six years. Falconer knew that, while Henry had had the stone in his grasp, he had felt safe from the angel of death. Some animation had returned to his flaccid face, and a sparkle to his formerly dull, cloudy eyes. Now the King was despondent, and his right eyelid, which had hung down over the orb beneath it all his life, fluttered but briefly. Falconer was reminded that many said Henry at his peak was the one designated by the prophet Merlin. He spoke of a King likened to the lynx – penetrating everything with his eye. That was no longer so. The King's eyes were dimmer, and his voice also weaker since the stone had been stolen.

'I must try to think clearly.' He turned to look sternly at Falconer. 'What is that word you used?'

'Syllogism, Majesty.'

The word reminded Falconer of when all this started.

He was despairing of this new batch of students who had started at the university a little while ago. It was late October, and the faculty of arts schoolroom he rented was an icy box. A bare room at the best of times, it now had the semblance of a monastic cold store. He scanned the three rows of low benches on which sat his class. He could barely discern more than their noses peeping out from between felt hats rammed on greasy heads, and woollen comforters wrapped around throats. And what he could see of their faces was pinched and reddened. Young Paul Mithian sniffled, and a dewdrop fell from the end of his nose. Falconer had taught his elder brother, Peter, and now it was the youngster's turn to apply his mind to logic and rhetoric. Both were beggar students with no money, relying on the charitable chest of the university and working as slaves to the wealthier students. Somehow they survived – Falconer saw to that. But every subsequent class now seemed to Falconer to be dimmer than its predecessor. He wondered if he, not they, was the problem. Perhaps he had been teaching for too long.

He took a deep breath, pressing on regardless.

'Syllogism. A discourse in which, certain things having been supposed, something different from the things supposed results of necessity because these things are so.'

These words were Aristotle's own, even if a little obscure. He looked around the blank, uncomprehending faces and groaned audibly. He waved a weary hand.

'Go. Your brains are clearly as frozen as are my fingers. Go, and thaw them out.'

Enlivened by this early and unexpected release from their toils, the reluctant students rose noisily from their benches, scraping them across the stained wooden floor of the schoolroom. Cheerful again, they made for the door out on to the narrow lane that wound northwards behind St Mary's Church on the High Street. Falconer gave them a final task, however.

'We will move on at the next lecture, though. Begin reading "On Sophistical Refutations" .'

The general groan of horror from his students gave him cause to smile broadly. He followed the ragged band out of the icy schoolroom, and as they dispersed to their respective halls he made his way back to his own. Aristotle's Hall stood in Kibald Street – a long lane south of the great High Street. One end of the lane terminated at the town walls and the other at Grope Lane, which was lined with brothels. Falconer always felt he thereby held a satisfying middle position between the order of the civil authority and the chaos of the dark world of personal pleasures. A good place for scholarship to inhabit. He ducked through the low doorway in the hall's narrow frontage and into the dimness of the communal hall behind. Once up the rickety staircase, he would be back in his private solar on the upper floor of the building. Safe among his prized possessions, he was in his own special world. The tenement building was only rented by him from the prior of Oseney Abbey, the great religious endowment that towered up beyond the western edge of Oxford, and he covered his costs by taking in students at whatever rent they could afford. Some years had been better than others, some worse, but he had always survived. Teaching also gave him time and opportunity to pursue his private interests, including understanding the world around him. And solving murder cases.

He had discovered this latter interest almost by chance, when one of his students had become embroiled in the curious death of a serving girl. He had quickly discovered that applying Aristotelean deductive logic to the material relating to the case – and not a little intuition – had led to identifying the murderer. He had repeated the process in several other cases since, assisting the town constable, Peter Bullock, in bringing killers to justice. Much to his embarrassment, Bullock had dubbed him the Great Deductive.

Pushing open the door to his solar, he was pleased to find Saphira standing behind his work table. The table was as usual cluttered with a myriad objects, including broken stones that revealed patterns in their interiors, animal and human bones, pots and vials containing liquids and pastes that emanated a mixture of vile and intoxicating odours, and old scrolls and texts in ancient languages. She put down the small and malodorous jar she had been sniffing and smiled.

'There you are. I have a gift for you that will outdo all these marvels.'

She swept her right hand across the jumble on the table.

'Indeed. And where is this marvel?'

She brought her left hand from behind her back and opened her fingers. In her palm nestled a dark stone. It was nondescript and quite small. Unconvinced of its uniqueness, he asked Saphira where she had come by it. She smiled sweetly at him.

'It was hard come by, and expensive. Covele, the talis-man seller, was reluctant to sell, but for us Jews business is business.'

She liked to tease him over the Christian contempt for her race, though she knew he was a good friend to the Jews of Oxford. Saphira Le Veske was a Jew herself and a widow, who had run her husband's business since his death. Well, to be frank she had run it long before his death. He had become deeply immersed in the Kabbalah – much to her concern – and had ignored the family business, which was based in Bordeaux in France. She had taken over, and run it successfully, handling the lending and transfer of money as well as initiating the dealing in wine shipping as a side-line. When her husband had died, she had not missed him. But her son, Menahem, had run away at the same time. Her search for him had caused her to neglect the business and had brought her to England – first to Canterbury, and then to Oxford. A chance meeting with William Falconer had led to her finding her son. And to a close relationship with the regent master, despite his nominal celibacy. She explained what had brought about the ownership of the object.

'Actually, he sold it for a song, as it was too heavy to hang around anyone's neck like his usual amulets. His dupes prefer the little angel texts – kimiyeh – sealed in silver cases that they can wear to ward off evil humours and illnesses. He did say this stone had the same miracu-lous properties.'

Falconer looked at what Saphira still held in her hands. 'Heavy? That little thing?'

Saphira smiled and held the dark stone out for him to take.

He lifted it from her open palm. 'Oh! I see what you mean.'

The smooth stone was heavier than it should have been. He swept aside the clutter on his table, and set it down. Only as big as the palm of his hand, from one angle it resembled a ship with curving prows at both ends, a cabin amidships and a small keel below. But then, as he walked around the table, it changed and became in his eyes a gliding bird, its curved wings outstretched like a swallow's. The keel became the bird's head and the cabin its tail. But he thought he saw that because of his own burning obsession. Falconer was consumed with a desire to solve the mystery of flight and to soar like a bird himself. He had got as far as building kites that he tossed off the tallest tower in Oxford – at Oseney Abbey. But when they plunged to earth and smashed, he decided not to risk his own life to one of them just yet.

'Has it been worked by hand? Or is its shape natural?'

Saphira's question caused Falconer to look closer at the stone. He could see some markings on its surface. He got out his eye-lenses and put them on his nose. Falconer was short-sighted and had been astonished when, a few years ago, an artisan had offered him these ground-down glass lenses to see through. He had first held them up to his eyes on a simple V-shaped frame. But now he had made his own frame with side hooks that went over his ears. He peered through the lenses at the marks.

'Could these be Hebrew letters?'

He pointed them out to Saphira. Though he could read Hebrew himself, he wanted her confirmation. She leaned over the stone, her head close to his with a stray lock of red hair suddenly spilling out of her modest widow's snood. She paled a little at what she saw. When she spoke her voice betrayed an uncertain note.

'They may be. It looks like *HaShem*, meaning *The Name*. But Covele often paints signs on the stones he sells as talismans.'

She stood up, tucking the stray lock back in her snood. Falconer frowned, knowing the Jewish proscription on saying the name of God out loud.

'Yes, but this is not painted on. It looks as if it is ingrained in the stone. Where did Covele get this, anyway? Did he say?'

'From an old woman with a scarred face in Norwich. He remembers it clearly because, when he was in the town earlier this year, a sudden flash of lightning struck the main tower of the Christian church towards the north so hard that it sent stones flying in every direction. There was much gossip about what evil it might portend. So Covele left as soon as he could for fear of an attack on the Jews of the town. I believe the month was June. The old woman who sold it was happy to be rid of the stone because it carried with it stories of strange events – some of them not particularly welcome, though some had said it cured all evils. She had kept it for nearly forty years and said that no good had ever come of owning it. The old woman was so glad to be rid of it in the end that she sold it to Covele for next to nothing. I only bought it as a curiosity because I thought you might like to see if it contained those strange patterns inside it that you like to find in stones.'

Falconer tapped the dark stone with the metal hilt of a knife that lay on the table. It almost rang like a bell. 'I don't think this will shatter like those other stones. It sounds as if it is made of iron.'

Saphira took the knife and tapped it too. 'The story that came with it from Norwich was that it had fallen from the sky already shaped as it is. But isn't that just myth? It is not possible, surely?'

'Don't be so fast to pour scorn on the idea of sky-stones. Almost a hundred years ago Gervase of Canterbury wrote an account of five eyewitnesses who saw something odd where the moon stood in the sky. They spoke of a flaming torch, and fire, hot coals and sparks. Others have seen falling stars in the sky and even claimed to have found stones such as this. I can understand why the ancients venerated them.'

He pointed at the object now lying between them on his table. Suddenly, it seemed to both of them to have taken on a mysterious aura, which it formerly did not possess. Saphira felt a deep sense of foreboding and almost regretted bringing it to William's attention.

'Where is it?'

Sir Thomas winced at the petulant sound of the King's voice. He turned to face Henry, a fixed and obsequious smile on his face.

'Your Majesty?'

He feigned lack of knowledge of the matter to which Henry referred, when in reality he knew exactly what he meant. The King hobbled over to his chamberlain, leaning heavily on the stick he now needed to get about. He was sixty-five, but the years had not been kind to him. No longer robust, he surrounded himself with doctors and other quacks, who gave pronouncements on his every bowel movement. Which was not saying a great deal, as Henry, King of England, was constipated. He screwed up his face, and Sir Thomas was not sure whether it was in anger at being crossed or from trapped wind.

'The stone, damn you. The stone.'

'Sire, if I can draw you back to the matter in hand. We must pass judgement on these townspeople. They must be punished.'

Henry shook his head in frustration. It was true. He had journeyed all the way to Norwich because the mob had broken into the town's priory and burned the church to the ground. What the cause of the riot had been now seemed to be unclear in most people's minds, but the result had been unequivocal. Property had been destroyed and precious gold items stolen. The townsfolk of Norwich had to pay the price, and Henry would make sure they did. But he had not been in the town long when he had heard tales of a strange stone. Though its reputation for attracting evil had been revived by the lightning strike on the church, he had been drawn to it by the assertion that it could cure all ills. The information fitted well with other hints he had received from abroad about a magic sky-stone. The problem was, he had been here two weeks already, and he couldn't find the stone. He was tired of the whole business.

'That bolt of lightning foretold the truth, then. Evil in the form of a riot has followed in its footsteps. Who do we have in gaol right now?'

Dalyson fumbled among the papers that lay piled on his desk and extracted the relevant list. He made a quick calculation.

'Thirty-four men and one woman, sire. They came to plead their case and were held at your pleasure.'

'Then hang them all, and burn some, too. They will be the example for the others. You can extract monies from the rest to pay for their crime.'

Dalyson nodded and picked up his quill pen to note down the King's justice. But the King had not finished. Twisting the seal ring that adorned the finger of his right hand, he piped up petulantly.

'And find me the stone.'

Covele was furious. He had recently returned to Norwich in his usual guise of a travelling German Jew, with a *pileum cornutum* – a spiked straw hat – on his head, only to find that everyone was looking for the sky-stone. He had sold it to that red-headed woman in Oxford, knowing her lover was fond of curiosities. And he had made a tidy profit on it, too, bearing in mind it had then seemed worthless. Now it was said the King himself desired it. His luck seemed to have been cursed ever since crossing paths with Saphira Le Veske and William Falconer. For it now looked as though he needed to turn right around and walk all the way back to Oxford again, to find a way of wheedling the sky-stone out of those two. But first he needed to rest, and he sent out his son, Hak, to perform two errands. One was to let it be known that he had the sky-stone – a little lie, but one he would rectify soon enough. The other was to fetch some food from the widow living down the lane from his lodgings.

Stowing his satchelful of kimiyeh and painted stones in one corner of the bare room that he and Hak shared, Covele slumped down on the creaky pallet that was the only furnishing. He tossed his spiked hat on top of the satchel and lay back exhausted. It was not long before his eyes closed, and he drifted off to sleep. His dream of untold wealth, however, was soon disturbed by a creaking sound from outside his room. He sat up, guessing that Hak had returned with some provisions. But the boy was usually boisterous, and he realized that the sound had not been followed by Hak's normal clamour.

'Hak? Is that you? Stop playing tricks on your father, boy. Bring me the food.'

Covele fancied he heard a low sigh, but nothing more. He started to feel a prickle of fear running down his spine. Barefoot, he pattered over to the door, putting his ear to it.

'Hak?'

This time he did not call out, but only whispered his query. He didn't really want anyone to answer. Better that the person behind the door was only in his imagination. He lifted the latch slowly.

Hak had delayed his return to his father because he had hoped to see the King. He first passed the message about the sky-stone on to the old man, Elias, who groaned at discovering that what he sought was now a hundred miles away. The boy had told him his father would get it back within days. But the old man knew Covele could not afford a horse and would have to walk, a journey that would take at least three weeks. He cursed the old woman, Magote, who he was sure was responsible for the stone being stolen from him in the first place. Just his luck that the King should turn up wanting the stone.

'The King is here now and is seeking the stone in order to cure him of his ailments. If anyone gets to know that I had it and lost it, I will be in grave trouble. And I will make sure your father shares the punishment, too.'

He put his grey-haired head in his hands and moaned over his ill luck. Hak quietly retreated. Free of the old man's interrogations, he scurried out into the street. He was excited. The King was in Norwich! So instead of immediately going to fetch the food his father wanted, he dawdled around the close where the cathedral stood. He knew that rich folk stayed there when they visited the town. Maybe, if he waited long enough, he would get to see King Henry himself. However, he managed to hang around only long enough for one of the black-garbed priests who wandered in and out of the big church to take note of him. Finally, the man hurried over and tried to strike him across the face.

'Get away from here, Jew. Go back to your own kind.'

Hak expertly dodged the flailing hand and ran off towards the Jewish quarter. He had lingered as long as he dared anyway without incurring his father's wrath. On the way back, he collected a dish of warm potage from the widow woman who cooked for other Jews, exchanging it for the few coins his father had given him. She covered the dish with a greyish, thin cloth and adjured the boy to hurry home before the broth got cold. Hak carefully negotiated the muddy lane back to the tenement where he and his father lived. At one point he slipped silently down a side alley when he saw some roistering Christian boys coming his way. He knew if he was not careful they would jostle him, and the broth would be all over the ground. Fortunately, they had not spotted his evasive action and ran past the end of the dark alley laughing and shouting. Safe from their attentions, but once again delayed, Hak hurried the final distance to the crumbling house where he and his father had a room. It was easy to negotiate the front door, even with a dish in both hands. The door had not closed properly in years, and it hung half off its hinges. Hak slipped through the gap and made for the back of the house. Closest to the midden in the backyard, the room Covele rented was the cheapest of all.

'Father, I am back. I am sorry it took so long. I had to wait at the widow's for—'

The excuse died on his lips when he saw that the door to their room was ajar. His father never left the door open under any circumstances. Covele preached safety and circumspection to his son. They were, after all, Jews in a Christian world, with precious items worth much money. Hak nudged the door further open with his foot. It gave that familiar creak, which almost reassured him that all was well. But then he saw his father sprawled out on the bed they shared at night, blood leaking from his mouth. He gasped, and dropped the dish of stew on the dirty rush-strewn floor. The pottery bowl shattered, and the contents bled through the cloth that clung to the mess and oozed across the beaten earth. Covele's dull, staring eyes slowly focused on his son. Hak sighed.

'Father. I thought you were dead.'

Covele seemed unable to comprehend for a while what Hak was saying. Then he saw the mess on the floor. 'The food . . . You dropped the bowl.'

Hak wasn't sure if he was more scared at thinking his father dead or at finding him alive but not the same father. Covele's normally sharp tones were dulled, and he appeared uncertain of his surroundings. He helped his father sit up, wiping the blood from his lips. He saw now that a swelling was coming on his jaw. Someone had hit his father hard in the face.

'Who did this, Father? Who hit you?'

Covele ignored his questions, glancing fearfully around him, as though his attacker could be hiding somewhere in the bare, small room. His fear was so palpable that Hak, too, found himself looking around the chamber. It was a foolish act. There was nowhere anyone could hide. The boy tried to cheer his father up by asking about Oxford.

'When do we start out for Oxford again, Father? The sooner we get the sky-stone back, the better things will be for us.'

For the first time since Hak had entered the room and found his father sprawled on the bed, Covele's voice had a touch of its usual harshness to it.

'Forget the stone. I don't want to hear you mention it again.'

Puzzled at the sudden about turn in his father's attitude, Hak rose and knelt on the floor, trying to salvage what he could of the potage. He still didn't know what had gone on in his absence, but it had clearly frightened his father. From behind him, as if reading the boy's mind, Covele finally answered his questions about who had beaten him.

'It was the Elagabal.'

Falconer was fascinated by the sky-stone. It was late into the night, but he still burned a precious candle down in order to examine its properties. It certainly wasn't any ordinary stone, as he had already suspected. He was used to stones he could shatter with a mason's hammer and chisel. Some he could cut into shards that showed marks inside them; others broke into pretty crystal shapes. He had tentatively tapped the sky-stone, only to get the ringing note he had first heard hitting it with his dagger. Then he had hit it with as heavy a blow as he could, and still it refused to break. Now he was sliding a magnetized piece of iron towards it.

He was following instructions from a document that lay at his elbow. It was in his own hand, and he had copied it from a manuscript received by his old friend Roger Bacon only months ago. The original document had been drafted by a military engineer in the service of Charles of Anjou, King of Cyprus. The man was called Peter de Maricourt, and he had some interesting ideas about magnetism. Bacon, a Franciscan monk and experimental scientist, was so taken by the work of Peter that he called him *magister experimentorum* – the master of experiments – which from such a man as Bacon, devoted to practical science as he was, was praise indeed. Peter, sometimes called Peregrinus – the pilgrim – had shown that a piece of magnetite, or magnetized iron, had very particular properties, always aligning north–south. And when a magnet was broken in two, both pieces preserved the north and south polarities that were in the original piece. He believed these properties came from the celestial poles, and a magnetic needle should be able to guide a traveller on his journey by land or sea. Falconer could see that the idea had possibilities, but for the time being he was concentrating on the basic properties of a magnet.

He had placed a magnetized piece of iron some distance away from the sky-stone on the table surface. And when nothing happened, he had moved it closer. And closer. Eventually, he found the point at which the small piece of magnetic iron slid of its own accord over the table surface and clung to the sky-stone. There were definitely large quantities of iron in the stone. It amused Falconer to watch the affinity of the two items, and he repeated the experiment over and over again.

'Is that black magic, or what?'

'Hello, Peter. No, it's not magic, just the natural actions of the universe.'

Peter Bullock, the constable of Oxford, eased his old bones down on to one of the two chairs in Falconer's solar. He was feeling his age of late, and his bent back was aching more than usual. He had broken his night patrol at his friend's house, hoping for some distraction. He sighed over his friend's comments.

'I am too old to understand the universe, William. I leave that to God. And you, of course.'

Falconer laughed nervously. Only in each other's company could they safely utter such profanities. But Falconer, on more than one occasion, had been brought before the chancellor of the university for expressing heretical ideas in the hearing of his students. It was only his celebrity in the academic world, and his wily disputational skills, that had saved him to date. But it was mere months since he had been on trial for his life, and he still felt somewhat that his luck had been sorely tested to its limit. He put a finger to his lips.

'Perhaps we should not speak of God and myself in the same breath, Peter. And certainly not of black magic. Who knows what ears are pressed to the door?'

Bullock waved his hand dismissively. 'You are becoming too cautious, old friend. When you get to my age, you care not what people think. Or of the censure of some meddling priest.'

He pointed to the black, strangely shaped stone on the table.

'I still say that looks like magic to me.' He licked his lips. 'Do you think it could magic up some ale?'

Sir Thomas Dalyson was getting concerned. Not only had he failed to find the sky-stone that Henry so desired, but the King had now fallen gravely ill. Someone more mired in superstition might have linked the two and seen cause and effect in it. Dalyson was more phlegmatic. The court had left Norwich after Henry had pronounced his death sentences. He had also burdened the town with a fine of three thousand marks of silver to pay for the rebuilding of the church the citizenry had burned down. Dalyson suspected his intemperance had something to do with not finding the sky-stone he so desired. But they had only got as far as the abbey of St Edmund's when the King complained of pains in his left arm and a weakness in his limbs. The doctors had been summoned, and the arguments had begun. Master Roger Megrim had at first prevailed, partly because he had been educated at Cambridge. Having observed the sweating fever that racked the monarch's body, the conclusion Megrim reached was an excess of the sanguine temper. This induced a warm, wet nature, and could be remedied with bloodletting.

As the King lay on his bed, staring apprehensively at his little group of doctors, Megrim stepped forward with a small lancet in one hand and a bowl in the other. Henry mewled like a kitten. But he meekly allowed the physician to move his left arm and push up the sleeve of his nightgown, so that the inside of his elbow was revealed. Megrim plumped the flesh as if he were testing a fowl for succulence, then pressed the small blade into the royal skin. A bead of red blood appeared and began to trickle down Henry's forearm. Megrim placed the bowl below the flow and could not help but pontificate on his skills.

'Look how the blood flows. Food turns to blood in the liver, and flows along these vessels to the heart, where it percolates from left to right by means of heart spasms. I am using the phlebotomic method of revulsion – tapping the vessel at an extremity.'

Henry stared with evident revulsion at his life's blood flowing out of his body, and fainted.

It had then been several days before Henry had improved enough for him to travel back to Westminster. By the time he got there however, he had to take to his bed again. Once more the arguments raged between his physicians as to the cause of his malady. Dalyson didn't know what the uncertainty was. Henry was old, and he was dying. In the meantime, it fell on Sir Thomas to continue with the day-to-day business of managing the realm, a task he carried out with relish. Towards the end of October, he also had some news for Henry that he thought might rally the King.

As he entered the King's bedchamber, he observed the same group of quacks hovering in one corner of the chilly room. Master Roger Megrim stood inches taller than his fellow physicians, a stature that emphasized his precedence, at least in his own eyes. Megrim's height made it seem as though he had been stretched on the rack. His limbs were unusually long, his chest concave and his stomach protuberant. He hunched over to disguise his height, and his beak of a nose poked forward like a bird's bill. He was once again pontificating on the causes of his patient's illnesses.

Brother Mark, a Dominican monk of medium height and nondescript features, had adopted his usual pose of dark disdain and half turned away from the voluble Megrim. The third member of the group, however, was hanging on to Megrim's every word, or apparently so. Dalyson knew that John Rixe, short, fat and of a jolly aspect, fawned on whoever was in favour with Henry. He would as easily denigrate Megrim to the Dominican once out of the Cambridge master's hearing. And vice versa, when the opportunity arose. As a mere guild apothecary, Rixe depended on the approval of the educated clerics for his very existence. But that did not mean he would defer to them in private, except in so far as they would approve his pills and potions. The fourth person in the bedchamber was seated close by the King's bed. He was already something of a mystery to Sir Thomas.

Pierre de Montbrun, Bishop of Narbonne, had appeared at Westminster a few days before the ailing Henry had returned from his vengeful trip to Norwich. Wandering darkly around the palace until the King and his court returned, he had then refused to reveal his business to Dalyson, hinting that it was for the ears of the King only. It now seemed he had that ear exclusively. And Henry was engrossed in whatever it was that the foreign bishop was whispering. Dalyson sidled over towards the pair, hoping to hear what it might be that so interested the King. But as soon as his shadow was cast on the bed, the bishop stopped talking and turned to see who it was had disturbed him. Not for the first time, Dalyson almost reeled from the dark pools that were Narbonne's eyes. They were the darkest of dark brown – almost black – and held no reflection in them. Dalyson was not sure if the lack of a spark of light was due to their depth or if they were like those of a fish on a slab. The eyes of something dead. And now they held the courtier in their cold gaze.

Henry wheezed and expressed his irritation at the intervention of his chamberlain. 'What is it, Sir Thomas? Can you not see I am busy?'

Dalyson inclined his head in deference to the King's righteous annoyance. But his tone of voice still betrayed his own irritation. 'Forgive me, Majesty. I had thought you wished to know about the matter I have come to advise you of. But as I can see that your conversation with the bishop is concerning greater matters of state, I will wait until a more . . . propitious time to tell you of the sky-stone.'

Dalyson knew that his final word would attract the attention of the King, but he was surprised to hear a gasp from the lips of the bishop, too. And then to witness the exchange of looks between the two powerful men. Had they been talking about the very item he had at last tracked down? He had thought it a distraction – a bauble to amuse the King in his dotage. Did it have more significance than he had first imagined? He stored the thought away in his head for further consideration.

'You have found it? Is it here?'

Dalyson shook his head. 'Not yet, Majesty. It appears that some Jew took it from Norwich and sold it to a teacher at the university in Oxford. Envoys have been sent to bring it to you, and it should be no more than a week before you will have it.'

Henry's piping, old-man's voice rose in horror. 'A week? I could be dead before then.'

Dalyson refrained from saying he hoped so, and shook his head in obsequious denial. 'No, no, Majesty. You will live for ever, I am sure of it. Do you wish me to call your . . . doctors over?'

Henry's face fell. 'No need, Dalyson. Look behind you. They anticipate my demise sooner than you do.'

Indeed, all three quacks had hurried over to the King's bedside at the first sound of pain and horror in their patient's voice. Brother Mark made it to the bedside first and asked his patient to show his tongue. As the King meekly stuck the aforementioned appendage out, the Dominican hovered like an angel of death, sucking in his breath. He clearly did not like what he saw. Dalyson left Mark and his colleagues to it, and turned to speak to the Bishop of Narbonne. But the man was no longer present, having silently left the bedchamber already. Dalyson felt a shiver run down his spine. The man was unnatural in his ability to appear and disappear so quietly.

Pierre of Narbonne was angry, but he did not show it. His emissary to the Norwich Jews had failed by a whisker, and now he was reliant on an old and petulant monarch. He prided himself on never showing any feelings, and knew how still and impenetrable his eyes were. But back in the sumptuous rooms he had been allocated in Westminster Palace, he picked up a silver platter and gave in to the pure pleasure of throwing it across the room. It thudded into the tapestry that hung on the wall and fell to the stone floor with a clatter. A whey-faced servant appeared at the open doorway, and the bishop, his temper spent, waved for him to clear the dish, now bent on one rim. When the man had left, his task complete, Narbonne knelt at the improvised altar in his room, lifting his palms so the purple sleeves of his tunic fell away from them. He began to pray, playing with the ancient words of Pope Leo the Great.

' "But this Nativity which is to be adored in heaven and on earth is suggested to us by no day more than this when, with the early light still shedding its rays on nature, there is borne in upon our senses the brightness of this wondrous mystery." '

Only he knew to what mystery he was referring, and he intended to keep the secret in his heart. Until the day he could lay his hands on the sky-stone.

The sacred stone.

Unconcerned by the scandalous nature of their relation-ship, Falconer and Saphira Le Veske walked through the streets of Oxford, exchanging opinions on all sorts of matters. Neither could say who was the tyro and who the dominie, for they could vie with each other in differ-ent areas of knowledge. At the moment they turned into Kibald Street, where stood Aristotle's Hall, Saphira had the upper hand. They were discussing medicines, and she had learned her trade from old Samson in Jewry.

'Belladonna may be a poison in itself, but it can be used in small quantities as an antidote to poisoning by amanita mushrooms.'

Falconer nodded, then came back with a rejoinder that he hoped would silence her. 'It is also written that cat's brain is a poison. As is menstrual blood.'

Saphira's laughter was like a peal of sweet-sounding bells. 'Do you think to shock me into submission, William? It will take more than a reference to a woman's curse to do that.'

She was about to continue when Falconer laid a hand on her bare arm. She looked at him, then followed his eyes down the lane. At the entrance to Aristotle's Hall stood a little knot of students, evidently in some sort of quandary. Saphira recognized the Mithian brothers, and one or two others who were William's students and lodgers in his hall.

'What is going on, William?'

'I'm not sure, but I think we are about to find out.'

He nodded his head in the direction of Peter Mithian, who, having spotted his master, was hurrying towards the couple. His eyes were wide with shock, and as he approached he waved his hand behind him. 'Master, they have come for you.'

Falconer grasped the older Mithian brother by the arm and tried to calm him down. 'Come for me? Who have come for me?'

The boy could hardly contain himself. 'They have. Envoys from the King, they said. They wanted to know where you were. And when we said you were not home, they went upstairs nevertheless. They are in your solar.'

'Are they indeed.'

Falconer's face was grim, and he made to go towards the hall, and its intruders. Saphira held him back, though.

'Think first, William. Why are they seeking you out? Would it not be better to retreat? You may be going into danger.'

It was not long since Falconer had been on trial for murder thanks to a trumped-up charge laid by the chancellor of the university. If this was more mischief of a similar type, she feared for Falconer's safety. But he refused to consider the danger.

'Chancellor Bek has been ousted from his post, and my reputation is unstained. Well, no more stained than it was before. No, I think I should find out what this is all about.'

'Then I shall come with you.'

He smiled at Saphira. 'With you to protect me, I cannot be in any danger. Come. Let us see what the King wants of me.'

Pushing through the group of students in the doorway, Falconer and Saphira crossed the communal hall and ascended the creaky wooden stairs up to the private room under the rafters. Falconer almost expected his solar to be in chaos, ravaged by a band of careless soldiers. What he found was an elegantly garbed young man seated at his oak table flanked by two armed soldiers. Falconer had been a mercenary in his youth, and he knew signs of good discipline when he saw them. The impassive look on the soldiers' faces barely flickered when he entered. The elegant youth, however, rose and smiled pleasantly.

'Please forgive this intrusion on your privacy, regent master, but I come on urgent business.'

'The King's business, I am led to believe.'

The courtier inclined his head slightly and almost blushed at the perceived compliment made to his importance.

'I must admit I am honoured to serve our King. My name is John Zellot. But may I first ask . . . these texts—' he indicated two scrolls that Falconer had pushed aside when he had placed the sky-stone on the table '—this is in Hebrew, and this in Arabic, yes?'

Falconer was surprised at Zellot's knowledge, for the two texts were indeed in the languages he ascribed to them. They were translations of the same treatise originally written in Greek by the great physician Galen. Falconer had been comparing them to come to a clearer understanding of the subject.

'Yes. They concern the medical practice of bloodletting.'

Zellot nodded, as if he was familiar with the topic. 'Ah, yes. His Majesty is well acquainted with that practice.' He could do little more than recognize the scripts but had deliberately used his limited knowledge of languages to seek a rapport with the master. Now he could move on. 'But I have come on another matter. It concerns this stone.'

He pointed with his neatly gloved hand to the dark grey sky-stone that lay in the centre of the table. Falconer cast a sideways glance at Saphira and stepped up to the table, quickly picking the stone up. Suddenly, it seemed as if the two soldiers flanking the courtier swayed in a breeze. Their initial aggressive movement was a reaction to Falconer's swift step forward. But almost immediately they were checked by a slight twitch of Zellot's gloved hand. They returned to their former impassivity as if nothing had happened except the slightest of movements. Falconer smiled and hefted the stone in his palm.

'The King is interested in this?'

'Yes. Or more accurately its . . . medicinal properties. We are prepared to pay well for it.'

Falconer snapped his fist closed over the stone. 'No.'

The courtier seemed a little perturbed by Falconer's refusal to part with the stone, but he recovered himself well. He managed a smile without actually feeling any pleasure – a useful attribute in the corridors of Westminster Palace – and inclined his head in curiosity.

'No?'

'It is not for sale. But I will make it a gift to the King, on the condition that I can present it to him myself.'

This time the courtier smiled genuinely. Zellot thought he had seen right through this Oxford master to the heart of his venality. He wanted to speak to the King in hopes of some worldly reward far greater than mere coinage. Some valuable sinecure, perhaps. Well, he would give him his day at court, but he would find out soon enough how petulant the old King could be. He held out his hand. 'Of course. It is a bargain.'

Falconer, who had seen a chance to observe for himself how the highest in the land behaved, and not thinking of any other reward but a satisfaction of his curiosity, added a condition. He cocked a thumb at Saphira Le Veske, who had stood silently in the corner marvelling at William's boldness. 'And I shall be accompanied by my companion, who is an expert on medicines. She may be of help to the King.'

He refrained from saying out loud that she was likely to be more help to him than a lump of stone that had fallen from the sky. Zellot nodded.

'You may bring her. The King is always eager to consult another physician.'

The two men shook hands on the deal, and within a short while the oddly matched party had readied themselves, hired horses at Zellot's expense and were on their way to London.

For the first time in days, Henry had struggled out of his bed and called for his wardroper, Ralph, to assist him in dressing. He always felt at a disadvantage when receiving the Bishop of Narbonne in his bedchamber. Truth to tell, the cleric scared him, what with his dark pools of eyes and his secretive talk of the sacred stone and its powers. Henry was determined the bishop was not going to lay his hands on the stone, however. It was for the sake of his own health that he had sought it out. Suddenly, he felt as if his arm was being torn out of its socket.

'What are you doing, man? You are ripping me apart.'

Ralph grovelled before His Majesty, apologizing for his rough awkwardness in pulling Henry's tunic over his arm. He was normally so adept in assisting the King to dress, but his son's illness weighed heavily on his mind. The boy was wasting away before his parents' eyes. And the healer woman he had paid out royally for had taken one look at little Robin and shook her head sadly. He could not accept, however, that there was nothing to be done. His sad thoughts were suddenly interrupted by a sharp prod. The King had dug a bony finger in his chest.

'Pay attention, Ralph, or I shall have to replace you.'

'Majesty, forgive me.'

Once again Ralph apologized abjectly. He had been wool-gathering, when his duty was to pay full attention to the King. He concentrated enough to help Henry don the rest of his clothes, and assisted him to the grand oak chair that stood at the other end of the chamber to the King's bed. Having eased his tired body down, Henry dismissed him with a wave of his hand. Ralph was glad to escape with his job still intact, but first he had to tidy the rest of the King's clothes that lay creased and rumpled in the chest at the foot of his bed. His presence was completely ignored as the King's chamberlain, Sir Thomas Dalyson, entered, followed by the French bishop. He concentrated on his task, making himself as insignificant as possible to these great men. But his son's fate still hung heavily on his mind.

Dalyson was surprised to see the King sitting up in his chair. The last time he had spoken to the physicians who attended Henry, they had assured him the King was near death. His face was indeed gaunt, resembling parchment stretched over a skull, but his eyes were unusually bright for once. The bishop strode over to the King of England and graciously bowed his head in deference. He even refrained from expressing any annoyance when Henry suggested he draw up a nearby stool, a seat that left the bishop perched at a lower level than the monarch. But for Narbonne what was at stake was more important than mere pride. The bishop's eyes fixed eagerly on the older man.

'Tell me, Majesty, have you found it?'

Henry looked at his chamberlain, who was hovering at the back of the room, close to the King's dishevelled bed. 'Tell him, Dalyson.'

Sir Thomas took a step or two closer. 'Indeed we have, my lord. The stone was said to have been in the possession of old Elias of Norwich. He denied it when . . . questioned, saying it had been stolen from him long ago. He did tell us that somehow it ended up in the hands of an itinerant Jew, who sold it to another of his kind in Oxford. However, as the Jews are no more than the property of the King, it should be no great problem to retrieve the stone. We have dispatched an eager young man called Zellot, who will be back with it by the end of the week. If he values his future.'

The bishop nodded and turned back to the King. 'Good. May we then talk in private, Majesty?'

Dalyson blushed at the rude dismissal but backed graciously out of the room, leaving the two great men to their business. Henry was a little surprised at his chamberlain's rapid acceding to Narbonne's request – he was normally prickly about his position at court – but put it out of his mind as the bishop began to tell him the story of the sky-stone. Engrossed, he went to touch the seal ring on his right hand, as he often did from habit, but realized the finger was bare. He reasoned that, as his fingers had grown thin of late, the ring must have slipped off. He would have to alert Dalyson to its loss as soon as possible, but the tale the bishop was telling was for the moment too intriguing to ignore. The power of the stone to heal and cure fascinated Henry. Neither man noticed the insignificant figure of the King's wardroper slipping quietly out of the bedchamber.

By pushing the horses to their limit, John Zellot ensured that his small party reached London in the middle of the third day after leaving Oxford. They were tired and covered in dust, but he had achieved his goal of returning within the week. The King would be well pleased, and Zellot hoped for a good reward. He settled the Oxford master and his red-haired strumpet in the guest rooms at Westminster and hurried off, still sweat-stained, to report to Sir Thomas Dalyson. Walking through the corridors of the court, he was suddenly a little fearful that he had not exactly done as he was told but had needed to bring two people with him. And they were people who still laid claim to the possession of the stone. He slowed his pace as his mind raced, trying to find the best way to explain the situation. Perhaps the King would excuse him, if he could present the two people as wise physicians. It was well known the King liked to surround himself with quacks and their opinions. He decided that was a plausible excuse, and once again strode more purposefully along the palace's gloomy corridors.

Meanwhile, Saphira Le Veske, unaware that she was perceived as William's whore, was pacing the rooms they had been put in. She began castigating Falconer for getting them into this mad situation. 'Do you not realize that we Jews are seen as the King's property? He has already mortgaged us once to his brother, Richard, who then taxed us to recoup his outlay. If he chose, Henry could merely demand I give him the sky-stone, and there is nothing I could do.'

Unperturbed, Falconer lounged comfortably on the cushions that adorned the outer room. He was unused to such luxury, but he thought he could come to like this life. He felt like a perfumed Saracen in his harem and waved a dismissive hand at Saphira. 'But there is no problem there. You gave the stone to me as a gift. So it is mine to dispose of as I wish. Not yours.'

Saphira stooped over him, poking his chest with an elegant finger. 'So you value my gift so slightly that you would give it away without a second thought?'

Falconer grabbed her outstretched arm and pulled her to him, laughing. 'I could always offer *you* as my gift to the King.'

Saphira pushed him away in horror. 'Don't even jest, William.'

Their situation did not seem to worry William, but she was frightened that there might be spies in every dark corner in this palace, listening to their every word. Falconer, realizing he had overstepped the mark, sat up. 'No, you are right. The situation is serious. It does occur to me, though, that you might use some of your expert knowledge of medicines. Mix him a potion. You might even make the King grateful to at least one Jew for prolonging his life.'

Saphira paled at the idea. 'And if he should die after taking my potion?'

Falconer's face creased in a frown. 'You are right again, and I am a fool. I should not have subjected you to this ordeal. I was being selfish in not wishing to be away from your company for any length of time.'

She hugged him and gave a throaty laugh, which promised much for later. But their private moment was disturbed, however, by a quiet cough. Standing in the doorway was a tall man with a regal bearing and long, well-coiffed locks. Falconer and Saphira stood up, a little embarrassed at being discovered embracing. The distinguished-looking man introduced himself.

'I am Sir Thomas Dalyson, chamberlain to the King. John Zellot has told me something of the situation, and who you are. Do you have the stone with you?'

Falconer spoke up. 'Yes, I do.'

'Then give it to me, and you can be on your way.'

Dalyson clearly hoped that his deliberately peremptory manner would cow this Oxford master, but he was wrong. He saw the grizzle-haired man bristle at the crude dismissal, his face turning stony. 'No. I told your envoy, Zellot, that I would present it to the King myself. If he did not pass on this stipulation, then you should punish him for his dereliction of duty. But I will see the King myself.'

Dalyson realized how much he had misjudged the master and swiftly changed course. 'I am sorry. I was misled by Zellot. Of course you may see the King. And Mistress—' he racked his brain for the woman's name, told him by Zellot '—Le Veske also. Come.'

Saphira cast a fearful glance at William, but he grasped her hand firmly and picked up the stone from where it lay beside him on the bed. Together, they followed Dalyson out of the room.

The King was struggling to breathe, and his doctors were clustered around him anxiously. The fear of wrongly prescribing a cure in such extreme circumstances made the three men nervous of suggesting anything radical. The herbalist, John Rixe, broke the impasse of their worried discussions with a bold suggestion.

'I recommend a tincture of lungwort with thyme and liquorice root.'

Master Roger Megrim hooted in derision. 'Lungwort? That will have the effect of a fleabite in an ox's back.' He poked a long, bony finger at their patient. 'Can't you see His Majesty is far beyond lungwort?'

The King's face turned an ashen grey, and he began gasping for air as if he were on the verge of drowning. Brother Mark frowned deeply. He crossed himself and put on his most solemn face. 'His Majesty is beset by demons. He must embark on a pilgrimage to Saint Madron's Well, for he is a saint who cures all pain.'

It was John Rixe's turn to question the proposition from the Dominican monk. 'And where is Saint Madron's Well, pray?'

'Cornwall.'

The herbalist and the erudite Cambridge master both burst out laughing. It was left to Megrim, once he could contain himself, to once again point out the error of the proposal. 'His Majesty is near to dying, and you propose to drag him hundreds of miles down roads no better than farm tracks, and across the wastes of Bodmin Moor? You will kill him for sure.'

By now none of the three physicians was taking note of the state of their patient, intent as they were on sniping at each other. Henry's breathing was becoming ever more wheezy, and his heart was pounding like a hammer in one of those newfangled iron workings. His vision became blurred, and the faces of his physicians swam before him in a red mist.

Unaware of the plight of the King, Megrim finally threw his cap into the ring. With sonorous tones, he laid out the scientific approach to cure as he saw it. 'The very latest writings of Albertus Magnus extol the virtues of magnetic stones, and lodestones are a cure for melancholy. This is what the King is suffering from – an excess of phlegm and melancholy. Powdered lodestone and milk will alleviate the symptoms of melancholy. Or he will surely die.'

Just as he reached this conclusion, and before his colleagues and rivals could comment, the bedchamber door opened. Sir Thomas Dalyson stepped into the room and, seeing the parlous state of King Henry, rushed to his master's side. For the first time, the three doctors noted that Henry was sinking fast. Indecision froze them in place, and they watched in consternation as the red-haired female who had followed Dalyson into the room, along with a tall, grey-haired man, took some action. She called out to the attendant she had passed in the corridor to bring some beer.

'A large tankard. Now, if you please.'

Then she turned her attentions to the King, abruptly grasping his thin and chilly hand. She patted it reassuringly while everyone else looked on in horror at her temerity. This unknown woman had touched the King. Something none of his physicians had ever done. She spoke in soft and comforting tones.

'Majesty, you are just panicked by these men. Drinking deep will slow your breathing and you will feel better. I assure you. Here.'

Ralph Wardroper entered and passed a large pewter tankard of ale to her. She helped Henry to sit up and held it to his lips. He took a sip then, encouraged by Saphira, he drank deeply in great gulps. She laughed.

'Steady, Majesty.'

He looked her in the eyes, his heart already slowing. He felt he had escaped death and grinned mischievously. 'I should have long ago had a nursemaid as pretty as you. Instead, I have these three gargoyles.'

Hiding a brief look of outrage, Megrim, Rixe and Brother Mark forced courteous smiles on their faces and bowed low at the King's comment. Saphira, who could not help but note the animosity hidden by their smiles, suddenly realized that she sat on the King of England's bed. And that she was holding his hand. Her face turned pale, and Falconer, seizing the moment, stepped forward. He helped the stricken woman rise to her feet.

'Majesty, I have something you have been looking for.'

He brought his left hand from behind his back and produced a dark stone in the shape of a ship. Henry's eyes glittered. 'Is this it? The sky-stone?'

'Yes, sire.'

Falconer proffered the stone and placed it in Henry's outstretched fingers, making sure the King didn't drop the unusually heavy object as he took it. Henry sighed deeply.

'The sacred stone.'

Falconer turned around at the sound of the resonant voice that had spoken the words. It had not been the voice of the King. In the doorway stood a stocky, powerful man in the garb of a senior cleric of the Church. Pierre de Montbrun, Bishop of Narbonne, strode into the room. Falconer could not help but see the glitter in the dark pools that were the Frenchman's eyes as he gazed at the sky-stone. Both Saphira and Falconer looked with renewed curiosity at the stone that now lay in King Henry's frail hands. They had heard of its claimed healing properties, but not that the established Church should see it as sacred. Falconer's interest was piqued, and he looked around the room. Everyone was staring at the stone, from the King down to his most lowly servant, who had brought the jug of ale. All perhaps saw something different in it, and it was something as a man of science he could not see. Hope. A cure. Deliverance.

He nudged Saphira and tipped his head towards the others in the room. She took the hint, and with her new-found authority spoke to the King.

'Majesty, I suggest you need your rest. If the others present would clear the room, I can stay to nurse you while Regent Master Falconer explains more about the stone.'

Henry waved aside the sharp intake of breath from the doctors, the bishop and Sir Thomas, and peered at Falconer.

'Falconer. I have heard of you. You stood up to that fool Thomas Bek, who was chancellor of Oxford University until recently.'

Falconer grinned broadly and bowed his head in acknowledgement. He had indeed been at loggerheads with Bek for some time. And trying Falconer for a murder he did not commit had been an audacious step. The chancellor of Oxford University had legal authority over students and masters except solely in the case of murder. That was the King's prerogative. Bek had attempted to extend his power and at the same time get rid of a thorn in his side – Regent Master William Falconer. He had failed miserably and paid the price. He was no longer chancellor of the university. And it seemed that Falconer's renown had come to the ears of the King.

'With a little help—' here he bowed to Saphira, who had aided him in finding the true perpetrator of the murder Falconer had stood accused of '—I solved the murder Bek had hung around my neck.'

'And you have done so in several other cases, I hear.'

Falconer was shocked the King knew so much about him. 'I am flattered that my name has come to your attention, Majesty.'

Henry sat up and waved a dismissive hand to the others in his bedchamber. 'Go. I would speak with Master Falconer alone.'

Reluctantly, those in attendance on the King turned to go, including Saphira. But the King grasped her arm with a surprisingly firm hand for one who a moment ago had been all but dying.

'You can stay, too, my pretty nursemaid.'

Saphira Le Veske blushed and averted her gaze from the envious eyes of the three physicians. She knew she could ill afford to make enemies, but she wished to remain nevertheless. Dalyson ushered the bishop out ahead of him, muttering apologies for the abruptness of Henry. The doctors followed, with Megrim taking precedence, and Ralph slipped out last, almost unnoticed.

Falconer looked at the sky-stone, held in Henry's claw-like grip, with renewed interest. 'The bishop called it a sacred stone. Why so, Majesty?'

A secretive grin broke out on the monarch's face, and his celebrated droopy right eyelid fell even further. Falconer realized he was winking conspiratorially. 'The Bishop of Narbonne hides a secret in his black robes and gilded cross. He thinks I do not understand how his desires are formed. But I haven't kept my position all these years through wars and conspiracies without sniffing out the truth a little.' He held a bony finger to the side of his nose and tapped it. Then he eased himself around uncomfortably, his bones creaking. 'You, my pretty nursemaid, you will have heard of a Beth-el stone.'

Saphira gasped, realizing that Henry knew her for a Jew in his reference to the pillar of Jacob. Henry chuckled at his little triumph and turned back to the regent master.

'And you scholars call it a baitylos, I believe. What can you tell me about it?'

Falconer wondered if Henry knew as much as he pretended to. To remain King for fifty-six years, he had probably perfected the art of allowing those around him to imagine he knew more than he really did. Especially about their own personal lives and dark, secret corners.

It must have given him great power over them. He tacitly played along with Henry's game.

'As Your Majesty knows well, there was an ancient cult in the Levant that venerated stones. And it persisted in Roman times as the cult of Sol Invictus. The god was a sun god, and the historian Herodian wrote of it. He mentioned a huge black stone with a pointed end and round base in the shape of a cone. The Phoenicians solemnly maintain that this stone came down from Zeus. But the cult has long since died out. Christianity has seen to that.'

Henry waved his hand impatiently as if he knew better. 'And the name of this god?'

Falconer frowned, looking across at Saphira in puzzlement. 'The name, Majesty? It was Elagabal.'

In his private chamber, the Bishop of Narbonne knelt in prayer. He often intoned this very psalm when he was frustrated. As he was today, being so close to his goal yet so far away from it.

'To you I call, O Lord my Rock;
do not turn a deaf ear to me.
For, if you remain silent,
I will be like those who have gone down to the pit.
Hear my cry for mercy
as I call to you for help,
as I lift up my hands
towards your Most Holy Place.
Do not drag me away with the wicked,
with those who do evil,
who speak cordially with their neighbours
but harbour malice in their hearts.
Repay them for their deeds
and for their evil work;

repay them for what their hands have done
and bring back upon them what they deserve.'

This time, the words gave him no comfort. God was truly
a rock for Pierre de Montbrun, and he had learned his
holy secrets from his father in the town of which he was
now the bishop. The old Roman town of Narbo still clung
tenaciously to its glorious past and its rituals. Now he had
at last seen the sacred stone, of which he had heard tell by
passing Crusaders over the years. He had shared part of
the secret with the English King, telling him in letters only
of its potency as a curative. He knew that Henry was ailing
and that he would seek out anything that might prolong his
life. Narbonne led him to seek out the stone and arranged
it so that he, the bishop, was present at Henry's court when
it was uncovered. He had not expected the old King to
be so possessive, though. And the presence of the Oxford
master and his Jewess complicated matters. It was obvious
the King had taken a fancy to the woman, and, through
her, the man and his strange interests. He would have to
find a way of turning the King back to favouring him, so
he could lay his hands on the stone. Perhaps the unctuous
chamberlain, Dalyson, was the avenue he could use.

Narbonne rose to his feet, brushed the dust off his robes
and went in search of Sir Thomas.

At the time, Dalyson was otherwise engaged. It was late, but
the King had refused to let Falconer and Saphira go. He
was too engrossed in William's tales of the murder cases
the regent master had solved in Oxford.

'Tell me more of this little man who cut up bodies for you.'

Falconer wondered how much he dare tell of Master
Richard Bonham's predilection for understanding the
inner workings of the human body. Dissecting the human

body was forbidden by the Church, except in the cases of convicted murderers, who had forfeited their humanity. But Bonham had carved open any body he could find, and sometimes these had been the sorry victims of murders Falconer had been investigating. But then, Bonham was now dead and could not be punished for his misdeeds. Falconer began to tell the King of an unfortunate serving girl who had been revealed as being with child when she had been killed. Suddenly, his monologue was disturbed by angry voices outside the King's bedchamber. One of the voices was that of Sir Thomas Dalyson. Falconer was surprised at hearing him shouting, as the man had always seemed in complete control of any situation.

The King waved a hand at Saphira. 'Go and find out what is going on, woman.'

Saphira rose, but, before she could reach the bedchamber door, a red-faced Dalyson stepped in the room. He bowed deeply towards the King, straightening his normally well-combed hair.

'Majesty, forgive me. There was an intruder. Some persistent petitioner desiring to speak to you. I told him it was impossible, but he would not take my word for it.'

Annoyance clouded Henry's pale, watery eyes. 'Who was it?'

Dalyson ducked his head and whispered in the King's ear to prevent Falconer or Saphira hearing. The King would have nothing of it, and told his chamberlain to speak out loud. Glancing at Falconer, Dalyson complied with the command.

'Majesty, it is of no importance. He has no proper reason to see you, and I have dealt with it. Your bodyguard has removed him.'

The King screwed up his eyes with suspicion. 'I asked you who it was, Dalyson.'

The chamberlain paled but stood his ground, a knowing look on his face. 'A cousin of the de Montforts, Majesty, seeking his lands back.'

The name he spoke had the desired effect on Henry. Not only had Simon de Montfort rebelled against the King less than ten years earlier, but more recently a couple of his offspring had slaughtered Henry's nephew at prayer in Viterbo. Henry's disinheriting of rebel families after the barons' war had been criticized at the time, but the King had stood firm. He would not waver now.

'Then you did well, Sir Thomas. Do not ever show the cur into my presence.'

Dalyson smiled in satisfaction and once more bowed deeply, then swept out of the room. The King sighed and fell back on his soft pillows.

'You will have to tell me some other time about the pregnant serving girl, Master Falconer. I am tired.'

Falconer and Saphira rose and bowed. As they left the chamber, Saphira thought how like a child the King looked, clutching the dark stone to his bosom like a comforting toy.

It was deep in the night, but Saphira could not sleep. She had woken hours earlier, imagining she heard someone passing their bedchamber, and subdued voices whispering outside the door. She feared, as most Jews did, that the King's hospitality could change to betrayal at any moment. To be within the walls of the King's palace placed her in double jeopardy. Beside her, Falconer snored gently, clearly unperturbed by their situation. He was loving every minute of his observations on the workings of government. Irritated beyond measure by his serenity, she nudged him only to find that he rolled over on his side and continued snoring. She poked him vigorously with her finger. He was suddenly alert, his distant past life as a mercenary asserting itself once again.

'What is it?'

She lay back on the too-soft pillow, her red hair spilling all over it. 'Tell me about Elagabal.'

Falconer groaned and propped himself up on his elbow, staring at her glorious profile. 'You have woken me up for a lesson in history?'

She sternly refused to respond, so he continued. 'Let me think. In ancient times the sun god Elagabal was worshipped as a black stone that was protected by an eagle. Herodian said it came down from Zeus, hence the connection with it being a meteorite. Such stones have been known by the name bethel, or baitylos. The Irish even have a word for them. Both-al.'

'The Irish? Was that where our stone came from? Covele, the talisman seller, reckoned it came from far beyond Ireland. But then he might have been inflating the story to get more money from me.'

Falconer shrugged. 'Who knows where it came from? But the truth is I don't imagine it was the actual stone the cult in Rome worshipped. Though some may think so. And it was a pretty nasty cult, by all accounts.'

Saphira sat up, holding the slipping blanket over her bare breasts, much to William's regret. 'Do tell.'

'The Roman emperor Heliogabalus was its high priest, and there were tales of castration and human sacrifice levelled against him by more conservative historians.'

Saphira frowned. 'Just the sort of accusations thrown at us Jews now, then.'

Falconer nodded. 'And probably for the same reasons. To denigrate and destroy the religion. It is said that the cult of Sol Invictus did not survive the death of Emperor Heliogabalus. Others say it was driven under ground. So who knows if it survives to this day?'

Saphira was about to respond when a great cry was heard far off in another part of the palace. Running feet could soon be heard pounding along the corridor outside their door. Saphira tensed and held the blanket close to her with clenched fists. Falconer stroked her bare shoulder to assuage her fears.

'It's all right. They are going elsewhere in the palace. Wait here. I will get dressed and see what is happening.'

He swung his legs out of the bed, half forgetting how high it was off the ground compared with the familiar pallet in his solar back in Oxford. Saphira grabbed his arm as he steadied himself.

'Take care.'

Falconer nodded his reassurance and quickly donned his old black robe and boots. Cramming his pileum on his head, he opened the door a crack and slipped through. After he had gone, Saphira could still hear cries of anger and alarm echoing down the corridors of Westminster. She sat on the bed for as long as she could bear, then she, too, got up and stepped into her gown. Curiosity overcoming her fears, she followed the sound of loud voices in the same direction Falconer had gone.

Falconer found that the babble of sound was leading him towards the King's chamber. He wondered if Henry had at last died, and the noise was the confusion associated with his passing. Henry had been King for so long that few people alive could recall anyone else ever being on the throne of England. And Henry's son and heir, Prince Edward, was in the Holy Lands on crusade. Such a situation could lead to total chaos. However, as Falconer turned the corner of the corridor that led to Henry's private bedchamber, he heard the piping voice of the King. He was still alive, and very perturbed, it seemed.

'Where is it? Where is it?'

Falconer could hear a note of panic in the tones as he approached the door. A bodyguard, who had clearly donned his coat of mail too hastily and was still struggling with it, made to prevent his entry. Then suddenly the King's cries turned into a hacking cough that went on and on without cease. Dalyson appeared at the door, dressed in a white and voluminous nightgown, damp at the edges. His hair for once was dishevelled. He stopped abruptly in front of Falconer.

'Get in there and try to calm him, for God's sake. I must call his physicians.'

The bodyguard reluctantly stepped back and allowed Falconer to pass. But before he entered the room, the regent master asked Dalyson a question. 'What is it the King has lost that perturbs him so?'

Dalyson grimaced. 'Not lost. Stolen, he says. It is that damned stone you brought him.'

As Dalyson retreated down the corridor in search of the three physicians, Falconer took a deep breath and went into the presence of the King.

Saphira had to admit her sense of direction was not as unerring as William's, and after the initial turmoil had died down there was nothing to guide her. She wished she had paid more attention when Sir Thomas Dalyson had led herself and Falconer to the King's chamber earlier. But she had been so wrapped up in her own fears that she had ignored which way they had turned. So when she came to the end of a narrow corridor and found a locked door before her, she paused. Turning back, she began to retrace her steps. At an unfamiliar junction, she realized she was lost and, thinking she heard the soft sound of bare feet, called out. 'Hello? Can you help me? I am lost.'

There was a moment's silence, then once again what sounded like bare feet hurrying away. She walked slowly in the direction the sounds had come from, suddenly cautious and alert to danger. She had called out loudly, so whoever it was had made the noises must have heard her. So why had they run away? Peering around a corner, she saw that she was entering an unlit room filled with large barrels. She must have found her way to the kitchens, or some storage room. The nearest barrel was almost chest high; whatever the contents were, some of it had splashed out very recently. Pools of liquid darkened the flagstones on the floor around the barrel. She crouched down and dipped her fingers in the puddle. Touching her fingers to her lips, she realized the liquid was merely water. Other equipment she could now discern in the gloom told her this was a brewhouse. She guessed that a palace the size of Westminster required prodigious quantities of ale. No one would drink plain water out of the river, so weak ale was required for everyday consumption. She hoped she had not caught anything by sucking on her wet fingers. She reasoned that it probably was not the case from such small quantities, even though there were many rats swimming in the Thames and its tributaries. Idly, she peered in the open top of the barrel. The dead eyes of Ralph Wardroper stared back up at her from under the water. She gasped and ran back down the dark corridor to call for help.

The man dressed in chain mail whom she ran into in the maze of corridors leading from the brewhouse took her for a dangerous intruder. Dressed as she was in a simple green gown, barefoot, with her thick red hair, uncovered and sticking out in tangles from her head, he assumed she was no lady. In fact, her wild claims of dead men in barrels made him think she was a madwoman. He called for assistance, and he and his two companions overpowered the lunatic, dragging her to the brewhouse to confront her delusion. The sight of the drowned man in the water barrel changed their minds. They now decided she was not only a madwoman but a murderer, too. Saphira soon sat shivering in a cold cell deep below the King's rooms. It was what seemed like an eternity before rescue came.

Sir Thomas Dalyson soon heard the reports of a madwoman loose in the palace and thanked God that she had been apprehended. When he heard that she had red hair, he knew who she was, and he knew he would have to look into the matter further. He didn't care about what William Falconer might say. But the regent master's whore had found a place in the heart of the King, and the King would probably want to know where she was. Especially when Megrim, Rixe and Brother Mark failed to calm him down over the loss of the stone. He then pondered the possibility of killing two birds with one stone, and ensuring that the woman was found guilty of the murder she stood accused of. He thought he could arrange that before even the King and Falconer heard of the matter. But before he was able to set the matter in train, he was summoned to the King's bedside. Entering the dark and stale-smelling room, he saw the familiar trio of physicians, heads together, arguing, as always. Close by the bed of the King sat the tall, calm figure of the regent master from Oxford. Shockingly, Falconer seemed to be laughing at one of Henry's tantrums. Did the man not know who he was mocking?

Falconer leaned towards the King as the figure of the chamberlain strode over. He whispered in Henry's ear. 'Here comes your trained monkey, Majesty. Too late, as always.'

The King momentarily forgot the gravity of the situation and sniggered. Then he put on his most serious face. 'Sir

Thomas, what have you done to get my stone back? This is a most serious affair.'

He could not help a whine growing in his voice. He was scared that without the sacred stone his health might deteriorate once more. Someone who wanted him dead must have taken it. He even suspected that one of his physicians might have secreted it away out of jealousy.

Dalyson bowed low. 'The matter is being looked into, Majesty. But many strange things are happening at the moment.'

The King looked at him with suspicion written on his face. 'Strange things? What strange things?'

Dalyson took a quick decision to change his angle of attack concerning the woman. 'There has been a murder.'

Falconer's eyes lit up, and he looked closely at the chamberlain. 'A murder? Who has been killed, and where?'

Dalyson chose to ignore the meddling master, and addressed the King. 'Majesty, I regret to inform you that your wardroper, Ralph, has been drowned.'

The King stirred weakly in his bed. 'Ralph? Damn the man for a fool; he knows I prefer him dressing me. He doesn't pull me about like the others.'

Henry made it seem as though Ralph had committed a treasonable act by allowing himself to be murdered, and thereby depriving his King of one of his little comforts in life.

Falconer ignored the man's petulance and pressed Dalyson for more information. 'Is there no hue and cry? I hear nothing.'

Dalyson smirked. 'There was no need. The killer was found immediately and is imprisoned already.'

'Who was it?'

Once again, Dalyson turned his back on Falconer's question, speaking only to Henry. 'Majesty, I regret to inform you that the woman, Le Veske, is the killer.'

To Dalyson's astonishment, the King suddenly screwed up his face, which was already turning bright red, and spat a command at his chamberlain. 'Do not be stupid, man. It could not be her. Go this instant and release her. And when you have apologized to her, bring her to me.'

Humiliated, Sir Thomas Dalyson scurried out of the room to do the King's bidding.

Meanwhile, Henry, calm once more, turned to Falconer and winked. 'Now, regent master, how are we to solve this little murder case of mine?'

Once Saphira had been restored to the bedside of the King, Falconer relaxed a little and coached the King in how he might pursue the case. He began with asking about the hours around the time Ralph was last seen alive.

'I remember Ralph was in the room when I gave you the stone. Right up to the point when the bishop called it a sacred stone. Was that the last time you saw him, Majesty?'

'No, no. Of course not. Who do you think undressed me last night? He left around compline, as I couldn't sleep.' The King seemed to drift off for a moment, then sat up. 'I still had the stone then.'

'Oh, yes, the stone. So that disappeared after Ralph had left your chamber?'

The King nodded. 'Do you think its theft has something to do with Ralph's death?'

Saphira answered the King's question. 'William does not believe in coincidences, Majesty. One event is more often than not connected with the other.'

Falconer was quick to throw in a word of caution. 'Even so, we should not rush to simple conclusions. Remember the syllogism. Many small truths, when seen all together, can add up to a larger truth not previously imagined.'

The King slapped the surface of the bed beside him in impatience. 'But what are these truths that we must gather? How can we tell what is significant and what is not?'

'That is the problem, Majesty. You never know an important fact from an insignificant one until you have accumulated them.'

Falconer could see that the King didn't appreciate the meticulous nature of deduction. He posed Henry a question. 'Did anything else unusual happen yesterday?'

'Well, you were here when some supplicant tried to wheedle his way into my presence. Does that count?'

'It depends. What do you recall of the occurrence?'

Henry tried to marshal his thoughts.

He was agitated and frustrated. He had now been confined to his bed for weeks, and none of the doctors would look him in the eye when he asked what ailed him. But they were all fools, because he knew anyway – the infirmities of age were catching up on him. More fool him for paying good money to doctors for not telling him this obvious truth. What frustrated him most were the gaps in his recollection of events. Only the other day he had lost his seal ring, and without it he could not endorse any of his edicts.

And had he not summoned the archbishop before sext, and was it not now nearly nones? He could have died unshriven in the time it took for that fat oaf to get to his bedside. He shuddered at the prospect of not reaching the kingdom of heaven, after all the money he had poured into the abbey and St Edward's tomb. The only crumb of comfort was the arrival of this Oxford master with the sky-stone. It now lay comforting and heavy on his stomach, reminding him of its presence. For the first time in ages he was taking an interest in his surroundings. He wanted to know more about William Falconer. And his pretty whore, the Jewess. Suddenly, he was aware of everyone in the chamber staring at the

stone, including Ralph, his wardroper, still fussing with his linen
as though reluctant to leave. That was when he ordered everyone
out of his chamber save the master and his woman.

The commotion had begun just after he was beginning to enjoy
their company. One voice was unfamiliar, but the other was clearly
Sir Thomas Dalyson's. Both voices were muffled by the trusty oak
door that protected the King's person, but for a moment the man's
voice rang out loud and clear. He remembered what was said.

'The King is being duped.'

Then the stranger's voice was suddenly stifled. Dalyson had
entered his bedchamber, and whoever it was had been seen off.

'Duped?' asked the curious master.

The King eased his bony frame against the cushions
whose softness seemed to have turned to stone. 'I'm always
having hangers-on questioning my decisions.'

Saphira then asked the question that had been on
Falconer's lips. Both had been recalling the scene they had
witnessed yesterday. 'Sir Thomas whispered something to
you when he first came in.'

The King looked a little furtive briefly, then passed off
the whispered exchange as unimportant. 'It was nothing
more than what he then said out loud in your presence.
The intruder was someone whose lands I had transferred
to another, and he had come to petition me. The man
must have committed some serious crime to warrant the
loss of his lands. Though be damned if I can remember
what it was.'

He sighed, and his eyes glazed over as once again he
drifted off towards the other world that beckoned him.
Anxiously, the regent master leaned forward to ensure that
Henry was doing no more than merely dozing. It would
not do to have the King of England expire in the presence
of a renegade Oxford master and a Jew. Henry's breathing

was shallow but regular, and Falconer silently beckoned Saphira to follow him out of the room.

Once outside, he whispered to her. 'Show me where you found the body. And then I would like to take a look at Ralph for myself.'

The Bishop of Narbonne waited until the wife of the dead man had left the little side chapel where Ralph's body lay. Events had overtaken his seeking out Dalyson and had led him to the corpse. Now he did not want anyone to know what he intended to do. The newly widowed woman spent what seemed like an interminable time with the skinny little corpse, weeping and touching him. She straightened his wet hair and tidied his robe, which was still clinging wetly to his frame. She appeared oblivious to the water that dripped off the edge of the slab on which Ralph lay. It pooled at her feet, and the hem of her dress got wetter and wetter as the woollen material soaked the water up. Finally, she gave up her vigil and, pulling her wet skirts around her ankles, hurried off.

Pierre de Montbrun took his chance and slipped out of the shadows. He wanted to finish what he had begun earlier in the night. But he could see instantly that the stone was not on the body. Ralph's clothes clung so tightly to him that there was no possibility the stone was hidden in them, and he had no purse about him. Maybe the wife had removed it. Instinctively, he turned and dashed away in the same direction as the stout lady with the wet hem. On the way, he almost bumped into the Oxford master and his delectable companion.

Once he had mumbled an apology and departed, Saphira offered an opinion. 'I would not have expected the great bishop to have been mourning at the bier of a lowly servant.'

Falconer tended to agree with Saphira's assessment. 'Perhaps he was here for another reason.'

He looked closely at the body on the slab but could see no sign of interference with it, other than his hair being tidied. Narbonne had not searched Ralph, or done anything to disturb the body. Neither could Falconer see anything that offered him a clue to the murder. Ralph had been drowned in a butt of water, presumably by a man bigger and stronger than he. Falconer had been shown the brewhouse by Saphira and noted that the upper edge of the barrel was chest high. Whoever tipped Ralph into it must have overpowered him sufficiently to lift him high in the air. But the former wardroper was a skinny individual and looked even more so in death, with his thin robe clinging to his frame. It would not have taken much for a well-made man to force him over the lip of the barrel and hold his head under the water. There had been considerable displacement of water, and many splash marks stretching out from the barrel. Enough to suggest that Ralph had struggled, but that it had all been in vain. He now lay as dead as a fish out of water in a dark side chapel at Westminster Palace, lit by a single flickering candle.

'Come, let us return to bed. There are still some hours before the sun will be up, and I need to rest.'

Saphira poked him in the ribs. 'Is it really sleep that you are thinking of, William?'

Falconer grinned like a sheepish boy caught peeping into a lady's chamber. 'It was, but if you have a better idea . . .'

Saphira took his arm and led him towards their rooms. 'Yes. I want you to tell me more about that Roman emperor, the cult of Elagabal and castration.'

Falconer winced and reminded himself never to take Saphira Le Veske for granted.

*   *   *

Henry, for whom the earliness of the hour meant nothing, levered his aching frame out of the bed. He had feigned tiredness and sleep when Master Falconer had begun asking him probing questions. It was a ploy he often used when bored or facing awkward situations. No one dared keep the King from his bed, after all. He shuffled his now scrawny shanks to the side of the bed, regretting the disappearance of all the muscle and fat that used to shield his bones. Now it was purgatory sitting on a throne without a thick cushion under his buttocks. As he swung his legs over the edge of the bed, he felt something sharp dig into his left hip. Lifting his leg, he slid his fingers under him, and felt around in the folds of the sweat-stained linen sheet. Pulling the offending article out, he lifted it to his rheumy eyes, recognizing it immediately. It was his seal ring that had gone missing a few days earlier. He had been afraid to tell his chamberlain about the loss. And when, on the night of the intruder, Dalyson had whispered in his ear that he might need a royal edict sealed in order to banish the man, Henry had become worried. Now it didn't matter. The ring must have slipped off his ever-scrawnier fingers to come to rest in the folds of his bed. Relieved, he slid it back on his finger and called for his wardroper.

Once dressed, he was going to show Falconer how to solve the murder without resorting to all that syllogism nonsense. But as he stood up he felt dizzy and slumped back down on the bed. He cursed the loss of the sky-stone, sure that he had felt healthier when he had held it in his hands. It occurred to him that whoever had stolen the stone might have done it to speed along his death. If Ralph had seen the thief take the stone, it would be a good motive for murdering his wardroper. Stealing the stone was tantamount to killing the King. High treason, no less. He clutched at his chest as he felt his heart race. When the new wardroper poked his head around the King's door, he went pale at the sight of his monarch leaning heavily on the edge of his bed, a cold sweat covering his brow. He called for the King's physicians.

Saphira tucked her unruly red hair under a modest snood and finished her dressing. 'So the Sol Invictus cult was a Syrian religion brought to Rome by soldiers.'

Falconer, whose entire morning wardrobe consisted of splashing water in his face and throwing on his undershirt and sturdy black robe, sat on the edge of the bed they had shared, watching in fascination at Saphira's preparations. 'Er, yes. And some members of the imperial family. Heliogabalus was part Syrian. And he it was who placed Elagabal above even Jupiter, building a temple to his god.'

Saphira's toilet was complete, and she turned to face William. This was a new experience for them both. In Oxford, they were a little more discreet, and Falconer always returned to Aristotle's Hall and the care of his students before daybreak. She liked their present intimacy, and wondered if she could somehow persuade him to take time away from Oxford more often. Probably not – the university and the boys were his life. She sighed, and Falconer's face creased up into a worried frown.

'Why are you looking at me like that? What's wrong?' he asked.

She waved aside his concerns. 'Nothing. I was just thinking how far the cult spread, and if it survived the death of Heliogabalus. I mean, it has been a thousand years, but the bishop comes from a town that was once Roman Narbo.'

Falconer waved an admonitory finger. 'Now don't you go jumping to conclusions without any evidence. I have enough trouble trying to convince the King he must stick to collecting truths, without you going out on a limb.'

'You are right. Let's go and see if we can help His Majesty solve his murder case.' She paused. 'It would go some way to explain the bishop's odd behaviour, though, wouldn't it?'

Falconer growled and strode out of the room.

When they once again sat with the King in his bedchamber, he was dressed. Though he looked a little pale, and his physicians were in attendance, he was eager to continue their conversation from the middle of the night. 'I have something important to tell you.'

But before he could continue, Master Roger Megrim stepped forward. 'Majesty, I must protest at this unnecessary strain. You have sustained another relapse, and you should be bled again. You have a worrying excess of melancholy.'

Henry's pale face quivered, and he spat his words out through clenched teeth. 'You will not take any more blood from me. I would be surprised if you found any, after all you have taken. I would prefer any treatment you wish rather than bloodletting.'

Megrim smirked, as though he had always intended working his patient into a corner.

'Then I recommend the use of the properties of magnetic stones. Pulverized magnetite and milk is a remedy against breathlessness I learned from Albertus Magnus himself. I have it already prepared.'

He produced a small glass vial and pewter mug from his capacious pouch and unstoppered the vial. Having poured the contents into the little mug, he proffered it to the King. Grimacing, Henry tipped the mug up and swallowed the vile concoction. Satisfied, Megrim backed away from the King, then ushered his colleagues out of the room ahead of him. Henry wiped his whiskery face with the back of his hand, then spoke.

'Now at last I can tell you who I think killed Ralph. You see, I spoke to my new wardroper this morning.'

The King had felt peevish that his usual wardroper was not present to attend to him. This new one, a callow youth, had dug him in the ribs as he changed out of his sleeping gown. Now he was all thumbs as he attempted to tie the shirt ribbons across the King's sunken chest.

'Where's Ralph?' whined Henry, thinking to sack the lazy man who had failed to come at his call. Then it all came back to him. He remembered that the man was dead, and why he had wanted to speak to his replacement.

'Tell me, boy, what is the opinion among Ralph's fellows? Who do they think murdered him?'

The substitute wardroper, a natural gossip, could not resist the invitation. He was inexperienced in protecting the royal personage from unpleasant facts, and he blurted out the truth as he saw it.

'It is said that Ralph was dallying with Marjorie, the usher's wife. Sir Thomas is ready to clap Godric in chains, apparently. Of course, since Ralph's son took ill, his wife has had precious little time for him. She devoted all her efforts to caring for the boy. And though Ralph was worried, too, about his son, he resented coming second. Hence the tales of his straying away from her. They say the boy will not live, and that cannot be good for a marriage. But still, despite his son's state, no one really liked Ralph, my lord. He gave himself airs and claimed to know many a secret of the bedchamber. So it could have been any one of many who did for him . . .'

Suddenly, the youth remembered to whom he was speaking and paled in horror. What if the King now asked him what secrets Ralph had passed on about the King? Fortunately, Henry was too preoccupied with all this new information and dismissed his new wardroper from his mind.

*   *   *

'So, you see, it was Godric killed Ralph, because he was playing him for a cuckold.'

Falconer grimaced. 'And do you have any proof for this allegation, Majesty? Have you ascertained where Godric was the night Ralph was murdered?'

Henry's face darkened. He was not used to being contradicted or questioned in this way. But he contained his temper. 'If you do not like that idea, then how about the servant who envied Ralph's position, or the potboy who owed him money? I can bring you several possible murderers, and a little torture would be guaranteed to loosen their tongues.'

'And no doubt that will result in several confessions as the pain becomes unbearable. Which one will you choose then?'

The King flapped his bony hand disdainfully in the air, as if that were not a problem. 'Then I would execute them all, and that way be sure of retribution falling on the true killer.'

Falconer and Saphira exchanged worried looks. If this was the King's way of dealing out justice, then heaven help the innocent. Falconer tried another tack. 'Majesty, you have cleverly winkled out several possible truths here. Perhaps you could leave it to myself and Madam Le Veske to verify them, while you continue to examine the larger scheme of things.'

Henry smiled broadly, glad to have his own superior cunning acknowledged in the presence of this Oxford master. But still he wasn't sure how to proceed as Falconer had suggested. What other possibilities were there? He had to plunder the master's brain without revealing his ignorance. 'If you were me, what other people would you suspect?'

'Anyone present in the palace at the time must be a suspect. Sir Thomas, Roger Megrim, John Rixe, Brother Mark . . .'

Before he could stop her, Saphira eagerly added to Falconer's list. 'And Pierre, Bishop of Narbonne.'

Henry snorted in amusement. 'And Master William Falconer and Madam Saphira Le Veske, too.'

Falconer nodded gravely, agreeing with the King's assessment. 'As Your Majesty wishes. But we can vouch for each other's innocence, if you take my meaning.'

For a moment Saphira felt that Henry's eyes, boring into her soul, had taken on his legendary lynx-like stare. She blushed and looked down at her feet. When she looked up again, the look had once again faded into a clouded blue. But the King's quiet smile showed he knew exactly what Falconer had meant by his profession of their lack of involvement in the murder. He turned his gaze slowly on to Falconer.

'I shall speak to all those you have mentioned.'

Hastily, Falconer interposed with a bit of advice. 'May I suggest you do it as part of your normal daily proceedings? Truths often emerge when suspects are lulled into believing they are above suspicion.'

Henry chortled, wiping away the saliva that had dribbled from the corner of his lips and down his jutting and whiskery chin. 'You mean to say that I should not subject any of them to torture. I wonder what would happen to our relationship with Philip of France if it emerged I had put one of his bishops on the rack. Of course, I have often thought of applying torture to my three physicians in return for all they put me through. Especially as I have often heard it said that doctors should have three qualities: to be able to lie cleverly, to seem to be honest and to be able to kill without caring.'

Falconer refrained from saying the same qualities could be said to be the prime attributes of being a monarch. He still needed Henry's cooperation to solve Ralph's murder. And besides, the King had rallied in health somewhat at the thought of playing at being a deductive. A game that had taken his mind off the loss of the sky-stone, for a while at least.

Having taken their leave of the King, Falconer's thoughts returned to the stone. Did its theft have a part to play in the murder? Had Ralph seen someone take it, and lost his life for being in the wrong place at the wrong time? If so, who had reason to steal it? The physicians all had cause to envy the place of the sky-stone in their patient's belief in a cure for his ills. Falconer tested the idea on Saphira. 'Do you think one of the doctors stole the stone because they thought it replaced the trust the King may have had in their own power to cure him? Or did one of them steal it to be able to use it himself on those who believed in its powers?'

Saphira squeezed his arm. 'Either possibility may be the truth. But why come up with a theory about the doctors, when we have someone who is proven to have had a desire to possess the stone?'

'You're back to the bishop again, aren't you?'

'Well, you haven't yet been able to convince me he is not involved. And if he did steal it, and Ralph happened to see him ...'

Falconer reluctantly nodded his agreement. 'Then Narbonne would have had cause to kill him. That is just what I was thinking. But what about the doctors? They have reason, too. It seems we cannot agree who to pursue first, so let us try to eliminate the servants. Let's see if those whom the King has cast doubt on can explain where they were when Ralph was killed. And let us do it without resorting to torture.'

*   *   *

As the day progressed, Henry was getting more and more frustrated. He had followed Falconer's advice and resolved to question his physicians without them knowing they were being interrogated as a murder suspect. First he wrapped a shawl around his shoulders, then he burrowed fully dressed under his bedclothes. He proposed to feign illness. Which was no great problem, because he soon began to feel hot and feverish, encumbered in clothing as he was. He called his physicians into his bedchamber one by one, rather than having them beside him bickering all together. Of course, he gave precedence to John Rixe the apothecary, knowing this would perturb both Brother Mark and Master Roger Megrim. When he came to speak to them, they would be worried about their position in the pecking order. Henry reckoned he could teach Master Falconer a thing or two about putting suspects on the wrong foot.

Rixe, when he entered, looked particularly solemn. He hurried over to the King's bedside. 'Majesty, you look very hot and fevered today.'

Henry put on a croaking voice, playing his part. 'Yes, and I think I have a toothache, too.'

John Rixe's chubby face broke into a wide smile. He looked over his shoulder, making sure he was free of the ridicule Megrim might pour on his ancient remedies. Then he leaned close to the King, and whispered his advice. 'You must say the words *argidam, margidam, sturgidam,* and then spit in the mouth of a frog and ask it to make off with your toothache. My grandam swore by this.'

'*Ardigam* . . .?'

'*Argidam, margidam, sturgidam.* Do you wish me to obtain a frog for you? There will be many in the margins of the river.'

Henry looked into the innocent round eyes of John Rixe. 'I think not, Master Rixe. I only . . .'

But before he could continue, the apothecary was making use of this rare time alone with the King to expound on his knowledge. 'Words are very powerful remedies. For a fever, I only have to say *agodes, platino, placete* into your right ear, and your recovery is guaranteed. Shall I do that, Majesty?'

Henry held up a firm hand to stop Rixe's eager stooping towards his ear. He was so close, Henry could see the beads of sweat on the fat man's brow. 'No. Stop, man.'

Rixe reared up, startled by his patient's peremptory, and loud, tones. Just now, the King had been weakened, and his voice had been hoarse. Now he seemed more robust. Perhaps his incantations had had the desired effect after all. He beamed cheerfully at his patient. 'Is there anything else Your Majesty wishes to ask me?'

Henry frowned. 'There is, actually. This sky-stone that has gone missing. Do you think it can have any curative powers?'

'Undoubtedly, Majesty. I am a firm believer in the powers of stones, herbs and animals.'

Henry poked a finger at the fat man. 'So you might have stolen it yourself to use on others.'

John Rixe paled, and the room swam around him dizzyingly. He could hardly get his words out. 'Ma . . . majesty?'

The interviews with the two other physicians went just as badly. Brother Mark, whom Henry called in next, insisted on intoning a prayer over the hot and sweating King. He fidgeted in his bed as Mark went on and on.

'I adjure you, ye fevers, by the Father, the Son and the Holy Ghost, by Emmanuel, Sabaoth, Adonai and the Mediator, by prophet and priest, by the Trinity and the Unity, by Almighty God, King of all, by Jesus Christ and in virtue of his blood, by the purity of the angels and archangels—'

Henry became impatient. 'Will this take long, Brother Mark?'

The Dominican's voice rose and continued inexorably.

'—by patriarchs, prophets, apostles, matrons, confessors and virgins, and because you have no power to hurt. For Christ was made obedient unto death, even the death of the cross. In the Name of the Father, and of the Son and of the Holy Ghost.'

Henry sighed with relief. Now he could begin his real task. 'Brother Mark, as a man of God, do you believe in the powers of the sky-stone?'

The monk's brow furrowed, and he began to expostulate on the Church's attitude to graven images.

Henry cut in. 'So could you have stolen it to remove me from its bad influence?'

As Henry proceeded to interrogate his physicians badly, William and Saphira had embarked on a far more gentle process of sifting through the servants. Falconer had asked Sir Thomas Dalyson to assemble those the King had mentioned, and he had agreed. In fact, he was so agreeable about the matter that Saphira wondered if he already had an inclination to believe one of them was at fault and merely wanted Falconer's corroboration. If that was the case, he was soon to be disappointed.

The first servant to be brought before William and Saphira was the putative cuckold Godric. A short, round man with food stains down his tunic, the usher was inclined to bluster his way out of trouble. When it was suggested to him why he had cause to have killed Ralph, he bubbled over in self-righteous indignation. 'It is a foul slur on my wife's honour to suggest she had anything to do with Ralph in that way. She expressed a neighbourly concern for his

301

boy, who is dying and no one can save him. I can vouch for Marjorie's behaviour.'

'And yours, Godric, who can vouch for yours?'

This abrupt question was from Dalyson, who had remained in the room allocated to Falconer for his enquiries.

Falconer gave him a piercing look and waved the question aside. 'That is of no consequence to me. But what is of importance—' here, Falconer did put on a serious look, using the fear that Dalyson had already instilled in the usher '—what I must know is where you were the night that Ralph was killed.'

Godric went pale but then rallied a little as his bluster returned. 'I was in bed with my wife, of course. Where else would I have been?'

The procession of other servants that Dalyson paraded before Falconer and Saphira proved as fruitless as the first. Two men who were said to be envious of Ralph's position were also proven to be safely tucked up with their respective wives on the night in question. The final one to be brought by Dalyson was Tod the potboy. In conformity to his name, his nose was long and prominent, turning his features foxy, a trait emphasized by his freckled skin and ginger hair. When asked about his debts, he admitted he did owe Ralph some money.

'But it weren't a lot. Only pennies. Not enough to kill over. I was in bed, I swear.'

Although he protested greatly, Falconer could see the sweat prickling on his brow. But then, was his interrogation any easier on the boy than the threat of torture Falconer himself disdained? Both were equally scaring in the circumstances. Saphira saw his fear too, and intervened.

'Tod. It will go well if you are honest with us. The truth is your best friend, and no one—' at this point Saphira stared hard at Sir Thomas, who still hovered in the door-way '—will punish you, unless you truly killed Ralph.'

Tod's freckles stood out even more as his face turned green. 'No. No. I wasn't in the brewhouse.'

'Then where were you on the night of Ralph's murder?' Saphira's tone of voice was low and coaxing.

Tod hung his head. 'I was playing at dice with some other lads. I done it before. That's why I needed Ralph to fund me, 'cause I was losing.' He looked up, his eyes wide and tearful. 'I won't tell you who the others was.'

Saphira patted his arm. 'That is not necessary, Tod. Now you can go. But stop gambling – it will only get you into trouble.'

The boy nodded and shambled out of the room, avoiding looking into Dalyson's eyes as he passed. Falconer and Saphira exchanged glances. They both tacitly agreed that the murderer still may have come from among the servants, but it now looked unlikely. Saphira leaned over towards Falconer in order to speak without Dalyson hearing.

'It's the bishop.'

Falconer grinned. 'Care to bet on it?'

'What did I just say to Tod about gambling?'

Later that evening, Sir Thomas Dalyson told them that the King wished to see them urgently. He also said that they were not to look shocked when they saw Henry. He was sinking fast, and only the quest for the murderer seemed to be keeping him alive. So William and Saphira were in a sombre mood when they entered the King's chamber. Henry was already in his nightclothes and in bed, his ashen face almost the colour of the yellowish linen pillow he lay back on. But his eyes glittered. When he saw the pair, he roused himself, struggling to sit up. Saphira hurried over to his side and helped him up. She instinctively grasped his hand, as she would any invalid. Under her fingers she felt a large ring that had not been there the last time she had comforted him. He noted her reaction and smiled weakly.

'That is the great seal ring of the monarch. All my documents have its impression in wax at the bottom to confirm their authenticity. Now tell me what you have found out about my servants. Who is the one I am to have executed for theft and murder?'

Falconer grimaced and sat next to Saphira on the bedside. 'I am afraid all of your servants who had reason to have killed Ralph claimed to have been elsewhere. Either in bed with their wives or with other servants.'

He refrained from exposing Tod's little gambling ring. Henry's wan face grew a little flushed, and he shook his head impatiently. 'But they may have been lying.' It was not a question but a bald statement that still spoke of a desire to seek the truth with torture.

Falconer pressed forward, trying to persuade the King to follow logic and the assembly of truths rather than those older methods of testing guilt.

'Your physicians – did you find out anything about them?'

'Any one of them could have stolen my stone. They have the freedom of the palace at all hours and have cause to resent the efficacy of the sky-stone.'

He settled back on his pillow and began to tell Falconer and Saphira what he had learned from Rixe and Brother Mark. And finally from Roger Megrim, who he felt was his chief suspect.

Henry was frustrated by the way his interviews with the apothecary and the Dominican had gone. He was determined to do better with Master Roger Megrim of Cambridge University. The man was his chief physician, and the one who would be most embarrassed by the way the sky-stone had caused him to rally. Henry resolved to try his hardest to avoid the sort of direct questions that had thrown the other two quacks into confusion. Megrim was a clever man and would be hard to bamboozle. He finally called the Cambridge master to his chamber, and, when Megrim entered, it was obvious he was perturbed by the other two having been asked to attend on the King before he did. Henry tried to set him at his ease.

'I am feeling unwell still, master, and your colleagues have failed to apply a cure for what afflicts me.'

Megrim nodded wisely, a feeling of relief and pleasure crossing his stern features. 'Well, naturally, Majesty, they do not have the learning that seven years at Cambridge have instilled in me.'

Henry refrained from commenting that most of that study would have been of theory, when Megrim's head would have been stuck inside books and ancient texts. Precious little time was devoted to practical work such as a surgeon might get on the field of battle. Instead, the King smiled and asked the master his opinion on the current state of his health and what might have an effect on it.

'Could the sky-stone have had any effect in truth?'

Megrim prevaricated, not wishing to contradict the King.

'That is difficult to say, Majesty. Now, if you were speaking of magnetic stones, I could state categorically that beneficial effects are proven. Aristotle himself has recorded the therapeutic benefits of natural magnets, and Galen used magnets to relieve pain. He also recommended their external use to draw out evil humours, and noted that lodestones had aphrodisiacal powers as well as being a cure for melancholy.' He sighed. 'But then the sky-stone is not magnetic, is it?'

Henry looked at Falconer triumphantly. 'You see? How could Megrim know that the sky-stone is not a magnet unless he had stolen it and tested it?'

Falconer was not sure if the King had found out an important fact. Had he said anything about the properties of the stone in the presence of the physicians? He would have to think about that. But in the meantime he assumed the King had a point. Megrim could have been the perpetrator of the crime. Though another idea had already begun to niggle at the back of his mind, revolving around something Saphira had observed about the King. It was an idea that turned the connection of the theft of the skystone and the murder on its head.

Saphira, meanwhile, was pursuing her own theories. 'Where is the bishop? I have not seen him recently.'

Henry chuckled, though it came out a wheezy struggle for air. 'You still think that Narbonne is our killer? He certainly coveted the stone, and there is something of the heretic in him. He hinted to me of the connection between the Feast of the Nativity and the worship of the rising sun.'

'Sol Invictus,' murmured Falconer, looking towards Saphira. But her look of triumph was shattered by what Henry said next.

'But it could not have been him who killed Ralph. He was here at my bedside when all the clamour started. And you haven't seen him because he has gone back to France.'

Falconer stood up and took a surprised Saphira firmly by the arm. 'Majesty, we have two more people to see, and then we can present you with all the truths. You will then be able to work out for yourself who the murderer was.'

The King waved a weary hand and let his eyes close. 'Very well. Go and collect your truths. But I want this settled by the end of the day.'

'Two more people? If the bishop has disappeared, who else is there to see?'

Saphira was buzzing with curiosity. She knew William, and he rarely made such statements unless they were completely accurate. Falconer smiled enigmatically.

'The bishop may no longer be in London, but there is someone who can tell us something about his actions before he left. When we went to see Ralph's body, who did we see hurrying away?'

'The bishop, of course.'

'And where was he bound?'

Saphira had to admit she had no idea, so William enlightened her.

'He wasn't going back to his quarters. He was hurrying off in the opposite direction, towards the—'

'Towards the servants' quarters. And who would have been at Ralph's side just before the bishop, but the grieving widow.'

Falconer nodded eagerly. 'We didn't see her, but it was certain she had been there. And her presence may have given the bishop an idea. If he didn't steal the stone himself, he was so eager to possess it that he would have been pursuing the one who he thought had stolen it.'

Ralph's widow, Megan, was packing a small bundle with her possessions. With her husband dead, she had no further purpose in being in the palace of the King. Her reddened, round face was framed by a white cloth head veil that was wound under her chin. She seemed stoical, cheered only by the little boy who played happily around her feet. In reply to Falconer's questions, she confirmed that the bishop had been to speak to her.

'The French priest? Yes, he came here the morning Ralph was . . . was . . . died. But he seemed interested only in the stone.'

'The stone?'

'Yes. Ralph had this stone he said he had found in the outer courtyard. He insisted on little Robin playing with it, though the child showed little interest. The boy has been ill, you see. But look at him now. He is so happy. It is a shame his father could not have witnessed the change in him. So I gave the priest this stone, and he gave me some coins for it, though it was worthless. I shall need them to see me through, until I can find work. And little Robin is so hungry now.'

William and Saphira left the widow to her packing, and the happy boy to his play. He had learned all he needed to know, hinting to Saphira that it was her action of holding the King's hand that had clarified everything. She was puzzled, but he said it only remained for them to make his second enquiry of the court scribes before they reported back to the King. By the time they had done that, it was late, and Henry looked wan and tired. But he insisted on sitting up in his bed, and hearing Falconer out. When he had finished telling the King everything, William was sure he had enough evidence to unmask the murderer. But this was the King's case, and he was merely the assistant.

Uncertain, Henry fixed him with a wary eye. 'Do I need more truths?'

Falconer shook his head. 'You have all you need to know. So now it may be useful to get Sir Thomas to round up your servants and physicians and bring them here.'

'So do you think it was one of the servants? Or a quack?'

Henry was trying to delve into Falconer's mind in an effort to uncover his conclusions. But the master kept a stony face and merely smiled non-committally at his monarch. Peevishly, Henry called out for Sir Thomas Dalyson, who clearly had been hovering close to the bedchamber door all this time. He hurried off about his task, and soon the bedchamber filled with some ten servants without whom the King's existence was clearly intolerable. Falconer marvelled how he had managed to look after himself so long, if it took this number to minister to just one man, be he King of England or not.

The faces, whether young or old, long or broad, slim or rounded, had one feature in common. They all exuded the sweat of fear – a helpful tongue-loosener the King was going to use to his benefit. He began with a bold statement.

'In this room stands the killer of my wardroper.'

Before anyone could protest, the King pointed a bony finger at his usher, Godric. 'You are accused of being cuckolded by the dead man. Reason aplenty to kill him. And you . . .' his finger moved on to one of his stewards '—envied his position, lusting after it. You—' again the accusing finger moved and landed on poor Tod '—owed him money, more than you could afford to repay.'

One by one, he pointed out the reason why each servant present might have wished the wardroper dead, until everyone marvelled at the King's insight into the dark secrets of those who surrounded him. But then who was the murderer? Were they all? The King came to his conclusions.

'But all these reasons have long existed. Why would any of you kill Ralph now? And so precipitately? My three physicians had more urgent reason to murder Ralph, for he may have witnessed one of them taking the stone for his own purposes.'

All three physicians blanched as all the eyes in the room turned on them. A flood of protest fell from their lips, which the King stilled with a peremptory lifting of his hand.

'However, laying the murder at the feet of my quacks . . .' Henry used the word with great pleasure, and enjoyed the pinched look of horror on Megrim's face at being so named. He pressed on. 'Laying the murder at the feet of my . . . physicians would depend on one of them having been the thief of the stone. And I know none of them was, because Ralph himself was the thief.'

A gasp escaped the lips of all those in the room. This was a complete turnaround from what had been supposed. But the King was the King, and he knew best. Henry lay back on his heap of pillows and smiled at Falconer, revealing the jagged points of his worn teeth. Falconer nodded his encouragement, knowing the King had seen the trail of evidence he had carefully laid before him. Ralph had been killed not because he witnessed the theft of the stone, but because he had seen something much more serious happen in the King's bedchamber. And he had been in the bedchamber in order to steal the stone to cure his ailing son.

Henry's eyes glittered, and his breath came in great gasps.

'I have a syllogism. My seal ring was missing between the twelfth and fourteenth days of this month. There is on record a document dated the thirteenth, and sealed with my ring, whereby Sir Anthony Ledsham was deprived of his lands by my authority. I did not have the ring then; therefore this action was a fraud.'

There was a confused muttering in the bedchamber, and those present glanced nervously at each other. If the King was correct, and not confused, such a misuse of the seal was treasonable.

'I have another syllogism.' The King's voice was firmer and more penetrating than it had been for some months. 'He who possessed my ring on that day is a thief and fraudster, who sought to gain Ledsham's land illegally. Second, anyone who saw that ring in the thief's possession on that day needed to be silenced. Ralph, in the process of . . . borrowing the sky-stone, saw the secretive returning of my ring while I slept. Therefore, I deduce the person who had the ring and placed it in my bedclothes so that I might think it had fallen off my finger is both a thief and a murderer. Is that not so, Sir Thomas?'

Sir Thomas Dalyson blanched and leaped towards the door. William Falconer swiftly blocked his path, the smile of satisfaction on his face matching that of his monarch.

Historical Note

King Henry III of England peacefully gave up his soul to the Lord on the sixteenth day of November 1272 after a reign of fifty-six years and twenty-nine days. But not before he had seen Sir Thomas Dalyson dance on the gibbet for his treasonable misdeeds.

ACT FIVE

London, 1606

This was the worst hangover ever, no question. It was not only the sour taste in my mouth or the pulse throbbing in my head or the cast-iron sensation in my limbs. It was the way the bed kept swaying. I was lying on my back, and I feared that if I opened my eyes – something I wasn't planning to do for a year or two – then I would see the dingy ceiling of my bedchamber in Tooley Street swooping and plunging above my head like a giant, demented bird.

Fortunately, I had no reason to open my eyes. No reason at all since it was night-time. There was a deep blackness beyond the glow-worms flitting across my inner eyelids. I felt justified in sinking back into a fume-filled slumber with the hope that when I awoke again, after a millennium or two, I might feel more like myself, more like Nick Revill.

Nick Revill of the King's Men . . . a company of players whose home is the Globe Theatre . . . which is an edifice in Southwark . . . which is a borough on the South Bank of the Thames. The South Bank? The unrespectable side, I hear you say. All those brothels and bear-pits and taverns and prisons. But what I say back to you is this: despite our brothels and bear-pits, we have some famous people for friends. Take the King, for example. Yes, King James – the first of that name to rule over England (but the sixth of that name in his native Scotland) – he is our patron. And William Shakespeare, he's one of our shareholders as well as our chief writer. He is famous, our Mr Shakespeare. You *have* heard of him, haven't you . . . ?

Rambling on like this to myself, I must have slipped back into an alcoholic stupor. I could even hear the sound of my own snoring, an odd effect. When I came to myself once more, the throbbing in my head had eased, and my limbs felt less like pieces of cast-iron. It was still the middle of the night, though. Blackness pressed against my eyelids, while the bed I lay on continued to sway gently as if I was afloat on a sea of ale.

And at that moment a doubt started to burrow into my clotted brain. I pinched at the material beneath my splayed hand. The fustian bedding supplied by my landlady, Mrs Ellis, might not be of the highest quality, but it was less coarse than what I now felt at my fingers' ends. Mrs Ellis's mattress would probably not have been good enough for the King of England (and Scotland) but it was a nest of luxury compared with what I was currently lying on.

I sniffed the air. I was used to the smell of my bedchamber, the mouldy odour of the plaster, the faint taint of soot in the air. I could smell damp here, too, but it was a different and more bracing style of damp. There was no sootiness in the air, either. Alert now, I strained my ears but heard nothing familiar. No ringing church bells, no neighbourly cries, no sound of cartwheels rising up from my street, Tooley Street. Instead, there were ominous creaking noises and what sounded like rain gurgling down the street-kennels. A lot of rain.

Only now did I dare to open my eyes, but slowly, as if afraid of what I was about to see. It was so dim that I sensed rather than saw a low wooden ceiling with cracks and empty knot-holes that admitted a little daylight. Only

313

a little light but sufficient to reveal that, wherever I was, it was not my top-floor bedchamber in Tooley Street. And the explanation, which I had been holding at bay for many minutes, now flooded in on me.

The continuous rocking motion was explained. So, too, were those creaks and gurgles. My God, how had I woken up on a boat? How, in the name of Christ, had I come to board a boat in the first place? And not one of those ferries that plies the Thames under the command of a foul-mouthed boatman, but a proper vessel equipped for the open seas! How did I know all this? I struggled to put together the fragments of the previous evening but the effort was too great.

I shut my eyes more quickly than I'd opened them. Maybe if I kept them closed for long enough, then the whole scene would disappear. Maybe when I looked again I would be restored, body and soul, to Tooley Street. But the brain, which had been befuddled, now began to bring back the circumstances that had landed me on a sea-going vessel. A vessel called . . .? Let me see. Yes, the *Argo*. That was it. I could hear the man saying it. What was *his* name? Case, yes, Jonathan Case. I could hear Case saying, 'My craft is the *Argo*. You're an educated man, Mr Revill. You recognize the name, don't you? The *Argo*. The vessel that Jason commanded in his quest for the golden fleece of antiquity.'

That was what Case had said, or as near as I can recall. After that, everything went a bit hazy – although in truth it had been hazy enough before.

With eyes still closed, I tried to put events in order, to make some sense of how I'd come to be on board the *Argo*. Because that was surely where I was, lying awkwardly in a swaying berth, listening to the groans of the ship's timbers and the gurgling waters as they rushed past inches from where I lay. Was I already at sea? The thought was almost too terrifying to contemplate. Instead, I clung to the notion of land, dry land.

The previous evening I had definitely been on dry land. Very dry land indeed. Legal land, since we of the King's Men were performing William Shakespeare's *Twelfth Night* in that den of lawyers, the Middle Temple. It was spring-time, and although *Twelfth Night* may seem unseasonal it is a play for all times and every audience.

We've performed in the Middle Temple on previous occasions, and I have to say that the fledgling lawmen make for a coarser and more noisy audience than the ground-lings at the Globe. Since they were well-off and educated, that's what you would expect. Unlike the groundlings, the young lawyers did not stand on their hind legs but rather perched on bum-numbing benches in the well of the dining hall while their seniors – benchers and serjeants-at-law and the like – were enthroned on a dais at the opposite end to our makeshift stage. Many of these were in the company of lady guests, whose incessant chatter did not signify much interest in anything we poor players were up to. Don't get me wrong. We were pleased enough with the audience. They paid well, and the men among them were (or soon would be) people of influence. More than other trades, players need friends in high places.

We had an especially elevated guest this evening. It was the French legate, the ambassador to England, a gentle-man by the name of Antoine le Fèvre de la Broderie. He and his entourage had pride of place in the middle of the dais. I don't know why he was gracing us with his pres-ence. Perhaps he was on friendly terms with the legal greybeards of the Temple. Perhaps he was a devotee of William Shakespeare. Certainly, a visit to this place was a simple enough matter for him, since the little patch of France-in-London which he inhabited was close by, in Salisbury Court off Fleet Street. However, my knowledge of Monsewer de la Broderie did not extend much further.

Where was I. . . ? Ah, yes.

It is a grand place, this Middle Temple, regardless of the quality of its occupants. Above the dais are banks of varnished portraits which glimmer in the light of countless candles. The mighty roof, with its tiers of beams, dissolves into mysterious shadows. On everything is the lustre of power and wealth. And solemnity, if you ignore the braying young lawyers.

They particularly brayed at me, for I was playing that foolish knight, Sir Andrew Aguecheek, who blusters and threatens but whose sword turns to a piece of limp string when it comes to fighting a duel. Even though I never came to proper blows against my opponent, Viola (attired as the masculine Cesario), I received a painful injury which caused plenty of amusement in the pit of the Temple hall. He – or rather she – made an unexpected thrust at me with the foil and, when I twisted clumsily away to avoid it, I fell with a resounding clunk on the boards of our makeshift stage. As I scrambled to my feet with the guffaws of the lawyers ringing in my ears, I felt a stabbing sensation in my side which made me fear I might have cracked a rib.

Once we were offstage, Michael Donegrace, who was playing Viola-Cesario, was all concern until I reassured him that no damage had been done. He shouldn't have lashed out at me unexpectedly, but, equally, I should have known how to avoid his foil or at least to have fallen without injuring myself. But I've noticed that accidents are more likely if you're playing on strange territory.

By the time that Feste the clown had finished the play of *Twelfth Night* with his bitter-sweet song and we players had done a little jig – a cautious little jig for me – to round off the action, and once we had bowed to the applause, made our final exits, changed out of costume and quit the Temple, night had fallen. It was cold outside with a draught coming off the river. We wrapped ourselves tighter in our street clothes and looked towards the rest of the evening. Some were going home to wives and families, some to idle away their time in an alehouse, some to do the second thing before the first if they were willing to face their wives afterwards. I, lacking wife and child, could visit the alehouse without a qualm.

There was a place called the Devil's Tavern not far from the Inns of Court which was convenient as well as a couple of cuts above the dives in Southwark. I'd already arranged with one of my fellows, Jack Wilson, to stop off at the Devil on the way to our respective lodgings. With my side still aching from the clumsy fall onstage, I thought that a draught or three would numb the pain before I sought the shelter of my bed.

I spotted Jack in conversation with a man and a woman near the entrance into Middle Temple Lane. Not players but members of the audience. They were fitfully lit by the flare outside the porter's lodge. Noticing me, Jack beckoned. I was going in that direction anyway.

'Nick,' he said, 'you will help me out here, I am sure. I have a question, or rather this gentleman has a question. He wants to know whether William Shakespeare has ever been to sea. I thought you might know, since you are closer to William than I.'

This was such an odd thing to ask that I wasn't sure what to answer, not that I knew the answer in any case. Instead, I glanced at the couple in the flickering torchlight by the lodge. The man was thickset, with firm features and a square-cut beard. He was wearing a long gown and holding an ornate but serviceable stick with one hand while the other grasped a bag. It was hard to see much of the woman, on account of her broad-brimmed hat, but I had an impression of a slight figure swathed in expensive clothes.

'I know no more than you, sir,' I said. 'Why do you ask?'

'Your Shakespeare writes of the sea and seamen and shipwrecks with real feeling,' said the man. 'The struggle of the brother and sister to reach the shore, their poignant separation, the quiet courage of the captain and Antonio here.'

He gestured at Jack Wilson, who had taken the part of Antonio in *Twelfth Night*. I wanted to say that WS had created these figures and their emotions from his imagination, or perhaps that he had copied them out of old books, but somehow it would have seemed like giving away a trade secret, so I just replied, 'Perhaps you'd better ask the author.'

I knew that they would be most unlikely to find Shakespeare, let alone ask him anything. The playwright was elusive, almost anonymous, unless he wanted you to know that he was there. But the large gentleman responded to my cursory answer with a warmth that made me feel slightly guilty.

'Perhaps I will ask him! Thank you. I know Richard Burbage.'

He knew Burbage. That was different. The Burbage brothers, Dick and Cuthbert, were the most senior figures among the Globe shareholders. Dick was also a player.

'We much enjoyed the play,' added the man. 'I believe that the French legate did, too. We were sitting near his party. A handsome fellow.'

'*Il est un favori du roi.*' This comment came from Jack who, after sensing rather than seeing our baffled expressions, said, 'Well, it's no secret, is it? Queen Anne favours the Spanish ambassador while the King is . . . partial to the French legate.'

Jokes and ribald comments about King James's tastes were everywhere in London, but those who voiced them tended to know and trust their audience. I was a bit surprised that Jack was speaking like this in front of a couple of strangers. Perhaps the man was, too, for he changed the subject by addressing me.

'Have you recovered from your fall this evening, sir?'

'Oh, that. It was just a piece of stage business.'

'Surely not,' said the man. 'I could tell from the way you tumbled down and, more important, from the way you got up afterwards that you were hurt. Some damage to your ribs, perhaps?'

Since this was not too far from what I was already thinking and feeling, I gave the feeble reply: 'It was nothing.'

'I am glad to hear it,' he said. 'In recompense for the enjoyment of the play, however, can I offer you both some hospitality? I am staying fairly close by.'

I glanced at Jack. We sometimes got such invitations from people who want to consort with players, for various reasons. Was this gentleman someone important? Or could he be thanked for his kindness and then ignored? A few companionable drinks in the Devil and then my solitary bed seemed preferable, to be honest. But if he knew the Burbages, who were our employers . . .

'I am a doctor,' the man said conclusively.

'Of law?' said Jack Wilson.

'No, a doctor of physic,' he said, raising his bag as if it contained the tools of his trade. 'Dr Jonathan Case. This lady is my young cousin, Thomasina.'

The lady dipped her head, or rather her hat, in acknowledgement but said not a word. Sensing reluctance to his offer on our part, Dr Case said to me in an oddly pressing way, 'If you accompany me, I can give you something to soothe the pain in your side, Mr. . . .?'

So both Jack and I were compelled to introduce ourselves. It would have been churlish to refuse the invitation now, particularly after Thomasina laid a gloved hand on my arm as if to reinforce the other's words.

Jack and I followed the couple from the lodge. I observed that they stopped on the threshold and that Jonathan Case looked in each direction as if he was about to cross a busy street. But the lane was empty as far as I could see. To the right was a glow of light from the top of the stairs leading to the river. The trees in Temple Gardens, newly in leaf, rustled unseen in the breeze.

As they walked up Middle Temple Lane and into Fleet Street, Dr Case put his stick and bag in one hand and offered the other arm to his female companion. But she seemed unwilling to move closer to him. When we reached the broader thoroughfare, the physician once more looked carefully around. This time there were a few passers-by, but none of them paid us any attention. Case rapped his stick sharply on the ground before waving it in the air. A covered coach drawn by a pair of horses materialized from the shadows of Temple Bar and lumbered in our direction.

The driver reined in his team and leaned down from his perch to listen to the physician's instructions, which I did not catch except for the name at the end. When Dr Case addressed the driver as Andrew, I realized that Jack Wilson and I were in the presence of an important gentleman, or at any rate one who was wealthy enough to own or to hire his own equipage. We clambered aboard, and the carriage pulled away up the gentle incline towards Ludgate.

'How did you enjoy the play, madam?' said Jack. Like all players, he wanted to talk about the most recent performance. It is what we would have discussed had we gone to the Devil's Tavern.

'She felt sorry for Malvolio,' said Dr Case, answering for his companion. 'The steward *was* most notoriously abused, but then he deserved to be.'

The cousins, young and middle-aged, were sitting opposite Jack and me. The seats were low, and the space between us was all knees. I had hoped to get a better look at them, but scarcely a glimmer penetrated the carriage from outside, since there was little enough illumination in the street and the window curtains were almost drawn. When we halted at Ludgate, instead of looking out as would have been natural, the physician pressed himself back into his seat, clutching his bag and his stick to himself. We heard the coachman exchange some words with one of the watchmen at the gates, which were not yet shut up for the night, and then we trundled on.

I wondered how far we were going. Where was Case's house? Already I regretted accepting this invitation. Could Jack and I contrive an excuse to stop the carriage and get off?

'Were you a guest of someone at Middle Temple, Dr Case?' I said. 'It was not Mr Burbage?'

'No,' he said curtly out of the gloom. Then, as if he owed us more of an explanation: 'I am acquainted with a gentleman in the French legation. He suggested that Thomasina and I might be diverted by the play.'

'Which you were.'

'Indeed,' said Case, as if he had forgotten his earlier compliments. 'Your Shakespeare writes most feelingly of . . . of . . . the sea. As I said.'

I couldn't help contrasting his manner now with his eagerness for our company while we were talking by the lodge. Something about the man or his manner obviously made Jack uneasy, too, for he said, 'I hope your dwelling is not too far off, Dr Case. Both Nick and I must return to our lodgings in good time. We have a rehearsal to attend tomorrow. We are fined a shilling if we are late.'

The physician gave a mild snort of derision, whether at the small size of the fine – although a shilling was a whole day's pay to us – or at the notion that a young man should be concerned about getting to bed on time.

'Don't worry,' he said. 'I shall see you safe home.'

We lapsed into silence as the carriage clattered along. It was not a comfortable ride. Quite apart from the hardness of the seats, we received frequent jars when the driver failed to see or was unable to avoid one of the many holes that pitted the road. I was glad I was not wealthy enough to have to employ any other means of transport than my legs. And now we seemed to be on a downward slope with the smell of the river wafting through the unglazed windows. After a few more minutes we drew up.

'Here we are,' said Case. 'After you, dear sir.'

I got down quickly enough, followed by Jack. A spasm from my side reminded me that the physician was supposed to be providing something to dull the discomfort. If he really was a physician . . . if he really lived here.

My doubts were on account of where the coach had stopped. We were by a wharf on the river, and the neighbouring buildings had the look of storehouses. This place was either Botolph's Wharf or the Lyon Key, I wasn't sure which in the darkness. To our right as we faced across the river was the great bulk of London Bridge. Against the night sky it stood like a mighty wall but one interrupted by pinpricks of light from the windows of the houses that line it. From below came the rumble of water as the tidal surge forced its way through the piers of the bridge. Was this our destination? It must be, for the next thing we heard was the doctor's carriage pulling away.

The sight of the bridge and the sound of the Thames were strangely reassuring. I had only to cross the river to be at my lodgings at Mrs Ellis's in Tooley Street within a few minutes. Jack Wilson also lived on the far side of the river, the unrespectable side. I was about to say to Jack that we should quit the scene now when I became aware that Jonathan Case and cousin Thomasina were behind us. I must have been jumpy, because I suspected some trick, even an ambush, and whirled around, causing me to groan involuntarily from the hurt in my side. But Case put his hand gently on my shoulder and used his stick to point ahead.

'We are down there,' he said. 'On the river.'

'You live on the river?' I said, incredulous.

'No, no. I am about to board a boat, because like you players I need to make an early start tomorrow morning, with the tide. Come on board and I shall explain. Oh, and I will find a remedy for that injury you gave yourself, Mr Revill.'

He went to the head of the stairs leading to a landing stage and, as he had done in Fleet Street, rapped with his stick on the cobbled ground. Within a few instants a figure puffed up the stairs, bearing a smoky torch. He stood as still as a statue to illuminate our descent down the greasy flight. In the diffused glow cast by the torch, I could see little of the boat which we boarded except that it was substantial enough to be a merchant vessel, with tree-like masts bearing furled sails. The low murmur of voices, together with the smell of pipe smoke and the embers of a brazier near the bow showed that the craft was manned.

Picking their way among various unidentifiable marine items on deck, Case and his cousin paused by a massy construction in the aft portion of the vessel. Do I have these terms right – aft and bow? I'm neither knowledge-able about boats nor happy away from dry land, to be truthful. I have never seen the open sea and have no great desire to catch sight of it. Even taking the ferry to cross the Thames, especially when on the broader stretches below the bridge and if there's a hint of bad weather, has me glancing nervously at the shore.

'Welcome to our quarters, gentlemen,' said Case, as he opened a door and ushered us through. We negotiated some steep wooden steps and emerged into a surprisingly spacious area below the deck. It was illuminated by candles and oil lamps and, on this chill spring evening, warmed by a metal tripod heaped with charcoal. The ceiling was low, scarcely above head height, but the other dimensions were generous enough. A table and benches occupied the centre. There were curtained-off spaces in the side walls but no windows or ports. At the far end were a pair of doors. A black cat was curled on the floor near the char-coal tripod, but it quickly roused itself and bolted up the steps we had just descended.

Jonathan Case and Thomasina stood in the centre of the cabin, watching as we took in the surroundings. The lady was still overshadowed by her hat, and the better light revealed no more than I'd seen already: a slim, almost lanky figure. Under a mantle, she was wearing a bodice and kirtle of fine scarlet taffeta. As for Case, the gentleman's cap and coif marked him out as a physician almost as clearly as if he'd been carrying a urine flask, but somehow this just deepened the mystery. I think Jack was as baffled as I. What business had caused this doctor of physic to board a vessel on the Thames? Furthermore, what business meant that he had to sail with the tide tomorrow morning?

Before anyone could speak, there was a clatter on the steps and a man entered the cabin. He was well dressed in a maroon doublet and elaborate ruffs. The only unexpected note was a whistle hanging on a cord around his neck.

'I did not expect—'

He was addressing the physician but, catching sight of Jack and me, he broke off.

'—expect us to return with company?' said Dr Case smoothly, as if in continuation of what the other man was about to say. 'These gentlemen are players from the King's Men. They were taking part in the piece at Middle Temple. The play we have recently attended. They have been gracious enough to accept my offer of hospitality on board.'

All this was said slowly and with care. The other man stroked his beard, square-cut like the doctor's, while his watchful gaze flicked between the two of us. 'Well, I suppose you are welcome on board the *Argo*,' he said, 'but know that we cast off at first light tomorrow.'

The last part of the remark seemed to be directed at Dr Case rather than us. I realized the two men were brothers. There was the same stocky build and the same firm expression, and that more elusive sense of being two individuals cut from the same length of cloth. Therefore, Thomasina must be cousin to this gentleman also, although neither had so much as looked at the other.

'You will join us in a glass, Colin?' said Case.

'No. The only glass I am concerned with is the half-hour glass. As I said, we leave early and there is much to be done.'

He nodded at us and clumped back up the stairs. Moments later, we heard him barking an order on deck.

It sounded as if he was taking out his irritation on one of the mariners.

'As you probably guessed, that is my brother,' said Dr Case. 'He is the captain of this vessel, the *Argo*. Forgive his terseness, but his mind is obviously full of tide-times and half-hour glasses and caulking and . . . things nautical.'

'This is his cabin?' I said, wondering if that was the reason for the other's gruff manner.

'This is the great cabin,' said the physician. 'It is where sailors of rank and any travelling gentlemen sleep and eat.'

We must have looked baffled at the absence of beds, for Dr Case proceeded to show us some hidden lodgings. Set into the walls on either side behind the curtains were alcove-like recesses containing mattresses. Once inside, the sleeper might make himself secure by drawing the curtain. Each space was provided with a shuttered port through which one could see a flicker or two of light from the world outside. The shipmaster had more elaborate quarters, a squared-off space behind one of the doors at the end of the great cabin. This was provided with a full-size bed which one did not have to contort oneself unduly to enter.

Case explained that a trading vessel like the *Argo* carried paying travellers from time to time, and that they required better sleeping arrangements than were available to the common mariners, who ate, slept and took their ease in the stench of the fo'c's'le under the bowsprit. The two things most to be valued at sea, he said, were a little area to oneself and a little bit of light. And, yes, he was presently occupying the bed belonging to his brother, the shipmaster.

'I am paying him well. The least I can require is to be accommodated in comfort on the journey.'

'Where are you travelling to, Dr Case?' said Jack.

'St-Malo.'

I had not thought he would answer so directly. I rather thought St-Malo was in France but did not like to ask for fear of appearing ignorant.

'To reply to your next question, Mr Wilson, I am going to meet a man in St-Malo about . . . a private matter. My brother, he is to pick up a cargo of French wine. He sails with empty tuns and substitutes them for full ones. He tells me that I am fortunate to be sailing on a wine trader. They smell sweeter and their seams are tighter than other vessels'. Talking of which, Thomasina, would you pour us some wine?'

The woman busied herself with a jug and glasses and brought the drinks across to us one by one. She kept her eyes averted and that, coupled with the shadowy hat brim, meant that we had yet to get a clear look at her. Oddest of all, she had not spoken a single word so far, but she performed the task of serving drinks gracefully enough. I noticed a mole on the back of her hand and, queerly, it seemed the only personal note about her.

We sipped appreciatively as the physician described the wine, which was an Osney – a fine specimen of its type – from Alsace (wherever that is). Then Jonathan Case said, 'Now, Mr Revill, if you wouldn't mind unfastening your doublet . . . so that I may examine you.'

I had forgotten the injury to my side, but the discomfort returned the moment it was mentioned. I put down my glass and unbuttoned my doublet. The doctor felt my ribs beneath my shirt and nodded when I drew a sharp breath or winced.

'No great damage done, although you may have cracked a rib,' he said. 'You will have to avoid exertion. No sudden movements. No leaping about or fighting duels, even mock ones.'

'Duels and leaping about are part and parcel of a player's lot,' said Jack. 'You'll have to play old men for a week or two, Nick.'

Case moved to open the bag, which had been resting by his feet all this time. There was some sort of complicated clasp to it, and he turned his back on us, as if to keep its precise operation a secret. When he turned to face us again, he was holding an object swathed in satin. He carefully unfolded it to reveal a lump of darkish rock about the size of his hand. He passed it to me. 'Hold it. It should bring a benefit.'

Not understanding, I nevertheless grasped the rock, which was so smooth and deliberately shaped that I assumed it had been carved and polished by hand. It was difficult to say exactly what the shape represented, however. Looked at one way, it was a bird with curved wings. Looked at in another, it might be a simple boat with a keel and a stubby mast. Or it was no such thing but a mere piece of rock, although curiously weighty. By the light of the candles in the cabin, I could make out a series of small grooves on one side. Accidental scratches or deliberate markings?

I observed Dr Case watching me intently. How was I meant to respond? What 'benefit' was the rock supposed to confer? But all at once I did experience a sort of access of energy even as the pain in my side dulled.

'What is it? Is it stone?'

'It has several properties,' said Case, putting out his hand for the rock. 'Look at this.'

He directed us towards the far end of the cabin by the pair of doors. A box with a glazed cover was set into the floor. Inside was an arrangement of metal hoops supporting a disc seemingly inscribed with the image of a sunburst surmounted by a pointer. An oil lamp was hanging overhead.

'That's a gimbal,' said Jack, indicating the arrangement of metal rings.

'Very good, my friend. However rough the seas and however violent the pitching of the boat that . . . item in the centre . . . will stay level.'

I had the idea that quick-witted Jack knew what we were looking at. As for me, I was confused and, in my mind's eye, could see the rough seas and the pitching boat.

'Watch,' said Dr Case.

He brought the black stone near to the glass cover of the box and moved it from side to side. At once, the pointer became agitated and swung about as if it was dancing in response to the stone. Dr Case looked at Jack for an explanation.

'The stone you are holding is acting as a magnet to the compass.'

So this object was a compass. I knew the *word*, of course, but had never seen the *thing*. But then I've never been to sea.

'This is no stone but a piece of iron,' said our physician.

'Where is it from?' said Jack.

'Not from this earth,' said the physician, pausing after this remark in a style that would have done him credit onstage. 'It fell from the heavens to a land of ice and who knows how many centuries ago. This is a sky-stone.'

As with the compass, I had heard of such things but never seen one, let alone held it in my hands. Fallen from the sky, eh? This idea was even stranger than the fact that the stone came from 'a land of ice', something which sounded as remote as the moon. I looked at the stone again and seemed to feel a strange vitality flowing from the thing. I passed it to Jack. Then, to show the refinement of my feelings, I said, 'Is it valuable?'

'Yes,' said Case, without enlarging on the subject.

I wondered whether his trip to St-Malo was connected to the stone. As if to reinforce his remark about its being a valuable item, he took the stone back from Jack and made a show of storing it inside a cabinet. This turned out to be another curious item. Not the cabinet itself, which was an ordinary if handsome piece of furniture made of cedar. No, it was the lock securing the cabinet which Case decided to demonstrate to us, his appreciative audience. He'd been about to open it, then paused.

'Look at this, gentlemen,' said Case.

We crouched down to join him as he played the light from a candle across the brass plate of a lock, which was about the size of an extended hand. There was the figure of a woman on it in relief, with frisky legs visible beneath a skirt and an arm extended as if she were about to dance. Her head was surmounted by a large hat rather like cousin Thomasina's. I glanced around to see where that lady was now, but we three men were alone in the cabin. She must have left while we were examining the compass.

Case pressed down on the figure's hat, which tilted back at a jaunty angle and which presumably operated a catch mechanism, for he was then able to swing open the door. Wrapping the sky-stone in the satin cloth once again, he deposited it with exaggerated care in the cabinet, closed the door and refastened the catch by nudging the woman's hat back to a level position. This didn't seem so very secure, since anyone familiar with the hat trick would have been able to unfasten the cabinet. But there was more to come.

Case flicked with a forefinger at one of the miniature legs, and it kicked up to reveal a keyhole whose widest point was in a position which combined suggestiveness with practicality. Jack and I looked at each other in amusement. The physician produced a key from the folds of his gown and gave it a couple of twists in the keyhole. I heard the soft click as a bolt slid home inside the device.

Case stood up with a satisfied look once he'd restored the female figure's leg to its former position and back to respectability as well. 'Made by Johannes Wilken of Dordrecht – in the Low Countries, you know. It has an additional feature which guarantees security. Look again.'

I noticed that the lock-plate held more puzzles. The woman's arm was extended not so much in preparation for the dance but so as to point at a clock-like dial, above which some words had been inscribed, although the light was not good enough for me to make them out. Jack took his turn to look.

'I have heard of this, I think,' he said.

'It is a detector lock, my friends,' said Case quickly, unwilling to find himself trumped. 'Every time the key is turned to lock up the cabinet, the dial moves around a notch so that the lady's hand indicates a higher number. Note that it presently stands at thirty-nine. So if, when I next open the door, I find my lady fingering the number forty I will know that some villain has been playing fast and loose with my key. And the inscription now, you must want to know what that says . . .'

He peered at the cabinet lock as if to familiarize himself with the words again and then recited:

> 'None but my master shall open me,
> Respect my virtue if you be not he.'

Having delivered himself of all this news and the rhyme, Jonathan Case urged us to make ourselves comfortable on one of the benches at the table while he refilled our glasses.

The good doctor proceeded to talk to Jack and me about our work. He was full of praise for our abilities as players. He complimented us on our nimbleness, the injury to my side nothwithstanding. He said that we must have remarkable memories to hold our parts in our heads for one day, only to have to discard them on the next in preparation for a fresh drama. He remarked that the common belief about players – that we were little better than uneducated vagabonds – was obviously untrue, for here (looking at Jack) was a fellow who knew about gimbals and spoke French. I gazed in surprise at Jack and then remembered that he'd said something about the French legate being *un favori du roi*, a favourite of King James. For his part, Jack mumbled some words about having had an aunt who came from Paris. For some reason this struck us as enormously funny – an aunt from Paris! – and we hooted with laughter.

By this time, as you'll probably have gathered, we were fairly pissed. Jonathan Case kept filling our glasses with the Osney and we kept on downing it. All thoughts of next day's rehearsals were forgotten. After all, it was only a short walk back across the river, and the gatehouses at each end of the bridge closed later than the city ones so as to accommodate the pleasure-seeking folk who frequented Southwark in the evening. We had time for another drink. Always time for another one.

We were well settled in when a man descended the short flight of steps to the cabin. None of us heard him enter. Case started up in surprise. He did not look pleased to see the newcomer.

'Mr Tallman,' he said. 'What are you doing here?'

'I do not know that it is your business, Dr Case, but your brother wanted to consult me about the voyage.'

'Well, it is I who have chartered the ship,' said the physician. 'He should have told me first.'

The other shrugged. He fitted his name, if I'd heard it right (by this point my senses were none too sharp). Tallman was a tall man, and a dry, austere-looking one. His black garb might have enabled him to pass for a puritan in a poor light, except that his fingers glittered with rings and the shoes on his feet were ornamented with fine silver buckles. He had not acknowledged Jack or me, by the by.

'You can see that Colin is not here. You must go and find him elsewhere.'

The stranger turned about without a word and went up the steps as silently as he'd come. Jack said, 'He is a navigator, a pilot?'

'No, no, Henry Tallman is . . .'

But whatever Tallman was exactly we were not to find out. Instead, Case let the sentence drift away and launched into a disquisition on sailors and their strange beliefs.

At one point I got up to go outside. Unsteady on my feet, I had to cling on to the edge of the table. I stumbled up the steps, across the deck and, since the bulwarks which prevented the mariners falling off the boat were quite low, urinated with ease over the side of the boat, managing the considerable feat of not tumbling into the river. The night was still and cold. Down the front end of the craft the embers in the brazier had almost died out and there was no sound of voices. My unease at being on board a boat had gone. But then rather than going anywhere we were moored tight against the bank. I wondered what had happened to Case's brother and his cousin, the silent Thomasina. Then I returned to the cabin and accepted Dr Case's offer of another glass. And another. He was a generous host, dispensing several glasses for every one he consumed himself.

I'm not sure how the rest of the evening went. Knowing that the bridge gatehouses would by now be shut, Jack and

I must have accepted Case's offer of accommodation for the night, or perhaps we simply slipped into a deep, fume-filled sleep without any offer being made. Either way, we did not leave the *Argo* that night.

I've got only a couple of other memories. One was of being half hoisted, half propped up, before being escorted down into a place that was dark and dank. The other memory was earlier, even though I was still far gone, with eyelids drooping while the candles in the great cabin guttered. The physician's cousin Thomasina finally returned – where had she been all this time? – and the middle-aged man and the young woman embraced in a close manner that, if I'd been in my right mind, I would have said was very un-cousin-like.

All of this, the extended story of the previous evening beginning in Middle Temple with *Twelfth Night* and ending in a stupefied state on board the *Argo*, unfolded behind my tightly closed eyes in much less time than it takes to tell it here. Nevertheless, even in my mind I stretched the story out longer for fear of opening those eyes a second time and discovering what I already knew.

I had to open them eventually. To glimpse a dark, cluttered space rather than the relatively comfortable cabin where Jack and I had drunk ourselves stupid. To realize that the fumy odours I was smelling emanated not just from my brain but from stacked and roped barrels. To understand that I was lying on a heap of sails or tarpaulins. To recall, when I made a slight movement, the injury I'd foolishly incurred on the Middle Temple stage. To realize that the snoring I'd heard was not my own but that of my friend and fellow, Jack Wilson.

It was some consolation not to be alone. And to hear his voice.

'Nick? You are awake?'

'Yes. In God's name, what's happening?'

'What's happened, more like. We drank deep last night on the *Argo*. So deep I fear we never left the vessel.'

'But the vessel has left . . . with us on board.'

With one accord, both of us staggered off our makeshift beds. There was a conveniently placed ladder and a hatch, which yielded to our urgent shoving. In seconds Jack and I were out on deck, swaying on our feet, dazzled by the sunlight off the water, almost overwhelmed by the buffeting air.

I suppose I'd imagined that, although we'd slipped our mooring by London Bridge, we couldn't have gone very far. That I'd look about and see the smoke of the city chimneys and the Tower of London standing proud above a huddle of dwellings. But none of this was visible. Instead, the river stretched out on either side, broader than I've ever seen it. Where there was land, it had the look of marsh, although in the hazy distance I discerned low hills.

Jack seized my arm. 'Have we been captured by pirates?'

'If we have, they'll get no ransom for a couple of players. In fact, I can think of one or two people who might pay for us not to be returned.'

I tried to speak lightly but, in truth, I was hardly able to grasp the reality of where we were. It was the first time I'd seen the boat, the *Argo*, by daylight.

It might have looked large in the dark and when attached to dry land but, out in the open water, its dimensions seemed to have shrunk. Jack Wilson and I were standing on a relatively uncluttered area of deck. To our backs was the entrance to the great cabin where we'd got so disgracefully drunk last night. The cabin was part of a larger structure at the back end – or rather to the aft – of the boat. This was balanced by another structure at the front end. Overhead, the sails clattered and banged in the tearing breeze, while

the three masts supporting them groaned in their housing. The boat progressed through the water, not smoothly
but as if it were hammering out its path like a smith beat-
ing out a piece of iron. From the position of the sun in the
sky it was still quite early in the day.

A lad passed us and I grabbed him by the elbow and
demanded to know where we were. He looked about in
confusion as if the question was meaningless.

'On the river,' he said eventually.

'Where are we going?'

'France.'

He shook himself free of my grip and went off about his
business.

There were a couple of older sailors only a few yards
away, half hanging over the side while they fiddled with
some ropes attached to the largest of the sails on the
centre mast. They took no notice of us, may not even
have been aware that we were there, but their posture
put an idea into my head, unfortunately. I rushed to
the opposite side and, clutching on to the bulwark,
cast the contents of my stomach on to the waters. Angled
into the wind, I only narrowly avoided receiving them
back in my face. I hung there, chest heaving, eyes streaming, clinging on for dear life, terrified of the racing waters
down below.

When I turned back, it was to see a half-familiar face.
There was a hint of pleasure on it, pleasure at my discomfort, that is. I recognized Colin Case, brother to the doctor
and captain of the *Argo*.

'Even the most lubberly fellows can usually hold off until
the open sea,' he said.

'You must put in to land at once,' I said, aware that I was
not cutting a dignified figure.

'Why?'

'To let us off,' said Jack Wilson. 'We are from the King's Men and have work to do in London.'

'And who will pay me for the lost time? We have a favouring wind and we are running with the tide. No, we are not going to "put in" for the King's Men or anyone else's men.'

'I shall speak to your brother,' I said. 'He has chartered this boat.'

'Please yourself,' said the shipmaster, jerking his thumb in the direction of the aft cabin before tugging his hat over his ears and turning his attention to the sailors still struggling with the rope.

'Wait a moment, Nick,' said Jack. 'Don't go storming in there. Think a moment. There is something very odd about where we find ourselves.'

'How so? I'm going to give Dr Case a piece of my mind. He is responsible for . . . for luring us on board and plying us with drink until we were incapable of movement.'

'*Luring* us? We had no responsibility at all for our plight, I suppose. But you are right even so, Nick. It is as if Dr Case deliberately set out to get us to accompany him back to this boat and then to cause us to stay on board after hours.'

I remembered that Case had seemed watchful yesterday evening while we were leaving the Middle Temple precincts, but I could not see how this would make him want our company. Unless . . .

My thoughts were interrupted by Jack's tugging at my sleeve. He cast his eyes upward. We were standing in the shelter of what I later learned was called the aftercastle. There was a figure half protected by some housing at the far end who I assumed was the helmsman. But there was another figure by the railing at the near end, and he was staring at Jack and me, very intently, as if wondering what we were doing on the boat. He was dressed not like a mariner in a jerkin and slop-hose but well wrapped up in a cloak while his head was enveloped by a hood. Nevertheless, I sensed his eyes boring into us. After a moment, he turned away towards the stern of the boat.

'Who was that?'

'No idea,' I said. 'We must confront this doctor.'

Jack and I clattered down the steps and burst into the great cabin. There was no sign of Dr Case, but the door to the little inner cabin was ajar and, spurred by our anger and the sound of someone clearing his throat from within, we crowded to the door, which opened outward. The physician was half sitting, half lying on the bed, knees drawn up, a large book balanced on them. He looked up as if annoyed to be disturbed. The cabin was compact but the items in it – a bed, a stool, a chest that could double as a table – were neatly arranged. There was a casement window a couple of feet from the end of the bed. Perhaps the captain enjoyed waking up in the morning and seeing from the comfort of his bed the waters the boat had just crossed over. More than the furniture, it was the casement that gave an odd domestic note to this chamber, as though it was inside a cottage and not aboard a seagoing vessel.

'Gentlemen,' said Jonathan Case. 'I am glad to see you have recovered from last night's potations. It was impossible to make you stand up, let alone walk, indeed almost impossible to rouse you both. I thought players had harder heads. We might have, ah, deposited you on Botolph's Wharf before we left but, considering the state you were in, I'm not sure you would have still been alive by daybreak. And even if you had been allowed to go on living, you would have been deprived of any items of value you were carrying, any items at all, in fact.'

This was all true enough. There are human rats on the wharfs as well as animal ones. But it didn't satisfy me. I felt my anger sparking afresh, as Case delivered this meandering speech from the comfort of his bed. He was showing no ill effects from the previous evening, and the suspicion grew that he had plied us with drink while being abstemious himself.

'So we had to take you down to the hold to sleep it off,' he added. 'No room in here. Yet you were better off in the hold than you would have been in the mariners' quarters in the fo'c's'le. Very squalid across there.'

I wondered about all those little sleeping nooks in the cabin which Case had demonstrated to us the previous evening, but there were other, more urgent protests to make.

'Dr Case, you must tell the captain, tell your brother, to put into shore straight away so that we can disembark.'

'Speak direct to my brother yourself,' said the physician. 'He *is* the captain, as you say. But I can imagine what his answer will be. Time and tide wait for no man . . .'

By now I felt almost murderous towards Case. Jack must have sensed this, for he put out a hand as if to restrain me.

'Dr Case,' said my friend, 'I realize that we have brought this on ourselves, Nick and I, by being stupid enough to get blind drunk on board last night. But our company was sought by you, very pressingly, and we are your guests. Yet we are reluctant guests. Indeed, we have a livelihood to earn on land at this very instant—'

'And you will be fined a shilling if you are late for rehearsals. Gentlemen, I will do what I can. We will likely have to put in for fresh water before we reach France and you may be put ashore then. Since I am partly responsible for where you find yourselves, I will write a letter to old Dick Burbage explaining the circumstances and pleading for you. I cannot say fairer than that.'

I wasn't mollified, not at all. I did not like the idea of slinking back to London, bearing a letter which must make us look like a couple of greenhorns carried off to sea by mistake. I visualized myself tearing up the letter to 'old Dick Burbage' and scattering the pieces to the winds. Jack Wilson and I weren't likely to lose our posts and nor would the King's Men be seriously inconvenienced by our brief absence, since they were adept at filling holes. And even members of the leading company in the land are not obliged to behave well at all times; a few have found themselves in clink or disgrace for worse reasons than ours. Nevertheless, Jack and I would be the butt of plenty of jokes. Oddly, this was almost a more dire prospect than being ferried willy-nilly across to France. Better to pretend that we were voluntary absentees from our work.

Gravesend

In the event we never got to France. We never got further than Gravesend, which turned out to be appropriate, since one of our party was to meet his death there. The day, which had begun bright and sunny, turned foul. Black clouds massed overhead and rain swirled everywhere, obscuring the view of both banks. A vicious east wind snaked down the river. Far from going forward, we seemed at times to be going backward or not moving at all. Water was every-where, above, around, below, and – most alarming of all – spurting freely through the decks and topsides (which I gathered was the name for the parts of the vessel that were above the waterline). At any moment I feared we might be overturned, although the sailors on the *Argo* seemed to regard the storm as little more than a spring shower.

Piercing through the noise of the wind and rain was the sound of the shipmaster's whistle whenever Colin Case summoned the mariners to a particular part of the boat.

He left it to a heavily bearded boatswain, whose name was Bennett, to issue most of the orders. This gentleman bellowed out instructions concerning topmasts and main courses. Every command was pushed home with the demand that the men do it yarely. It was all Greek to me – apart from the 'yarely', which is sailor-speak for 'quick' – but the men went at it like monkeys, tugging at ropes, climbing up masts, lowering the sails and cursing their heads off . . . cursing most of all.

Jack and I spent the day clinging to ropes or any fixed object on the deck, receiving our ration of oaths if we were in anyone's way and sometimes when we weren't. Some of the sailors not only sounded but looked threatening, carrying poles with hooks for some obscure nautical purpose. I observed that Henry Tallman, the black-garbed man, was still on the boat. We might have gone back to the great cabin, which is where Tallman and the shipmaster Colin Case spent some of their time, but neither Jack nor I had much desire to keep company with our fellow travellers, especially Dr Jonathan, whom I held responsible for our plight. Besides, the rocking of the boat stirred me up to fresh bouts of sickness – even though I could've sworn that not a particle of anything solid remained in my guts – and I preferred to suffer without unnecessary witnesses.

We tried taking shelter in the hold, where the wine barrels were stored and where we'd been deposited the previous night, but there was something about being shaken about in the dark that was worse than remaining out in the open. I also believed we weren't alone down there. There were rats in the hold, scuttering and scurrying, but also a human presence. A dark shape in a corner. A mariner, perhaps, or another unfortunate individual being carried away from his homeland. I thought of the hooded figure I'd seen on the afterdeck, and I shivered from more than the cold and wet alone. Jack saw – or sensed – this individual, too, so to the deck we returned. To face the wind and the rain, a combination which reminded me of Feste's song at the end of *Twelfth Night* – 'the rain it raineth every day' and all that – and caused me to wonder whether I'd ever again see my companions in the King's Men, so low did I feel.

In the late afternoon we put in at Gravesend, where the river grows less wide and looks out to Tilbury on the northern side. Now I decided that, however unpleasant the bad weather, I preferred it a thousand times over to blue skies, since it had compelled us to put in at a port whereas, otherwise, we might have anchored offshore or by some desolate marshy stretch.

It took us some time and trouble to moor. The rough waters meant that we slammed into another boat as we were docking, or rather the other boat slammed into us. The jar threw Jack and me to the deck. It was a herring buss, I was told, also coming in to moor. The boat was smaller than ours, but with a great bowsprit. Canvas was stretched on hoops arching above the main deck presumably to protect the fish catch.

If I thought I'd heard enough of sailors' curses before, I realized that it was as nothing to the torrent that swept between the *Argo* and the fishing boat as the men on each vessel struggled to push away from the other with staves and those vicious-looking hooked implements. Finally, we got ourselves clear of the herring buss and securely tied up to some mighty stakes that stood near the Gravesend wharf. A couple of precarious planks were stretched across the void between the bulwarks of the boat and the dockside. Below was the turbulent river.

Speaking as if he had done us a favour, Dr Case said we would be able to return to London on the morrow. Of course, it was too late to travel now. He advised us to go by river on the so-called 'long ferry', since the route overland was dangerous on account of robbers, particularly in the area around Blackheath. He talked as if he had our best interests at heart. Yet I no longer trusted him, especially when he tried to press Jack Wilson to stay on board because it would be useful to have a French speaker to help him with his business in St-Malo. I recalled our laughter on the previous evening over Jack's French aunt. Had we been tricked into remaining on the *Argo* solely in order that Jonathan Case might have a translator to accompany him?

We stayed on board that night and shared a supper with Case and others. He insisted we join him, as a small recompense for the trouble we had been put to. Even so, Jack and I drank very sparingly and we extracted a promise from Colin Case – despite his rough exterior, the captain seemed a more reasonable man than his brother – that they would not depart next morning without leaving us behind. He reassured us that high tide was not due until a couple of hours after sunrise.

I must describe the supper, since it has a bearing on what happened afterwards. Food and drink were brought across the precarious planks from a Gravesend ordinary, and we ate in the great cabin, sitting on the benches and resting our elbows on the table. The food and drink were served by the lad I'd stopped on deck. Looking at him more closely, I realized that he was closer to man than lad, despite his smooth and downy features. Attending at supper apart from Jack and me there were the Case brothers and Henry Tallman, the fellow with the appearance of a puritan and the shoe buckles of a man of fashion. I'd seen no sign of cousin Thomasina and assumed she'd quit the boat at London Bridge. Nor had I glimpsed again the hooded figure seen on the aftercastle and, perhaps, below deck.

The mood of the meal was argumentative from the start. Colin Case and Henry Tallman came in from enjoying a smoke on deck and, their pipes scarcely stowed away, were met with a comment from Jonathan Case that smoking was a filthy habit. Furthermore, it was a habit that had incurred the displeasure of their sovereign. Did they not know that King James was the author of an anonymous pamphlet that had recently been circulating in London, called *A Counterblast to Tobacco*? Tallman yawningly indicated that he was aware of it, while Colin laughed either at his brother or at the King's opinion or both. Dr Case took even more offence and made some pompous remark about James being well within his rights to pronounce on the bad habits of his subjects as he was the 'physician of the body politic'.

Then there was some bad-tempered discussion between the brothers over how long the weather would detain them. Jonathan wanted to proceed as soon and as fast as possible, while Colin pointed out that they were at the mercy of wind and tide.

'I have heard that there is a sure way to raise a favourable wind,' said Jonathan Case. 'You must drown a cat.'

'Then you will have to catch one in Gravesend,' said Colin Case. 'Lay a hand on Gog and Magog and I will lay both hands on you.'

Gog and Magog? I was baffled by this reference to the two giant figures carried in London processions until Colin made a comment on their ratting skills and I realized he was talking about the ship's cats.

'Well, maybe I will go catch a cat in Gravesend,' said Dr Jonathan before adding, with a relish that caused me to shudder inwardly, 'and drown it in a bucket.'

'Rather than kill a cat, maybe my brother could use the influence of his magic stone to get favourable weather,' said Captain Case to the rest of us.

'Oh, I have heard of this magic stone,' said Henry Tallman. 'It originated in the polar regions, did it not?'

It was plain that Jonathan Case was unwilling to answer. This was most likely the reason Tallman pressed him further, saying, 'Won't you show it to us, Dr Case? I understand it is in this very chamber.'

Jonathan glanced automatically at the cabinet and its weird detector lock before looking daggers at his brother for raising the subject. Even so, I could see that he was half tempted by the chance of showing off what he'd called 'the sky-stone' once more. He sighed but nevertheless reached for his keys and went across to the cabinet. Stooping, he was about to insert the key into the lock when he suddenly straightened and whirled around. The expression on his face was somewhere between fury and panic.

'Someone has been tampering with this. The lady's finger points at forty. Someone has opened the cabinet.'

He looked at our four faces as if one of us might have been responsible. I could vouch for Jack and me, although I didn't know about Captain Case or Henry Tallman. While Dr Case jabbed at the keyhole with the key – failing several times on account of his angry state – I recalled that the extended arm of the dancing lady had indicated the number thirty-nine on the dial. If it was now reading forty, then the cabinet must have been opened. Unless Jonathan Case had done it himself and somehow forgotten.

By now the physician had succeeded in turning the key in the lock. He scrabbled blindly inside until his hand closed on something. He brought out the satin-swathed item he'd deposited there the previous evening. He unwrapped it

345

and brought the contents close to his eyes. He pored over its surface. To me it looked very like the sky-stone. Case's shoulders slumped in relief. An involuntary 'Thank God' escaped his lips. It was the sky-stone.

He carried the dark stone back to where we were sitting. He was reluctant to let it out of his hands but allowed Mr Tallman to hold it for a few instants. This black-clad individual weighed it in his palm before holding it up so that he could study its outline. I was still unable to decide whether it most resembled a bird or a boat. I noticed Colin Case looking curiously at it. Tallman sniffed at the sky-stone. He, too, scanned its surface.

'Why, there appear to be characters inscribed here,' he said. 'Strange markings. Letters, perhaps, although not English ones.'

'Perhaps so, perhaps so,' said the doctor.

'It has curative properties?'

'It may do.'

'My friend Dr John Dee of Mortlake would be interested in this,' said Tallman.

'No doubt,' said Dr Jonathan Case.

I picked up the reference to a much more famous doctor, the aforesaid Dee, the aged occultist and astrologer who was an occasional counsellor to kings and queens. Tallman probably mentioned him to show the reach of his acquaintance. If so, Case was determined not to be impressed, as his terse answer showed.

Trying again, Tallman said, 'I am sometimes troubled by the head-ache. I could sleep with the stone under my bolster to test its curative powers.'

Case was having none of it. He held out his hand but Tallman wasn't quite done.

'I was under the impression that this was the property of an important foreigner, one residing in London.'

'It may have been,' said Jonathan Case, now practically seizing the sky-stone from Tallman. The physician replaced the black stone in the cabinet, once more making a show of turning the key in the lock and examining the dial.

I had a sense of strong animosity between the three men, or at least between Jonathan Case on the one side and his brother Colin Case and Henry Tallman on the other. I was not sure what Tallman did but, from his mention of Dr Dee and other not-so-casual comments, I rather thought he, too, was one of those individuals who claim to be able to unpick the mysteries of heaven and earth, and most likely of hell as well. That would explain his interest in the sky-stone. Each man had his specialism, whether it was seamanship or physic or occultism, and each man looked down on the others'. With Colin Case there was the additional irritation of having to defer to his brother, who had chartered the *Argo*. I hoped the ship's captain was getting well rewarded for it.

Jack and I kept fairly quiet and tucked into the mutton stew provided by the Gravesend ordinary. We were glad enough to be at the end of our voyage, as we thought. I hadn't eaten all day and my appetite had returned. We listened to the bickering of these individuals with mild interest, no more. There was a revealing comment made by Dr Case later in the meal. Tallman brought up the subject of the sky-stone once more, remarking that many people would like get their hands on it by fair means or foul. As Tallman said this, Jonathan Case glanced at Jack Wilson and me. Not in suspicion, as if we wanted to steal the thing, but with a momentary unease, as if he were touched by guilt.

'Is that why you requested our company from Middle Temple to the riverside yesterday?' said Jack. 'Were we to act as protection against any attempt to seize the stone?'

'I was delighted to have you with me,' said Case. 'Strength in numbers.'

'But why did you take the stone to the Temple in the first place?' persisted Jack.

'Tell them, Jonathan,' said Colin Case. 'It is the least you owe these players for having imposed on them. Tell them, or I shall.'

'I went to the Middle Temple with a dual purpose,' said Case with great reluctance. 'To see you players in the King's Men and to, ah, collect an object that another member of the audience wished to entrust into my hands . . .'

'Nonsense!' said Captain Case, a very mild reaction for a sailor. 'As usual, my brother can't help making himself out to be much more important than he really is, as when he conveys to us the King's opinion on smoking. Brother Jonathan is merely acting on commission, carrying that precious sky-stone from London to St-Malo. He is being paid for his pains, and I in turn am being paid for the pain of enduring his company and his chatter.'

'You collected the sky-stone from someone in the French ambassador's party,' I said. This was not much of a stab in the dark, since Tallman had already referred to 'an important foreigner in London', but I could see from the expression on Case's face that it had gone home. 'That was really why you were at the Middle Temple. You and your cousin.'

'Ha!' snorted Colin in derision, so that another of my suspicions seemed to be confirmed. Thomasina was no cousin to the physician. As if to prevent any further outburst, Jonathan rapidly agreed that, yes, it was so, he had been in conversation with an individual from the ambassador's entourage – whom he was not at liberty to name – and that he was now responsible for delivering the sky-stone to another unnameable individual in St-Malo.

Henry Tallman had been staring hard at the doctor all this time. He tapped his long, beringed fingers on the table.

'I knew it,' he said. 'It is Maître Renard you are taking it to, no? He is the only man in St-Malo who would be concerned with such things.'

'It may be Renard.'

'The only one who would have the resources to pay for it, too. He must trust you, Dr Case.'

'I have a certain reputation,' said Jonathan.

'That is what I mean,' said Tallman. 'And I would wager that the individual you obtained the sky-stone from was acting – how shall I put it? – sub rosa? That he perhaps does not have full title to the thing since he is not the "important foreigner" I referred to but one of his underlings.'

Having relieved himself with these insults and imputations, he settled back, satisfied, and fiddled with a pipe. Lighting it from the charcoal brazier, he was soon filling the low cabin with layers of aromatic smoke as a way of further irritating the good doctor.

Jonathan Case said nothing in response to Tallman's comments. Instead, he changed the subject by announcing that Jack and I might sleep in the great cabin tonight. It would be preferable, he said, to going down to the hold, where the wine barrels were stored, and much preferable to sleeping with the mariners in the fo'c's'le. He indicated the little curtained alcoves where we might rest our heads. All of this was performed with the air of bestowing a great favour on us. I gathered that Tallman was also sleeping in the cabin, so it may have been that Jonathan wanted protection from his persecutor. Colin Case, however, planned to lay his head elsewhere. Probably he could not bear bedding down near his brother, particularly if Jonathan was occupying the space that would normally be his.

Jack said he wanted to take a turn on deck before putting his head down. He spoke for both of us. In truth, we wanted to escape the stifling air of the cabin, stifling not so much on account of the pipe smoke as for the bad feeling between the other diners.

Outside, the air was bracingly chill. The bad weather had blown itself out for the time being, and, not far above the horizon, a waxing moon bobbed like a boat among the clouds. It was quiet on deck and I wondered whether the mariners were happily asleep in the squalor of the fo'c's'le or out and about among the delights of Gravesend.

'Do you know what was going on in there?' said Jack.

'It's fairly obvious, isn't it? The sky-stone doesn't belong to Dr Jonathan and probably not the person he acquired it from either. According to Tallman, it is the property of an important foreigner. Probably the legate, de la Broderie. I reckon that someone in de la Broderie's entourage has passed it to Case for disposal in France. He's no more than an agent for stolen goods.'

'We don't know that,' said Jack.

'No, but I do know I don't like him. And it would explain why he wanted us with him last night. He felt more confident in company. Perhaps he was fearful that someone would attempt to take back the sky-stone.'

Jack was about to answer but suddenly paused. I sensed rather than saw him hold up his hand. From somewhere close by came a muttering sound. Jack moved towards it, stumbled and swore.

A human shape started up from where it had been lying or crouching on deck and made to dart off. But we were too quick for him. Jack had him by one side and I by the other. Although I could see little, I was fairly sure it was the individual we'd glimpsed on the afterdeck and perhaps down in the hold. His hood fell back to reveal a round face, whitened by the moon. He wriggled but he was smaller than us and after a moment he gave up the struggle. I was glad, because the tussle gave me twinges from my injury the previous evening in Middle Temple.

'I did not know anyone was there,' he said, as if to explain his reaction. Even though it was high-pitched in fear, his voice sounded educated.

'You were talking to yourself,' said Jack.

'Was I?' said the other. 'Yes, that's it. I must have been talking to myself.'

'Who are you, sir?' I said. 'You are not a mariner, for sure. You've been spying on us.'

'My name is Nicholas,' said this person, and I started slightly at meeting in the dark someone who shared my name. Then he said in a more controlled tone, 'I am no spy but a traveller like you.'

'Well, we are the most unwilling travellers on earth,' said Jack. 'We leave this boat tomorrow.'

'While I am hoping to sail on,' said the other meekly.

By this time we had altogether slackened our hold on Nicholas's person. Whatever he was doing on board was none of our business. Once he was free he immediately bent down and began scrabbling on the wooden boards.

'Lost something?' I said.

'Yes.'

Perhaps we felt slightly guilty for having accosted this harmless gent, for Jack and I also stooped, cautiously in my case, and began to fumble about on deck with splayed hands. I found the dropped object first. It had the feel of a beaded necklace. Before handing it back I said, 'We share a name, you and I, although people usually call me Nick. Is this what you are looking for, Nicholas?' As he snatched it from me, I added, half in curiosity, half in mischief, 'Deo Gratias.'

He repeated 'Deo gratias,' then stiffened as if he'd given himself away. Which he had, since his unthinking quickness in responding to the phrase and the discovery of the necklace – or rosary – were signs of his religion. He had not been talking to himself but kneeling in prayer, and so absorbed in his devotions that he was unaware of our presence.

'You are taking a risk coming out on deck,' I said.

'I need some fresh air after a few hours in the hold,' he said.

'Some persons of your sort might spend days and nights inside a priest-hole,' said Jack, showing by his words that he had also realized who – or what – this man was.

'They have more endurance than I,' Nicholas said. 'I cannot bear being cooped up for long. Not that I have ever been in a priest-hole.'

'You have a . . . warrant to be aboard the *Argo*? You are here by arrangement?'

'My presence is known,' said the other, choosing his words with care. 'I do not want to say who knows.'

'Well, my friend and I mean you no harm, I am sure,' said Jack. 'In fact, I am not certain that we have ever met. So goodnight to you.'

Nicholas muttered some indistinct words, presumably of gratitude, and scuttled away. Moments later we heard the sound of the hatch being opened. Jack and I remained out in the dark, as if giving Nicholas a decent interval to hide himself away once more. Neither of us said anything even if the same thoughts were probably running in both our heads. Thoughts to do with treason and conspiracy.

Ever since the Powder-treason and the attempt to blow up the Parliament in the November of '05 the authorities had shown a new determination to root out the plotters in the Catholic families as well as to hunt down their priests. Rather than face the Pursuivants, more than a few were making their escape to safety overseas. I'd no idea whether Nicholas was a member of a Catholic family or a fugitive priest, though something in his garb and manner suggested the latter. Nor did I know whether Captain Case was a sympathizer with the old religion or was merely being bribed to ferry this individual to St-Malo. It also occurred to me that perhaps Nicholas was on the *Argo* without the shipmaster's knowledge. Possibly it was another of Jonathan Case's enterprises. Or even Henry Tallman's.

Whatever the answer, it was best that Jack or I stayed ignorant, not so much out of fellow feeling as to avoid trouble. Why, as Jack said, we'd never even met the man. We returned to the great cabin, passing on our way the lad who'd served at table. He was carrying some leftovers of food and a jug of wine, awkwardly cradled in his arms. Perhaps he was taking them forward to share with his fellows. Crumbs from the rich man's table . . .

The aura of pipe smoke still hung in the air together with the odours of food and drink, but of our fellow diners there was no sign. I assumed that everyone was tucked up in their beds, Jonathan Case in his privileged quarters at the far end of the great cabin, and Tallman in one of the alcoves, with Colin Case having disappeared elsewhere, although I had heard no steps behind us on deck. A little oil light still burned near the compass, but the candles had been snuffed out. There was nothing for it but to turn in, though I did cast a curious eye at the cabinet containing the sacred stone or, more precisely, I ran my hand over its intricate lock. As I did so, something snagged against my fingers. It was a piece of thread. I rolled it into a little coil and tucked it into a pocket.

Jack and I squeezed into the tiny, neighbouring alcoves and drew the curtains. I could almost stretch

353

out at full length. The wind was getting up again, and the ship groaned and creaked around me as if it were alive. I was aware of the river water just below my berth. Above it was a tiny port that was closed with a kind of shutter. I did not open it. What was there to look at? The *Argo* was swaying gently but this was not reassuring, not like being rocked in a cradle. The straw mattress was less uncomfortable than our lodgings in the hold on the night before, but the pinched sides of the berth were reminiscent of a coffin and I thought of my bed at Mrs Ellis's in Tooley Street. Then I wondered how we were going to account for our absence to the Globe shareholders. We'd be fined, for certain. I was reluctant to go to sleep for fear of waking up and finding that we'd set sail once more.

But I did sleep in a fitful fashion. Once I awoke with a start, imagining we were under way. There was a grinding sound and distant, raised voices. But although the *Argo* seemed to be, as it were, shivering with cold, we were not actually moving. I slept again. The next I knew I was tearing aside the curtain and stumbling away from my little recess and up the steps and out of the great cabin into the open. The sun was just lightening the sky with glaring streaks of red. There was not a living thing on deck apart from a cat slinking along. Gog or Magog? The cats were free to come and go. I recalled Colin Case declaring that the *Argo* would not be leaving until the day was well begun. I breathed in clammy draughts of morning air and saw isolated threads of chimney smoke rising from the dwellings that marked Gravesend.

The day looked to be a fair one even if the sky's red message was hardly a good omen. For shepherds or sailors, that is. Not that I cared much about shepherds – and even less about sailors. I'd go back and rouse Jack Wilson and we'd make our exit from the *Argo* without bothering to say any goodbyes. Then we would either wait in Gravesend for the long ferry or, perhaps, hire horses to return to London. We had enough money for that, Jack and I. Jonathan Case had not mentioned again the letter to 'old Dick Burbage', but by this stage I did not trust him or believe anything he said. Would rather never see him again.

But see him again I did, and in the worst of circumstances.

I went through the entrance to the great cabin. Reaching the bottom of the steps, I paused. Coming from the outside, I could not see clearly at first, but the door to the inner cabin appeared to be open. This was where Dr Jonathan Case was sleeping, usurping the captain's place. But no, the physician was up and about. There was a figure stooping over the bed that took up most of the space of the little chamber. The figure was outlined against the red light of dawn. As I've already mentioned, the occupant of this room was fortunate enough to have a window that offered a fine view from the stern of the boat, that and a bigger bed to sleep in.

The figure remained where it was, stooping slightly. Something about the pose made me uneasy. I coughed and shuffled my feet, and the figure raised its head. It wasn't Jonathan Case but Jack Wilson.

'Nick?'

'What's wrong?'

'Come here.'

I crossed the few paces to the doorway of the tiny cabin and saw a terrible sight. Dr Case lay sprawled on his front on the bed, his feet by the tiny window and his head nearest the door. His prone body was washed by the red light of dawn as it poured through the casement window. Oddly, the casement was open.

However red the sun, its light was pale enough in comparison to the blood which had issued from a great rent in the centre of Case's back and which covered his nightshirt. Case's hands were clasping at the bedcovers, while his head was jerked back so that he seemed to be resting on his chin. His eyes were cast up in his head, and his mouth was gaping as if he were about to scream or laugh. But he would never make another sound in this world. I noticed a great egg-like swelling on his forehead. The skin had split and there was dried blood on his forehead. I glanced up in the direction of the doctor's dead gaze and saw what appeared to be more blood on the beams of the low ceiling.

'In God's name—'

'I found him like this, Nick. I got up and the door was partly open and I was curious to have another peek inside the captain's quarters. I found him like this.'

Jack sounded calm but somehow weary, too, while I heard a slight tremble in my own voice. A tremble of frustration as much as fear. I foresaw hours and hours of complications before we would be permitted to quit the *Argo*. I glanced at Jack's hands. They were clenched tight, like the dead doctor's. My friend was grasping not bedclothes but, in his right hand, something more solid. I touched the back of his hand. In surprise, he dropped whatever he was holding. It landed on the bed by the dead man. I picked it up and felt the surface of the sacred stone, the sky-stone, polished smooth apart from those queer little incisions which might be letters.

'That was on the floor,' said Jack.

'How did the doctor die?'

'That is obvious, Nick. There is a great hole in his back and there is also a knife on the floor. Look. Someone was probably attempting to steal the stone.'

'Then why is the stone still here?'

'I don't know. What I do know is that Dr Case has been attacked with great force. With fury.'

Rather than examine the gaping wound, I peered more closely at the knife where it lay on the floor. On the blade were markings that could be dried blood. I did not want to pick up the knife; it seemed inadvisable, and I was already holding the sky-stone. Instead, I averted my eyes from the body and went to examine the open window. Why was it open? Did Jonathan Case have a taste for the night air? That was unlikely. Of all people, physicians are the ones who know that the night is full of unwholesome vapours.

'Could someone have come through there?' I said. 'The base of the frame has been damaged. The wood is cracked and splintered, as if someone had attempted to force his way in.'

Jack didn't bother to look. He shrugged and said, 'Anyone who succeeded in that would have to be very small, almost a child.'

It was true. The window aperture was about a foot and a half square. I'd observed that most of the mariners on the *Argo*, even the slighter fellows, had well-developed arms and shoulders, the result, no doubt, of years of hauling and carrying and climbing. Nevertheless, I tried the window space for myself. I could get my head through but reckoned I would have got stuck had I attempted to go further. Besides, how could anyone reach the window? Below, perhaps fifteen feet or more below, swirled the dirty river water. No way up from there. Above my head was the overhang of the after-end of the poop deck. A nimble man – a sailor, say, particularly if he was secured with a rope – might have been able to descend to this level if he had a mind to spy on Dr Case as he was preparing for bed. But it would have been almost impossible for an intruder to have made an entry through the casement window even if the damage to the frame suggested that someone might have tried. Moored directly behind us was the herring buss which had collided with the *Argo* yesterday. I wondered if anyone on board had witnessed anything, but there was no sign of life on that deck either.

Without more words, Jack and I moved out of the tiny cabin. One of us, I'm not sure which, instinctively pushed the door to so that we no longer had to gaze at the outstretched corpse.

'We must raise the alarm,' said Jack.

'Yes. Is Tallman here?'

I gestured towards the third of the curtained alcoves. But the gesture wasn't necessary. The curtain wasn't fully drawn and it was apparent that no occultist was sleeping there.

'Must raise the alarm,' repeated Jack.

But neither of us moved.

In the half-light of the great cabin I examined the sky-stone, which I still held. I could not decide whether it was a bird shape or a ship shape or something else altogether.

It wasn't until this point that it occurred to Jack and me to look towards the cabinet that had kept the sky-stone secure. The door to the cabinet was shut, but it must have been opened during the night. If you examined the dial, the lady's finger would be indicating the number. Which number now – forty-one? But what did the figure on the dial matter? The cabinet must have been opened. The simplest evidence of that lay in my hand. Had the doctor unlocked it so as to take out and gloat over the stone which was promised to Maître Renard of St-Malo? Or had someone else got hold of the key and unlocked the thing, intending to filch the stone?

'We don't *have* to raise the alarm,' said Jack.

'We could simply leave the ship,' I said, the image of a slinking cat passing through my mind.

'This is nothing to do with us.'

'*We* know that, but others don't. A man has been murdered, violently murdered. If we run away, we become fugitives.'

'We'd probably get no further than Gravesend. A hue and cry would be raised.'

'Yes.'

It was almost a relief when Captain Case and Henry Tallman entered the cabin. They took in the scene in an instant. So quickly, in fact – as I realized within another couple of instants – that there was no need to raise the alarm or even to say anything. They must have had some inkling of what they were going to find. Colin Case paced across to the inner cabin and opened the door. He grunted, gave a cursory glance at his brother's body and reached out a hand to touch the swelling on the forehead. Meanwhile, Tallman remained by the bottom of the steps, keeping a wary eye on both of us. The captain rejoined Tallman. Both men looked at us. If Captain Case was distressed by the violent death of his brother Jonathan, he was doing a good job of hiding it.

'A murder has been done,' I said.

'I am sorry for it,' said Jack.

'If that is so, Colin,' said Tallman, 'it looks as though you have found your murderer, or should I say murderers?'

'Not so fast, Henry. Jonathan has been dead a little time. He is scarcely warm to the touch. If these two gentlemen had a hand in it, wouldn't they have run away? Look elsewhere before suspecting them.'

My thoughts exactly. My respect for the captain went up a couple of notches.

'You do not suspect *me*, I hope,' said Tallman, raising his hands in a defensive gesture. I noticed that his right hand was wrapped around with a makeshift bandage, a handkerchief. 'After all, I came to inform you of what had occurred.'

I gave a sigh of relief. This meant that Jack had not been the first to discover Dr Case's body. Tallman must have also peered through the open door and gone off to rouse the captain. That is, if he was not the one responsible for the physician's death. Whatever happened must have happened before Jack or I was awake.

Colin Case ignored Tallman's remark and instead said, 'Anyway, what reason would a pair of players have for . . . disposing of my brother?'

The good captain rose another notch or two in my estimation. He was doing an excellent job in our defence.

'I rather think Mr Revill might be holding the reason in his hand,' said Tallman.

I became aware that I had not relinquished the sky-stone. Rather than drop it as Jack had done, I handed it to Captain Case. I was reluctant to give it to Tallman. Case examined it, as did everyone who picked up the sky-stone. Instead of commenting on the markings, he said, 'This might be blood. It is hard to see in here, though.'

'Perhaps an outsider has done this deed,' I said. 'I have examined the casement window in the little cabin, and although I do not think anyone could have entered that way—'

'You are right, Mr Revill. No one could possibly have entered through the window. No one but a child or a . . .' said the shipmaster, his voice tailing away. There was an unreadable expression on his face. I might have believed he was toying with us, if I could have come up with any explanation why he should be doing so. Grasping at straws,

I said, 'Maybe a thief sneaked on to the boat in the night and was taken by surprise by your brother.'

'There I think you are wrong,' said Colin Case, pocketing the sky-stone, which might have been stained with his brother's blood. 'Come with me.'

We trooped on to the deck, the four of us. The sun had risen higher, and the red bands in the sky were thinning out. There were a few mariners about, including the bearded Bennett. Colin Case summoned his boatswain, had a conversation and gave some instructions. The only bit I heard concerned the departure of the *Argo*. We would not be sailing with the tide. He gave no reason for his order, which is the shipmaster's privilege. Case returned to where we were standing and indicated a place in the bulwarks which was marked by ropes rather than wooden panels. This was the point where people and goods boarded the *Argo*. There was an equivalent gap on the other side of the boat. When we'd arrived at Gravesend, a couple of planks had been extended to connect us to the wharfside.

Case explained that a boat the size of the *Argo* could not moor right up against the ancient wharf because of the shallowness of the river at this point. The wharf had been constructed when boats were smaller. The planks that served as a makeshift bridge between ship and shore now lay stowed against the bulwark. The captain said that, on his orders, the planks were drawn inboard at night to prevent the very thievery or intrusion which I had mentioned. We could see that the boarding planks were tucked away on the ship. Therefore, no one had come aboard the *Argo* since the previous evening.

'I have confirmed that with Bennett,' added Case. 'A few of the men went into Gravesend, but they were back well before midnight when the planks were drawn inboard.'

'No one came on board after hours but a particular type of person might have *left* the ship,' said Jack Wilson, leaning over the bulwark and estimating the gap that separated us from the muddy wharfside, which lay a couple of feet below the level of the deck and several yards away. The gap between was filled with the dark waters of the Thames, now scarcely stirring. 'A reckless or desperate individual might leap this distance.'

'Possibly,' said Case. 'But you are forgetting that the *Argo* has risen with the tide over the last couple of hours. If an outsider was making his escape in the middle of the night, not only would he have to contend with the darkness and a jump of twelve or more feet, but he would also be jumping upwards. The deck of the *Argo* would have been below the level of the wharf. Besides, there are few sailors who'd risk falling into water, even shallow water. Mostly they cannot swim, you see.'

'Why's that?' said Jack.

'It would show a lack of faith if they were able to swim.'

I wasn't sure whether he meant a lack of faith in the ship or the shipmaster or even in God. More questions seemed beside the point.

'Perhaps we must look beyond the merely mortal for this murder,' said Tallman.

'A spirit, you mean,' said Case. 'An imp or demon.'

'Your words, Colin.'

'More likely, isn't it, Henry, that the action against my brother was undertaken by someone who is still on board the boat? Isn't that what you're all thinking?'

The logic of this seemed strong enough. The shipmaster had a word with another mariner, then the four of us went back to the great cabin. Colin Case suggested we sit at the table. He commanded rather than suggested. He had taken charge. Now that the physician was dead, he was the sole authority on the *Argo*. Case opened the door to the inner cabin, as if to ascertain that his brother's body was still there. He spent some time inside, doing what I had done as far as I could see. Poking his head through the still-open casement window, examining the low ceiling.

After that the shipmaster locked the door, using a key from a ring containing several, and joined us at the table. Jack and I were sitting on a bench on one side, Tallman and Case on the other. The shipmaster looked thoughtful. He stroked his beard with one hand. The other held the knife that had been lying on the floor of the little cabin. He handed it to Tallman, handle first.

'Yours, I think. It was in there.'

Tallman took the knife in his left hand. The right was bandaged, a handkerchief wound around the palm. It was fortunate, perhaps, that the linen of the handkerchief was dyed red; otherwise the blood on Tallman's hand might have shown through. If there was blood to show in the first place. Confronted with the knife, Tallman seemed uncertain how to respond.

There was a silence before he said, 'I must have dropped it when I was in there last night. I asked Jonathan to show me the sky-stone again. I let him think I might make a counter-offer for the sky-stone. An offer which he could report to his French principal at the London legation rather than deliver the object to Maître Renard of St-Malo. In truth, I had – and have – no desire to possess the stone, which I believe that Jonathan came by illicitly. But I wanted to make a copy of the markings on it to show to my friend Dr Dee. It was while you two players were out on deck. You weren't here either, Colin.'

'Well . . . what happened?' asked the shipmaster.

'When I persisted, Jonathan obliged. He opened that cabinet and produced the stone, although not very willingly. He insisted we retreat to his cabin on account of the stinking pipe smoke in the great cabin. His words, the stinking pipe smoke. He opened the window to let the air in, even though night had fallen.'

I caught Jack's eye. So much for the notion that someone had tried to enter the little cabin by forcing open the casement window.

'I asked to look at the sky-stone, and all the while I did so Jonathan was watching me like a hawk. I didn't get the chance to copy the markings because when I produced a knife – this knife – to scrape at the surface of the stone, to test the substance it is made of, Jonathan became very anxious. He snatched it back. He was anxious and angry. As he seized the stone out of my grasp he caused me to cut myself with my own knife.'

Tallman held up his bandaged hand.

'So it is your blood on the stone,' said Colin.

'Very likely. And on my knife, too, now that I look at it properly. Anyway, the good doctor was so out of temper that he ordered me to quit his cabin. Realizing that I was not going to get any further, I did so—'

'Leaving him with the sky-stone. He didn't put it back in the cabinet?'

'I don't think so. I staunched the cut on my hand with this kerchief and withdrew to my little nook.'

In the ensuing pause, Colin Case said that when we were out on deck he had ordered some breakfast – bread and ale – brought in for us. We must be hungry. He was certainly hungry, he said. The shipmaster seemed not only dispassionate about Jonathan's death but unaffected by it.

I was curious about something and thought the shipmaster could enlighten me. The answer might even have a bearing on the death of Jonathan Case.

'Where does the other door lead to?'

Case glanced over his shoulder at the second door alongside the one giving on to the small cabin.

'It leads to a platform and a ladder that descends to the bowels of the ship and ascends to the poop deck. The whipstaff passes through there.'

Seeing our bafflement, he explained that the helmsman on the afterdeck controlled the direction of the boat by means of the whipstaff, a stout piece of timber which passed through a hole in the deck and shifted the tiller through a narrow arc by means of a pivot. Once out in the open sea, the shipmaster would consult the compass and then issue instructions to the helmsman by opening the second door and climbing the ladder or, more likely, ordering someone else to do it.

'We have grown soft and easy of late, we mariners,' said Case. 'In the old days the sole compass would have been housed on the poop alongside the helmsman so that the shipmaster had to brave the elements to give direction. But now I may do it from the comfort of the great cabin. Nevertheless, the helmsman still steers most of the time by using his own compass and the log. The method is called dead reckoning.'

Henry Tallman looked increasingly impatient with all this maritime chat. In the meantime he had been lighting his pipe. Now he felt confident enough to make a joke. 'Well, that is why we are here. A dead reckoning. Or a reckoning with the dead.'

'Yes,' sighed Colin Case. The absorbed expression which had settled on his face as he outlined the function of the whipstaff was replaced by a more dogged look. 'Gentlemen, we should alert the watch or the headborough in Gravesend to what we have discovered. But I do not expect great things from the constable in such a place. It is true that I am on good terms with one of the justices in north Kent but, even so, we might be detained for days. Meanwhile, I have a ship to take across the British Sea to France, where there is a cargo of wine to collect—'

'—as well as a sky-stone to deliver to Maître Renard of St-Malo?' said Tallman.

'Perhaps,' said Case. For the first time he seemed slightly unsure of himself.

'What do you intend to do?' said Jack. 'Sail on and ignore your brother's murder?'

'Murder, eh?'

'What would you call it?'

'Let's say murder, then. You think the best course would be if we handed over the responsible person to the local justice, his guilt signed and sealed.'

'To do that, one of us has to confess or be detected in his guilt,' said Tallman.

'It would be as well if we were clear about our movements last night,' said the shipmaster. 'Once they are established we can turn our attention elsewhere.'

'That is easily answered for Nick and me,' said Jack. 'After we'd eaten last night we went to get some fresh air on deck. There we . . . took a turn or two before coming back here.'

I noticed the way Jack had glided over our meeting with Nicholas the priest (or whatever he was) in the dark. My namesake was presumably lurking in the hold at this very moment. Fearing persecution and fleeing to France, he would not be likely to disembark at Gravesend. Did the shipmaster know of his presence? Surely he must do. Was it Nicholas who had disposed of Dr Case? He could have had access to the great cabin by climbing up from the hold and entering through the second door. Possibly that's what had happened. But, if so, why?

'There was no one here when we got back from our walk on deck,' I said. 'You two had gone. The three of you had gone if you include Dr Case.'

'I was tucked up in there, as I said,' said Henry Tallman, indicating the curtained alcove with his pipe-stem. 'Jonathan had already retreated to his cabin after the business with the sky-stone, as I also said.'

'I left the cabin by that other door,' said the shipmaster. 'I went up to the afterdeck to take a final look around before turning in. It is my custom even when we are moored up.'

'You didn't sleep in here?' I said, even though I already knew the answer.

'My brother had rented this space just as he had chartered this boat. I preferred to leave him to it. I slept up in the fo'c's'le. I had no wish to be near him.'

'You did not like your brother?' said Jack.

'I never troubled to hide that when he was alive, and I see no reason to hide it even if he has just been the victim of – what should I call it? – a fatal attack. He was an arrogant, self-important fellow. Dishonest, too, for all his airs.'

'So are plenty of others,' I said.

'You do not know the half of it. Ask Henry Tallman here.'

'I am a doctor of physic, too, although my interest spreads to many other areas. Because of old rivalries and his jealous nature, Dr Case made many aspersions about me. He spoiled my business and damaged my reputation. He put it abroad that I was not qualified to practise astrological physic.'

I was amazed that Tallman would speak this frankly before strangers and within a few yards of the dead man. It was as if he wanted to talk himself into a noose. Unless he believed that, by making a play of being so blunt, he was diverting suspicion from himself. We were interrupted for a moment as our breakfast was brought in by the same lad who had served us at supper last night. He was carrying tankards of ale and had a loaf tucked under one arm, yet he managed to place it all on the table without dropping or spilling anything.

He glanced towards the closed door of the small cabin behind which lay the dead body. Something about his manner showed that he knew who – or what – was in there. This impression was confirmed by a nod from Colin Case in the direction of the potboy. It was hardly surprising that news of Dr Jonathan's death should be spreading around the ship. If so, the lad seemed to be taking the information with the same equanimity as everyone else. More than equanimity, if one considered that no one had yet attempted to arrange the body more decently or reverently. I wondered what would be the reaction to the death on the part of Thomasina, the brothers' cousin – except that she was more likely the mistress of one than cousin to both.

As I had this thought, the potboy placed a tankard at my elbow. Something about this individual's manner and, more specifically, about his hand nudged my memory.

'Thank you, Thomas,' said Colin Case.

After he had gone I took a long draught of ale to fortify myself for what I was about to say. I jerked my head in the direction of the steps.

'I wondered what had happened to Dr Case's young cousin. She never left the boat, did she? Or *he* never left the boat, I should say.'

'Cards on the table, eh?' said the shipmaster.

'Yes, cards on the table,' I said. 'We must be near the end of the game.'

'It is not so difficult to guess, I suppose,' said Colin Case, not even attempting a denial. 'There is the coincidence of names, Thomas and Thomasina, which is not a coincidence at all, of course. Then there is the fact that both have the same height and build.'

'And a mole just here,' I said, indicating a point at the base of the thumb on my right hand.

'I feel as though I have wandered into a real-life play,' said Jack Wilson. 'Young men dressing up as women, identification by means of a mole. What in God's name is going on?'

'My late brother had a preference for young men,' said Colin Case. 'There is no great shame in that, or at least it did not perturb me greatly. It is common enough among seagoing folk and, I dare say, in the stage-play world. Jonathan has – had – always been that way inclined.'

'He followed the example of the King in two ways at least,' said Henry Tallman, speaking with a mixture of amusement and disdain. 'In his inclination towards youth and in his aversion to smoking.'

'But Jonathan went further,' said his brother. 'He enjoyed sporting with others.'

'Like encouraging Thomas to dress up as a young woman and taking him – her – to a play at the Middle Temple, a play in which a male plays a girl who disguises herself as a man.'

'Yes. I thought it was an absurd thing to do. But Thomas agreed or was persuaded to agree, even though it seemed a kind of humiliation to me. And Jonathan actually went to collect the sky-stone rather than to watch a play. I am not sure whether he took Thomas along for colour, to make his presence at the Middle Temple more plausible, or whether he simply enjoyed the danger, the risk . . .'

'The risk of pretending to be accompanied by his female cousin.'

'That part at least was no pretence, Mr Revill. Thomas really is his cousin – and therefore he is mine, too. But a very distant one. There is no additional impropriety involved. Or not much impropriety. I believe, though, that Thomas was becoming tired of Jonathan. Not a tear has yet been shed for his death.'

'Tired enough to put an end to him?'

'You are very eager to find a murderer, Mr Revill.'

I do not know that I was very eager but suddenly I grew very irritated. Or simply tired. Tired of the whole thing. Tired of having been inveigled with Jack Wilson on to the *Argo* and carried away, if not out to sea then at least as far as Gravesend. Tired of having been taken from our fellows and our livelihoods at the Globe. Tired of being confined aboard a boat for what seemed like weeks rather than a couple of nights, and in company I wouldn't have chosen. Tired, above all, of involvement in the violent murder of a physician who had a taste for dressed-up young men and who was about to trade a mysterious sky-stone, an object he had possibly acquired illegally and which might (or might not) be linked to his abrupt death. It was this irritation that caused me to say, 'What about your other passenger, your hidden passenger, the person down in the hold? Couldn't he have had a part in all this?'

Colin Case glanced at Henry Tallman. It was the occultist who answered me with the same phrase as the shipmaster. 'Cards on the table?'

I nodded. So did Jack.

'The person you are talking about is also called Nicholas – Nicholas Tallman. My brother, but dearer to me than Jonathan is or was to Colin here. For reasons that you can probably guess at, gentlemen, Nicholas needs to leave our country for a while, and perhaps leave for ever. I can assure you that he is not part of any plot or treason, but these are dark days for everyone who adheres to the old religion, the innocent as well as the guilty.'

'You are such an adherent?' said Jack.

'No longer. I tell you I am interested in more arcane matters,' said the occultist, swathing himself in a cloud of tobacco smoke. 'But a brother is a brother. I arranged with Colin here that he should transport Nicholas to France. Nicholas was instructed to keep quiet in the hold until we were well clear of land, but he is a restless spirit and told me that he had encountered you. He also said that you had listened to him with, ah, deaf ears. For which I thank you.'

'Was *your* brother aware that you were ferrying a priest to France?' said Jack to Colin Case, nodding his head in the direction of the corpse behind the door.

'Oh, no. He would not have been so understanding, not at all. In fact, knowing Jonathan, he might well have told the authorities, not so much to prove that he is a loyal citizen but out of malice.'

'So neither one of you had a reason to love Jonathan Case,' I said. 'Not you, the ship's master, nor you, Mr Tallman.'

'And cousin Thomas and Nicholas the priest can be added to the roll,' said Jack.

'Let us fetch them in here,' said Colin. 'You can confront them and us with your suspicions. Perhaps one of us will confess. Isn't that how things should be done at the end of the game?'

While the shipmaster was out gathering up the other suspects, Henry Tallman turned his attention to the loaf brought in by Thomas. He sawed the bread into sections using the knife that Colin Case had given back to him. True, he dabbed a little ale on the blade before wiping it on his sleeve to remove the marks of blood. His own blood, if we were to believe him. But I rejected the proffered chunk of bread, as did Jack. We sat in silence waiting for the captain's return.

I would have welcomed the chance to discuss this peculiar situation with Jack, but it seemed somehow out of place in front of one of the individuals who might have killed Dr Case. There were at least four of them: the priest Nicholas Tallman, who feared exposure, the young man Thomas, who was said to be weary or even humiliated by his link with the physician, the occultist Henry Tallman, who bore a grudge (and might have wanted the sky-stone for himself – although, if so, why hadn't he simply taken it after disposing of Case?), and the shipmaster Colin, whose distaste for his brother was not far from hatred.

Colin Case returned with Thomas and Nicholas. The young man was blushing, although that could have been the result of the fresh morning air. Nicholas was no longer wrapped up in his cloak and hood but dressed in a sailor's jacket and slops. Wisely, he was adopting a disguise. His skin was pallid, as if he had spent his whole life shut up in small spaces. The Tallman brothers nodded at each other. There was no likeness between them. Henry was tall and gaunt, Nicholas was short and round in the face. Everyone sat down on the benches. The shipmaster opened proceedings without ceremony.

'As you know, my brother is dead. The circumstances suggest that it might be murder, and our two player friends are keen to see that justice is done. Accordingly, the four of us are gathered here as the most likely suspects. Have you any question you wish to put to us, Mr Revill, Mr Wilson?'

There was more than a tinge of mockery in his voice. What was going on here? Why was there not more concern in Colin Case's manner? He might not be sorry, might even be glad, that his brother was dead, but, surely, he should be showing a little concern for himself as a suspect? I could have said this but instead kept silent. Fortunately, Jack spoke up.

'There was a disturbance last night. I heard voices raised overhead. This was long after everyone had gone to bed.'

'I heard it, too,' I said.

'Don't look at me,' said Henry Tallman. 'I was tucked up snug. Slept well after my altercation with Jonathan.'

'I was down in the hold among the rats and the wine casks,' said Nicholas Tallman. 'I am not certain I heard anything, although the ship did give a jar at one point.'

'I was in the fo'c's'le,' said Thomas. 'I have nothing to do with any of this. I've done nothing.'

These were the first words I'd heard him speak, apart from the brief exchange on deck the day before. I retrieved from a pocket the length of thread I had found snagged around the complex lock of the cabinet.

'I do not know where you were last night,' I said, finding my voice, 'but you have done one thing at least. While you were playing the woman's part during that first night when Jack and I first boarded the *Argo*, you went to the cabinet and opened it, or tried to. Dr Jonathan realized the dial had moved around by a single number at supper last night, but he must have overlooked this little piece of evidence, this coil of taffeta. No one else is wearing or has worn anything of this bright scarlet material. No one except Thomasina on the night of the play.'

Thomas hung his head. His face went a brighter red, almost the colour of the thread I now held up. I felt my own face heating up. I did not like the exposure of this young man but, by now, I was a fierce hound for truth and justice. What did it matter that no one cared for Dr Jonathan Case, in fact that everyone positively disliked if not hated him? He had been murdered and someone had to be held accountable.

'Yes,' he said, keeping his head down and speaking scarcely above a whisper. 'I admit I got the key from . . . from cousin Jonathan . . . when he was sleeping and that I opened that cabinet there. I meant to take the sky-stone. I knew it was important, valuable. It was the reason we went to the Middle Temple, to collect it. Cousin Jonathan was full of talk about how he was going to sell it in France and make a handsome profit.'

'You meant to steal it?' said Colin Case. He looked stern, but his voice was surprisingly gentle.

'I . . . I don't know. Perhaps. I thought if I had the sky-stone I could use it against cousin Jonathan. He said it was powerful, that it had magic properties. I wanted to escape from him. I had become afraid of him, and the more afraid I was the more he liked toying with me. He was kind in the beginning but not later . . .'

'Anyway, you did not take the stone,' said Henry Tallman. 'You couldn't have done, because it was still there last night at supper.'

'I took it out and looked at it in the candlelight and thought that it was a strange object, almost beautiful,' said Thomas, his tone getting firmer. 'I could not take it. I wrapped it up again and put it back in the cabinet and turned the lock and replaced the keys. I had nothing to do with what happened afterwards. I cannot say how cousin Jonathan died or who did it. I was sleeping in the fo'c's'le, as I said. I did no murder.'

I believed him, not because he looked abject but because I found it hard to associate this willowy, blushing youth with the furious assault on Jonathan Case. I wondered how he managed among the rough mariners in the fo'c's'le and remembered that the shipmaster had also been lodging there. Cousin Colin would have kept an eye on him. If he needed an eye kept. I thought of one or two of the boy players in the London acting companies and how, even though younger than Thomas, they had the power to wind some susceptible older players around their fingers.

There was a pause before we looked to the shipmaster for his account of last night. He was the last to speak.

'Yes, there was a disturbance,' said Colin Case. 'I was called to the poop deck in the early hours of the morning. The boat moored next to us was drifting with the incoming tide. It was poorly manned and worse secured. Fortunately, a direct collision was averted. Our watch shouted loud enough to alert the mariners on the other vessel, and they fended themselves off with their staves. In fact, the two vessels touched only fleetingly.'

I was baffled. What had all this to do with the death of Jonathan Case? Had someone from the other boat leaped on to the *Argo* and disposed of the physician? The shipmaster seemed to be relishing this particular story, just as he'd enjoyed instructing us in the mysteries of the whipstaff.

He now instructed us to follow him outside once more. So Jack and I, together with the Tallman brothers and Thomas, went back on deck. We climbed the ladder to the poop – by now I was growing quite familiar with these marine terms – and made our way to the overhang of the stern. Above us was a furled aftersail and to one side the housing that offered a little shelter for the helmsman and also gave access to the ladder down to the great cabin and, beneath that, the hold. There was no helmsman on the poop deck since the boat was not under way.

We went to the bulwark at the far end. We were right above the spot where Dr Jonathan Case still lay. Beyond was the eastward stretch of the river, with a cluster of boats either moored tight against the wharf or standing slightly out from it if, like the *Argo*, their draughts were not shallow enough. The closest boat was the herring buss, which had put in rather clumsily on the previous day. I recalled the curses that had flown to and fro like musket balls.

If one forgot the dead body downstairs, the day looked to be set fair despite that red-streaked sunrise. Men were carrying cargo on and off the boats. There was a general bustle as preparations were made to sail with the tide. On the *Argo*, though, business was suspended. I noticed the mariners looking curiously at the captain and his little party up on the poop. No one questioned what he was doing (or not doing). It struck me that a shipmaster was an absolute monarch in his little kingdom.

Colin Case indicated the herring buss, one of the vessels readying to depart. In fact, about to cast off.

'I am acquainted with the master of that boat,' he said. 'He has a bad name on the river. He drinks like one of the fish in his catch. He runs a sloppy vessel. It isn't surprising that we have twice had to fend off the *Draco*.'

'The *Draco*?' said Henry Tallman.

'A foolish name for a fishing boat. And her master is a foolish man. If you want to catch a murderer, Mr Revill, then you had better hurry to lay hold of him before the *Draco* departs. Or perhaps it would be more correct to say that you should apprehend the vessel herself.'

'I don't understand.'

'Nor did I until I had a closer look at the cabin where my brother lies dead. I examined his corpse also. The wound in his back was a large one, wasn't it?'

Thomas turned away at this point as if he was about to be sick. Perhaps the realization of the death of his erstwhile friend, his protector, was only just sinking in. Colin put a steadying hand on the young man's shoulder.

'Yes,' I said. 'A great tear in the flesh.'

'It would have taken a deal more than my little knife to cause that,' said Henry Tallman.

'The instrument that killed him was much larger than a mere knife. But its . . . appearance in the shipmaster's cabin was the merest chance. A thousand-to-one chance. No, ten-thousand-to-one. If only my brother had not opened the casement to get rid of the smell of pipe smoke . . . Yes, he might have survived if the window had remained shut. But he left it open as he prepared for bed.'

'What in God's name happened?' I said.

'It would have been like threading a needle. A fine operation, requiring a sharp eye and a steady hand. Except that this needle was being threaded on the waters of the Thames and there was no eye or hand involved.'

'Are you losing your mind, Colin?' said Henry Tallman. 'Why all this talk of needles and eyes and hands?'

'There is your murder weapon,' said the shipmaster. 'Behold.'

As one we turned to watch the herring buss, the *Draco*, swing away from the Gravesend wharf, eased off by the staves of the herring fishers and turning with the tide. The boat sat much lower in the water than the *Argo* so that we peered down on to her deck with its canvas-covered hoops. A couple of the mariners glanced up and raised their fists at us, half salute, half insult. The end of the bowsprit was itself surmounted with an extension that glinted in the sun. The bowsprit was made of stout wood, but its tip was sheathed in metal.

And then I realized what Colin Case was talking about. Or thought I did.

'Your brother had the ill luck to be standing with his back to the open casement,' I said.

'He should not have been up so late,' said Colin. 'I

expect he could not sleep in his greedy excitement. He was examining his precious sky-stone, cradling it in his hands, working out his profit, oblivious to what was happening behind his back beyond the still-open casement . . .'

'That boat there, the herring buss, floated straight towards the *Argo* in the night—'

Colin Case nodded. I could have sworn that he was smiling, but he was standing against the sun and it was hard to be sure. I went on.

'—and the tip of the bowsprit entered through the aperture provided by the window like . . . like the point of a giant foil—'

'—a closed window would have shattered, even provided some defence,' added Tallman.

'I understand the talk about needles now,' said Jack.

'Jonathan was struck by the tip of the bowsprit. The jib boom, if we want to be precise. It delivered a great blow with the whole mass of the vessel behind it. The tip ripped into his back and flung him up so his head hit the roof. Almost at once the other vessel was fended off from doing further damage. No one on board was aware of more than a violent jarring or jolting while all this was going on. The *Draco* slipped back and the bowsprit – or the very end of the thing – withdrew from the cabin as neatly as it had entered while its tip withdrew from my brother's body, yes, like a sword's point. It did some slight damage to the frame of the cabin window, but not one of us was aware that it left a dead man in its wake.'

Nicholas Tallman performed a priestly act at this point. He lowered his head and crossed himself. The rest of us stood silent, dumfounded by Colin Case's explanation. Yet it was surely correct.

I watched as the herring buss manoeuvred itself nearer the centre of the stream. Then, with sails hoist so as to catch the gentle wind, it set off with the outgoing tide to find fish.

Jack and I left the boat at Gravesend. We sailed on the long ferry back to London, and that journey took us another day, so we missed two days' work and were fined and berated accordingly. We preferred to pretend that we had been playing truant – the kind of misbehaviour which is not unknown among players – rather than recount the strange tale of the travellers on the *Argo* and death by bowsprit.

Colin Case must have managed to square things with his friendly local justice, for the boat soon sailed on for France. The death of Dr Jonathan was presented as the peculiar accident which it was, and it has to be said that nobody much mourned the passing of this unpleasant individual. Nicholas Tallman, I assume, reached the safety of a friendlier country, while Thomas served under the tutelage of his kindlier cousin, Colin Case.

As for what happened to the sky-stone I remain ignorant. Ignorant whether it found its way to Maître Renard in St-Malo or whether Henry Tallman returned it to London to the 'important foreigner'. Or perhaps kept it for himself. After all, he had been eager to show it to his friend Dr Dee. I don't know, though. Some things are destined to remain mysteries.

And there is another mystery, too. It was only when Jack and I discussed it later that we realized how willingly both of us had accepted Colin Case's story of the death of his brother. That it was an accident disguised as a murder. It was hardly surprising we'd leaped to the conclusion of murder. The unlamented physician was the victim of a violent, bloody assault, and there were several individuals on board with the motive and opportunity to kill him. We were just as quick to seize hold of the comforting notion that Jonathan Case's death was a freakish chance. But what if it wasn't? What if it was not the bowsprit of the *Draco* which had done the damage after all but – say – one of those vicious, hooked implements the mariners made so free with on deck?

Perhaps it had been the other way about, a murder disguised as an accident. If so, Colin Case's story was a brilliant piece of improvisation to cover himself . . . or to cover someone else . . . just a story.

EPILOGUE

London, 2010

Greg edged his hand along the rim of the crater. The profile was ragged and unclear, but he reckoned he could make out a distinct circular shape. In fact, he was sure he could see a central peak indicative of the crater floor rebounding from the compressional shock of an impact. This is what was so exciting about scrambling over a new crater. Checking his coordinates, he noted them down on the pad he carried with him. 61 10N: 45 25W. Scanning across it, he estimated the diameter of the crater to be over two kilometres. Big enough to be a medium-size meteorite impact on this part of Greenland. He would have to measure it more accurately later. But for now visual observation was enough to get his pulse racing.

He looked south to the airstrip at Narsarsuaq, where other research team members could make their landing if he was right about the crater. No terrestrial impact craters had so far been identified on the surface of Greenland, covered as it mostly was with snow and ice. But the nearby landmass of continental North America was peppered with them. He ached to be the first person to identify a genuine impact crater on Greenland. He scanned across the deep blue fjord to the tiny settlement of Qassiarsuk hanging on to the small strip of green below the snowfields and glaciers. He thought he could just make out the site of Brattahli∂, the ancient Viking settlement at the head of the fjord. It was a sheltered location almost a hundred kilometres from the ocean, and no one knew exactly why it had been abandoned. Some scientists simply reckoned the weather had got worse, and the settlers had retreated from the encroaching ice and snow. Other people, more inclined to believe the old legends, said some evil had taken place there, driving the settlers out. Greg was a sceptic when it came to the supernatural, preferring hard facts and common sense to the unspeakable and the unprovable. Once more he returned his gaze to the impact crater and looked across the far rim towards the whiteness of the mountains that angled away from him. The sudden and insistent burble of his landline cut across his excitement.

He sighed and flicked the knob situated under his right hand in order to turn the motorized wheelchair to the left. The hum of the electric motor, which he hardly noticed normally, seemed like the angry buzzing of a cloud of bees. He felt as though a dull, leaden weight was filling his chest, which was ironic. As a T2 paraplegic, he had no feeling at all from somewhere just above his nipple line. When the accident had first happened, and he was lying in hospital, he had been told by an inexperienced doctor that he was lucky because he still had full use of his arms and hands. Greg had sworn at the poor man with all the vehemence he could muster. He sure as hell didn't feel lucky just at that moment.

Until two years ago, Greg Janic had called himself a hunter and explorer. Among other things, he explored the world for evidence of meteorite craters, enjoying the freedom of the outdoors and the exhilaration of climbing in often mountainous and dangerous terrain. Greenland had drawn him for years as one of the last wildernesses on the planet. It had turned out to be his nemesis. Climbing Allerulik, one of the peaks in the Narsaq region, a spring-loaded camming device had failed him, and he had plunged a hundred feet down a glacier. His only consolation had been suing the cam's manufacturer, and getting enough compensation to meet all his new and complex needs as a paraplegic. And to make him reasonably wealthy into the bargain.

He had set himself up in an apartment in central London with enough computer equipment to freak out even the geekiest of nerds. When he had first been looking for somewhere to live, one estate agent had shown him a loft apartment overlooking the Thames. It had a magnificent view, and he could have well afforded the flat. He had been sitting in his wheelchair staring out at the sun sparkling on the river. The view had been full of activity – boats on the water and people with the full use of their limbs hurrying around like ants. He had suddenly felt nauseous. It was as though he was trapped in a picture looking out on the real world. He had abruptly turned his wheelchair away from the window and exited the apartment. The place he ended up buying was in a warehouse conversion. It had restricted views, and it suited him. He wanted to see the world only through the medium of a computer screen.

For a year he had had mood swings and had thought of suicide, refusing to even talk to his old friends, most of whom he had known through his work. He could not bear to think of them able still to climb mountains and dig for evidence of meteorites. Finally, he had answered the persistent phone calls made by an old friend and colleague, June Piper. She had eventually convinced him that he could contribute to the research team she led, and which he had done fieldwork for. So he returned to impact crater hunting, and he did it without ever leaving his home. It was remarkable what could be done using Google Earth.

He picked up the phone. It was June on a very bad line. 'Hi, Greg. What kept you?'

He felt annoyed that his Google search had been interrupted and showed his displeasure. 'Nothing. Just a small case of T2 paraplegia. I had to drag my useless limbs across the floor. It took some time.'

He could hear June laughing down the phone. She was never embarrassed by his condition, as others were when they saw him in a wheelchair. He pictured her short, stocky frame topped by her round, ruddy face and cropped hair. Always dressed in a check shirt and jeans with sturdy walking boots on her feet, her appearance screamed 'I'm a lesbian; deal with it'. And she didn't cut Greg any slack about being a paraplegic, either. Where others sometimes treated him like a child, or, even worse, a brave little soldier, her attitude to him was 'So, you're in a wheelchair; deal with it'. His self-pity didn't work on her, so he became all business.

'I've got a new site for you. It's just north of Narsarsuaq Airfield, so it shouldn't be difficult to get to. Where are you now?'

The line crackled, rendering June's reply inaudible.

'Say again.'

'Kulusuk. Would you believe the population here is about three hundred and they have an international airport? It's not quite as big as Heathrow, mind.'

Greg twiddled his control and reversed the chair back towards his computer, still talking on the cordless phone. He moved the hand cursor on Google Earth and zoomed out to seven hundred kilometres. From there, he could see how far the two spots were apart. It didn't seem a problem, especially with airstrips at both locations.

'OK. If the search is not bearing fruit where you are, I suggest you skip down to Narsaq. It looks far more promising.'

'Nothing bears fruit here, Greg. It's ice, snow and more ice. But you have the big picture, so we'll do as you suggest.'

He ignored her feeble joke and idly moved the hand-shaped cursor around the rim of his crater, caressing it. 'It's what I'm paid for.'

There was a moment's silence from the other end of the line, and Greg thought he had lost the connection. Then he heard June's voice again. 'Oh, I nearly forgot the reason why I phoned you. There's a meteorite for sale on eBay. Looks interesting. Its curious shape might appeal to you.'

'Curious shape?'

'Take a look.'

Annoyingly, she rang off before he could question her further, so he opened Google Chrome and went into eBay. He bought lots of items on the website, so his access was smooth and easy. He soon saw what June had meant about the meteorite on offer being a strange shape. From the picture, it looked like one of those stealth planes from the 1980s. Boomerang-shaped with a small tail, and smooth. Later stealth aircraft got all angular to prevent radar working on them. This was like an early prototype, all rounded and smooth. And to Greg it looked old. New meteorites had a fusion crust, making them dark and glossy. This was brownish, and the surface looked grainy. But when he zoomed in on the picture, he could just make out some markings on the surface, half hidden by its granular nature. He thought it might be a fake, but he was prepared to take the risk to get a good look at it. And to add it to his collection. The seller, a guy with the handle Tallman, claimed it was an iron meteorite, which made it quite rare. Less than six per cent of meteorites were iron. He looked at the auction bid and at the time left. It had already reached $2,000 with an hour left, so he put in a bid of $2,200. Within a few minutes someone bid $2,500. Greg added another $500, only to be topped again a few minutes later. He grinned, knowing the guy bidding against him was an amateur. With only an hour – less now – to go, he should have been holding off until the last minute. This was going to be Greg's strategy before he pushed the bidding higher than it needed to go. He eased back in his wheelchair, rearranged his lifeless legs that had slipped awkwardly and poured himself a glass of Tall Horse. The South African Merlot washed down his throat with its characteristic smoothness as he relaxed and held his nerve. Leaving eBay open, he returned to Google Earth. He ran his electronic hand over the Greenland crater rim once more.

Fifty minutes later, he had won. The iron meteorite was his for a paltry $3,600. He quickly sorted out the payment and arranged delivery. It was very late, and he should have been going through the tedious ritual that got him into bed by now. But he couldn't bear it, when he knew he had to do the whole thing in reverse in only a few hours' time. Not for the first time since his accident, he carried on through the night searching for craters that might provide remains of extraterrestrial life. The one he had found was very promising, as the outline was hard and jagged. He really needed to find craters without an outline eroded by Ice Age glaciers and the millennia. A crater formed by a meteorite that had come down recently – in other words, no more than 100,000 years ago. Even better if it was one that had impacted within living memory. And in a cold place.

When he told people he worked for a research team who were looking for extraterrestrial life, he had to fend off the inevitable inane questions about ET, little grey men with big eyes and flying saucers. The research team, led by Dr June Piper, would be overjoyed if they found something as lowly as frozen bacteria. Which is why Greenland was a great place in which to hunt for impact craters. The only drawback was that most of it was covered with snow and ice. The possible crater north of Qassiarsuk was an excellent prospect, as it was on bare terrain but close to the ice sheet. He ploughed on through the night looking at all the smaller dots and hollows on Google Earth that might be part of the scatter from the original meteorite fall. He hardly noticed the creeping greyness that began to fill the room as dawn approached. Suddenly, his email service pinged, alerting him to an incoming email. He scrubbed his stubbly chin, and yawned, aware for the first time that he felt hugely exhausted. He opened his email box and clicked on the new item in the inbox. The message was so unexpected as to immediately wake him up. It was from someone signing himself V. A. Bassianus, who claimed to be a representative of the Sol Invictus Trust. He explained that he had been very interested in buying the iron meteorite and regretted losing out on the eBay auction. He invited Greg to name a price for selling it to the trust. Greg stared at the screen as though it might have the answers to a myriad questions that were buzzing in his brain. He gave in to a persistent habit, developed since his accident, of talking to himself.

'How the hell did you know I had bought it, and how did you get my email address?'

Any information on eBay had to be confidential. If it wasn't, and the site had given – or, even worse, sold – his details to this individual, he would sue them. He trusted the site, though, and quickly dismissed the notion. But he still couldn't work out how V. A. Bassianus could have got his address. He typed a short reply, asking those very questions, and ended by saying the meteorite was not for sale. He sent the email on its way and put it out of his mind for the time being.

A week later, when a heavy packet arrived at his apartment, the mystery was revived in his mind. Opening the packet, he found inside a battered wooden box with a label stuck to the lid. The label itself was ancient and almost worn away. Only strips remained on which Greg could discern faded brown writing in a crabbed hand. Some of the text was lost completely, along with the paper on which it had been written. What was left would take him a while to decipher. Intrigued, he opened the box. Inside lay the iron meteorite just as he remembered it from the photograph on eBay. The surface looked darker than in the picture, and smoother – as though someone had tried to polish it. Maybe Tallman, whoever he was, had thought he should do so before passing it on to his buyer. Greg could see the characteristic regmaglypts that covered the surface. They were popularly called 'thumbprints' because that was what they looked like – as though someone had pressed their thumb into the surface over and over again while the rock had been malleable. He could also see the marks he had at first thought had been painted on the surface. Looking closely at the rock, he could tell they were an integral part of the material. Curiously, they looked like Hebrew letters. He turned the rock over and over in his hand. It was heavy, and, if it conformed to the normal make-up of an iron meteorite, it held iron, nickel and perhaps some kamacite and taenite. He rolled his wheelchair along his workbench and put the rock on some electronic scales. He whistled quietly. It was almost 1,700 grams, so, taking its dimensions into account, it probably had a specific gravity of 8. Definitely within the range of an iron meteorite. He placed it on the bench and looked hard at it.

The email message from Bassianus came into his mind, and he wondered what was so special about this stone that the man was prepared to pay any price to get it. He picked the stone up again and nestled it in his lap while he motored back to his computer. Once there, he looked in his email service's deleted file and called up the message again. He scanned the text, and the email address of the sender.

'What the hell is the Sol Invictus Trust when it's at home? And why were you so keen to get the stone in the first place, Mr V. A. Bassianus?'

He tried the obvious first route, typing the name of the trust into Google. He had plenty of hits, including an online gaming site, and information about an English neofolk band addicted to electronic experimentation. There was nothing about a trust. However, there was another entry on an historical site that caught his eye. It was about a Roman emperor called Heliogabalus who had been responsible for promoting a version of sun worship. He replaced Jupiter with the god of the cult called Elagabalus, and renamed him Deus Sol Invictus – God the Undefeated Sun. Greg's inclination was to be sceptical about anything he couldn't measure or define, so he didn't believe in the supernatural. But he knew equally that it didn't stop some cranks thinking they had powers greater than science could encompass. Someone probably wanted to revive this old cult seriously enough to spend big money on obtaining the meteorite. Then he spotted Emperor Heliogabalus's birth name, Varius Avitus Bassianus. He clicked back on the email text on his computer screen.

'Just who do you think you are, Mr V. A. Bassianus? A ghost, a reincarnation or a god?'

He recalled the old box the stone had been delivered in and reached out for it. The label that had been glued on the lid was tantalizing. The words were in English, but an old form of it, and broken up by the missing pieces of paper that had been shed like dry skin. He pored over it, and slowly he began to piece it together. He noted down what he could decipher, then interpolated some possible words into the text. What emerged was startling.

With this sky-st[one] comes a legend. It is [said] to be a force for great good, and a cure. But ev[il?] is drawn to it also. It has travelled through m[any h]ands [or maybe many lands], but its origin is thought to be Greenland [. . .] where the evil began. HT, 16[??].

Could it be? Was the missing place name Brattahli∂? Greg's mind reeled. It was only a week since he had first had sight of Brattahli∂ on Google Earth. Before then, he was unaware of the ancient site. And maybe that was the rational answer – he was making an incorrect jump based on limited knowledge. How many places in Greenland started with those three letters? On Google, he did a place names search. It didn't take long, and showed him that no modern town at least had a name beginning with the letters 'Bra'. Nor were there any other ancient sites so entitled. It was not conclusive, but it was disturbing nevertheless. He lifted the stone from his lap and stared at it. It felt hot, and he could feel it pulsing in his grip. Hastily, he put it down on the workbench top. He tried to clear his head, rationalizing that he had just felt his own pulse. But the thought kept returning to him that this very stone could have been the meteorite that had impacted in the crater he had discovered last week. Or at least part of the original meteor, because the crater was larger than this small stone could have made. He began again searching Google Earth for smaller impact craters in the vicinity of the larger one. And on the same side of the fjord as the ancient settlement of Brattahlið.

It was the early hours of the morning before he took a break and rolled his wheelchair into the kitchen. He needed coffee to keep him awake. The last time he pulled an overnighter, he had been drinking red wine, and it didn't help his powers of concentration. He made some of the real stuff in a cafetière, balanced the hot jug between his insensitive thighs and rolled back to the computer. He depressed the plunger, poured the hot coffee into his mug and took a sip. The phone rang jarringly in the deep silence, and he almost spilled the mug into his lap. He wondered who was calling him in the depths of the night. Picking the cordless up, he heard the voice of June Piper, and she was excited. Before he could say anything about the meteorite, which sat, dark and mysterious, in front of him, she babbled out her news.

'We've found something. It's from your new impact crater site. Well, not exactly from that but around it. There are the fingers of some glaciers running down the valleys quite close, and Don sashayed down there on to the surface.'

Greg felt a pang of jealousy. Don Tremlett was the mountain goat who had replaced him after his accident. He did all the risky manoeuvres that had been Greg's forte. He could just imagine him scrambling down on to

391

the uneven and no doubt fissured surface of the glacier. As June pressed on, he idly moved his cursor hand on Google Earth, grasping the image and sliding it east, back over the fjord. One stretch of the satellite image had been taken in winter, and Greg could see a grey river snaking through ice just below where he had identified the crater. He followed it up and found the glacier terminus – a mass of shattered ice. Above it he could almost picture Don walking on the crumpled surface and finding a good point at which to bore down with his core sampler. June's sharp tones alerted him to the fact that she didn't know if he was still on the line.

'Yes, I'm here, June. Just looking at the Google image. What did you find?'

'That's what I've been telling you. We found microbes – a species of bacterium in a spore-like state. They must have been under the ice for a long time, moving very slowly towards the terminus. Whether they are associated with your impact crater we aren't sure yet. But we're going to thaw them out in the lab and coax them back to life.'

'Isn't that a little dangerous? It sounds like the sort of doomsday scenario Michael Crichton would conjure up.'

June snorted. 'You've been reading too much science fiction, and anyway Crichton's dead. As for thawing out bugs, it's been done before at Penn State, and nobody's died yet. Look, I've got to go. We're celebrating here, and Alicia has just waved a bottle of beer in my face.'

Greg pictured the gorgeous Alicia in his mind and wondered if June had got her into bed yet. He had tried and failed. He wished the team good luck and rang off. Greg felt totally dissociated from that world out there, where at this very moment scientists were getting paralytic because they had found a bacterium. All he had was a mug of rapidly cooling coffee and an empty room. Tired of looking for craters, and depressed at being in London when all the action was in Greenland, he returned to Googling Sol Invictus, Bassianus and Elagabal. He flipped from site to site, and after a while the information began to repeat itself, as it frequently did on the net with one site pirating another. Then something caught his eye. A site describing the sun god Elagabal said he was the 'god of the black stone'. He clicked on this highlighted text and found himself reading about the Baetyl – a black stone venerated as the house of God. There was a quote from the historian Herodian suggesting the stone came down from Zeus. The clincher was the final sentence, which Greg read out loud.

'In the third century, the stone was believed to be a meteorite.'

Greg knew that the stone lying on the bench in front of him couldn't be that very stone, if it had come down in Greenland. But if the original stone was lost, who's to say that some crank wasn't seeking a suitable substitute? A crank like V. A. Bassianus, for example. It was a little scary that, since the man's email and Greg's rebuff, Bassianus had gone silent. Suddenly, the warehouse conversion didn't feel so safe. A wave of exhaustion rolled over Greg, and he hunched over in his chair. He felt a tingling sensation in his left toes and sighed, reaching out to close Google Earth. Before he managed to hit the keyboard, though, he suddenly pushed himself upright. How could he have had any sensation in his toes? He was a T2 paraplegic. He shook his head, guessing he was more tired than he thought. He was having delusions now. The meteorite still lay on his workbench, and he picked it up, hefting the weight in his hands.

Then it happened again. He felt something in his right foot this time. It was like weak radio signals beaming in from outer space, almost lost in the background wash of white noise. But this time he knew it was real. He needed something stronger than coffee to deal with this, so he tucked the meteorite down between his thigh and the side of the wheelchair and flicked the switch to motor into the kitchen and get a bottle of wine. When he returned, there was a man standing in the middle of the room. He was tall, well muscled and looked quite at ease. His hair was thick and dark, slicked back from a bronzed forehead. His eyes were pale blue and steady.

'Who the hell . . .?' Greg stopped his wheelchair abruptly, and the tyres squeaked on the wooden surface. The man smiled with a lopsided grin that had no doubt charmed many a woman and held out his hand.

'Greg Janic? My name's Bassianus.'

Greg's mind was racing. He couldn't figure out how the man had got in, and done it so quietly. Then he felt a draught on his neck. Half turning in the chair, he saw that one of the windows that looked out on to the street was open. If Bassianus had come in that way, he was as good a climber as himself. As he once had been. Greg's apartment was three floors up. He went to move the switch on the arm of his chair so that he could swing out of the room and escape. Maybe he could barricade himself in the bedroom. But the man was too quick for him. Bassianus strode over to him, reached behind the chair and pulled the battery leads free. Greg was disabled all over again. He thought briefly of the bottle that was nestled in his lap, but Bassianus must have thought of it, too, and he gently lifted the wine away from Greg and placed it safely on the workbench.

'Now, Mr Janic, please may I have what I have come for? Just give me the stone, and I will be on my way. No harm done.'

Greg waved a hand at the shelves on the other side of the room, where his display of meteorites was arranged. 'Help yourself.'

Bassianus sniggered and shook his head. 'I've already had a look, Mr Janic. The one I want is not there. I want the sacred stone you stole from me on eBay.'

Suddenly, the man surged forward and pushed Greg's wheelchair roughly back until it was under the open window. Greg felt his legs tense even as the air whooshed out of his lungs with the force of the crash against the wall. His head pitched forward on to Bassianus's chest. The man grabbed him by his hair and pulled his head cruelly back. He thrust his contorted, red face into Greg's, all appearance of the urbane man draining away from his features to be replaced by a wild and uncontrollable beast.

'Where the fuck is it, you miserable cripple? Tell me before you go out that window.'

Greg kept his mouth shut, even as he felt the back of his neck forced over the sill of the window. His head sang as the blood rushed to it, and the night sky hung above him, the stars mocking his terror. The struggle was all too brief and one-sided.

DS Dave Skye leaned out of the window and looked at the body of the man that lay sprawled out on the pavement below. He called down to the police surgeon, who was examining the corpse.

'Cause of death?'

Andy Topley, who was used to this question from detectives at the scene of a crime, gave a deep sigh. Why did they all think it was like on the TV? The DS would be asking for a time of death next, which in reality was often impossible to specify even after a post-mortem. He looked up to where the red-haired Scot hung out of the window three floors up.

'How about multiple injuries, consistent with a fall from three storeys up?'

Skye's head disappeared. No doubt the DS was moaning to someone about the doctor having got out of bed on the wrong side. He thought he had seen DC Harry Parris trailing upstairs after the DS. Perhaps he could deal with him. At least he was a sensible older cop, who would not bother the doctor too much. Then Skye's head appeared again, and Dr Topley just knew it was the next inevitable question coming, so he pre-empted it with a comment of his own.

'There is an unusual depressed fracture on his forehead. Dish-shaped. As though he has been hit with something rounded. Of course, there may be something down here that caused it. There is an iron bollard over there.' He pointed to the old-fashioned cannon-shaped black object by the pavement edge. 'It's near the body, but your forensics team will have to check it out first.'

The red-headed policeman waved at the doctor and disappeared yet again.

'Wanker,' muttered Topley.

'What's up with him?' said Skye. 'Male PMT, or something?'

Parris, stolid as ever, ignored the unnecessary comment. He was used to his boss, university educated and a high flier, behaving like a prat. He just shrugged his shoulders non-committally. Never take sides, was his guiding principle in life. The DS carried on his musings.

'Still, it's interesting what he was saying about the skull fracture. A blow to the head makes this an interesting case after all.'

When he had got the call about the dead body lying in the street in what was now a fashionable part of London that used to be warehouse land, his ears had pricked up. A murder in yuppie-dom would do his career no harm at all. Then he had learned that the apartment the body appeared to have flown out of was owned by someone called Greg Janic. And that the guy was wheelchair-bound. It suddenly looked like Janic must have accidentally fallen out of the window, or maybe thrown himself out. Suicide or accidental death loomed large, and a celebrity murder case dissipated like ice cream in hot sunshine. But with the doctor's observation, things were looking up again.

Harry Parris wasn't convinced. Gloomily, the DC looked out of the window for himself.

'That bollard looks awfully close to the body.'

'What? No, it can't be the cause of the guy's fracture. He would have had to have flown to hit it. And if it's not the bollard that caused the injury, what was it?'

The sound of rubber tyres squeaking on the woodblock floor of the apartment's living room caused both policemen to turn away from the window and plaster unconvincing smiles on their faces. It was Skye who spoke first. 'Mr Janic, are you OK now?'

Greg nodded and waved to the long sofa that ran down the centre of the room facing the big TV screen on the wall.

'Thank you for letting me dress. I didn't really want to entertain you in just my boxer shorts.'

The policemen sat down and watched as Greg Janic expertly manoeuvred the motorized wheelchair around the coffee table to stop opposite them.

'You were asking me when I first became suspicious there was someone in the apartment.'

Skye nodded. 'Yes. You said you had gone to bed early, undressed, and had been reading.'

'That's right. One of those historical crime novels that seem so popular now. By ... Sorry, I've forgotten the author already.'

'No matter. I wasn't looking for a recommendation. I can't stand the things myself. And then you heard a noise, you say?'

'Yes. I thought at first it was the window making a noise. I had recalled leaving it open as soon as I had got into bed. But I didn't feel like doing something about it.' By way of explanation, he pointed down to his useless legs and the chair. 'It takes so long to get back up again, once I've settled down.'

Skye smiled sympathetically. 'Quite. But then ...?'

'Then I definitely heard something else. Footsteps, and a bleep from my laptop.'

He pointed at the bank of equipment that was arrayed down the far side of the room, surmounted by the shelf full of meteorites.

'Someone had to be playing with it. It took a little while to get in my chair, and I could hear whoever it was moving things around. Maybe he was looking for money or valuables. But he was disappointed, I suppose. All I have is a collection of stones.'

'Meteorites, you say?'

'That's right. Curiosities, but not worth a lot. I came into the room as quietly as I could. But I suppose my tyres must have squeaked on the wooden floor, and alerted him – the burglar – to my presence. Just like they did with you.'

'You say the burglar.'

Greg looked a little puzzled. 'What else could he have been? He must have seen my window open and thought he would take a chance. When he heard me, he made a dash for the window and must have slipped. He went out of the window without a sound.' Greg looked down into his lap, as if recalling the terrible event. 'I called the police and ambulance straight away.'

'You did all you could, sir.'

Skye leaned over and patted Greg consolingly on the thigh. The sensation Greg felt was something he had not experienced in two years, and he had to stop his leg from twitching. Skye sat back and looked Greg solemnly in the face. 'After all, in your condition you could hardly leap down the stairs and offer the kiss of life. Or have beaten the intruder to death yourself.'

As Skye laughed at his own tasteless joke, Greg smiled thinly and thought of the last moments of life of the mysterious V. A. Bassianus. Sure he had the poor cripple at his mercy, Bassianus had been astonished when Greg had heaved himself out of his chair, the sky-stone in his right hand. He had lurched sideways across the window sill. Greg, standing on his feet for the first time since his accident, swung the precious meteorite hard against Bassianus's forehead. The man's eyes went blank, as though his life was snuffed out instantly. He pitched backwards out of the window, carried off by the weight of Greg's blow. Greg, his legs trembling, leaned out and looked down at the street below. Bassianus was surely dead. If the blow hadn't killed him, the fall must have done. He fell back in his wheelchair and tucked the murder weapon down beside his thigh again. It nestled there now, and he reckoned he could feel its warmth against his legs, a sensation he should not have. Whether it was the effect of the stone, or a spontaneous return of sensation, Greg didn't know.

But he was no longer inclined to total scepticism about the supernatural. Making sure he didn't move his newly restored legs, he smiled sadly at the red-haired policeman.

'No, detective sergeant, I'm afraid I'm stuck in this wheelchair for life.'

Simon & Schuster proudly presents

hILL OF BONES

By

The MEDIEVAL MURDERERS

July 2011 in trade paperback

An intriguing new collection of mysteries
is about to unfold.

Turn the page for a sneak preview . . .

PROLOGUE

I

Geraint watched the lizard basking in the sun on the tiled floor. Its head was canted towards where Geraint sat a few feet away on the grassy slope. The creature was so still it might have been carved out of stone apart from the tiny pulse that throbbed on the underside of its silver-grey neck.

The lizard, about the length of a man's hand, was crouching above a fish with a great mouth and with water spouting from the top of its head. The lizard was directly over the gaping mouth. Geraint amused himself with the idea of the lizard's surprise if the fish were to come to sudden life and swallow it down in a single gulp. Geraint knew the fish could not come to life, of course, since it was made up of countless little tiles that were coloured red and blue and green and silver.

Shifting his gaze without moving his head, Geraint looked across the rest of the ornamented floor beyond the lizard and the great fish. It lay bare to the sky but was edged with random blocks of stone, the remains of the walls to the chamber. Beyond were the outlines of other rooms and even fragments of columns. The house had been built on a ledge of land on a hillside. It looked out on a circle of hills and a town below in the valley basin. Geraint wondered how the inhabitants of the villa had defended themselves, isolated, far from other habitations. Perhaps they had not needed to.

He returned his attention to the tiled floor, which showed a picture of the sea and its inhabitants but quite unlike any that Geraint had ever seen. There were creatures with swollen heads and many arms, and others whose foreparts were similar to birds, with beaks and claws, but whose hindquarters were those of fish. Among these monsters sailed small ships containing smaller men holding nets and spears.

Closer to Geraint and riding out of the sea was a great bare-chested man or god, twenty times the size of the men in boats. He was in a chariot drawn by horses with scaly fins for tails. The face of the man-god – wise and vigorous – reminded Geraint of their leader, Arthur. He had seen Arthur astride a horse holding the reins in the same easy fashion as the man-god in the chariot. Arthur had even spoken to Geraint as he rode by. He had scarcely been able to look at him nor had he heard the leader's words, his ears were buzzing so. But he knew the words were firm and, in their way, kindly. Kinder than he was used to hearing from Caradoc, for example.

A rustling in the grass behind him did not cause him to look round – he already knew who it must be – but, instead, to flick his gaze back towards the lizard. But the lizard had gone. For an instant, Geraint wondered whether the creature had been swallowed up by the great spouting fish. But that could not be, because the fish's jaws were still gaping with hunger. And because although the lizard was real, the fish was no more than an image.

Someone clumped down the slope and clouted Geraint across the back of his head. He sighed and clambered to his feet. He turned to look at his brother, Caradoc, standing on the higher ground above. The sun was behind him so Geraint couldn't see his brother's expression but he sensed it was showing the usual mixture of irritation and impatience.

'What are you doing?' said Caradoc. 'We must be on our way. There's no time to waste.'

As if to show that his own time had not been wasted, Caradoc held up a cony by the hind legs.

'Tribute,' he said. 'A contribution to supper. When we get there.'

The dead animal swayed in the evening air, its white front speckled with blood. Further up the slope sat Caradoc's dog, Cynric. It stared fixedly at the rabbit, but gave no sign of anger at being deprived of its prey.

Geraint did not move. He thought of the much more valuable tribute he was bringing and his hand closed about the pouch that was attached to his belt. Then, as if to distract Caradoc from the gesture, he swept his arm over the mosaic sea-scene.

'What happened to them?' he said.

'What are you talking about?'

'The ones who lived here. The Roman people who made these pictures.'

'Who knows?' said Caradoc in a tone that meant, 'Who cares?'.

'They left long before the time of our father's father but their traces are all around us,' said Geraint. He was thinking of other villas, in better condition, that they had passed on their journey up from the south. Not just villas, either, but terraces of land with strangled vines and neglected orchard plots. Now Geraint looked in the direction of the old town tucked into the fold of the river below. He knew this was Aquae Sulis. The upper parts of the buildings glowed in the evening sun but even while the brothers watched, the light dimmed and died as if an invisible hand were wiping it away. In reality it was only the sun slipping down behind a neighbouring hill but Geraint shivered.

'Dreamer,' said Caradoc. 'And trust you to miss the only thing of value here.'

He bent down and picked up a battered coin from the edge of the mosaic floor. It was true, Geraint had been so intent on the sea picture that he had overlooked the little tarnished disc. Then Caradoc swung away in a downhill direction, still holding the dead rabbit and skirting the remains of the villa, with its exposed floors and weather-beaten columns. Cynric leaped from a sitting position and bounded after him.

Geraint paused for a moment longer. Perhaps it was the image of the sea on the floor that made him think of waves of people, waves of men, flowing across this land. Men who were of a different race from him. Men such as the ones who had built this villa on the outskirts of the town in the valley and then, in a time before his father's father, abandoned it and withdrawn like the tide. Or perhaps they had not withdrawn at all but simply died out. Which came to the same thing.

And now there were different waves of men from the east and north, fresh and fierce, Saxon barbarians, threatening this land with fire and slaughter. For years, they had advanced like the incoming tide but now there had come a chance to stem the tide, even to turn it back. The only chance perhaps, but a fair one under their leader, Arthur.

He stood up and gazed across the valley towards the hills to the north-east. One hill stood slightly separate from the others and was distinguished by a flattened top. In the clear light of evening Geraint was able to see that the lines of the hill top looked too straight to be completely natural. There were few trees growing on the lower slopes and none at all on the upper, which meant that any approaching group would be easily seen. It reminded him of the great hill town in the south, near the village that he and Caradoc had come from. The town called Cadwy's Fort, which Arthur used as his headquarters when he was in the region. The size of Cadwy's, with its towering grassy flanks and deep defensive ditches surmounted by walls of pale stone, made Geraint think of the work of gods rather than mere men.

The hill opposite where he stood was less imposing than Cadwy's, but that it was occupied by men was not in doubt, for he now saw a thick column of black smoke rising from a point near the centre of the flattened top. Then other spirals of smoke sprang up, and carried on the breeze there came cries and screams, the scrape of metal on metal, the thud of blows. Geraint had never been in battle, never been close to the scene of battle, but he recognised this for what it was. Had he and Caradoc arrived too late? Was the decisive encounter already taking place?

He felt confused and dizzy and almost sank down on the ground. When he looked again at the flattened hill, its top was placid and the pillars of smoke had vanished. In his ears there rang no sound except birdsong. Geraint was familiar with these moments, which overcame him occasionally. He had told no one of them, except one person.

Geraint blinked and followed his brother downhill towards the town in the valley. It was an open evening on the edge of midsummer. Threads of innocent white smoke wavered from the encampments set around the town of Aquae Sulis. The distance and the fading light made it impossible to judge numbers. You would scarcely know that there was an army camped about the town. You would not know that there was another army on the march in this direction.

Caradoc and Geraint crossed the lower-lying meadows, where the ground was soft underfoot and the breeze rippled through willows and rows of poplars. Geraint said nothing of the battle-scene he had witnessed on the opposite hill top. Either it had happened in the past, in which case there was nothing to be done about it, or – and this was more likely – it was still to come. The question was, would the battle take place in Geraint's presence? Was he one of the fighters? Was his own voice among the screams and cries he had heard? Or Caradoc's?

As they drew nearer to the encampments, with Caradoc still in the lead and the dog off to one side on some mission of its own, they could smell distant wood smoke and roasting meat, could hear a whinnying horse. It seemed to Geraint that his brother knew exactly where he was going, he walked with such confidence. Then Caradoc halted. He was standing on the edge of a marshy, reed-fringed stretch of water. They might have been able to wade through it, but beyond the reeds was a faster-flowing current, which caught up all the light remaining in the sky. Geraint realised that this must be the Abona. From their vantage point up in the hills the course of the river down here had been concealed. Now it was going to require a detour before they could reach the encampments or the town.

'There must be a crossing point further along,' said Caradoc, gesturing towards the west. 'There must be a ford.'

How much further along? thought Geraint. He saw the pair of them blundering about in the gathering dark, their nostrils tickled by the smells from the other side of the river and their eyes distracted by the twinkle of fires. He suddenly felt hungry. Caradoc whistled for Cynric and the black shape came crashing through the long grass.

Distracted by the return of the dog, neither brother

noticed the small boat sliding noiselessly out of the reeds. When they did, Caradoc dropped the dead rabbit and his hand jumped to his sword hilt. Geraint tensed and Cynric growled. The occupant of the boat had seen them before they were aware of him. He was a lean and wrinkled man – quite old, to Geraint's eyes – and he was crouching in the centre of the boat, which was about half as broad as it was long. He was pushing himself towards the bank with one hand but there was a paddle resting across his knees.

'I had my eye on you as you came across the meadows,' said the boatman.

'Where is the crossing place?' said Caradoc.

The boatman did not answer until, with a final flick of his wrist, he caused his craft to crunch softly into the mud and reeds a few feet from where Caradoc and Geraint were standing.

'Over there, but you will not reach it this side of night,' he said, jerking his head in the direction of the now vanished sun.

'We are here to join Arthur's host,' said Caradoc.

The boatman cleared his throat and spat into the water. Evidently he was not impressed. 'Is Arthur here?' he said.

'Yes,' said Caradoc with a confidence that was based more on belief than knowledge.

The boatman cast his eyes up and down the length of the brothers as if assessing their fitness as warriors. Geraint was conscious that he cut a boyish figure but his brother now, Caradoc, he had more bone and sinew on him.

'You will carry us over,' said Caradoc.

'And you will pay what?'

'We are here to fight our common enemy,' said Geraint, speaking for the first time. 'The Saxon horde.'

'Oh that enemy,' said the boatman. He flexed his arms

and the oval boat rocked in the water. 'What are your names?'

'I am Caradoc and this is my brother, Geraint.'

'And I am Brennus,' said the boatman. He had a high-pitched voice, disagreeable. Geraint was reminded of an ungreased axle on a cart. 'Talking of enemies, mine are the cold in winter and the hunger and thirst all the time. You've got something to drink?'

'The dregs of some water only,' said Caradoc, 'warm and stale from being carried all day.'

The boatman laughed, an odd sound like the squeak of some water bird.

'You must surely be carrying something of value,' he said. Instinctively, Geraint's hand tightened on the pouch, which was fixed to his belt across from his sword. Despite the growing gloom, he could have sworn that Brennus the boatman observed this slight gesture.

Caradoc retrieved the coin he'd picked up from the villa floor. He held it towards the boatman.

'This will more than do,' he said. 'It's a coin from the old days and it is silver. You can have it if you ferry us both across. And the dog.'

'The dog will swim behind us. You can't have a dog in a small boat like this on account of the balance,' said Brennus, stretching out a sinewy arm and waggling his hand to illustrate his point. He gathered a coil of rope from the bottom of the boat. 'Here. Tie a stick to this and throw it out when we are afloat. The dog will seize hold of the stick.'

Caradoc found a fallen branch along the bank and, using his knife, sawed off a section. He secured one end of the boatman's rope to the piece of wood. Cynric sat and stared with his head on one side, baffled by his master's actions. The boatman watched with almost as much interest, stroking his chin with one hand and grasping the long paddle on his knees with the other. At one point his gaze wandered casually towards Geraint, then flicked away again – too quickly, Geraint thought. Clouds of midges hovered in the half-light.

Brennus was suddenly struck with a fresh idea. 'Come to think of it, my little craft will not carry three at once. I will take one of you over and come back for the other. Out of goodness of heart, and seeing as you are to join the fight against the Saxon horde – our common enemy – I will do two journeys for the price of one, and in any order you please.'

Geraint was about to protest at their separation but stopped himself. It would sound feeble and unmanly. This Brennus was quite old and withered, for all his sinewy arms. The brothers were young and strong.

If Caradoc had any doubts he did not show them. He nodded. 'Very well. But you will not be paid until we are both standing on the far bank.'

'Step in,' said the boatman, 'but carefully now.'

Geraint nodded at his brother as if to say, you go first. Brennus shuffled backwards as Caradoc, holding the coiled rope, stepped into the boat and sat down at the near end. Cynric quivered on the edge of the reedy bank, uncertain of the next stage in this game. The boatman shoved off with his paddle. When they had pushed out a little way, he indicated that Caradoc should throw out the rope. The stick-end landed on the mud and Cynric snatched it up in his jaws, floundered out into the water and began paddling as if he was born to it.

Geraint heard the old boatman instructing Caradoc to keep the rope slack so that the dog's struggles would not drag the boat down. He watched as the boat cleared the reeds and shallows and bobbed out into the clearer stretch of the Abona, the black head of the dog just visible. At once he felt very alone. Suppose the boat overturned and his brother was drowned? It did not look very stable, more like an over-sized platter thrown onto the water. Suppose that, once they reached the other side, the ferryman refused to return? But then he would not be paid. Geraint did not believe that Brennus would be able to overpower Caradoc, his older, stronger brother, equipped with knife and sword. He breathed deeply, taking in cool draughts of evening air. He gazed back at the willows and poplars that fringed the shore.

By the time he looked again across the river it was to see Caradoc clambering out of the little boat on the far bank, followed a few moments later by Cynric. Geraint sensed rather than saw the dog shaking itself violently, sending spray everywhere. Then the boat, paddled by Brennus, was making progress back over the water. With one hand Geraint grasped his sword hilt, while the other kept firm hold on the pouch attached to his belt. Inside was his tribute, intended for some purpose that he did not yet know. He was tempted for an instant to unfasten the pouch, to unwrap the precious item, examine it once more in the twilight. But, hearing the splash of the paddle as the boat pushed through the outer-most reeds on this side, he resisted the temptation. He glanced at the ground and noticed the white, blood-speckled front of the dead rabbit. Caradoc had forgotten his contri-bution to the supper that they hoped to get on arrival. Geraint picked up the dead animal by its stiff hind legs. Carrying it somehow distracted attention from the contents of the pouch.

Brennus grounded the boat once more in the mud of the shore.

'Come on, sir,' he said. 'No time to waste. We must get across before nightfall.'

Geraint stepped in the boat and sat down clumsily as Caradoc had done.

For the second time, the boatman used the paddle to push them off the bank and the craft bobbled its way out into the open.

The river seemed immense once you were in the middle of it and the willow frame and stretched skin of the boat offered very thin protection. The current carried them at an angle, but Brennus was familiar with its twists and turns for, with a slight touch or stroke of the paddle, he aimed for the point at which Geraint could see his brother standing with the dog. The rushing of the water threatened to swamp the boat but it was more stable than it looked and, after a time, Geraint started to relax and study Brennus, helped by the fact that the boatman's face was half averted. He wondered what the man did for a living. Ferrying travellers across the Abona? Fishing? Certainly a strong, disagreeable odour of fish came off him now that he was at close quarters.

Then the boat came to a halt or, rather, began to spin about in a slow circular motion as if they were trapped on the edge of a whirlpool. Geraint found himself looking at the bank they'd left behind. Brennus withdrew his paddle from the water and laid it, dripping, across his bony knees. He reached over and stroked the fur of the rabbit, which Geraint was holding. The young man suddenly felt foolish for bringing this insignificant dead tribute.

'I've changed my mind, sir,' said Brennus. His voice grew higher, more disagreeable and grating. 'The coin your brother is offering is only enough for one passage. I need something more before I take you to the other side.'

'I haven't got anything,' said Geraint, somehow unsurprised by this new demand. He had not trusted Brennus from the instant the boatman slid out of the reeds. He indicated the rabbit that nestled in his lap. 'Nothing except this cony. You are welcome to it.'

'I want more than a dead thing,' said Brennus. 'You have got something else on your very person. I saw the way your hand went towards your belt on the bank earlier. I see the way you're gripping that pouch on your belt even now.'

It was true. Geraint was holding on to the leather pouch even more tightly than he was using his other hand to cling to the side of the boat. He had his short sword, but it was tucked awkwardly down by his side and would be slow to draw. Besides, he had never used it in anger, scarcely knew how to wield it.

'Can you swim?' said the boatman.

'Yes,' said Geraint promptly.

'You're a liar, and a bad one at that. Whatever you say, you *have* got something in that pouch of yours and, whatever else you say, you cannot swim. Not one in a hundred men can swim. I'll turn the boat over and you'll sink like a stone.'

'Then you lose whatever I'm carrying. You lose your boat.'

'Boats float,' said Brennus. 'And you will lose rather more when you're at the bottom of the river.'

Geraint sensed that Brennus was enjoying this: the teasing, the control of what was happening on his boat. He looked towards the far bank where Caradoc and Cynric were standing expectantly. He thought of shouting out, but what could his brother do? Then he noticed that although they were still spinning round, the figure of his brother was growing larger. The current was gradually pushing them to the other shore while the boatman, intent on his threats, was neglecting to use the paddle to keep them in the centre of the stream. If he could only manage to distract Brennus for a little longer . . .

'So *you* are able to swim?' he said.

'Like a fish. Come on now, just open up your pouch and hand whatever's inside it to me. I'll take it in exchange for a safe landing. A blind bargain on my side, can't say fairer than that.'

'It is a keepsake from my mother,' said Geraint.

This was a lie too, more or less, but one the boatman seemed eager to accept.

'Then she'd be pleased if you handed it over to save yourself from death by water.'

'She is dead now, my mother,' said Geraint, his eyes growing moist as he said the words but still seeing the outline of Caradoc, standing rigid on the bank. From his posture, Geraint's brother knew something was wrong.

'I don't care what she is,' said the boatman, tiring of his chat. 'Give me what you're carrying or you'll be dead alongside her.'

'Here you are then,' said Geraint, angry now. He made to open the leather pouch. Instead he seized the rabbit by the hind legs and swung it straight at Brennus's face. It connected with a satisfying thwack. The dead cony was no club but the shock of the blow was enough to surprise and distract the boatman, who jerked back and put up his hands to protect himself. Geraint rose to his feet, the boat swaying wildly beneath him, and before he should lose his balance altogether he pressed down against the side of the shallow craft and made to leap into a clump of feathery reeds, one of several outcrops not so far from the bank. He felt something holding him and realised that Brennus had made a grab at the region of his waist. There was a tearing sound and Geraint toppled rather than jumped into the water.

His body sank through the reeds into the murk. His mouth filled with choking water and his feet flailed for the bottom.

Through his mind flashed the image he'd glimpsed on the villa floor, the sea with the strange beasts that lived there, and he wondered whether his final moments had come. He could not swim, that was no lie. Then his feet came to rest on something that was neither hard nor soft, perhaps a submerged clump of vegetation, and it gave him enough purchase to push himself above the surface of the water. Gasping for air, he scrabbled about among the reeds, pulling himself forward, kicking out with his legs and feeling his wool clothes growing heavier by the second.

He touched bottom but, far from giving him support, the mud of the river-bed grabbed at his boots as if it wanted to tear them from his feet. His head was above the surface but he could not keep upright. Something struck him in the face and he heard shouting. At first he thought it was the boatman, but then he recognised his brother. He was calling out, 'Take hold! Take hold!' Caradoc was too far off to reach Geraint but he had tossed out the boatman's rope to which was still fastened the stick the dog had used. Geraint grabbed it and, half by dint of his own struggling, half by being tugged in on the rope, found himself drawn up onto the bank, the last few feet in his brother's hands.

He lay on his front, a landed fish, water pouring from his hair, his eyes, his garments. The black shape of Cynric panted above him while his brother stood off a distance to allow him to recover. Geraint sat up. He wiped his eyes and looked out across the Abona. He glanced at the bank on either side of him. He half expected to see the treacherous boatman emerging from the river, dripping wet and vengeful. It was only then that he realised, in the struggle, the pouch had been torn away from his belt. It was lost, presumably at the bottom of the river. Or in the watery grasp of the boatman.

He felt more angry than he could remember feeling in his life. He would have attacked the boatman with his bare hands if he had appeared onshore. But of Brennus there was no sign, not an arm or head visible in the twilight above the swirling current. Then he caught sight of the man's upturned boat, like a giant's hat in midstream. Boats float. But he prayed that Brennus had gone to the bottom.

'What in God's name was going on out there?' said Caradoc. He sounded more irritated than relieved.

'He tried to rob me,' said Geraint. 'He said the coin you'd promised him wasn't enough. He thought I was carrying something of value.'

Caradoc looked curiously at his brother. He made to say something but stopped himself. Geraint stood up. His clothes clung to him. The anger had gone and now he was cold and shivery.

'At least you have saved yourself a silver coin.' The bitterness of losing his pouch and its contents was like a bad taste in Geraint's mouth. He said nothing of the loss to his brother.

'And I have got the man's rope,' said Caradoc, rolling it up into a coil.

'We should use it to hang him with if we find him again.'

'I see there's some spark in you after all, brother. Save it for the Saxons. Come on.'

They tramped across the fields to the nearest encampment, marked by fires and makeshift shelters. They struck lucky almost straight away. Caradoc did not give the name of their village or steading – a place-name that few were likely to know or remember among the occupants of so many villages that had flocked to Aquae Sulis – but he spoke instead of a very tall man with reddish hair by the name of Aelric. The second person to whom he mentioned

Aelric indicated a dilapidated farm building in the twilight next to a cluster of willows. Approaching, Geraint and Caradoc saw a cluster of men sprawled about a fire by the entrance. Hobbled horses champed the grass close by. Red-headed Aelric seemed surprised to see them but grudgingly welcomed the young brothers to the circle. Geraint was ribbed about his wet clothes but allowed to get close to the fire.

It was only later, after the food and drink and the talk, that Geraint, now lying at a little distance from the cooking fire, finally began to think of what he had lost or had been snatched from him. The pouch that hung from his belt and the precious object that he had been carrying for three days on his journey from the south. Although he had been guarding it for longer than that.

II

It was on his third and last visit to the old woman that Geraint was presented with the gift. She lived inside one of the hollowed-out mounds that dotted a flat area of ground not far from the village. The field, with its tussocky hummocks, was a place that the villagers avoided because it was believed to hold the dead. Not their dead, the recent ones, but the dead of long ago. At least, that was what was suggested by the things that had been discovered (and allowed to remain undisturbed) within the hummocks: the remains of skeletons and scraps of old leather and potsherds; even knives and axe-heads fashioned from stone.

There must have been some powerful magic preventing the villagers from using these places for shelter or storage, since they were dry and warm in winter, as well as cool in summer. Perhaps it was not only the partial skeletons but the presence of the woman that frightened people. She had flowing white hair and a face through which the bones showed as if she was more than half-way towards joining her underground companions for ever. She was so tall that, when she stood, she had to stoop within the quite generous confines of the burial chambers. At first, Geraint had not realised she was blind. There was a little light by the outer parts of the old woman's lair because during the day she was in the habit of sitting near the entrance, which was made out of two stone uprights and a crosspiece. Geraint thought she sat there because she wanted to see who was coming, before he realised that there was no sight in her large, glazed eyes. And then he understood that she did not need to see in order to know who was coming. She had, after all, greeted him by name on his first visit.

Geraint was not frightened. He did not see why he should be frightened. Unlike the other villagers – unlike his brother, Caradoc, for example – he did not question why the woman – she had no name, she was simply the *woman* – should not live there in the place of the dead, by herself. If she really was alone. Once or twice during their conversations, Geraint had caught the tremor and sound of movement further back in the chamber, not some animal but human, he thought. Who it was he never discovered.

But the woman already knew much about Geraint. Knew that his mother was ill and must shortly die, knew that his father had been killed in a skirmish with the Saxons when Geraint was little, knew that he regarded his only surviving brother with a mixture of respect and love and resentment. Above all, she knew of his waking dreams, of those moments when something seemed to slide between him and the reality surrounding him. When he first began to experience these, around the time of his father's death, Geraint had been truly frightened. He told no one and suffered in silence.

In one vision he saw two men tussling on the bank of a nearby river. One fell in, or was pushed, and the other stumbled after him. He recognised the two men. Geraint was actually within sight of the river but by the time he plucked up the courage to go closer, they had disappeared. The death by drowning – which occurred a few days later – was accounted an accident but Geraint had seen in his vision the way in which Deri's opponent, who desired Deri's wife, had held his rival's head underwater. Perhaps he did not intend to get rid of Deri but had taken the opportunity as it arose. The man who held the other underwater was redheaded Aelric, the head of the village. Later Geraint heard Aelric describe to the other villagers how he had been several fields away when Deri drowned, and this seemed to allay any suspicions they might have. Geraint said nothing to contradict him but, afterwards, he was more wary and frightened of Aelric than ever.

On another occasion during the winter Geraint dreamed several times of a sunless summer of cloud and constant rain, and how the village went hungry when the crops failed. Sure enough, it happened and the village sent petitioners to Cadwys for help.

When, on his second visit to the burial ground, he started to tell the woman who lived there of these things – and he had never mentioned them to anyone before – she merely nodded and grasped his arm with her claw-like hand. She reassured Geraint, telling him he was possessed by a gift, not a curse. All men and women could see with their eyes, she said, save those few unfortunates like herself who lacked sight. And everyone, even the blind, was able to see backwards in time thanks to the gift of memory. A few, a lucky few, had the ability also to see *forwards* in time.

'What can I do with it, this gift?' said Geraint. 'I should have warned Deri that his neighbour was going to kill him.'

'You would not have been believed.'

'I could have told the others that the crops would fail.'

'You would not have been believed.'

'So what use is it?'

'Everything has a place,' she said, 'but not everything has a use.'

The third time he visited the burial place the woman told Geraint that he would soon be leaving the village where he had been born; he and most of the other able-bodied men. Geraint was pleased to be thought a man. It put him on the same level as his brother, Caradoc. A great crisis was coming, the woman said. They would be summoned away to face it. Geraint knew nothing of this but accepted the truth of her words without question. He wanted to ask if he and the others would ever return but he was afraid of the answer. The woman sensed his mood and said that it was a time of danger but also of hope. Geraint would experience grief but gladness as well. There is no victory without tears, she said.

'Will Caradoc go too?'

'He will accompany you,' she said.

She had a gift for him. He was to take it on his journey when the call came. She reached into a bag that lay at her side and extracted a small object. He was surprised to see that it was knife, but small, almost ornamental, rather than practical. She held it in the palm of one hand and ran the fingers of the other across the surface of the hilt before passing it to Geraint. The blade glinted with a metallic blue threat but the hilt was finely worked. It was made from some off-white substance that Geraint did not recognise, like stone but with a smooth, living feel to it that stone did not possess. The hilt depicted an animal that Geraint also didn't recognise. The beast stood on its hind legs with its forelegs wrapped around the trunk of a tree. Its upright posture was disturbing, neither man-like nor animal.

'What is the beast on the hilt?'

'A bear.'

'I have never seen one.'

'Are you sure of that?'

Geraint did not answer. Instead he said, 'What am I to do with it?'

'Keep it with you, safe. Take it with you when you are called away. You will know what to do with it when the time comes.'

And Geraint had to be content with that. A few weeks afterwards the call came. Arthur was summoning his countrymen to confront the Saxon hordes at a place several days' travel from the village, near the old Roman town of Aquae Sulis. Caradoc explained what was happening. It might all have been rumour but he told his younger brother as if it were fact (which it was, more or less). Caradoc said that for many months Arthur, using pedlars and paid informants as well as reputable travelling merchants, had caused a story to be spread among the Saxon enemy. The story was that the Picts, the people of the far north, were preparing to march south as soon as the winter retreated. Arthur had made a great show of sending some of his men north, apparently to face the Pictish threat and leaving the southlands undefended. But the British army had halted near the mouth of the Sabrina, far from their supposed destination. The Saxons, deceived, saw their chance to swing round and cut the country in two, like a woodman cleaving an upturned log at a single stroke. They massed to march west and south towards the river Abona, ignorant of the existence of the army lying hidden at their heels.

When Arthur received news of the Saxon preparation to march, he made the general call to arms. It was the final crisis, as predicted by the woman in the burial ground. If the Saxons were not dealt with now, they would surely over-run the whole land.

Caradoc and Geraint might have left with the other men of the village although they had not got the explicit permission of Aelric to go. But, as it happened, they had to delay their departure by a couple of days since their mother, so long dying during the spring and early summer, was now at the very point of extinction. They departed on the morning following her death, each young man sunk in his thoughts and letting the breeze dry the occasional tear. Hence it was that they eventually arrived near Aquae Sulis, accompanied by the dog Cynric, but behind the rest of their neighbours.

Now Geraint sat not far from the men's campfire and wondered about the coming battle. He heard the sound of his brother's voice, protesting amid some laughter that he did know how to use the sword and knife that he carried. Geraint remembered the knife and its ornamental hilt. The bear with its arms clasped around the tree trunk. *You will know what to do with it when the time comes.* What would he have to do? When? Too late now. He had been robbed by the old boatman. The leather pouch and the knife were at the bottom of the river Abona. He had failed. He felt ashamed.

His thoughts were interrupted by the arrival of a tall man near the dying fire. Aelric welcomed him and asked him where he was from. The man said, 'I am with the Company of the Bear.'

Geraint started at the words, since they chimed with his recent thoughts. The newcomer settled himself close to the embers as if he had a right to be there and the others accepted him without question. He was wearing a hooded mantle, grey, and his great height was evident even though he carried himself with a stoop.

'What news?' he said to no one in particular.

Aelric said, 'The enemy draws nearer.'

'And what are our chances?'

It was either a foolish or an inappropriate question for there was an uneasy shifting among the group by the fire.

Then Caradoc piped up, 'Under our leader, how can we fail?'

'You mean Arthur guards us against defeat?'

There was a general mutter of agreement at this but the man was firm in contradicting his own question. 'No, each man must guard himself against defeat. Arthur is not one of the gods, as in the religion of the olden days.'

'He is not an ordinary man,' said Aelric. 'You, of all people, must know that if you are truly with the Company of the Bear.'

'Perhaps so,' said the newcomer, 'but the outcome of battle is always uncertain. What do you think, you over there? Do you expect victory?'

As he said these last words he turned to look at Geraint, who was sitting in shadow. Disconcertingly Geraint could see nothing of the face under the hood except the glitter of the man's eyes – that and a grizzled beard.

'No victory without tears,' said Geraint, repeating what the sightless woman in the burial ground had told him.

'True enough,' said the man.

'That is my young brother, Geraint,' said Caradoc.

'Whoever he is, he speaks sense,' said the man.

After that the group about the fire fell silent and after a time the man got up and, with a muttered farewell, left them.

III

The next morning Geraint woke early, cramped and stiff from where he'd been sleeping on the rough ground. There was a thin mist lying across the valley and the damp had crept under his clothes. He clambered to his feet. Cynric, who had edged himself close to the dying fire during the night, staggered up, looking expectantly at Geraint. No one else was awake, not even Caradoc.

Geraint and the dog wandered away to stretch their legs. Quite soon Geraint heard the sound of the river, although at first he saw nothing but the blurred outline of the willows along the bank. He pushed through some low-lying shrubs and entered a flat, grassy area fronting the water. Suddenly Cynric stopped and the hackles on his back rose. Through the mist Geraint strained to see what the dog had sensed. A few yards in front of him a man was sitting on the edge of the water. His knees were drawn up under him and his head was bowed. He looked like a large grey stone. Something about his posture and the cowl that covered his head reminded Geraint of the individual who'd joined them at the campfire the previous evening. He gave no sign of being aware of their presence. Perhaps he was asleep or praying.

Geraint was about to move away. Then out of the corner of his eye he saw movement on the far side of the clearing. Another man was emerging from the undergrowth. This one Geraint also recognized, and his heart thumped and his mouth went dry. It was the boatman, Brennus. He had survived the spill from his coracle! Moving through the long grass with exaggerated gestures, raising his legs high with each step, he advanced towards the man on the bank, who remained still as a stone. In his hand he held a knife. Geraint recognised this too. It was his, the knife with the bear-hilt.

The treacherous boatman was within a few strides of the other, the one huddled up on the bank. His intention was plain: to take the other by surprise, to stab him in the back or the neck.

Geraint had no weapon. His sword was left, carelessly, inexcusably, where he had been sleeping. But his unarmed state did not cross his mind. Seeing Brennus once more, stepping like a malevolent spirit through the tendrils of mist, grasping *his* bear-knife, was sufficient to cause Geraint to launch himself across the clearing. He almost took Brennus by surprise but the wrinkled man turned just in time and slashed out with the knife. He was aiming too high and the sweeping stroke passed over Geraint's back as the lad hit him around the knees. Both of them tumbled into the dank grass and rolled over, now one on top, now the other. Geraint seized hold of Brennus's forearm and exerted all his strength to keep the knife blade away from his face and eyes. His nostrils filled with the stench of fish from the boatman.

Cynric joined in but he was no dog for a fight. Rather, he lunged at the tangle of legs and impeded Geraint instead of helping him. Brennus might have been old but he was tough and wiry as a strip of tanned leather. At one moment, Geraint levered himself up and sat astride Brennus. As he did so, his grip on the other's knife-hand slackened. The boatman's arm wriggled away and would have slashed Geraint across the face had he not raised his own arm to protect himself. So instead the blade sliced through the coarse fabric of Geraint's sleeve and ripped down the under-side of his arm. He was conscious of no pain but the blood welled through the cloth and blotted Brennus's withered face. Wounded with his own weapon, Geraint managed to seize the other's knife-hand once again but his hold was not as tight as it had been. Now the boatman had the advantage and, arching his back, he threw Geraint off. Positions were reversed, with the boatman lying at an angle across the younger man and attempting to twist his hand and arm about so that he might pierce Geraint in the flank.

Then there loomed above them both a man's shape, a very tall man in cloak and hood. With one hand, it seemed, he grabbed Brennus about the nape of his neck and lifted him clear of Geraint. He held the boatman at a distance as one would a poisonous viper, and his grip on the other's neck was so firm that Brennus appeared to hang like a sack from the man's hand.

With his other arm and in almost leisurely fashion, the tall man reached about and twisted the knife-hand of the boatman. Twisted it so sharply Geraint could have sworn he heard the crack of bone. Brennus gave a screech like a bird and let go of the bear-knife. The man dropped the boatman on the ground and then planted a foot on the side of his head. All this time he looked not at Brennus, who might have been so much discarded rubbish, but at Geraint. The lad was standing up by this time but felt very unsteady. It was not only as a consequence of his wound but also because he recognised the man for certain. In the struggle his hood had fallen away and Geraint realised this was indeed the individual from the night before, the man with glittering eyes and grizzled beard. His stooping posture then had disguised his true height: he was almost a giant, in Geraint's eyes. Cynric the dog crouched uneasily at the edge of the clearing, watching the trio.

'Thank you,' said the man. 'You have protected me. I know this traitor. He would have killed me while I was sunk deep in my thoughts and was lost to the world. Each man must guard himself, I said, but I forgot my own teaching.'

'Thoughts about the battle – the battle to come?' said Geraint, surprising himself by the evenness of his voice. But he could not look at the tall man and instead cast his glance down to where Brennus, writhing, was pinned under the other's foot.

'Yes. I was thinking of the battle.'

'I am here to take part,' said Geraint.

'How old are you?'

'Old enough to fight,' he said, then, seeing the man staring hard at him,

'Twelve years, I think.'

'And your brother, the one who identified you last night?'

'I do not know,' said Geraint. 'Two years older maybe.'

The man seemed about to say something then turned his head to one side. 'You must be attended to,' he said.

By now blood was beginning to issue from his arm in some quantity and, before he knew it, Geraint was sitting back on the rank grass and then lying down as he heard rather than saw a rush of people enter the clearing. Then the morning mist seemed to enter his own mind too.

Geraint dreamed he was in a desperate fight but, even though he was once again equipped with the bear-knife, he could not lift his arm to strike out against his unseen enemy, who was jabbing at him out of a mist. Then he woke and when he glanced sideways at his arm he saw it was swathed in blood-soaked bandages and, although it was throbbing slightly, it seemed not to be part of him. He was lying on a plain bed in a plain room, illuminated by sun pouring through a high narrow aperture. Caradoc was standing nearby, awkward.

'Brother,' he said simply.

He squatted down on his hams so that he almost on a level with Geraint.

In a corner of the room lay Cynric. The dog's tail fluttered to see Geraint awake. It was cool and dry in the chamber.

'This is a storage room of one of the villas in Aquae Sulis,' said Caradoc. 'You have been brought here to recover. One of the woman of the town has been ordered to tend to you.'

'It is my fighting arm,' said Geraint.

'You will not be doing any fighting for a while,' said Caradoc, and the remark sounded like something he had heard someone else say.

'What happened? Did you see Brennus?'

'Who? Oh, the boatman. Yes, he has been ... questioned. It seems he was more than a petty thief and ferryman. He was in the pay of the Saxons. We have agents among them and they keep traitors among us.'

'Brennus was trying to attack the man by the river. The hooded man.'

'Thanks to you he did not succeed. You know who the hooded man is?'

'Arthur,' said Geraint, remembering the time when he had seen him near Cadwy's Fort. On that occasion he had ridden past in splendour, high and easy, like a god. Very different from the man still as stone in a grey mantle by the river-bank. 'Arthur, our leader.'

'Arthur knew Brennus of old. He was a steward at Cadwy's Fort. He had stolen from the stores and kept false records. Arthur showed mercy by driving him from the realm in disgrace instead of taking his life. He was not grateful but twisted with bitterness. He would have harmed Arthur.'

'Arthur was the stranger by the fire last night. The one who said he was not a god.'

'It is his custom, they say, to walk unknown among his men and listen to what they are saying.'

'We are his men,' said Geraint.

'Yes,' said Caradoc. 'Boys no longer.'

There was an awkward pause before Caradoc said, 'He told me to return something to you. Arthur spoke to me! I could scarcely meet his gaze. He told me to give this back to you. He assured me it was your property even though I have never seen it before.' He fumbled in his garments and produced the knife with the bear-hilt. Geraint took it with his good hand. 'Where did it come from? It is not our father's.'

'The bear is Arthur's image, isn't it?' said Geraint, not replying to his brother's question. 'The Company of the Bear. Brennus could surely not have killed Arthur with a weapon bearing his own image on the hilt.'

'In any case, you alerted him.'

'He was deep in thought. Or he was praying for success in battle.'

'The battle that is coming,' said Caradoc.

'I am afraid for you,' said Geraint, struggling to rise from the narrow bed.

'Be still, little brother. Recover your strength and the use of your arm.'

The battle of Badon Hill, which Geraint had witnessed as plumes of smoke and cries and screams, began within a matter of days. The Saxons were ambushed by Arthur's men as they approached Aquae Sulis, in a pass between the hills to the east of the Roman town. Taken by surprise and temporarily overwhelmed, they retreated to the old fortified hill top called Badon and there the Britons lay siege to them. The hill top was barren, without water or any resources.

When the enemy was weakened by hunger and thirst and constant harrying, Arthur's men stormed the bare slopes and swept over the plateau with sword and fire.

It was a great struggle, and a great victory for Arthur and the Britons against the Saxons. Arthur was reputed to have slain over nine hundred of the foe single-handed – or so the story went centuries later when he was no longer a mere man but a god once more. There were losses on the British side too, among them red-headed Aelric and young Caradoc from an anonymous village not far from Cadwy's.

Geraint, kept from the battle by his wound, knew of Caradoc's death before the woman who was tending to him informed him of it. He knew of it not because of any vision but because one morning Cynric, who stayed in the store-room and would not leave Geraint's side, was restless for hours and then raised the hairs on the boy's neck with a long-drawn-out ghostly howl. Geraint turned his head to one side and wept for his brother, following so hard at the heels of their departed mother.

He might be glad of the happy outcome of the battle but he grieved for the loss of Caradoc. In commemoration of his brother and before returning to his village, Geraint went to the hill of Badon outside the town. The day was overcast and the clouds pressed down low. Geraint did not walk to the very top of the hill from which smoke drifted, acrid, smelling of meat. The dead were still burning, the corpses of Saxons and the Britons, or it was merely the carcasses of the horses. Nevertheless Geraint did not want to climb any higher. He did not want to go searching for the exact spot where Caradoc had fallen. He did not want the possibility of glimpsing his brother's mangled, roasting corpse among the slain.

Instead he faced about to the south-west in the direction

of his village. The gentle hills slept under the low sky. Geraint saw no vision of any battle to come. Perhaps the talk that he had heard while he was recovering his strength was true: that the battle of Badon was the last battle, or the last for many years. The Saxons were routed. For all the bitter scent in his nostrils, thought Geraint, perhaps the Saxon threat was sleeping or even at an end. Then, in the company of the dog Cynric and, choosing a secluded spot on the slope, Geraint buried the dagger with the ivory bear-hilt.

SIMON &
SCHUSTER

The Medieval Murderers

THE TAINTED RELIC

July, 1100. Jerusalem has fallen to the Crusader armies, the
Holy City lies ransacked. Amidst the chaos, an English knight
is entrusted with a valuable religious relic: a fragment of the
True Cross, allegedly stained with the blood of Christ. The
relic is said to be cursed: anyone who touches it will meet an
untimely and gruesome end as soon as it leaves their
possession.

Thus begins a series of intriguing interlocking mysteries by
Britain's best-known medieval crime writers. A decapitated
monk. A savage impaling. A mysterious talking raven. At the
heart of it all lies the lethal influence of the evil relic . . .

'Monks, mists, madness, taverns: a must for historical crime
buffs' *Tangled Web*

ISBN 978-1-41650-213-5

SIMON &
SCHUSTER

The Medieval Murderers

SWORD OF SHAME

**Five enthralling interlinked mysteries from Michael Jecks,
Susanna Gregory, Bernard Knight, Ian Morson
and Philip Gooden.**

Qui falsitate vivit, animam occidit. Falsus in ore, caret honore.
The Latin inscription carved on the gleaming blade read: *He who
lives in falsehood slays his soul; he who lies, his honour.* If only
they had known how true those words would prove to be . . .

Lovingly crafted by a Saxon swordsmith shortly before the
Norman invasion, treachery and deceit are the Sword of Shame's
constant companions. From the Norman conquest of 1066 to the
murder of Thomas a' Becket, from an attempted coup against
Richard the Lionheart to the bloodstained battle of Poitiers: at the
heart of every treasonous plot, murder and betrayal lies the malign
influence of the cursed sword. As it passes from owner to owner
in this intriguing series of interlinked mysteries, ill fortune and
disgrace befall all who wield its glittering but deadly blade.

Sword of Shame is the second series of gripping medieval
mysteries from the acclaimed authors of *The Tainted Relic*.

ISBN 978-1-41652-190-7

SIMON &
SCHUSTER

The Medieval Murderers

HOUSE OF SHADOWS

Five enthralling interlinked mysteries from Michael Jecks, Susanna Gregory, Bernard Knight, Ian Morson and Philip Gooden.

Bermondsey Priory, 1114. A young chaplain succumbs to the temptations of the flesh – and suffers a gruesome fate.

From that moment, the monastery is cursed and over the next five hundred years murder and treachery abound within its hallowed walls.

A beautiful young bride found dead two days before her wedding. A ghostly figure that warns of impending doom. A daring plot to depose King Edward II. Mad monks and errant priests . . . even the poet Chaucer finds himself drawn into the dark deeds and violent death which pervade this unhappy place.

ISBN 978-1-41652-680-3

SIMON &
SCHUSTER

The Medieval Murderers

THE LOST PROPHECIES

A mysterious book of prophecies written by a sixth century Irish
monk has puzzled scholars through the ages. Foretelling wars,
plagues and rebellions, the Black Book of Bran is said to have
predicted the Black Death and the Gunpowder Plot. It is even said
to foresee the Day of Judgement. But is it the result of divine
inspiration or the ravings of a madman?

A hidden hoard of Saxon gold. A poisoned priest. A monk skinned
alive in Westminster Abbey. Only one thing is certain: whoever
comes into possession of the cursed book meets a gruesome
and untimely end.

'The various excellent crime writers each weave a clever and
inventive tale around a central theme' *Good Book Guide*

ISBN 978-1-84739-121-6

SIMON &
SCHUSTER

The Medieval Murderers

KING ARTHUR'S BONES

Glastonbury Abbey, 1191. During excavation work, an ancient
leaden cross is discovered, buried several feet below ground.
Inscribed upon it the words: *hic iacet sepultus inclitus rex arturius*
. . . here lies buried the renowned King Arthur. Beneath the cross
are skeletal remains. Could this really be the legendary King
Arthur and his queen, Guinevere?

As the monks debate the implications of this extraordinary
discovery, the bones themselves disappear: spirited away by the
mysterious Guardians, determined to protect King Arthur until the
ancient legend is fulfilled, and he returns to defend his country in
the hour of its greatest need.

A missing right hand. A gang of ruthless bodysnatchers. Brother
accused of killing brother. As the secret of the bones' hiding place
is passed from generation to generation, those entrusted to
safeguard the king's remains must withstand treachery, theft,
blackmail and murder in order to keep the legend intact.

ISBN 978-1-84739-365-4

This book and other titles by the **Medieval Murderers** are available from your local bookshop or can be ordered direct from the publisher.

978-0-85720-426-4	Hill of Bones	£12.99
978-1-84739-832-1	The Sacred Stone	£6.99
978-1-84739-365-4	King Arthur's Bones	£6.99
978-1-84739-121-6	The Lost Prophecies	£6.99
978-1-41652-680-3	House of Shadows	£6.99
978-1-41652-190-7	Sword of Shame	£6.99
978-1-41650-213-5	The Tainted Relic	£6.99